Son of Prophecy

Ratna Chandra

SON OF PROPHECY

Publisher: Ratna Chandra

Contact Info: Website: www.ratna-chandra.com
Email: ratnachandra414@gmail.com

Copyright January 2025 - First Edition

Publisher's Cataloging-in-Publication Data

Names: Chandra, Ratna, author.

Title: Son of prophecy / Ratna Chandra.

Description: Orlando, FL: Ratna Chandra, 2025. | Summary: Fourteen-year-old Devin Reelms finds his life irrevocably altered when a prophecy reveals his destiny: to restore light to the fallen realm.

Identifiers: LCCN: 2024927298 | ISBN: 979-8-9922011-0-9 (paperback) | 979-8-9922011-1-6 (ebook) | Hardcover: 979-8-9922011-2-3

Subjects: LCSH Prophecy--Fiction. | Good and evil--Fiction. | Friendship--Fiction. | Fantasy fiction. | BISAC YOUNG ADULT FICTION / Fantasy / General | YOUNG ADULT FICTION / Fantasy / Epic

Classification: LCC PS3603 .H36 S66 2025 | DDC 813.6--dc23

DEDICATION

*To the Unicorn who insisted this be
brought to Light – Endless Thank Yous!*

ACKNOWLEDGEMENTS

Immense Gratitude to The Light in allowing me to be the Channel.

Mariswaran Selvarajan – This has been made a reality by your support and unwavering drive in every step of the process in bringing it to fruition. You're truly appreciated. Thank you. I'm in Gratitude.

To Dr. Priyanka De – My Editor and Mind Observer – For understanding Devin's journey and allowing my story to stay authentic. Knowing you got lost in the reading tells me I did it right. Thank You!

Shabbir Hussain Badshah – Cover Art and Book Layout Design – Your patience and professionalism throughout the rounds of changes is much appreciated. Thank you!

Chapter Images: Mariswaran Selvarajan - With help by Copilot, FontSnap & Gemini

For those not named here - You know yourselves and how you matter – even when it slept in the shadows with no real idea it would one day truly be birthed. My appreciation and thanks.

CONTENTS

1

A KINGDOM FALLS

Legend has it that the tiny Kingdom of Ohhm existed hundreds of years earlier in the Celestial Hills, in the countryside of Veil. A warm and sunny place with a friendly climate year-long, it lay within the vast valley of the Seven Sisters' Hills.

The Castle of Ohhm, housing seven magnificent towers, with each dome covered in gold, lay sprawling in stunning beauty, amid lush vegetation and enchanting forests, with the flowing river nearby and its plentiful streams, brooks, and waterways completing its idyllic kingdom.

Its riches drew all sorts of characters—from the very strange and bizarre to the mystical and mysterious. But the glory days of Ohhm had come to an end. After having stood victorious against warring regions fighting for control, it seemed that the heavens themselves had cast a dark cloud to descend and the fate of Ohhm was sealed.

★ ★ ★

Chad Asgeir, Commander and Chief of Ohhm's armies, flinched as a flock of vultures landed nearby. It was a sure sign that the kingdom had been penetrated by outside forces. He had to get to the castle quickly, knowing that they'd take heavy losses with the approaching darkness.

His men were the best and fiercest in the land, the most loyal he could find. Knowing that they would gladly die rather than be defeated, he secretly worried. Fighting against a physical threat was one thing, fighting against the unseen and unknown, another.

That he was chosen to head Ohhm's armies was beyond any honor that he could have dreamed of. His past had made him ruthless, and it had driven him to heights in the command chain, leaving him unrivaled. His only loyalty was in serving his king and kingdom and now his duty lay in saving his king.

News had reached him that the sister gems had been weakened and under attack, and as he rode by a string of fallen soldiers, he dreaded the news that he was about to give to King Aeon. Surrounding kingdoms had fallen under the Shadows' siege of terror and with them, Ohhm's allies and their support.

Elders, Ancients, and Wise Ones had been killed as battles were lost and armies conquered. Women and children, old and sickly, were destroyed, leaving the land to perish.

With his assistant in charge, Chad had left to escort the King to safety but his efforts had been frustrated by the many ambushes of the Shadows. Having lost many of his men to horrific deaths, Chad knew that it was only a matter of time before all was lost.

With a heart heavy, he rode on — his thoughts turning to Serena. He'd loved her from the moment he first saw her. She gave him a reason to live again and to dream of a future filled with bright possibilities.

But as guardians of the realm, as well as a Princess of Ohhm, her first duty lay in protecting the kingdom. He knew that it was his own fault for having fallen in love. It would be the end to any dreams he had of being with her. The fates had spoken, and he sighed in bitterness.

Pushing his horse on, knowing that there was not a moment to rest, now that every second counted, he worried even more at the lack of anyone greeting him this far into the grounds.

Ohhm was proud of its history of travelers over the millennium who had gained knowledge and the ways of the beyond in using their gifts in securing their kingdom.

He rode on, reflecting on the ancients he'd turned to for help in times of turmoil. Their knowledge always gave him strength. In veiling the gems, they had paid a heavy price as the Shadows' retaliation was merciless, and many of the great ones were now no more.

He'd met with what had remained of his tribe and had seen them to a hidden valley. Fortified with eons of sacredness and divine worship, he knew it would offer protection. His people had their own gifts, and he didn't doubt that they'd give the Shadows reason to leave them alone.

He prayed that he would reach the King in time and spurred his horse forward. A short while later, he arrived at the castle, even more worried as Serena appeared.

"Father got news you were on the way. He said it was of utmost importance that he attended the meeting," she greeted him.

Chad's eyebrows rose. "Your father left?"

With the kingdoms at war and Ohhm at stake, how could King Aeon still try to attend the meeting and leave Serena at their mercies? It was unheard of.

"He went to see the Elders?"

"Yes." Serena nodded. "But only because he said you'd know what to do. He needed to give information before everything was lost."

Chad fumed on the inside but kept an outward calm. He couldn't believe that the king had been so cavalier in his safety. He could have told him that the Elders were no more.

Dismounting, he grasped her arm and started forward with the only choice he had left. "Let's go!"

★ ★ ★

The Symbolic Tower was the safest place within the castle. Every possible precaution, prayer, barrier, sign, and means of protection had been installed; and it was exactly where he needed to get to. A string of young women appeared around the corner with exclamations of relief on seeing them, and then falling silent at Chad's grim expression.

At his nod, they followed with urgent footsteps, hurrying through hallways and up the winding staircases, passing by grand halls. Chad ignored the splendor that beckoned, knowing that the secret passageways within would be useless to them.

Urging the maidens on, he silently sent up a prayer of thanks as the arches leading to the tower appeared ahead. Yelling for everyone to run, he sent Serena ahead, falling behind as a sudden blast of coldness swept in, filling the castle.

Less than a few feet away from the Mystic Fountain, windows exploded. Chad shoved the maidens into a sign of the falcon and uttered the words for their safety. He felt the air move against him as the portal opened, and they melted from view. Grabbing Serena, he activated a beam of mist and kept going.

An orb exploded and a blast of energy sent them flying. He reached for Serena, barely encircling her in protection as they landed inches away from the broken fountain, amidst shards of marble and scattered debris.

Warmth seeped into him as water gushed by, and he was sure he'd cracked a few ribs as pain seared his every breath. He reached over, touching Serena who'd been motionless. Shaking her gently, he watched as she reoriented herself.

"Get the crystal! Go. Now," he said. "We only have a few minutes. They'll be here any second!"

Watching as she struggled to crawl forward, he prayed that she would make it in time. The chill intensified, and Chad felt a dread flowing through his veins.

"Get it, Serena! It's now or never!"

The shout startled her, and Serena lunged. With hands outstretched, she grasped the slippery crystal sitting in the flow of milky water. A spark of connection flared, sending an electric surge through her. A gurgling, sucking noise roared, and she was airborne.

Flashes of color and bits of scenery swirled by as she hurtled on with nauseating speed. Close to swooning at the unfamiliar sensations coursing through her, and tears streaming down her face, Serena felt a heaviness squeezing at her, compressing her vision. Scrunching her eyes and gasping for the breath she had forgotten to take, she hurtled on.

A blur of mixed odors was her only clue something was different, and seconds later, she landed with a bone-jarring thud that racked her to the core. Surrounded by blackness, she felt a torrent of rain and forks of lightning greeting her. Within seconds, she was drenched.

"Just what I needed," she muttered, blinking water out of her eyes.

Her stomach roiled, and she doubled over. Minutes went by as she retched, and when it had passed, Serena slowly sat up, feeling a tree against her back. With her stomach still feeling queasy, she peered around.

Chad! She hadn't heard him coming through. Panic flared, and she shivered. Crawling gingerly around, feeling for him, she forced herself to remain calm.

Unable to find him and knowing that she couldn't risk calling out, dread filled her at the thought that he might be hurt, or worse, that he might have died back at the castle.

She had been so focused on getting to the crystal, clueless it would activate a light beam and become an escape portal, she realized Chad must have known of its secret all along.

Water ran in rivulets over her, and she huddled against the wind, her teeth chattering. Delayed tremors shook her entire being, and she took a deep breath and vomited again, feeling like her brain was on fire.

Much later, Serena found herself lying on soggy ground, soaked and spent. She groggily sat up, her thoughts turning to Chad again, trying to deny what the Shadows might have done to him. They were creatures of the dark, existing between realms.

Tears fell unchecked as she sat in misery until the sudden movements and neighing of horses nearby startled her. A flash of lightning showed her that the crystal had landed about a dozen feet in front of her.

She sat for a long while as the rain abated to a soft, steady drizzle. She felt her mind working again.

But Serena knew she didn't have the luxury of worrying. Chad was a warrior first. His duty lay in the protection of

Ohhm. And with that fact, he would have been prepared to give his life if the need ever arose. As it should be with her, she reminded herself.

She tried to focus, knowing that she had to get the crystal and find shelter. Clueless about where she was at and knowing that her kingdom had been destroyed, Serena closed her thoughts to the pain and slowly inched her way forward, hoping another flash of lightning would show her the exact spot where the crystal lay.

A twig snapped ahead of her, and she paused, listening. Sensing a presence, she stayed still. The next flash of lightning showed her a man approaching. He knelt, hands stretching toward the crystal. Her heart pounded painfully and a sudden glow and startled gasp told her what she had feared.

She was about to call out, when a scream of utmost terror wrenched the air. Serena froze as flitting movements went by. It could only mean one thing. They had penetrated this foreign land. For Ohhm to have fallen, it meant that the veil was either no more or was too weak to prevent them.

She sat up, focusing on her energies. Saving herself was her only choice. The crystal had made human contact before they could get a hold of it. It was as safe as she could have wanted it to be.

"Quickly, quickly," she heard her mom's voice echoing instructions in her ears, her voice urgent.

Serena slowed her breathing, allowing the chaos around her to recede. She felt herself starting to shake. Raising her arms, she made the sacred sign. The ancient language whispered softly in her mind, and she flowed in soft release.

She suffered a second's ungainly tilt as another scream rented the air. Steadying herself, she felt an odd sensation and watched herself become a cloud of golden dust.

Amazed she could see in the inky blackness, she sensed a sudden change as the air constricted around her and an ominous silence descended.

Too late, Serena realized that her body still sat exposed to the elements. In anguish, she searched her memories for ways to protect it. She watched in revulsion as a patch of slimy, sticky blackness orbed itself where her body lay.

It hovered a while, sniffing undecidedly, sensing something strange. More arrived and, the fact that they couldn't see a soul, yet found her body without one struck Serena as very funny. She grinned and then instantly regretted it as the orbs of blackness flung themselves in violent jets, echoes of terror sounding at places of contact.

Fear flooded her as she realized that being invisible hadn't made her immune to their evil. Their wrath at finding her body useless, yet unable to find her soul increased with each passing second, and Serena found herself praying desperately.

"Some help. Some sign." Calling on all her ancestors, she pleaded, "Please give me strength. Protect me. Somebody!

Anybody! Angel of this land, I call to you, save me from this evil!"

As the balls of blackness hovered again around her still form, she felt a change. As she watched, beams of silvery dust poured in and the darkness disappeared. Morning had miraculously dawned! Threads of bright sunlight filtered through the leaves, revealing a dense forest surrounding her. Serena silently thanked the heavens and felt her nose twitch at the smell of burnt odor. The shadows had been vaporized.

A deep sigh of relief coursed through her. They hadn't understood the repercussions of destroying the Mystic Fountain. If they had, well . . . she didn't want to think of the result.

Now that the crystal was safe for a while, what was she supposed to do? The folks had gone. She would have to find them. The crystal wasn't useless even though it was out of its element. She took some comfort in the knowledge that no one else knew that fact. She was still its Guardian, and if she had to stay till eternity to recover it, it was what she had to do. Ohhm had fallen. Chad was gone. The crystal was lost. What did she do?

Serena approached her still body.

* * *

Ohhm had fallen. Slowly, it withered and died. Folks who survived fled, leaving the land to fend for itself; the castle lay in ruins, its inhabitants having disappeared after the battle of the Shadows almost as mysteriously as they had appeared.

Ohhm became history. What remained were intriguing tales told by elders of tiny villages that lay sprawled around the foothills in the valleys. While some were quaint and quiet, others were loud and colorful. Of these, Foxwood, Realm Point, and Cruxbury were the largest.

Little did anyone know that strange events were about to descend upon them on a blue moon's night in May.

FULL MOON'S GATHERING

"**D**evin! Dev! Where are you?"

"In the henhouse," Devin hollered, peering inquisitively through the doorway as his fifteen-year-old sister, Lexi, called.

At fourteen, he was wiry, of olive complexion, and already a little over five feet tall. With dark brown eyes set in a thin, oval-shaped face, his mop of tangled black hair gave the impression of constant untidiness. His khaki overalls, tattered and shredded, only emphasized the fact that he was doing his least favorite chore—cleaning their poultry droppings.

Shoveling vigorously into a pile, he hollered again in case Lexi hadn't heard him. Scraping and scooping, he shoved at an especially tough spot that gave way, giving momentum that sent the pile squarely into the entrance, right as Lexi stepped in.

"Eeeeew.., did you have to do that?" Scrambling backwards, Lexi barely managed to avoid a disaster. Twitching her nose at the stench, she breathed the fresh air deeply.

"Didn't see you, Sis." Devin huffed, heaving from his effort and the sudden give of the stubborn pile.

"You would, if you get that bush off your head."

"Aw, you like my hair."

"Phfff. Don't fool yourself."

He grinned at Lexi's frown of indignation and couldn't help needling her.

"You came to tell me to get rid of my hair?" Scooping the pile and dumping it into a bucket that would go to the burning pit, he rested the shovel against the wall and picked up the water he'd brought in earlier to wash the floor.

"Gramps says he has a treat for everyone tonight!"

Water sloshed, spilling on his boots, the tray rocking in his hands. "I wanted to check out the load of rocks he had delivered today," Devin muttered, unsure he wanted company.

"Your loss then." The sound of her receding footsteps told him Lexi had already left.

"Be there later," he yelled.

"Whatever," he heard her reply.

Devin sighed. Lexi could be irritating. Attractive, with thick, curly lashes, dark eyes and full lips, she was the local beauty, and Devin was secretly proud of her, but she was no fun to hang with. Since his cousins had moved away, life had become dull, and Lexi thought all boys, including him, were stupid.

Chucking feed into the troughs, he added water into the pans and finished cleaning. Locking up for the night, he headed for a shower thinking about the meet-up later.

Gramps always said that he'd tell them some big secret when the time was right. There must be a full moon tonight. Gramps did say nights on full moon were powerful times.

Devin used the special mixture of herbs his mom had prepared to thoroughly wash the grime and stink off. Smelling and feeling refreshed, he finished and headed for a dinner of roasted chicken, mixed rice, and vegetables.

In a short while, he'd finished dinner and arrived in Gramps's yard, knowing that the evening light was fading fast with the approaching night. Gazing at the pile, he felt a thread of energy zing through him. About to pick up one that sparked and shimmered at him, Devin heard his mom calling. He left, knowing he'd have to wait well into the next day before he could visit again. Heading for the kitchen, he began helping with the preparations.

Half an hour later, folks started arriving: neighbors from down the street, Cheryl and Rufus and their three kids - Teryl, Cindy, and Mark, along with two of his cousins' friends, Austin and Joe, and behind them, giggling and being silly, some of Lexi's girlfriends - Patsy, Rose, Julie, and the self-appointed head of their little clique, Cassie.

Other folks of various ages straggled in, and Devin wondered how word had spread so quickly. But the meet-ups were always fun, and he didn't mind.

Gathering on full moon nights had become something of a tradition. Everyone would gather for a few hours when Gramps, a tall, robust man of seventy with a prominent nose, large eyes and thick mustache, told his tales. He'd heard it all from his dad, the lovable but eccentric Hums. Celeste, Devin's grandmother, a big-boned, plump lady, with love to cover the world and a hug to match, would nod her contribution or tell funny stories of her own.

At other times, Elders from various parts of the villages would share their own adventures. Devin always felt braver on the nights of full moon than any other time, and he had a niggling feeling Gramps understood, even though he didn't know why.

One of the nice things about the meet-ups was the makeshift swing that kids would hitch together, using a limb of one of the many trees in the yard as a place to ride the wind. It wasn't unusual for someone to be dropped unexpectedly when the ropes gave way.

A yell of pain sounded, followed by laughter, proving the evening was proceeding normally. With only his pride injured and a few scrapes and bruises, Teryl wandered away, anxious to avoid everyone's stares.

Devin's home, like most in the village, had the sleeping quarters on the second floor and the kitchen taking up half of the ground floor. The other half flowed to an open area, giving a glimpse of their garden, street, and the neighbors on every side.

Old rattans were set out as everyone gathered around, with a few kids sitting on the various limbs of the gnarled guava tree that stood nearby.

Austin and Joe took out playing cards, exchanging stories of their latest scrapes – their lively banter filling the air. Snacks and drinks were shared as the adults busied themselves while trading news.

★ ★ ★

He always wondered how folks who came by would confide things to his mom, almost as if she was their secret keeper. It puzzled him since he didn't think his mom ever took the time to listen to him or even understood him. Always preaching at him, he'd long since learned to tune her out whenever he sensed a lecture coming on.

As he watched, he saw she was busy passing out cucumber sandwiches and hot tea, while Lexi was in charge of a concoction she had discovered. Suspecting this was their mom's way of teaching her what little social etiquette existed, Devin wondered what tactic she might be using on him.

A string of kids flew past him, squealing in welcome as Gramps and Celeste, his grandmother, made their way over, amidst a flurry of hugs and hellos, distracting him.

Gramps's smile rivaled that of the full moon over the horizon.

"It's really good seeing everyone. What's with the crowd? You're having a party, Rae? Gramps greeted impishly.

"Me?" Rae spluttered, her astonishment making Devin grin. Leave it to Gramps to needle his mom, he thought.

"Don't give him the satisfaction, Rae, you know your dad," his grandmother interrupted. "The old goat told Fina yesterday we might be here tonight. And you know Fina. You might as well be broadcasting to the village. But it's okay," she added, patting Rae on the shoulder.

Devin laughed, quickly turning it into a cough on seeing his mom's expression.

"Of course, it's okay. We love company."

The quick reassurance brought a sigh of relief to the group, making Devin smile. "Come, let's get comfortable, everyone."

The sound of light-hearted chatter and good-natured ribbing, followed by laughter, flowed well into the next hour, and it was only the sound of Gramps clearing his throat, "umh, mmhh," that brought silence.

"I've wanted to say something for a long time," he began, "but somehow the time was never right."

Folks settled themselves and when all was quiet, some leaning forward in anticipation, he began, "I had to wait to be sure what I thought was happening was really happening."

Feeling sure Gramps was about to regale them with tales of visitations by ghosts at the dam again, Devin burrowed deeper into his seat.

"I was coming home one night after work at the Locks and found a fellow with a travel bag, who'd collapsed by the gate," he finished, pointing to the entrance of his yard.

Devin straightened. He hadn't heard this one before.

"Real old too," Gramps began . . .

"Like you?" Zeke snickered.

"Like me," answered Gramps, sounding amused. "I don't know how he ended up at our gate, but he was really weak."

"I remember," Celeste interjected.

"I took him inside and Celeste offered him soup. He managed to eat a bowl before—"

"What was his name?" Old Stanley interrupted.

After a moment, Gramps said, "I think it might have been Alb or Abe." He continued, "he slept on the cot and we went to bed. The next morning, he was gone."

"Gone?" Cindy repeated.

"Yes, we never saw nor heard from him again. But," he paused, and Devin felt he was searching for the right words. Finally, he said, "he left a very odd package."

"What was it?" Stanley interrupted again.

Devin sighed loudly, rolling his eyes.

Gramps glanced at him before saying, "Anybody want to guess what I found?"

"His life savings?" asked Patsy.

"No," said Gramps.

"His pipe?"

"No."

"His harmonica?" said Zeke again. "I always wanted one."

"Shut up, Zeke!" his sister cuffed him on the shoulder. "Why does everything have to be about that stupid harmonica, anyway?"

"Stop, both of you," their mom checked both of them. "Zeke, we'll talk about your harmonica later."

"It's okay. I'll tell you." With a dramatic flair, Gramps pointed to the gazebo and said, "it's the crystal!"

A babble of questions and silly giggles broke out from Lexi's friends. Devin clamped his lips shut to keep himself from sounding rude.

When the twittering and chatter stopped, Gramps said, "I thought maybe he was confused."

"So, was he?" Julie asked the question everyone else seemed to be wondering.

"I still don't know, but Celeste opened the package."

"And I couldn't be happier that I did," agreed Celeste. "That was the day I became whole again."

Devin grounded his teeth as giggles broke out again.

"What happened?" Julie whispered.

"What do you mean?" rasped Becky, a dried-up, old bat from five houses away, known for her ill-tempered nature and a candidate for mischief by the boys in the village. Devin was always sorry when he'd hear of her mishaps.

"Well," Celeste patted Gramps's arm, saying, "It started glowing! Faintly at first. But it became so bright, we couldn't bear it. I've never seen anything so beautiful. It was a shimmering silvery ball. I couldn't move."

Devin felt his fingers clutching at his seat. He forced himself to relax and heard Celeste say, "Then I felt it."

"What?" Old Stanley asked again.

Devin wanted his grandmother to hurry up with the telling, but Old Stanley was becoming the voice for everyone's questions, so he kept his impatience in check.

"It felt like an electric shock was going through my body. I don't know how long I stood there. I couldn't think properly. I became really happy. Then later, I found all my aches, pains, and sickness had left."

Turning to Becky, she said, "I used to have such problems, remember, Becky?"

"So that's why you don't crawl around anymore," Becky snapped.

Startled, Devin saw the same shock cross the faces of everyone present. He took a quick peek at his grandmother, and saw her staring at Becky, her expression unreadable.

"What do you mean you weren't thinking?" continued Old Becky. "You were thinking all right. Only you could have told me at the same time and saved me my pains too. I've become a cripple."

Pain flooded Celeste's eyes at the flow of bitterness from Old Becky, making him think that the kids were right when they messed with the old prune. She deserved every nasty thing that they ever did to her.

"Becky, don't be bitter. Your pains have nothing to do with Celeste. And the healing wasn't something we advertised." The sound of Gramps's voice, reasonable and quiet, startled Devin.

"Of course, you didn't," snapped Becky.

"What are you implying, Becky?" Gramps said with determined calmness.

"We helped everyone that came by over the years, and you know it."

She sniffed. "Helped? You helped everyone?

"Imagine that," Gramps said, with an edge to his voice.

She sniffed. "Well, where's everybody who's been healed then? I still think they said that not to hurt your feelings."

"Feelings? Feelings, Becky?" Gramps repeated, incredulously. "Everyone who came by thought I'd do a funny ritual or give a silly jig or two. I have you to thank for that. You spread those tales that I was loony! Years have gone by, Becky. You should open your heart, or you'll end up a sad, old woman."

"I'm already sad. And old! What difference does it make?"

Devin's gaze, like everyone else's, kept swinging from Becky to Celeste to Gramps in open-mouthed disbelief.

"You can choose to be happy or be bitter," Celeste's tone was mild and gentle. Any sign of anger from before, gone.

"Easy for you to say, Miss Eternal Youth," Old Becky snapped, getting up stiffly and setting off, the sound of her walking stick tapping angrily as she headed home.

Having never seen anyone be nasty to his grandparents, Devin wondered if there was more to what had just transpired. He watched as folks shifted uncomfortably in their seats at Old Becky's unexpected departure, unsure as to how to behave.

"There's someone determined to be miserable." The unexpected sound of Lexi's voice eased the tension and the group settled down.

* ★ *

"Tell us what happened next, Gramps?" The voice of Zeke broke the awkwardness.

"I will, unless anyone else has more complaints?" Gramps said, looking around at the group. None did and after a satisfied nod, he wiggled his eyebrows saying, "I guess I can now, Zeke."

Zeke gave him a thumbs-up sign.

"Well, I built the gazebo and installed the crystal. After that I started the garden."

Listening as Gramps spoke, it reminded Devin that theirs was a steady love in an otherwise drama-filled valley. His wandering mind caught only a bit of what Celeste said, as he stared with renewed interest at the crystal sitting in the white gazebo in Gramps Garden.

Rocks that Gramps had collected from his travels had been placed around the gazebo. Flowers of every type bloomed and danced in the night air, and he'd always thought it was the prettiest garden in the village. Hearing its story, made him wonder what exactly the crystal was supposed to do.

"I think the crystal's alive," Gramps announced.

"Alive?"

The instant chorus of voices told Devin that Gramps had just said the wrong thing.

"Just a minute, let me explain. I've seen the crystal light up at times," Gramps rushed on.

"Light up?" said Gail excitedly, a girl of ten from two houses away.

"How?" exclaimed little Brett.

"When was this? And what color was it?" Zeke chimed in.

Gramps raised his hands, halting the flow. "It stopped healing as far as I know. It happened when I returned late from work, and was going up to the house. The whole crystal was lit up. The front yard was bright white. I couldn't move."

"What did you do then?" said Zeke in a hushed voice.

"Well, I watched. Everywhere was glowing and the air felt different. I remember feeling like bubbles were floating everywhere."

"What happened?" Devin felt the words leaving his mouth, unwilling to break the moment, but intrigued.

"It disappeared," Gramps said quietly. "I went up and touched it. It felt warm but no light."

"What did you do then?" Zeke continued.

"I went upstairs and kept watching, but it didn't happen again. I saw it again on the next full moon and kept track. I've followed it ever since."

"Wow," whispered Devin, knowing things were never going to be as they were before. It was pointless, trying to tell everyone that their evening was at an end.

"I gotta see this stuff," said old Stanley.

"Me too," several voices echoed.

"And me," said Zeke.

Devin saw his mom looking around helplessly.

Gramps scratched his head, cautiously saying, "Well, I don't know. It has to be okay with Rae."

Everyone turned to his mom, and Devin was secretly happy when his mom nodded.

"Sleepover! Yeah!" Zeke hoorayed, getting up and dancing a jig.

Devin smiled, thinking that it was Gramps's intention all along and wondered what the old geezer was up to. But an odd sensation flickered through him, and he paused as strange thoughts entered his mind.

He loved Gramps dearly, but people didn't really understand the old man. Even the ones listening would change the story in the retelling. New meanings would be added and simple words would take on new meanings. Suddenly he wished Gramps hadn't said anything, the odd feeling refusing to leave.

Amid much bantering and friendly pushing around, every old blanket, sheet, jute bag, pillow, and anything that could make a bed, was gathered. Anticipation filled the air and time passed quickly. Almost two hours later, with the youngest ones having nodded off, a hushed expectancy descended. Devin felt the unfamiliar sensation in the pit of his stomach, making him shiver.

"Gramps is just playing with us, aren't you, Gramps?" Zeke called out. "All the time everybody made fun of you. I bet this is payback, right?"

Lexi flung a pillow, hitting him in the face. "Hey! Why'd do that?" he snapped, flinging it back in a huff. It fell on Skippy, their dog who rrhh in annoyance.

"Shut up, Zeke!" Austin flung the pillow back at Zeke who ducked and laughed. It landed on the sleeping Brett, and in a second, a pained wail erupted. Zeke made a hurried escape, deciding he needed a visit to the outhouse. Devin breathed a sigh of relief. It was eleven thirty and everyone was in countdown mode. He really had no patience for Zeke's antics.

* * *

The odd sensation deepened in his stomach, and in the next moment, lightning erupted across the sky, streaking in fierce slashes that traveled like fingers of fire snaking down at them. Thunder clapped directly overhead, and Devin felt the undulating reverberation across the village.

The confused cries of the children sounded as they found themselves jolted awake by the thunder. With the adults trying to calm them down, Devin saw the same stunned look on their faces at the suddenness of the changing weather. The wind picked up, howling around, and a bone-jarring crack of thunder rumbled overhead.

Devin felt their home, No. 5 Blessings Way, had mysteriously become the focus of some unknown wrath from the heavens and watched as blips of silver mist jetted out in arches around them. The beams flew forth in splinters, and the glittering dust flowed in waves around the yard.

He watched as Gramps stared at the crystal and knew his grandfather's stories had finally made the most dramatic of appearances. The gazebo sat serenely amidst the raging storm. As the storm intensified, the wind shrieked in an unrecognized offense and the beautiful moonlit night changed into the weird, with an undefined mood seeping in.

Jolted into action, Devin, his mom and Lexi rushed to get the little ones into the safety of their first-floor kitchen. Wet and miserable, they all gathered inside and soon he got a nice fire going in the old fireplace, adding warmth to their chilled bones.

Lexi helped their mom do her best to ease the strangeness, and as the little ones sat in quiet fear, the storm went on before eventually abating. Devin noticed the mood shifting as a stillness descended, erasing any remnant unease from before. Folks slowly began to make themselves comfortable and gradually nodded off.

★ ★ ★

It was a long and weary night for the neighbors, and as morning approached, on awakening, it was the first thing they all talked about. Disappointed they didn't get a chance to see the crystal come alive, Devin listened on as everyone endlessly speculated about why the strange storm happened.

"Well, I think you should have warned us, Gramps," said Patsy.

Devin left the kitchen, a silly chuckle escaping his lips. He caught sight of Lexi standing with arms folded, watching him.

"It's been a really strange night, Devin. You shouldn't laugh at people."

"Well, I can't help it," he replied. "Warned her? How could Gramps have warned anybody?"

Lexi gave him a dark look saying, "Well, he's the one always going on about strange stuff, isn't he?"

"I think that's what he was doing, Lex." Devin answered.

Lexi shook her head, muttered something rude and headed back inside. He left it alone, anxious for everyone to leave.

Going back into the kitchen, he saw folks were busy bidding farewell and knew that they couldn't wait to tell their version of what had happened. It would be the main topic for weeks to come. He sighed and hid his disappointment when Gramps and Celeste went home, fatigued from the strange night.

It wasn't until later when he had finished his chores that Devin remembered the rocks and quickly headed for the pile. He'd been busy making sure that the poultry was taken care of and didn't want to have his mom yelling.

Now, standing beside them, something felt out of place, an absence of sort. Unable to figure out what was odd, he looked around. Other than broken branches and scattered leaves from the night before, things seemed fine. But that nagging feeling wouldn't budge. He walked slowly around the pile, his mind going back to the events from last night. The storm was beyond spooky, but it didn't explain the emptiness he felt.

It wasn't the first time Gramps was expanding his garden and had rocks delivered. So, what had changed this time? He had quite a collection of odd rocks and stones he had stashed by the gazebo. Gramps would look at him and grin every time he added a new one.

"What's so funny, Gramps?" he'd asked several times.

Gramps would only chuckle, saying "I'm not the only odd one in the family, Dev."

And then it hit him! Devin felt the breath sucked out of him as he watched the vibrant, sparkling pile of rocks from the evening before lay dull and sad beneath him. That was it! That's what was missing! With all the weird goings-on with the storm, how was he supposed to know this would happen? Rocks didn't die!

He grabbed a handful. Nothing! No fuzzy current zinging up his hands. Digging through the pile, he found a coating of dust everywhere. It couldn't be.

"Now you see what I mean?"

He hopped around, startled to find Gramps watching him.

Devin's heart pounded wildly for a moment. He hadn't heard Gramps' approach.

"Even you can tell something's wrong." Gramps continued staring at him.

Thinking that it was the perfect opening, he asked, "What does it mean, Gramps? Just look at this stuff! Rocks don't die!"

Gramps was silent, looking around.

"I'm scared," Devin blurted out, and then, realizing what he had just admitted, fell quiet.

Gramps's expression softened and he nodded. "Me too, Dev. Didn't think I would say it, but I am." He moved over, motioning for Devin to sit down and did the same.

"Strange things have been happening for some time now. I don't know exactly what it means."

"Strange good or strange bad?" asked Devin.

"Well, I'm not really sure," replied Gramps. "One doesn't happen without the other. If it's a bad thing, some good will follow, but . . ." After a long silence, he started again. "If it's something good, I'm scared to think about the bad that will follow."

Devin digested this bit, unsure he wanted to know any more. His fear deepened, knowing Gramps being this worried was not a good sign.

"Gramps, you think it was because we tried to see the things you talked about?"

"I really don't know, Dev. I thought the same thing. I just wanted folks to know that I was really telling the truth. I always figured it had something to do with Ohhm."

"Why?" asked Devin.

"Well, everything around here started with Ohhm. Everybody I know of has some link to Ohhm. All we have are stories of Ohhm. I remember hearing of amazing animals and magical folks. I heard of people living for hundreds of years."

"Hundreds of years!"

"Yes," continued Gramps, "prophecies, strange powers, and things. I guess I convinced myself that it meant something. Don't really know what. I kinda had this thing in my head."

"What kinds of things?" asked Devin, thinking he'd gotten his first clue.

"Well," said Gramps, "if the crystal was special, we know it healed a lot of people, and I saw it coming to life, I think you'd have to agree that it was alive. Right?"

"I—," began Devin.

"Everything was magical, strange, and extraordinary," interrupted Gramps. "It's not unreasonable to think that it came from Ohhm."

"Ah, Gramps, you think . . ."

"The thing I've been trying to figure out," continued Gramps as if he hadn't spoken, "is what it means. I don't know if something's about to happen or—"

Devin could tell Gramps was worrying too much and said hurriedly, "Do you think it's okay now that folks know about it then?" Devin was worried himself now.

"Well, I can't exactly change that now, can I?"

He couldn't argue. Knowing Gramps already regretted saying the things that he had said last night, he kept quiet. Gramps seemed scared, almost as if he himself believed that they had somehow brought an unknown wrath upon themselves.

It dawned on him that Gramps was trying to prove to everyone that he wasn't loony. As much as Gramps had told off the old bat, it did bother him. Now guilt was added to his worries.

"Gramps, you don't know for sure that the storm happened because you talked about the crystal. You don't even know if it came from Ohhm. And how were you supposed to know anything would happen anyway?"

"Yes, Dev, but I'm the one who saw it coming alive over the years. Celeste was healed, I swear. Other people too. I didn't make any of that stuff up."

"I believe you, Gramps," replied Devin. "Maybe that's all they'll ever talk about now. You don't have to worry about people disbelieving you anymore. We all saw what happened."

"I just wanted everyone to see what I have been able to do," said Gramps, his voice cracking as he fell silent.

"Well, it's like you said. We can't change any of that now. We'll just have to wait and see."

Devin felt Gramps reach out and hug him. It felt strange to comfort Gramps. Confused and sad, for the first time, he felt Gramps was an old man. He reached out, returning the hug tightly.

NIGHT WATCH

Devin lay under his tattered, grungy blanket on an old but comfortable mattress he'd rescued for his little platform. It was perfect for what he had planned. Their parents had gone to a remote village for some seeds and supplies his father needed for the next gardening season, leaving Lexi in charge.

No neighbors tonight. When they had asked earlier that afternoon, he'd told them his parents were away and had decided to stay up and watch all by himself. He didn't tell Lexi what he'd planned, but had snuck out, leaving the upstairs backdoor closed but unlocked. If nothing happened, no one would be the wiser. But boy, he couldn't wait to tell Gramps if he saw the phenomenon tonight.

As lights from neighbors slowly started going out, he felt better. The lamp across the street flickered and went dark. Eventually, even Gramps's home had just a single oil lamp burning.

His cousins and grandparents shared one huge plot of land, boundaries divided by small clumps of hedges and rows of wildflowers. Their home was already in darkness as they had recently moved away, and as memories of the fun times they once shared flooded him, he wondered when he would see them again.

To his right was the vegetable garden his dad grew. Further along was a small pond and just behind it, to the right was their henhouse under coconut palms. He had a good position to observe anyone approaching and kept an eye out for anything unusual.

With the crickets serenading the night air, Devin gazed at the stars twinkling above and checked the time on a small watch he'd brought along. He still had a while to wait, so he decided to read an old book that he had randomly gotten from his mom's collection.

A strange sensation washed over him and as it increased, he peeked through the eye holes in the blanket. The swaying clump of young bamboos directly in front of him, offered protection from anyone looking his way. Seeing nothing unusual, he went back to the book.

He was surprised to read the title of the book: *Ohhm, A Forgotten Land.*

"My lucky night after all," he thought, opening the cover and reading the first page.

In years to come and on full moon's shine
The one reading this will be Him
Darkness threatens and That which was taken
Becomes known
The quest will be started,
Yet he knows it not
A gift he'll be given,
But still remains unknown
In gaining, he will lose
In loss lies strength
Once done, will not be undone
A journey filled with darkness should he waver,
Conquer
And Man's way shall be eternal,
It begins now with the call answered . . .

He closed it shut, feeling a shiver down his spine. "It couldn't be! It's just a book. It didn't mean anything," he kept telling himself, slowly opening the book and re-reading the verse. He felt the words vibrating, connecting him with an unknown force. He closed it, unwilling to accept what it said.

Forcing himself to look away, he saw patches of water glinting off the tiny brook flowing beneath the bamboo, the rustle of leaves whispering into the night. Gramps' garden bloomed in secret romance under the moonlight. Everything was normal.

Which made him wonder how his grandfather was able to have the fruit trees bearing year-round and flowers and shrubs flowering nonstop. There was something secretive about Gramps' way that said there was a lot to the old man he didn't quite know.

He was still afraid to think about what he'd just read and tried convincing himself it was pure coincidence. He searched for ordinary things to think about and remembered the recent activities around the schools, the rice-harvesting season and the release of a movie that had scandalized the locals. Devin wondered what The Village Beat, the local newspaper, would make of everything.

So far, he was surprised to see that the strange storm which had disrupted their meet-up last month hadn't made its way to the newspaper, but was glad Gramps was spared another round of ridicule.

* * *

The sound of faint music drifted in, signaling the local bar would soon be closing. As loud voices approached, he watched two drunks stagger their way home, stumbling and singing off-tuned on their way.

They soon disappeared and a heavy silence crept in.

He felt his breathing quickened and the sensation of butterflies fluttering inside his stomach. Strange thoughts flitted through his mind, gone before they had solidified and a whisper in his ear, "You have nothing to fear."

He jumped, his heart pounding against his chest, his head swiveling from side to side. He heard a hoarse croak, "Who's there?" before realizing he'd spoken aloud. His eyes searched every nook and corner, every little crevice that he could find but saw no one. Could Lexi be playing a joke on him? He waited and, eventually feeling stupid, settled down. He felt his panic dissipate and the constricting emotion ooze itself out.

It was still only eleven-fifteen. Feeling a bit hungry, he ate the sandwich he'd made earlier and drank some water. Feeling refreshed, he settled down to wait for midnight.

Thumping and creaking noises sounded above, telling him Lexi was getting ready for bed. He remembered how she'd run screaming on finding earthworms in her trinket box. He grinned, but it faded quickly and his nose twitched as he recalled the now all-too familiar stench — the stench that came from a week's worth of cleaning the droppings in the henhouse as punishment. Now it was a regular chore and he had no one but himself to blame for that particular piece of mischief.

Sighing, he returned to the present, hoping he wasn't wasting his time sneaking out and waiting up. The odd sensation of being talked to flooded him and he listened, but only silence met his ears, broken only when a hoot from an owl gave him a start.

The village sat in sleepy silence as midnight struck and a sweet smell wafted in. He sniffed. It wasn't from the fruits from the nearby orchard. He tried again, thinking of honeysuckles. Maybe jasmine? No.

The stillness deepened and he watched as a sparkling, spangled veil of moonbeams danced across his vision. Thousands of bubbles appeared, floating by, hovering in front of him, silvery and delicate. He reached out, touching one. It popped and a needle of warmth shot through his finger, filling him with joy.

Not a sound filtered in the deep silence that descended as the crystal glowed and slowly became a bright, white, shimmering ball. Sitting in front of him was proof that Gramps hadn't lied. It was really true. He wasn't crazy after all!

He watched as bright sparks emitted from it. Devin felt a faint movement as tiny droplets fell. He left his seat and crossed the yard to stand in front of the gazebo, feeling a coolness against his skin. Stretching his hands out, he felt the silvery droplets gather in his palms.

"Holy moonlight! It couldn't be!" He watched as beads of liquid moonlight like little mercury drops he'd seen in class, sprinkle everywhere. He tilted his face up, letting himself be covered in their magic as everything around glowed with shimmering beauty.

He felt the crystal drawing him forward and walked into the gazebo. Reaching out, he touched it, feeling a rush of warmth travel up his arms. He felt a strange, pulsating rhythm through his spine to the head and found himself unable to move. It continued for a long time, keeping him connected. He felt a sense of joy pouring forth.

How long it went on Devin couldn't say but the bubbles vanished just as suddenly as they had appeared. The crystal too gradually dimmed and stopped glowing. Disoriented, he stumbled back to his platform, breathing like he'd just finished running a marathon.

He sat down, feeling his mind expand and his awareness becoming filled with a symphony of sensations. When his mind began working properly again, he remembered that his grandmother had been healed by touching the crystal. What did it mean for him? He didn't have sickness of any sort. Devin searched for an answer but came up empty.

A NEW FRIEND

Movement at the entrance of Gramps' yard startled him. Devin blinked, trying to get his focus clear. Who could be at the gate at this hour of the night? Did Gramps go to work and was now coming home? He thought they were home.

But then he spotted someone crouching down outside the gate and felt his chest flutter in fear as the form rose and came into view — a person slowly peering into the yard. Who was sneaking into Gramps' yard and why? he wondered.

The gate slowly opened. Devin felt his palms grow sweaty and his heart pounding loudly against his chest. He worried that whoever was out there could hear his heart thumping. Torn between running with his club at the intruder and rushing back to safety upstairs, fear paralyzed him. By the time he could move, it was already too late. He was ready to yell but found, to his great surprise, a calm settled over him.

The intruder was still working at the chain that looped around the gate and fence. He heard the chain snap and drop with a thud to the ground. A small figure came into view. It was a kid like himself — crawling on all fours and heading toward the gazebo.

"No, no, no!" he stared in disbelief as the kid reached the gazebo, rose up and lifted the crystal off the base and stashed it in his shoulder pouch.

"No, no, no!" Devin tried to yell, but found his lips sealed. He decided to go and demand it back, but stopped on hearing a voice call out.

The kid replied in silent gestures and Devin felt his fear deepen when the form of a large man detached itself from the gate and stepped inside the yard.

"Give it over kid!" The man demanded.

A chill shot up Devin's spine. Eager to get a clearer view, he shifted and felt his foot upset an old spade that had been leaning against the platform. Desperately he reached out for the spade and caught it just as it was about to crash on the ground. He laid it down as quietly as he could but nearly jumped out of his skin as a loud "meow" sounded. He saw Carrots, their pet cat, go streaking away from the platform.

The intruders stood like statues, gazing intently in his direction. Devin thanked the gods that they didn't decide to investigate. "What timing!" he thought, betting Carrots had gotten a whiff of the sandwich he'd eaten earlier and had kept him company. As she made her way across Gramps' yard, meowing and rubbing herself against the man's legs, they visibly relaxed.

"Hand it over kid!"

The kid didn't move.

"Now! Give it over."

The kid stood stubbornly clutching the pouch that now held the crystal.

"I won't ask again," the man snarled again.

"You'll leave us alone now?"

A resounding "whack" sounded and the kid fell over.

Devin felt his jaw drop and watched the man grab the sack and tug. The kid struggled, trying to sit up.

"You'll be still if you know what's good for you. A deal's a deal. Now let go."

Devin wanted to yell and demand the return of the crystal, certain that the kid was being stupid. But, he found himself rooted to his seat, feeling like his lips were glued together. No matter how hard he tried, he couldn't move. So, he sat there watching them, frozen in frustration.

The kid grabbed onto the man's leg the same moment the sack came free. The man kicked out to dislodge him and the kid doubled over with a howl. The man ignored him, grabbed the sack and backed away, hurrying through the gate and disappearing down the street.

Relief flooded Devin as he felt himself released from the strange frozenness that had engulfed him and watched the kid crawl forward, whimpering softly and reaching down into the small brook which ran in between the yard separating theirs from his grandparents. Devin watched him splash water on his face. His pain was evident as he stayed huddled over for a long time.

A million thoughts flitted in and out of Devin's head. He'd come prepared to do some spying to see the mysterious glow from the crystal. But, nothing had prepared him for this.

The kid looked up and found his eyes locked with Devin's. Wild fright flooded his face.

"Shh," Devin indicated, putting his finger to his lips. "Friend." Pointing to the gate, he said, "He's gone."

Without waiting for the kid to respond, he went over to the kid, relieved to find himself able to move again.

"I'm Devin, what's your name?"

"Rusty," the voice came out small and scared.

"Are you okay?" Devin wasn't sure how badly the kid was hurt. "Come, let's go inside."

After a few moments, the kid nodded and Devin reached out, grabbing him by the arm. Putting his shoulder under Rusty's shoulder, he pulled him upright while supporting him. Rusty groaned, leaning heavily on him, and hobbled along.

Hoping no one had woken up, Devin hauled Rusty to their kitchen and settled him on a wooden chair, before returning to secure the bolt on the door. Feeling for a box of matches, he lit a small lamp.

He went about getting some bread, cheese, chicken legs from the earlier roast and some fruit along with a mug of water.

Placing them on the small table in front of Rusty, he sat down and motioned his guest to help himself.

Rusty sat up and then leaned back hurriedly. Devin said nothing. Moments passed but Rusty still said nothing. After a while, he timidly took some water and sipped then slowly began to eat, before picking up his pace. Devin watched as Rusty devoured the food.

* * *

Devin kept his silence and waited, watching Rusty closely. Rusty squirmed under his scrutiny, his eyes becoming guarded.

"Why did you take the crystal?"

"I had to", he said simply, offering neither denial nor excuses.

"Why?"

"He made me."

Irritated, Devin snapped, "Who is that man?"

Rusty bent his head, staying quiet. Devin could see tears glistening in his eyes.

"Listen," he tried again, "I know you're scared, but that crystal belongs to my grandfather. You just can't take it the way you did!"

More silence followed.

"Okay, maybe I should get Gramps here. He'll know what to do."

Rusty jumped out of his chair. "No, no. Don't. Please don't get anyone! Please!"

Devin felt a tiny shred of shame on hearing how Rusty pleaded and paused, taking in the unkempt hair, the patched shirt and pants, and the way the holes in the knees had been darned. The kid was rather good looking with dark brown eyes accented by long, curly lashes. He seemed ready to bolt and Devin knew he had to think of something quickly.

"Tell you what? I promise I won't get Gramps if you tell me everything," he said, fingers crossed behind his back.

Rusty gave him a long, considering look, before taking his seat again.

"My family lives at the edge of the village, next to the beach. We're gypsies. Our camp is hidden by the woods."

Devin repeated, "Gypsies? Camp? What camp?"

Rusty smiled. "Yeah, I'm a Gypsy. Something happened a long time ago and ever since we've been here. Zoie, my grandma, says not to worry why we got stuck in Foxwood Village because it coulda been anywhere."

Curiosity flooded Devin, his anger for the moment forgotten.

"I've never heard of Gypsies. What do you do? How do you live?" Then realizing how it sounded, he muttered, "Sorry I meant like what is a Gypsy anyway?"

Rusty didn't seem to take offense. "We're tribes of wandering people, or at least, that's what I've been told. Zoie says it was different long ago and I don't know the details."

"I see," said Devin. "I'm amazed you live so close and I've never heard of your people. What do your people do?"

Rusty shrugged. "We get by. We haven't been on the road in years. Some of us are allowed at school. Zoie is old but takes care of the little ones at camp. Mom works at the Hibiscus Inn . . ." An odd look crossed his face for a brief second, disappearing just as quickly. But Devin had noticed.

"What's wrong?" asked Devin.

"Nothing"

Devin looked at him.

"Just the drunks can be creeps."

Devin nodded, knowing how ugly the village drunks and their antics got at times. He shelved that particular thought aside for the moment and waited.

"My dad, well, I don't know too much about him," Rusty started.

"Wait a minute!" Devin stared at Rusty. "You said you go to school?"

"Yeah," replied Rusty.

"Where?" said Devin.

"Beachside Academy," he answered, seeming scared that he had said the wrong thing.

"But I go there! How come I've never seen you?"

Rusty shrugged. "I'm not like you, you know. Kids from my camp sit in the old room under the office."

"But that's a kind of a storage room of sorts. At least that's what we were told," he corrected.

"Kinda," replied Rusty, shrugging again. "But it's the only place we can go to."

Devin was appalled. "How could they do this?"

"I want to learn," Rusty said defiantly, as if daring Devin to laugh at him.

Devin nodded, unwilling to believe what he'd heard.

"People treat us as outcasts. Some kids attack us."

"You mean like . . . like even now?"

"Yup." Rusty nodded, then delivered another shocker. "But we work. We clean the toilets and take out the trash when everyone's gone. We sweep the yard . . ."

"What!" bellowed Devin, almost falling off his seat, "You . . . !" Seeing Rusty's expression, he lowered his voice. "You what? Why? How?"

Devin was speechless for a moment before saying, "They have people to do those kinds of things."

"Yeah . . . us," Rusty agreed.

Devin couldn't find a proper response. Eventually he managed, "I'm sorry."

Rusty nodded.

Then he asked the question topmost in his thoughts. "So, what do we do about the crystal?"

Rusty's eyes grew large, unsure if Devin was still angry. Finally, he said, "I don't know. What's so important about it anyway?"

Devin stared at him and Rusty had the grace to look embarrassed. "Did you ask that fellow why he had you steal it?" Devin shot back.

"Ohhh…! Rusty. "Yes, true. I didn't think. Maybe it's valuable or does something special."

"Gramps said an old fellow gave it to him a long, long time ago. And it's supposed to heal folks." Devin didn't say he himself had witnessed the crystal come alive, but it wasn't anyone's business anyways. He just wanted to get the crystal back before anyone found out.

Rusty sat up, a grimace of pain crossing his features. "I wonder . . ." Rusty mused.

Devin cleared his throat in annoyance. "What?" he said impatiently.

"Zoie's always telling us how things used to be that I've kinda stopped listening. But she did talk about a crystal from a long time ago."

"Hmm," Devin tapped his foot.

"Wish I could remember," Rusty said. "She always talks of stuff from when she was little. There was a wise one then."

"Wise one?"

"Yeah," said Rusty. We have Rupert but he's not what he used to be."

Devin was confused. "Yes, but how would a wise one help us if Zoie was telling you stories?" Devin couldn't follow.

"Oh, they know everything," Rusty said simply.

Devin sighed. He must be more tired than he realized.

"Why don't we speak to Gramps?"

Rusty shook his head vigorously, looking sorry he'd said anything.

"Okay, tell me about the guy who hit you. Who is he?" Devin tried again.

"That's Rennie, the Renegade. He works for Ole Higue," Rusty whispered.

Devin stared blankly. "Old. . . . who?"

"Ole Higue," Rusty replied. "You mean . . . you don't know? You never heard of her?"

Devin shook his head. "Nope."

"Well, she's the most evil, nasty, old hag there is. A witch is what she is. You know," he continued . . . "you hardly see her, but she's there. She's always there. She's been there for a long time. Before I was born. Zoie said she remembers stories since she was little. The great storm blew her in." He stopped, seeming scared he'd said so much.

"Are you talking about the old woman down by the beach?" said Devin with a frown. "There're a few of them around. I've heard a lot of stories from Gramps but never any about Ole Higue."

"Then, you don't think it's true? You think because I'm a gypsy, I lie?"

"What? When did I say you lied? You come here, steal Gramps' crystal, tell me some story and because I don't agree with you, you're angry. You're angry?" He snapped again, his voice rising. "I should just forget about feeling sorry for you!" Anger and fear had built up, and it felt good to yell.

When Rusty said nothing, they both sat, breathing hard, staring at each other.

Finally, Rusty said, "I didn't mean that."

"Good," said Devin, relieved. "Now tell me what you know."

"Well, I know she's a witch. Zoie wouldn't lie, and we've seen things. Stuff is always missing from our garden."

"Okay," said Devin. "The old lady . . . I don't think you're lying. It's just I've never had any reason to be scared of her. If it's the same person," he added as an afterthought. Then seeing Rusty's expression, he hurried on, "Anyway, about the crystal."

"The Renegade grabbed me on the way to school. He threatened to tell the authorities I've been stealing from people if I didn't help him get something he needed," Rusty said. Then continued, "I didn't know he'd have me steal the crystal."

"Well, it's lucky I was sleeping out then."

Rusty nodded, seeming untroubled at this.

The hours had flown by, and they had become friends of sorts.

"Thanks for helping me."

The simple statement gave Devin a warm feeling. But since they'd talked themselves out for the time being, he nodded. Tiredness had crept in and he said, "Let's get some sleep."

Rusty nodded.

Yawning, he got up and helped Rusty over to the cot. Taking some old comforters to the floor next to the cot, he made a bed for himself and asked, "What about your folks? Wouldn't they worry about you?"

Rusty gave him an odd look before saying, "It's okay. Mom knows I sleep out. Sometimes by the beach to get fish. Or . . . well, sometimes when the boats come in."

Tired, Devin said goodnight and settled down, keeping an ear out in case Rusty tried to escape. His last thought as he drifted off was who was Ole Higue and what did she and Rennie have to do with the missing crystal.

* * *

He was in a strange cave, reaching almost a hundred feet high. Sunlight poured in from a large hole in the roof where a huge tree sat precariously at the edge, its roots hanging down like an enormous bundle of ropes, ending at a small mound covered in greenery, sitting in the center of a small pool of water.

He looked around, seeing rocks and boulders scattered about. Strange ferns, vines, and ivies grew in the shaded areas, with flowers blooming from nooks and crannies. Reflections from the water danced on the wall, reminding him of the night he'd connected with the crystal. Something glowed on the mound in the pool, and he felt his heart beginning to race.

He watched the glow becoming brighter and brighter and walked forward, stepping into the shallow water, hands reaching out to it.

Bang! Bang! Bang!

He reeled backwards, spinning in a whirl of empty space.

Bang!

"Devin, are you in there? Open up! What are you up to now?"

He scrambled up stupidly, fuzzy with sleep. Stumbling to the door, he hastily unlocked it and felt his mind clearing quickly. He'd completely forgotten Lexi had to get in the kitchen in the morning. He blinked, trying to adjust to the sudden brightness.

"Shhh . . ." he indicated to Lexi, jamming his finger to his lip.

"It's about time . . ." Lexi stopped mid-sentence, surprised to see Rusty on the cot. Eyebrows shooting upward, she silently mouthed, "Who's that?"

Devin led her way over to the sink, away from Rusty but still within eyesight of him. He whispered, telling her only necessary parts.

When she said nothing, he grimaced inwardly, wondering if he'd be in for severe punishment. A small sound came as Rusty woke up and on seeing Lexi, he sat up, swinging his legs to the floor.

Lexi walked over, extending her hand. "Hey, I'm Lexi. Devin was telling me about last night."

Rusty stared at her hand a minute before reaching out and shaking it, clearly surprised at her friendliness.

"Uh . . . yeah, nice to meet you too," he stuttered.

"How're you feeling?" she asked.

"Like an elephant ran over me," he returned.

"Maybe you'll feel better after we eat. Wanna help?"

"Sure."

She grinned, saying "Dev'll show you where to wash up. You guys hurry up and get the eggs."

★ ★ ★

The events of the night on hold, Devin felt alive, and happy to have someone around. Rusty was badly bruised but otherwise quite fun. After dunking their heads in the tub by the washstand and washing up, Devin proceeded to the henhouse to feed the hens and gather eggs.

Breakfast turned out to be quite lively and with his initial fear gone, Rusty was good in the kitchen. Lexi bustled around with the frying pan and kettle on the small kerosene stove. In no time, breakfast was ready.

As Rusty sat wolfing down scrambled eggs and bread with jam while swallowing cups of tea, Devin grinned as he watched Lexi's unamused expression at Rusty's lack of etiquette. "Chill, Sis. It's just us," he warbled, his mouth stuffed with a handful of fruit.

Lexi sighed but curiosity got the better of her and she began asking Rusty endless questions, who bloomed under her attention.

Devin wanted to point out it was rude to eat and talk, but knowing Lexi, it wouldn't do any good. He quashed his impatience, hoping Rusty would give some other clues away in his chatter. Giving Rusty a kick under the table, he indicated the door. Rusty was quick to take the hint.

"Zoie is the one you want to speak with. She knows stuff that'll scare the pants off you."

"Lex, I want Rusty to meet Gramps and Celeste," he said, keeping his expression innocent of any frustration.

"Yeah, okay," she said. "I think Celeste said they needed to pick fruits. Maybe Rusty could help?"

"Pick fruits?" Rusty repeated desperately.

When she looked at him, he muttered, "Okay, sure."

Devin was sure that Rusty remembered his suggestion from last night about meeting Gramps, but said nothing.

"Mom makes jam, Lexi said. "Sometimes we have to give them away because it's a lot, and they go bad. Gramps is older now and it's a lot for him to do all on his own."

"I'll help Lex. I don't mind," Rusty agreed.

Devin knew even if Rusty did mind, he couldn't back out now and with breakfast over, they cleaned up with a thank you from Rusty and headed over to Gramps's place.

With his milk cans clanking and jangling on the gravel street, they watched as Slink, a medium-sized man, wearing a dirty t-shirt and a pair of worn, baggy jeans rode his bicycle along, heading for the day ahead.

Devin laughed when Rusty told him how the guys at the Mill had given him the name since he was always "slinking" away for his "medicinal drink."

"That fella hangs out with the Renegade down by the inn where Mom works."

"Ohh," said Devin. He could feel a memory lodged at the edge of his mind, refusing to fully come forth. He knew Slink to be Jesse, the stone carver's grandson who'd inherited the little property when the old man passed away. But he didn't get to finish the thought as they spotted Gramps leaning out the doorway, his face breaking into a welcome smile. Devin felt even more nervous to give him the bad news.

"I wondered if you'd be coming over. And who's this?" He looked at Rusty stepping aside as they entered.

"Hey, Gramps. Hi, Gran. Lexi said you wanted to pick fruits." Without pausing, Devin continued, "This is my friend, Rusty. Rusty, these are my grandparents, Gramps and my Gran Celeste."

"Hello, Rusty," said Gramps, shaking his hand.

Wisps of gray hair straggled out of its habitual bun giving his Gran a rather flighty look, making Devin grin. She hugged him and smiled at Rusty, laying a hand on his shoulder.

"You must be new around here. I haven't seen you before."

Rusty's face lit up when she said, "Devin needs a friend around here. Since his cousins left, he's been lonely."

"Yes, Devin's a good friend," he agreed. "I live down by the beach."

Gramps turned a surprised but interested look at Rusty. "Down by the beach? You mean you're a Gypsy?"

Devin felt surprised that Gramps knew of them.

Rusty nodded, happy to be recognized.

"Well, son, it's good to know your folks are still around," Gramps said. "I knew some people a long while back. I thought your tribe had left. What happened?"

"Dunno. Zoie might, though," he replied with a smile.

"Zoie?" Gran asked.

"My grandmother," Rusty answered.

Devin was happy he'd befriended him but he was anxious, wondering how to break the news of the missing crystal to Gramps.

"Rusty's helping us with the fruits, Gramps."

"We better get a start before it gets any hotter then," replied Gramps. "Will you get the baskets, Dev, and meet us in the orchard? Come Rusty, let's get moving. Getting his hat from its rack by the door, Gramps led the way out, leaving Devin gathering his wits.

His heart fluttering in fear, knowing they might get to the crystal before he had time to say anything, Devin flung out the doorway and rushed to get the baskets. Furiously thinking of an explanation, he hurried after them, breathing easier on spotting they had stopped to look at some fruit trees along the pathway.

With Gramps doing the talking, time passed and the baskets filled up quickly. Devin still wasn't any closer to telling Gramps about the Crystal. He decided he had to try.

"Hey, Gramps, can you tell me about Ole Higue?" he asked.

Gramps sent him a strange look, "Why do you want to know? And who's been telling you of such a creature?"

Rusty stopped picking and Devin could see his head tilted in alarm. He ignored him, watching his grandfather's face go through a series of strange expressions.

* * *

Gramps felt the memories of the old events they'd all had to deal with flooding him again. Cattle that died in strange ways, children who'd been victims of mysterious ailments, suffering weird symptoms. Many had never recovered, causing people to believe a dark and sinister force had moved in. Ole Higue was birthed and stories became wilder as the years progressed. Villagers far and wide had gone to great lengths to protect themselves.

He remembered how he'd comforted many who'd lost family members under the belief they'd been victims of dark and ugly things. Superstitions and strange remedies had come alive. Then, the stories went quiet when folks thought if the name was called it would invite Ole Higue's attention. They'd done their best to ignore its presence and pretend it didn't exist, but people still talk about it in hushed tones when unusual happenings occurred.

Whether this was true or not, Gramps didn't want to entertain it. The last thing young minds needed to hear was anything to do with the dark. He deliberately took his time in responding and when he did, he said, "Anything I know is pretty much what I've told you before, Dev."

"Yeah, but you never said anything about Ole Higue. And I know you know stuff. I didn't know you knew about Rusty's people until just now."

"Well, I never had any reason to talk about them. I'm just surprised they're still around."

Rusty, religiously picking fruits, seemed oblivious to the conversation, but Devin wasn't fooled. He knew there was something to the story. Why would Gramps avoid telling him?

Thinking maybe Gramps would say once Rusty left, he went back to picking, still having said nothing of the stolen crystal.

Celeste brought them out a jug of lemonade and some sandwiches.

He drank thirstily and then, finding a shaded spot, sat down. With a sandwich almost to his mouth, he heard Rusty announce, "I should be going. It's getting late."

He couldn't let Rusty leave this way. He needed to know more, and by hook or crook, Gramps needed to know about the crystal! Now that he knew Gramps had known of the gypsy folks, he might learn even more things.

Gramps cleared his throat.

Rusty looked at him and said, "Thanks, Gramps."

"You're welcome, son. And next time, tell me what you were doing here last night." The boys jumped, with Rusty dropping his sandwich.

"How did you? I mean what did you . . ." he couldn't finish. He sat down.

"Devin wasn't the only one up last night," said Gramps.

They jumped again, color draining from Rusty's face. "I can explain," he began.

"Okay," said Gramps.

Devin saw Gramps was looking at him. Silence grew.

A chickadee chirped in the branches above. Devin felt his stomach flutter. It wasn't his fault the crystal was stolen. He'd only been guilty of being out when it happened.

"Well, it's really not his fault," began Rusty.

Gramps looked at Devin. "Devin's fault? That you slept over?" A bewildered look crossed his face. "I thought you two were friends."

"We are," said Rusty.

"We are, Gramps," echoed Devin in alarm. This wasn't going as he'd planned.

"So, what's not Devin's fault?" Gramps questioned, head swinging from Rusty to Devin.

"He meant the crystal," Devin said, seeing the helpless look on Rusty's face.

"The crystal?" Gramps repeated, his gaze confused. "What about the crystal?" he called, already walking toward the gazebo.

"That's what he's trying to tell you," Devin replied, quite scared.

"The Renegade . . . the Renegade made me steal it last night, and that's how Devin knows me!" Rusty cut him off. "I was scared. I know it was wrong. I'm sorry."

Devin felt he had to say something and started to interrupt, but Rusty rudely cut him off, speaking nonstop. Even filling in bits and pieces he hadn't told Devin last night.

Gramps listened, his expression changing several times as Rusty spoke.

At his continued silence, Rusty continued, "I am sorry, Gramps. Devin only helped me after Rennie beat me up. He didn't have to, but he helped me when I was hurt and...."

Gramps put up his hand, halting the flow of words and looked at Devin.

"Devin helped you?"

Rusty nodded, telling him what had happened. A long silence followed, broken only by the sound of Celeste being busy in the kitchen and the leaves rustling overhead.

"I was turning in last night and had a quick look. I left and when I came back, I saw you helping Rusty here in the kitchen. I wondered what was going on, but thought you boys were up to some mischief and was going to talk to Devin about it later."

Gramps gazed in the direction of the empty gazebo, with a deep sadness etched in his face. Devin cringed, exchanging a look with Rusty who moments before was pouring his heart out.

"I'm glad you told me, son. It takes courage to do what you did, and I'm just glad no one's hurt."

Rusty visibly relaxed then asked, "Gramps, do you know Slink?"

"Why?" Devin asked before Gramps could respond, a sliver of hurt passing through him. His tone must have seeped through because Rusty gave him a funny look and fell quiet, leaving another awkward silence.

Gramps meanwhile said, "Hmm, Jesse's grandson? Yes, his grandfather was the stone carver who made the base that held the crystal." He paused a moment then said aloud, "I wonder, though. It makes no sense. Why now? Everyone's known of that crystal since I first got it. Who'd want to steal it now?" His tone wasn't encouraging, and Devin wasn't sure he wanted to say anything.

"Why did you ask about Slink, Rusty?" Gramps asked Rusty.

"Because I've seen him with the Renegade," Rusty replied.

Gramps gave him a look, but Devin interrupted.

"Last month at the gathering you said the crystal healed people. And that strange storm . . . do you think . . . well, do you think anyone thinks they can take it to cure people and that's why someone had Rusty steal it?"

"I can't really say. You were there, Dev. I guess it could've made someone greedy. I have to tell Celeste. It was her baby. We'll miss it terribly."

Rusty bowed his head in misery, and Devin felt a rush of sympathy for him.

"I told him to come to you, Gramps, but . . ."

"I was too scared," replied Rusty. "Do you have to tell my mom and the rest?"

Devin felt a tug of admiration, remembering when he too had put up a bravado.

Gramps wasn't fooled. In a gentler tone, he said, "I have to think what to do. I can't make you any promises, Rusty. I'm really happy Devin helped you. Remember that when you go stealing from people again, not everyone's like my grandson here."

"I'm glad Devin is my friend."

Gramps nodded and said, "Good, now that we understand each other, I want you two to listen carefully. "This Renegade fellow, he's bad. I want you two to steer clear of him, okay? I mean it!"

Seeing both of them about to protest, he continued, "It seems like eons ago, but I still remember the trouble I got into."

"Really?" Devin breathed a sigh of relief. "Can you tell me anything?"

"Yes, I can."

Devin sat up, excitement flushing his face.

"But I won't. It'll give you two ideas and you'll get into even more trouble."

Hurt stabbed at Devin. He felt Gramps blamed him for the loss of the crystal.

"Listen, Dev, and you too, Rusty. I got into a ton of trouble when I was your age. I got lots of punishment too. That's why I'm so concerned about you two. Promise me you wouldn't do anything like this again."

"This is unfair!" exclaimed Devin. "I didn't do anything! He did. Make him promise," he grounded out furiously.

"Promise," was all Gramps said, not budging.

"Fine, I promise," he almost shouted, turning to Rusty. "Happy? Now look at what you did!"

Rusty watched him before turning to Gramps, saying, "I promise, Gramps, I won't steal any of your stuff again."

Gramps turned to Devin and began, "I didn't make you promise because I want to punish you. I'm trying to make you see I love you, Dev. I have to go tell your grandmother the news." He gathered a heavy basket, turned and left, leaving two very confused boys behind.

Devin sat in miserable silence as Rusty scrambled up. With a quick wave he headed home, leaving silence behind him, his small bundle of gifts from Celeste grasped closely to his chest as he walked out the gate.

"See you around, Rusty," Devin muttered to empty air as he got up and headed to his room.

OLE HIGUE

The years had not been kind to the old woman living in the small cave down by the sea. Stories had grown and spread, becoming wilder as time passed. "Ole Higue" as she was branded, was claimed to be an old hag - a form of human vampire.

Accused of doing hideous things, like sucking the lives out of innocent babies and changing out of her skin, it was claimed she became a ball of flames, shooting through the night sky in wicked glee, terrorizing the community.

It was also believed the marking of an "X" on the doors and windows of homes with children and babies would deter her. Some were known to have left bowls of rice and a clock next to cradles where babies slept as protection. It was hoped the rice would force her to count the grains and the constant clicking of the time would confuse her, keeping her counting till morning, when she would be caught.

Babies were dressed in blue clothes to repel her and dried coconut flowers were hung over doorways to prevent her from entering their homes. Some claimed she shed and stored her skin in a dried gourd before going on her nightly travels. Powdered pepper and salt were kept handy to lace her skin in the hopes of having Ole Higue burn to death on putting her skin back on.

* * *

Confused and hurt, wandering endlessly, often spotted from the hilltops to the rocks by the beach, Ole Higue had cried until she had no more tears. Forced to keep to her beachside dwelling, she'd retreated further and further away as her attempts at friendliness had been seen as enticement to get victims.

As time passed, and with it, the permanence of her situation, she tried reaching out to the villagers again. But her days of wandering and bouts of crying had earned her their fear, and she'd seen terror dawn on their faces as she approached.

Her strange ways had sealed her faith, and none sought to understand her. Gloom had once again settled heavily on her. Deciding to use her alienation to her benefit, she had searched and found the perfect location to call home. Knowing it was the first bit of happiness she had felt, she settled down to live in the woods. It only enhanced her vile reputation further, but for Ole Higue, it was a good thing.

Being alone had given her time to think, and she knew things would work in her favor in due course. And so, she waited. The years had come and gone. Time passed. Seasons came and left. What little force remained with her had to be kept in reserve for that special moment.

Since none showed her friendship, she had been forced to seek sustenance on her own. From eating wild berries and fruits along the beachside, she soon found great joy in small gardens planted along the edge of the villages.

She learned when to make trips and when to wait unseen to get what they would never miss. She couldn't take much at a time as the farmers would notice their bounty disappearing, and she also didn't want her meals to rot before she could eat them.

Sitting on her favorite rock at the beach, watching the tide roll in, she remembered how she'd met "The Renegade" and theirs had become an odd friendship. Fearless he might be around the villages far and wide, but not to her. Saving him from the tribe of Dark worshippers in the hills, having stumbled upon them on their sacrificial night, she remembered how he'd refused to kill another. Their friendship had blossomed, and it was one she came to truly cherish.

* * *

She knew the time was close. She had waited, following the stars. The moons had been many, but by her record, the planets would be aligning soon, and she needed to get her plan into action. After much thought, she'd come upon one and headed to find the renegade. Asking the favor which he agreed to, joy filled her, and she headed homewards, her feet feeling like they had sprouted wings.

With the knowledge her wish would soon be fulfilled, a wave of uncertainty flooded her as she looked at herself. The years had been cruel, the weather harsh at times. She had aged miserably. Her once glowing, healthy hair was now streaked with patches of gray, hanging wildly around her face, down to her waist. Her nails were brittle and broken and her once supple body now sagging and wrinkled.

"No, indeed, the years have not been kind to me," she muttered. "But soon, soon I'll be right again. Ole Higue . . . if only they knew!"

Sighing deeply, a secret smile danced on her lips as she headed for the woods.

6

THE GYPSIES

School and homework flew by in a whirl of fun. Devin had searched Rusty and his classmates out and kept their company. At first, the other kids from his class weren't sure how to behave, but Devin ignored them. Their curiosity got the better of them however, and soon they were vying for Rusty's and the other boys' friendship. He could tell Rusty was unsure how to deal with this sudden interest, but soon his laughter became freer, and slowly he and the others were regular pals. Devin met Hunter, Toby, and David.

With the end-of-term exams behind them and not having to worry about homework, his mom was happy he'd once again found friends.

Gramps still hadn't said a word about the theft of the crystal. Rusty was delighted his mom had extended an invitation to Devin's family to their Annual Festival in two weeks' time.

* * *

The day arrived quickly with a magnificent expanse of blue sky as far as the eye could see, giving Devin a good feeling. Gramps and Gran had prepared baskets of goodies to take along, having made preparations the night before. He helped load their old jalopy with freshly plucked chickens, corn, bottles of seasoning, freshly baked bread, and scrumptious pies, biscuits, jams, and fresh fruits.

Gramps packed one of the biggest, most succulent ducks Devin had ever seen. Already seasoned, the aroma of mixed spices filled the car. He knew Rusty and his friends would be eating like princes that night.

Lexi had packed towels and blankets in the event they made it to the nearby beach. Gramps with his old hat on, dressed in grey shorts and a button-down white shirt and Gran Celeste with a headband to keep her fly-away hair off her eyes, wore her favorite green gingham dress, along with a pair of sturdy, old moccasins. They piled into their jalopy and, with Gramps driving, were soon off.

* * *

Turning right on their street, along the old tree-lined beach road, they passed the little church that sat in the grounds of their school, the Agricultural Station on the left and further on, passed a field, at the moment occupied by kids and their families at play.

Soon they went by a huge "Guest House Compound" that not even Gramps could say what it was used for. At the end of the village, the old road ended and meandered off into a sand-worn path.

Maneuvering along, they drove past a smattering of broken-down huts, past the once beautiful Hibiscus Inn where Rusty's mom worked, and kept going. A short while later, they slowed through a tiny trail, inching forward and soon entered a large clearing. Surrounded by a lush growth of forest, it lay hidden to outsiders.

Caravans of all sizes sat in a circle with small tents and huts lying further back forming a horseshoe-shaped settlement that backed up to the forest. With the dense growth offering protection on all sides, it made Devin think someone had put together a play-town and then forgotten to dismantle it.

"Oh, how cool!" exclaimed Lexi. "A real Gypsy Camp!"

"Shh," Gran Celeste admonished.

Parking under a huge tree, they clambered out and Devin spotted Rusty who must have been on the lookout for them. A beautiful woman advanced towards them, with a little boy at her side.

"Welcome, I'm Ginger. I'm so happy to finally meet you," she continued.

"You're beautiful!"

Gran Celeste's typical outspokenness caused a rush of color to flood Ginger's face.

As she stammered thanks, Devin gazed at the neglected huts, tents, and caravans they lived in. He felt emotions clutching at his throat, but was saved from embarrassing himself when Ginger approached and extended both arms in welcome.

"I'm so happy to meet you, Devin."

"And its good to meet you Miss Ginger," Devin said, returning the hug of friendship she gave, feeling an unfamiliar emotion blooming within his chest.

Ginger pulled a little boy from behind her, and introduced him. "This is Remy, Rusty's little brother."

Remy smiled shyly, dimpling at them.

"Let's get started then. Lots to do," Celeste said when the introductions were over. She soon had them busy and Devin had to forget about rushing away. Remy kept getting in the way, busy with investigating the car rather than helping out.

After several trips, everything was loaded onto a very long table and Devin made sure he wasn't needed before taking off with Rusty.

A surge of excitement danced up his chest on noticing a huge tree overhanging the caravan belonging to Rusty's family. Sturdy pieces of wood nailed to its trunk formed a ladder leading up to a tree house.

Folks had begun appearing and Devin felt curious looks directed his way. He smiled at them. But they had to forget about climbing to the treehouse for the moment when a yell sounded and three other boys he'd met at school came rushing up.

"Hey, Dev," Hunter called.

Devin smiled when Toby and David waved to him.

"Hi guys! Came to help?"

"Nope! We were trying to escape," Toby confessed.

"Fine, you guys go on. Rusty and I'll finish up soon."

They didn't need telling a second time, and even before he could say "see you later", they'd taken off.

They set to and did as much as they could, helping wherever things needed to be helped and soon colorful sheets took the place of a tablecloth and strings of colored ribbons were strung from caravan to caravan, dancing like butterflies in the sky.

Devin spotted a huge circle of rocks with driftwood in a large pile nearby and a small bundle of kindling for a bonfire later.

* * *

"Come along, everyone's getting ready," Toby called.

They headed back to the cooking pit where a large group had gathered and a table set, laden with the things his family had brought. The nearby fire pit had a mixture of corn, chickens, duck, and lamb merrily roasting, carefully tended to over the flames by kids of varying ages.

"Ouch."

One little fellow fell back as his eyebrows got singed. Giggles and loud laughter met his expression of constant surprise. As the aromas teased his nostrils, Devin felt his stomach rumble and was handed a plate laden with pilaf and tender meat with mixed vegetables.

Finding seats along the table, he saw an old man making his way down from a smaller caravan. Wearing an extremely old pair of green trousers, a long faded green shirt, patched in many places, and an old pair of boots with a faded, threadbare scarf draped across his shoulder, Devin watched him approach, feeling a stillness entering himself.

As the old man neared, he could see his black eyes were sunken in his weathered face. Wrinkles were in abundance as he smiled, and a quiet dignity exuded as he slowly passed by. The entire group bowed and remained quiet.

He paused before Devin, who immediately felt himself in awe of the little man. Something told him he was standing before a very wise soul. He knew for sure when a surge of knowing filled him.

"I'm Rupert," the old man said, extending a hand. Feeling as if he wanted to spill his guts, revealing all his silly secrets, and surprised at the strong voice, Devin couldn't tell how long he stood, holding the frail, leathery hand of Rupert.

Rupert smiled, laying his other hand on Devin's shoulder. "Welcome, Devin. Our home and family are like yours. Thank you for your friendship."

Devin swallowed, unsure of what to say. He was still trying to figure out all the strange emotions flooding him. Feeling himself flush and his tongue stuck to the roof of his mouth, his mind was confused. Wondering if the others thought him weird, he stood mutely, unable to respond.

Rupert, however, seemed to understand, for he patted him gently on the shoulder and turned, heading around the group of people under the trees and the long table.

Devin knew they had gone to great lengths for their celebration and wondered how they'd eat for the next month. Knowing they'd be insulted if he said anything, he was grateful when Rusty joined and distracted him.

Chatter ceased when everyone had gathered and joined hands in prayers. Rupert gave thanks for the Reelms family's generosity and kindness, speaking of honor and friendship and wished everyone a good time.

Devin ate in silence, savoring each mouthful, listening to light-hearted banter and laughter flowing as everyone ate.

With dinner over, he went looking for Rusty who'd been called away for some chore. He spotted his grandparents seated in the shadow of a giant tree, along with an older woman squinting in his direction.

Rusty was in the midst of a game of jump-rope, and on spotting him, quickly hopped out and headed over to him.

"What's up?"

"Oh, I finished eating and didn't know what else you guys had planned."

"Come on," Rusty said, "I want you to meet Gran Zoie." Rusty clapped him on the shoulders, and started walking towards the old lady sitting with his grandparents.

Devin almost turned back on seeing how keenly Zoie was watching him as they approached.

Surprisingly wrinkle-free with a smooth, clear complexion, she had a small, straight nose in a pear-shaped face and a halo of grey hair and was a bit on the heavier side. A bright red-and-yellow scarf hung loosely around her shoulders.

With introductions made, she thanked him again for helping Rusty.

He nodded.

With twinkling eyes, she grinned and said, "Even when he stole from you."

Devin felt his cheeks getting flushed, and muttered an inane comment, which brought rich laughter from her.

"Yes, it was the decent thing to do," she agreed, making him aware of what his response was. Zoie seemed wise and knowing, and he knew she was to Rusty what Gramps and Celeste were to him.

"I was just thanking your grandfather for keeping Rusty's secret."

Rusty, however, seemed to have suddenly been given the moon.

"Thank you, Gramps," he shouted, rushing up to Gramps and dipping into a deep bow. And fell flat on his face. Devin leaned down to give him a hand up as loud laughter erupted and he thought Zoie was in danger of falling off her seat.

Rusty was unfazed, taking the offered hand and laughing along with everyone else. He stood up, dipped again in a brief bow and then stood back in pride. "There, that's better," he said, to the sound of renewed laughter.

Devin was steering Rusty away just as Lexi breezed by, plunking herself down by Gran.

"Don't know when I've ever had such fun!"

"I can tell you something that might complete today," Zoie told her.

"Shucks," thought Devin, knowing how Lexi was, but he was intrigued as Zoie took out and shuffled a pack of strange cards with odd symbols. He stopped, staring.

"Come on, Dev. All the legs are gonna be gone if we don't hurry up."

"You go on, Rust," he said, wondering how Rusty could still be hungry after the meal they'd just had. "This looks interesting."

Rusty snorted, then hid it behind a cough as Lexi shot him a look. "You sure?" he said.

"Yeah. You go on."

"Don't say I didn't warn you then," Rusty sang to him, heading off.

"I won't," Devin promised, leaning against a tree and watched as Lexi pulled and placed the cards as Zoie instructed.

As they waited, he tapped his foot, earning a look from his mom.

Too late he realized. Rusty was trying to save him the silliness. He felt stupid but couldn't be rude and leave now.

"A gift for the mystical, still undiscovered," Zoie said, hmming. "You have an old talent in you."

"What kind of talent?" Lexi asked. "And what is old talent?"

Devin's curiosity deepened. Like Lexi, he wasn't aware of any gifts in their family anyone had to inherit.

"The cards show some old knowledge linking people who'll come into your life," Zoie answered.

Devin saw an odd look pass between his grandparents and his mom looked at Zoie with new interest.

Lexi asked the question going through his own mind. "Like whom? And when do I meet them?"

"It didn't say." Zoie smiled at her. "Just be happy. Yours is a happy reading I've done in a long time."

"Yes, but—"

"Lexi," her mom chided softly.

Lexi gave her mom a quick smile.

"Ah, yes. Thank you, Zoie," she said.

As she got up and floated off, Devin knew she'd be preoccupied with this for a good while. He was relieved, knowing he wouldn't be the butt of her sour mood for at least the next several days.

Zoie read for his grandparents, filled with silly nonsense that left them laughing and giggling. "And here I see a member of the family, gifted and destined to do great things in life," she finished, causing them to look at each other as if "great things" were stamped on their forehead.

He tried edging away.

"Now you, Dev," Zoie called.

He didn't care to know what was in the cards for him, silly or not. He'd already tempted the fates when he went looking at the crystal coming alive. "Nope. Not happening. Definitely don't care to know what the cards said," he told himself.

"Um, I . . ." he stalled.

"Come on Devin," Zoie chided him. "It's all part of the evening's fun. You can't leave now," she said, fumbling in a small pouch.

"Ahh, here they are!" she exclaimed looking up at him and seeing he'd backed away.

"Surely you're not leaving?" she said. "After all, this whole evening happened because of you. You can't just leave. I haven't done my readings in many years."

"Sure, guilt me into it," he thought to himself, walking over with a smile on his lips and sat down in front of her.

She shuffled the cards and he noticed they were very different from the ones she had used before.

Cutting them, she spread them in a half circle, saying, "Now, Dev, I know you think this is all mumbo jumbo stuff, but indulge me."

"You may think of anything you'd like to know and then draw a card."

His mind went blank and he sat mindless for a while.

Gramps cleared his throat.

Devin felt stupid. It didn't help as the moments ticked on before it came to him in a rush.

The image of the crystal flashed before his eyes. He gathered his thoughts and looked at the cards. Reaching out, he picked one up and was surprised to see it lying blank.

They were weathered and fragile and as he started to ask what was going on, he fell quiet when Zoie lifted a finger to her lips to silence him.

He watched as a small screen had opened on the card lying before him. Turning as black as midnight, it made him feel like he'd stepped into the heavens. Little twinkling dots appeared, like those appearing with the approaching night. A swirling motion brought bubbles floating into the picture and a number of tiny, silvery streaks began connecting each.

"Pull another, Dev," Zoie directed.

Reluctantly breaking his gaze from the image, Devin pulled the second card and set it down as Zoie had indicated. Gran Celeste and Gramps had come up behind him and watched. Within moments, a bluish tinge emanated from the card and an iridescent light glimmered within.

Devin bent closer and spotted the inside of a dark cavern. Like a large bundle of ropes, they glittered like silvery cords, streaking and winding their way from the top of the chamber before disappearing downwards. He felt a jolt of shock on seeing a large white orb sitting where the ropes ended. Something nagged fleetingly, but was gone in an instant.

Zoie quickly shifted her eyes and he watched as he felt the strange sensation again, making the hair on the back of his neck rise. It had happened the night he thought the leaves were whispering to him.

He leaned back wondering if Zoie was using some trick she knew. When the third and final card was drawn, he watched her. He knew the moment the card came alive as her face said a silent "Oh . . . !" and her hand came up to her lips.

He knew that expression. A bit of fear mixed together with wonder. A startled gasp from those around them, and he glanced down and kept looking. This card was even stranger than the last two. The black screen was dotted with tiny, silver dots. An arrow pointed directly out, a small key floated around and, strangest of all, a small, beautiful lady smiled up at him. An instant of recognition flashed before disappearing.

But Devin was disappointed to hear her say "Well, Devin, it seems you'll be going on many journeys." A faint swirling movement caught his eyes and the cards became blank, staring at him.

"Which one says that?" he asked.

"The first one. And the second one showed you . . ."

Incredulous, Devin cut her off. "You're joking, right?"

Rusty had returned and stood listening.

Devin turned to him. "Your grandmother said . . ."

"I know what she said," replied Rusty. "I saw and I heard. She's neither." He fell silent when Zoie nodded.

"Your second card said you've been chosen to discover something of great importance," she continued.

Devin pointed to the third card and said, "And this one?"

"Well," a pause, then, "the arrow shows you finding the right direction in life, the key means you hold something dear, and the beautiful lady means you'll be blessed with guidance in life."

Then as if it had taken a large chunk of energy from her, she suddenly announced, "I feel fatigued. I'll get some rest now."

Devin scrambled up and quickly helped her gather her things, watching as Rusty helped her up to her caravan. Something had changed even though he wasn't told where the crystal was. The second card with the orb reminded him of his dream the morning after Rusty had stolen the crystal. There was some connection, but it eluded him at the moment. Suddenly he felt impatient for the night to be over.

★ ★ ★

"That stuff's scary," began Rusty hesitantly after returning from seeing Zoie to her caravan. "You must be real special."

"Well, I'm still me," Devin said with a laugh, trying to lighten things up, knowing Rusty was unsure how to be around him.

★ ★ ★

They walked back to the cooking pit and found comfortable seats with views to the activities. Devin felt his mind wandering to the strange cards but kept up normal chatter to distract Rusty from questioning him further.

He spotted a tall, well-muscled fellow about eighteen with a thick mane of hair, scrutinizing him from the edge of the forest.

"Who's that?"

Rusty looked over. "Galeb. Zoie said he's part of the old blood-line of Gypsies. Some Prince of sort."

"Prince?"

"Yah, Prince. He would continue our tradition if things were different. But since that day..."

"What day?" interrupted Devin.

"The one Zoie talks about. Galeb's great-great-great-grand-ancestors were killed the day the storm came. Dark stuff happened. Men in our families leave camp for some odd reason or the other. We don't know if or when Galeb will too."

"Where do they go?" Devin asked as a feeling of foreboding crept over him.

Rusty shrugged, "Beats me. Maybe they're dead or just deserted and no one knows."

Devin left it alone. "So why do you think Galeb might leave if no one knows where the menfolk go?"

"I dunno really. I think because we don't do celebrations or special events anymore. Galeb thinks it's unfair to be a prince and can't be recognized for it."

"He's proud then?" Devin wondered, unaware he'd spoken aloud.

"Not the way you mean," replied Rusty. "We're simple folks, but have you ever wondered where you came from? Can you imagine knowing you came from great people but you can't honor them?"

The question struck a chord within him. "When did this start then?" he asked.

"Years and years ago. I think it goes back to Ohhm."

"Ohhm!" Devin didn't know where exactly the conversation was going but kept his feelings to himself. Some of what Rusty was saying didn't make sense to him but he didn't want to make Rusty feel insulted.

Rusty nodded. "Zoie and Rupert talked of our ancestors who lived in Ohhm. They said our people had 'gifts' and . . ."

"What kind of gifts?" interrupted Devin, his ears perking up.

"I don't remember. You should talk to Zoie. She knows stuff."

"Okay, but what about Galeb?" Devin persisted.

"Rupert's great, great, grand ancestors had knowledge of Ohhm," Rusty began. "Somebody betrayed them . . ."

"Betrayed them?" repeated Devin, beginning to think it was quite a tale.

"Betrayed them," Rusty continued, "then the battle of the Shadows happened and Ohhm fell. Did you know our families came from a line of great warriors?" he asked.

Devin shook his head "no."

"Well Zoie and Rupert say we were responsible for protecting Ohhm. Well, my ancestors, that is," he corrected.

It sounded like something out of a book. Unless Rusty was a pretty good storyteller, he couldn't see how he'd be able to come up with such a good story so quickly.

"Ever since then," Rusty spoke again, "our generations have suffered. We've moved from place to place, settling wherever we could. It was only when people started treating us like . . ." he stopped, a strange expression on his face. "I guess like the Foxies do," he finished.

Devin, afraid to say the wrong thing, moved over and sat down next to Rusty. "You okay?" he asked softly.

Rusty looked at him. "I finally get it, Dev. It's not just some stories they made up. Our families were great people. They failed at protecting Ohhm because someone betrayed them. That's why they became outcasts!" He shook his head.

Unsure what to say, Devin stayed quiet.

"We were protectors of the land, failed, and . . . wow! These people still ridicule us, and they don't even know why they're doing it. I wonder if that's why the menfolk leave. Out of shame maybe?" His one-sided conversation sounded like Rusty was having a whole lot of revelation and Devin didn't interrupt. His questions could wait. Rusty seemed different with what he'd just gotten, or thought he got, Devin corrected himself.

"And I can't be a prince when our people have been dishonored. We'll stop being outcasts when we can restore glory and honor to our ancestors."

Devin turned around, seeing Galeb who'd approached and heard their conversation. He got up and extended his hand.

"It is good to meet you, Devin."

Devin shook his hand, feeling an instant liking for him. Galeb had an air of confidence about him.

"It is good meeting you too, Galeb."

"Do you think we'll ever know who betrayed our people and what happened?"

Surprised, Devin thought for a moment then said cautiously, "maybe we should ask Zoie or Rupert. Rusty says they always speak of old stories."

"I think that's the problem. Everyone thinks they're stories and never bother," Galeb replied.

"If they have gifts . . ." Devin began.

"Our people didn't save a kingdom before with all their gifts. I think to say we can now, is an insult to the memory of Ohhm and our ancestors."

Devin thought of what he'd witnessed with the crystal and his reading. "Things have changed," he said. "What if there was a way? What if you could right that wrong or finally find the truth? Rupert and Zoie know a lot. Maybe there are many more we have to find to hear what they know. Maybe elders from the other villages can put their memories together, and we could try and figure things out."

A flicker of hope played in Galeb's eyes and he smiled. "Us Gypsies and the village elders. That's rich."

Devin realized his blunder too late. After all, the villagers old or young didn't care for the Gypsies. He cringed inwardly.

"Even if we do find out the truth, there's no Ohhm. What then?" said Rusty.

"We would know the truth", Galeb said. "Our people, whatever is left of us, wouldn't be a disgraced people."

Devin saw, like in Rusty from a little while ago, a transformation in Galeb.

"Thanks for giving me hope, Devin." Galeb extended his hand again and Rusty joined his hand with theirs and said, "To our honor!"

Devin knew for the first time they had something happy to look forward to. He wasn't about to spoil that for them.

7
JUDGMENT CIRCLE

A while later, the sun having gone down, Devin, Gramps, and Rusty were ushered into a circle of nine Elder Gypsy men, which included Rupert, a distance from the camp, and made to wait under a tree.

"What's going on?" he whispered.

"Not sure", Rusty whispered back.

He watched the Elders as they sat straight and proud, wrinkled and lined. Their simple clothes and tattered booths spoke of old power. He wondered what story they had each lived and how sad it was that their lives had deteriorated the way it had. His chest tightened as he felt the unfairness of their situation.

"Don't let their looks fool you, Dev," Rusty said as they watched Gramps being led to the circle and given a seat next to Rupert.

"First we bow to each other," he told Gramps. As Gramps bowed, he said, "I am Rupert."

Devin watched as the second repeated, "I'm John."

The third continued, "I'm Otto."

The fourth took it up, "I'm Erik."

The fifth said in a deep, baritone voice, "I'm Orrin."

The sixth continued saying, "I'm Pias."

The seventh said, "I'm Wen."

The eighth looked around and announced, "I'm Shandor."

Finally, the last cleared his throat—slowly and proudly, he said, "I'm Nathan."

With their names stated, Rupert proceeded,

"We've gathered here to thank Devin Reelms and his family for their friendship and kindness to our people, even when a member of our tribe, Rusty, was caught stealing from them."

Devin felt Rusty stir beside him.

"It is a known fact we live off the land and do what we do to survive," Wen said.

Nods of agreement greeted his statement.

"We're forced to live how we do because outsiders hate and fear us," Rupert said. "Singy," he continued, nodding at Gramps, "and his grandson Devin, are here at my invitation."

All present nodded and Devin wondered what their tribal laws said about befriending outsiders and if any had ever been present at their Circle of Elders' meetings.

"It's been many, many years since we've gathered," Rupert spoke again and Devin watched as a collective smile echoed around the group.

"Can't fight for no reason. Barely surviving," Elder John said. "No one listens to us anyway."

Loud agreements followed, some so colorful it had the boys grinning, and Devin felt the mood lighten.

"Today," continued Rupert, "we have among us someone who's been good to our kind and we respect that."

Devin flushed at the unexpected praise even as he saw they nodded their silver-grey, unkempt heads.

"Gone are the days when we lived as we should. But tradition has to be observed," he continued. "Here we are one. Equals."

"What are they doing?" Devin asked.

"Dunno. Looks like stuff from the old days."

"Cool stuff," whispered back Devin.

"Scary stuff," Rusty answered in a shaky voice.

"Since when are you scared?" he was surprised.

"Didn't know they'd do this 'cause I took something. We do it all the time."

"Ya, well . . . ," Devin left unfinished, silence falling between them.

"Let Devin Reelms come forward then," Elder Erik boomed in a loud voice.

Rupert beckoned him forward, nodding to Rusty, "You too, Rusty. Both of you."

"Say your name to them," Rupert said.

"I am Devin Reelms." He bowed to each of the Elders who nodded back. Rusty croaked his name out and fell silent.

"Devin Reelms, did you, on your own, decide to help Rusty knowing he stole from your family?" The directness of the question took Devin by surprise.

"Of course, I did it on my own!" he exclaimed at Elder Pias who'd questioned him.

"Why did you? It was something valuable. That's unusual." Devin bristled.

"I saw what the renegade did to him. It could've been me he did that to."

"Just too. And he has compassion, I like that. Good, good," Elder Pias said. Then as an afterthought, he continued, "We don't want anybody trying to trick us."

"Trick?" Devin bristled.

"Trick," answered Elder Otto.

"Why would I trick you?" Devin felt anger building.

"What you did was a brave thing boy. But strange."

"What my grandson did was admirable. Something not even I would have thought of in that moment." Gramps's steely voice interjected, heavy with reprimand. "What Devin did wasn't for recognition nor to force friendships."

Devin, sure Gramps was about to embark on a lecture, saw Rupert quickly lean forward and touch his grandfather with a restraining hand.

"Forgive us Devin, Singy. We are not a trusting lot these days. You have our gratitude and thanks for being kind to Rusty even at the loss of something valuable." He looked around at the group, now quiet.

Devin waited. Rusty fidgeted.

"It is not often we see a gift as yours." Elder Pias spoke. "This act of compassion shows a deep love. Love enough to care for another human being means a lot to our people."

"Singy has supplied our people with food and necessities over the past months. That is compassion if you ask me," Rupert reminded them.

Elder Nathan, who had been silent till now said, "Devin Reelms , you're family now. Do you accept this?"

Devin looked at Gramps who raised his eyebrows. He turned to Rusty, who gave a shrug but offered no help. He knew nothing of what was expected of him, except that Rusty was the best friend that had come into his life.

"I accept," he said.

Rusty grinned from ear to ear.

Clapping broke out. Gramps nodded at him but otherwise stayed quiet. Rupert nodded at him. Unsure of how to proceed, Devin waited and was surprised when Elder Nathan got up and approached.

Bowing, he waited as Devin returned the bow. The Elder smiled, extending a hand which Devin shook and then watched as the burly Elder took an object out of his pocket.

"As a token of our thanks and welcoming you to our family, Devin Reelms, this is our gift to you."

Devin saw a silvery string glinting in Elder Nathan's hand. "We all helped make this." Devin stared. It was a necklace unlike anything he'd ever seen. Made of bright, silvery thread, it had nine circular knots, each inscribed with a symbol unfamiliar to him. "You'll discover its secrets when you have the need for it. Not before."

He fastened it and Devin felt the necklace settle against his skin, with a sudden strong energy coursing through his limbs as a rush of emotions filled him. He felt small. Then he felt stupid that everyone was making such a big deal because he'd helped Rusty. He didn't want the old men to feel like they owed him something. He felt embarrassed when tears began to well up in his eyes but he couldn't cry and blinked them away. Managing a hoarse, "Thank You" to Elder Nathan, he bowed and saw it return before the Elder returned to his seat.

"Devin, what you've done here is not just a kind act to one of our kind. It's a sign from the heavens we'll be delivered from darkness. It's been foretold it would happen. It is good to know that day has come, and we're still here. Just remember your purpose is beyond helping one of our kind."

The sound of Elder Otto interrupted Devin's confused mind, and he wondered why they were putting such significance to everything. And what did it mean? Delivering them from darkness. From what darkness? And when was it foretold? Did it say specifically it would be him? Unable to roll his eyes as he would at Lexi, he smiled hoping things would be over quickly even as the verse he'd read on the night of the full moon came to mind.

He hoped with all his might all of this was just a way of them saying a proper thank you, and not that they truly consider him some kind of savior. He glanced at Rusty, who seemed to know his thoughts and looked away.

Keeping his voice warm and firm, he said, "Thank you. I'll treasure it." Fervently, he sent up a prayer for the meeting to be over.

"See you do that. It'll be your saving grace someday soon." The soft words came from Elder Wen who'd been observing him.

Devin nodded his thanks.

"Come. Come now," the voice of Rupert interrupted and Devin was thankful.

"We've prepared a celebration honoring our friendship."

Devin gave a sigh of relief as they gathered their things. Rupert headed over to him.

"Let's go," he said, laying a hand on his shoulders. "You did good, Devin. Welcome to our family." Giving him a brief squeeze on the shoulder, Rupert turned away, walking off with Gramps.

Several others approached with welcoming handshakes and words of advice, offering to tell him of their history. Devin eagerly accepted, saying he'd come by as he had time, and they'd talk. Satisfied, they headed off.

He looked around, feeling a strange sensation and spotted several young men who'd lingered at the back of the circle and were glaring at him. He looked for Rusty to ask who they were but Rusty had somehow disappeared as well.

The moment passed and when he looked over again, the little group had vanished. Devin tried to assure himself that no one would question the actions of Rupert and the Elders. But he suspected that the decision to make him a part of their tribe had caused some unknown issue. Something about them worried him but he'd have to figure it out later since the activities were picking up.

* * *

He started towards the assembled crowd and was surprised to see it grow in number. It dawned on him they were from many tribes and other camps hidden in the hills.

Cheery chatter picked up and after a while, fell quiet as the beating of drums announced the start of things, followed by the appearance of dancers.

Ginger and the girls floated in, decked in simple finery and flowing dresses, bowing amidst applause and loud whistling. The tempo of the drums increased, and as one, they moved. When the sounds of harmonicas and flutes mingled, it created a familiar, yet foreign rhythm, and Devin found himself tapping his feet and swaying to the beat.

A wild, primal energy filled the air, keeping him transfixed, the sound seeping into his pores, his bones and soon his very being. He watched the dancers gracefully twirl and flow in an undulating, hypnotizing flow with an agility he thought was impossible. The intricate movements were stunning as the beating of the drums increased only to flow into a slow sway. A hauntingly beautiful music echoed into the night, and mesmerized he sat, feeling himself flow into another world.

Soon the sound of the drumbeats built and reverberated into the night, the figures became a blur, their movements frenzied, and in moments, it reached a crescendo before crashing into silence. A magical throbbing filled the air long after everything had stopped, and Devin experienced an odd moment of hanging between realms of consciousness.

The sound of thunderous applause snapped him out of his trance as the dancers bowed and retreated with whistles and calls after the dancers had left.

"That was really special. Thank you."

The unexpected sound of his mom's voice reminded him of his manners and he nodded his agreement, seeing they were surrounded by Elders, some of whom had been at his meeting. "That was awesome. Thank you," he said.

"I'm glad you're pleased, Devin. We haven't had anything like this in years," Rupert replied, his smile wide with his own happiness. "I think you've brought the sunshine to us again."

Devin was spared an answer as Rusty called.

"Be right there, Rust," he called, relieved.

"Go have fun. You deserve it." Rupert waved to him before turning to talk with his mom.

He hurried off, spotting Lexi flitting past him, squealing and laughing, several kids in tow.

Reaching an excited Rusty, he was dismayed when they got roped into egg-balancing. He decided to give it a go and lost to a little girl who grinned impishly at him, showing the gap in her front teeth. "Nice," he thought, "beaten by a baby."

Noisy chatter echoed around them as folks gathered for the bonfire. Loud squeals and laughter filled the night air as a roaring fire burned. He strolled back to his mom and sat with Gramps, watching as kids ran by. He laughed at their antics and when they called on him, he joined in singing off-keyed and being silly. Happiness made him giddy. He missed a step, tripped, and fell. Then laughed along with everyone else, completely uncaring.

A boy had his harmonica out, another had a small violin, and a third began singing. Devin listened to the lyrics, thinking what trouble they'd be in if Miss Nelly heard them.

Silly Miss Nelly
Was walking . . .
Fetching her well water
To wash her belly
Spilling her stories
Thinking folks would be merry

'Bout how she was feeling
Till Old Man Helgie told her
To cut it out
'Cause we didn't care! No boy! We didn't care
To know which of her jellies was hurtin'!
Slipping and slidin' . . .
Poor Miss Nelly fell on her jellies
Silly Miss Nelly! Silly Miss Nelly!

Devin laughed, at the same moment spotting Rusty waving to him from up in the tree-house. He headed over and climbed up, hopping onto the little platform.

A moment later, he heard the sound of his mom's voice calling. Disappointed, he peered over the ledge. "Be right there, Mom."

Back down, as everyone gathered, there were hugs and thanks all around. Soon they were in the car on their way back home, with Gramps peering owlishly into the night, guided only by the moonlight overhead.

"I didn't get to hear what Zoie said about you," Lexi began. "Tell me."

"I'm tired," he said.

"You're not. I saw you in the tree," she argued.

The last thing he wanted to do was talk about it, but knowing Lexi, she'd badger him till morning. I don't remember everything," he hedged.

"Yes, you do…," she began.

He sighed in frustration, his mind conflicted in wanting to know and secretly dreading what it all meant.

"Let him be Lex," his mom said.

She huffed, falling quiet, and Devin settled against the seat, relieved.

8

SIGNS

Inclement weather blew in the next day, reminding him of the night everyone had decided to wait up for the crystal to come alive. Only this time, it didn't let up. The influx of storms and surges in their normally quiet countryside was unlike anything anyone had experienced before.

Cold blasts swept in, barreling through the villages. Fishing boats went in confused directions, and the temperatures changed dramatically from day to day. People found themselves short-tempered and irritable as the changes brought a flurry of activities.

Devin, like everyone else, was fatigued to the bone, trying to keep the poultry clean and warm. Some of their fields had suffered like everyone else's, and the local stores were running short on supplies.

Chaos followed a week's worth of flooding, and Gramps had wisely decided to hunker down and wait for whatever it was to blow itself out. Celeste had them gather things they needed and everyone moved into Devin's kitchen on the first floor.

Lexi complained endlessly before realizing that things weren't going to change because she was in a bad mood. Especially when Celeste ruthlessly pointed out that others were suffering more than she was. A quiet peace descended.

As days turned into weeks, everyone's patience was at an all-time low. Rae and Lexi were always out, helping out the wives and mothers in the village and tending to the sick and needy. His dad, grudgingly helped folks as well. Devin and Gramps stayed close to home, keeping their yards protected as best as they could.

Getting up early in the day, resting a bit by noon, and then staying up late at night caused people to become desperate and turn to thievery. It was a wearying time.

Devin finished feeding the poultry and made a quick trip to the orchard, fighting to stay warm from the cold that had seeped in. But everything lay in silent beauty and he watched in amazement as large snowflakes floated by. He reached out with opened palms, catching some and felt fear engulf him. The hills and surrounding countryside had never had snow. Theirs was a warm and friendly place.

Devin hurried to the front of their yards and saw Celeste's flower garden sitting in icy splendor. Icicles hung in sharp needles from trees laden down with snow. He hurried back inside and watched as Gramps consulted some strange calendar of his. Why did Gramps think he could find a forecast about what was happening if they'd never had this kind of situation before?

It didn't help when Gramps began "ahhing," and "hmming." He left, going up to his room. The whole situation was driving everyone crazy and he wondered if Gramps was starting to show signs of madness.

Strange forces were on the prowl and the poultry, crops, and livestock were suffering. The only ones profiting from all of this were the shops. Supplies and clothing were in great demand. Fuel was running low as folks tried stocking up, unsure as to how long the bitter weather would last. Firewood was the latest item being fought over.

Soon it entered the fifth week and the constant vigilance, the poor conditions, and the inability to visit Rusty and the gang, had Devin in a sour mood.

It was with welcome surprise he heard Gramps say, "It's full moon tonight!" The sudden return of Gramps' oddity had him laughing.

"It's good hearing you laugh again, Dev. I was beginning to think you had forgotten to live." He smiled at Devin and came over, giving him a hearty hug.

Devin was too happy to see signs of normalcy returning to argue over whether it was full moon's night or not. He didn't care if chickens talked. And Gramps was right!

That night, the moon was more glorious than he ever remembered seeing. A strange hush entered the countryside, and the next morning, the dark, ugly clouds had given way to sunny skies and mild temperatures. The soggy grounds slowly dried and gardens bloomed overnight.

Every day and night that followed was brighter and happier than the previous one, with kids squealing and playing in the streets and adults socializing again in happy voices. He was anxious to see Rusty and the gang.

As the days passed and life became more routine again, he heard his mom call,

"Dev, you'll need to see how everyone fared at the camp."

"Sure mom," he called, already doing a happy dance but paused as his mom came out of the kitchen.

He watched her. Something about her had changed, but he couldn't tell what. She'd been busy seeing to the older folks. He shrugged. Mom was mom. It was how she filled her days. He didn't want to start her off by asking questions.

He checked in with Celeste who'd packed a bag of things and in a short while, he was off. Making quick work of the trip by bicycle, he hopped off as the boys rushed up.

Toby hopped about. "Man, have you ever seen anything like it?" he said.

"I was worried, actually," said Devin, knowing their caravans were old, and the storms were merciless. It couldn't have been easy on them.

Rusty came up and they hugged. "How'd you all do? We were worried but I couldn't leave," Devin told them.

"We managed," said Rusty, accepting the bag of things Celeste had packed.

"They came."

"Who?" said Devin.

"The Housing Office."

Astonished, Devin repeated, "The Housing Office? They actually know you exist?"

"Yeah. Hard to believe, eh?" replied Hunter. "They said they'd be clearing this stuff away soon."

Helping himself to some cheese from the bag, he pointed to some fallen logs and broken limbs lying in piles nearby. "They've been supplying us with fuel till the weather warms up again."

Devin couldn't figure that one out. He was glad everyone was fine. There weren't any signs of significant damage. The entire camp was better off than the rest of the village from what he was seeing.

A new growth of wildflowers had taken over every scrap of ground he could see. Lush covering of new leaves had emerged, and birds and butterflies of every species were flitting about. The air had a freshness that made him feel light-headed.

Rupert had approached quietly and was now standing beside him. "The veil's been lifted," he said.

The simple words had a message of mystery but Devin stayed quiet, unsure of what to say.

"They're here," Rupert said again.

"Who's here?" repeated Rusty, coming up behind them, asking the same question Devin was about to.

"The fairies, of course. Just look at their handiwork," he gestured around, patting Devin's shoulder as other kids excitedly rushed up and the mood was lost. Devin stayed a while catching up with everyone before heading home, Rupert's words still lingering in his thoughts.

* * *

In the following days as life settled down, Devin noticed how people took note of Gramps helping the Gypsies and how they seemed a bit warmer towards the gypsies as well, especially when he spotted several women smiling and greeting on seeing Ginger and the men-folk from the camp.

He later found out from Rusty that the Gypsies' gardens were flourishing while the villages were drying up. Devin laughed but it quickly changed when Rusty said, "When they're dying or have some kind of disease, they'd come in secret to meet my folks for healing herbs. Go to the Gypsies," they would whisper. And we've never turned anyone away."

After his initial surprise, Devin felt a thread of hope, thinking it was a nice first step on the villagers' part to accept the gypsies. A part of him felt it was still early to gauge if it was going to last. People were fickle, he thought, knowing how quickly they rejected anything they felt they didn't need. The storm had created a need. His hope was it would last and the gypsies wouldn't be left out again.

FRIENDSHIP

Two weeks later, on a Saturday morning, his mom dropped him by Rusty's where she and Ginger, who had the day off, were happy to catch up.

Since it was still a cool morning, he and Rusty left to gather firewood and were soon heading out with a small machete and lengths of strings and ropes to secure their bundles.

"Be careful," Ginger called.

"We will," Rusty called back, already leading Devin off into the woods.

A radio was blaring from one of the caravans they passed and he heard "Now that all those terrible storms and snow have left, spring seems to be smiling on us. Some folks fared better than we had expected but some areas were damaged with only minor injuries to be reported. Thankfully there were no deaths."

The voice floated on as they walked by and he dodged a limb, only to lose his footing a moment later and slid forward. Swearing, he got up just as another limb trashed his shoulder as they walked into a particularly dense area.

Rusty however, kept up a lively chatter, pointing out rabbit holes, bird nests, wild berries, and a host of stuff that made him forget the weather reports. Deeper and further away from camp, they went. Rusty showed him small tracks he normally followed during his trips to the beach.

In a short while, they had bundles of wood stacked along the way. Every hundred yards or so, Rusty cut lengths of rope and deftly secured each bundle.

"How come you got so good at this?" asked Devin.

"Oh, I've been doing this for ages," said Rusty.

Devin was surprised when he looked at his watch and saw almost three hours had passed since they'd started out.

Rusty left the woods they gathered into small bundles and headed deeper into the forest. "We all got chores," he called out. "I like to wander, so I get the firewood. Plus," he continued, "I get stuff when the boats come in."

"Boats?" repeated Devin thinking it strange the Gypsies had boats, but knew better than to voice his feelings aloud.

Rusty had a sheepish look. "Well, I'm not supposed to tell."

"What?" said Devin as suspicion took root.

"The renegade. He smuggles," replied Rusty, grinning.

"Really?"

"Really," Rusty nodded. "I don't feel guilty taking stuff from him. Come on, Dev," he continued quickly seeing the expression on Devin's face. "He can't just complain now, can he?"

Devin laughed thinking of Rusty stealing from the smugglers.

"Crazy, huh?" Rusty said to no one in particular.

Devin took his time replying. He'd gotten to know Rusty better since that fateful night. Now he was cautious.

"Um, Rust," he began, then stopped, unsure how to say what he wanted to.

Rusty shot him a curious look, saying, "Spit it out, Dev. You won't hurt my feelings."

"I feel badly you have to do that," he blurted out.

Rusty looked at him for several moments before saying, "Listen, Dev. You can say "steal", you know. It is what I do. And yes, all of us know it's wrong. I don't think you know what it is to be poor. I mean, really poor," he emphasized.

"I have an idea," said Devin quickly. "Well," he amended, "what I mean is, we have our gardens like everyone else. Dad works, and Gramps takes care of our poultry. But the point is," he continued without giving Rusty a chance to cut in, "we get by like everyone else. There's no need to do that stuff," he finished.

"Yeah," came back the bitter answer. "Why would you need to? I mean, you've never had to go hungry because if you ate, someone in your family might still be hungry. Or maybe if you got a proper haircut, then your mom wouldn't have to work overtime to get leftovers for a whole week. No one laughs at you at school, right? You're not the one wearing patched clothes, going barefoot to school, right? Right?" Rusty was almost shouting by this time. "So yeah, why would we need money?" He heaved.

Unprepared at the bitterness pouring out of Rusty, Devin threw his hands up. "Cut it out, Rust. I wasn't belittling you. I was only letting you know I understood how you must feel."

"Well, you don't, so don't try to pretend."

This time it was Devin who stared. Hurt stabbed him.

"I'm worried about you. I don't think you should steal. And I'm sure Zoie feels that way too."

"You spoke to Zoie? When?"

His sudden hostility made Devin pause. "The day of the picnic. You'd gone to get food. She was talking to us till you got back. Anyway, she said she wouldn't make excuses for being poor, and I don't think you should either."

"Well, quit thinking I like stealing because I don't," shot back Rusty, glowering more than ever.

Clearly, he'd missed the point. Devin fell silent, thinking it was bad enough having to listen to how miserable Rusty thought being poor was, but to try and make him feel guilty like he had something to do with their misfortune was too much.

"Listen," he said, "we're friends, and you're the best thing that's happened to me, so quit feeling sorry for yourself. I'm worried about you. Gramps and Celeste care. They didn't turn you into the authorities only for you to get caught out here. Think how it's gonna make everyone feel if stuff like that happens! And what about the Elders? What will they do?"

Rusty stayed quiet as shame washed over him. It was true. Devin had nothing to do with them falling on hard times. He didn't mind being poor, but how did he begin to explain things to Devin who'd never had to struggle for anything?

Devin had a point. His family had been given a lot and he really shouldn't be complaining. Every week Rusty had seen jars of jams, bags of peas, fruits, and rice being delivered by Devin's family. He'd witnessed the frequent smiles now on everyone's faces in the camp.

He realized how much more chatty and friendly everyone had become. Before, it was a rush to finish the chores, distribute the meager meals, scuttling to their caravans; just surviving. But now, he thought, there was happiness, and it was reflected in the small "thank-yous" he'd heard and the little smiles the older folks greeted everyone with.

A long silence passed. Rusty turned back to his branch he'd been whacking at and then finally back to Devin. "You're right, Dev. I have a lot to be happy for, and I'm . . . I didn't mean to yell at you. I'm . . . I'm . . ." He stopped, took a deep breath, and said, "I'm sorry."

"It's okay. I'm sorry too," Devin said quietly.

Rusty felt a relieved grin spread across his face. For a minute he was nervous, wondering if he had offended his best friend. "My only friend," he corrected silently.

"They won't mind. You're important."

It took Devin a minute before realizing Rusty was referring to the elders. He sighed, then hurried after him. "Hey, Rusty," he yelled as Rusty had walked ahead.

"Talk, I'm listening," hollered back Rusty.

"Okay, here goes then," replied Devin a bit out of breath. "Only don't get all mad again."

"Okay," said Rusty.

Devin waited and when nothing else was forthcoming, began, "I don't know how to say what I really want to, but I'm going to try. Just let me finish, okay?"

Rusty laughed, saying, "So, we gonna argue then?"

"Not really," replied Devin.

Rusty turned around. Something in his expression made Devin wince, but he continued.

"You're not really ashamed of being poor. Most people here in Foxwood are. I know what's making you angry."

This time Rusty stared at him. "You do?"

"Yes," Devin said determinedly and stopped. "Let's sit and talk," he pointed to an old stump under a shaded patch of branches nearby.

Dropping his bundles, Rusty took out his little pouch and began picking some berries he had spotted.

"I know you're angry because of the way everyone treats you and your folks." A tense pause followed before Devin said again. "I'm right, aren't I?"

* * *

At his words, Rusty felt the familiar rush of anger flood through him. He could hear the jeering from the villagers, the kids at school calling him names, the times no one would sell their produce to his family, and the times when men at the bar would talk dirty things to his mom.

Rusty remembered how the kids weren't allowed to play with him. Memories kept flooding him. He recalled vividly, when he was seven, he and Zoie had gone to the Agricultural Station for some sweet potatoes that were being thrown out. The old man there had saved a box and left it for them to pick up. Rusty was so happy, skipping along with Zoie, and hearing an owl in the huge tree overhead, he'd asked Zoie to hoot like it. Zoie had indulged him, and they were giggling, hearing a reply.

It was unfortunate at that very moment, a number of the female Foxies happened to come along. Seeing Zoie and him behaving strangely, one particularly skinny lady laughingly called, "So you left your sty open again, Violet?"

Laughing loudly, they had crossed to the other side of the road and moved on. Zoie scrambled his arm, grasped the box of sweet potatoes in the other, and hustled home, unable to hide her tears.

He was brought out of his reverie by Devin gathering berries and was glad when he didn't ask anything. He really didn't want to talk about it. He just knew he couldn't wait for the day when . . . well . . .

Turning back, he said, "Yes, but how did you know?"

Devin looked taken aback for a moment, realizing Rusty had given him an honest answer, in spite of the length of time it had taken him to answer.

"I don't really know how I know."

Rusty looked at him oddly, shrugged, and turned away. "Seems like you have a story," he said after a while.

Devin froze.

"You know my story. What's yours?" He heard Rusty say.

Awkwardly, he puttered a bit before turning back, squaring his shoulders. Maybe Rusty would finally understand why he needed to care about things.

The shadows extended and lengthened as time went by, unnoticed by the two. Devin told what he knew. How his mom was mistreated and the things he and Lexi had had to witness and hear, pretending all was well. The bits and pieces he'd put together that his mom had revealed during unguarded moments. Anytime he'd asked, she would tell him he wouldn't understand and to wait until he got older.

"Slimy old bags!" he heard and then realized Rusty was outraged on his behalf.

"The toads! I hope they rot!" A string of ugly wishes came venting from Rusty, but Devin was unaware of the rest as an emotional pipe seemed to burst forth from within. It seemed he spoke for hours, and Rusty let him.

His shock at hearing Devin's story had him coming up with what seemed like the most ridiculous ideas to take revenge that kept them laughing until Devin got a stitch in his side. Finally, wiping his eyes, he said, "If my mom fought back, she would have been better off."

After a while, he continued, "I love my mom, and I know she loves me. But there's this thing between us. It's like she is always so distant, you know?" Not waiting for an answer, he said quickly, "I almost wish I could hurry and grow up so I can show them!"

A sparkle of interest lit Rusty's eyes. "You got a plan?" he whispered.

"My mom does," replied Devin.

"What do you mean?" asked Rusty, his gaze not leaving Devin's face.

"Let's just say Mom's got an image in her head about how I should be."

"What's wrong with that? All parents have dreams for their kids," continued Rusty, wisely. "My mom thinks I'm somehow responsible for the other kids at camp towing the line. I'm supposed to be a role model of sorts. Some role model," he muttered. "Me, Rusty, leader of the band to nowhere anytime soon, anywhere at all!" he ended viciously.

Devin knew exactly how Rusty felt. "Well, mom thinks if I finish school with good grades, I'll get to go places. She thinks traveling will make me 'cultured'," he said.

"Well, heck! What's wrong with that?" Rusty exclaimed. "I'd do that any day than sit out here gathering wood and stealing from fishing boats just to get a meal!"

"I guess when you put it like that, it doesn't look so bad," said Devin. "The only problem is I won't have fun. I want to enjoy being a kid. I kinda like the things you do and the simple way you guys live," he finished, feeling stupid with the changing expressions on Rusty's face.

A moment's silence passed before he heard, "Well, man, if it's so difficult to live the easy life and have people love you enough to have high expectations of you, you got it real bad!"

But Rusty wasn't finished.

"I gotta say," Rusty continued, flopping down in the sand and starting to doodle, a wrinkle in his forehead, "ya, it stinks. I guess it's not so bad when I think about it."

"Look at me!" he pointed to himself. "What do I have to look forward to?" Then without waiting for an answer, he went on, "Let's see now, going to that school and sitting in filth. Cleaning toilets and fetching for the Foxies! Maybe when I get older, I might get a chance to become a smuggler myself and then who knows? I might even find a girl and settle down right there! In that camp!" He jerked his thumb toward his campsite.

"And the beach, quite a world out there!" he said. "By the way, tell me again why your mom wants you to do all that stuff?"

Feeling really, really stupid, Devin muttered, "I guess it'd show them what class really is. Stupid . . . small-minded," he paused, kicking a rock that had him hissing in pain. "Ugly," he said, with another kick. "Miserable old bats," he spat out, wincing in pain as his toes connected at the rock. Hobbling to the stump, he said, "Mom says when I'm grown, I'll be the person they never could."

"Well, there you have it then!" exclaimed Rusty. "Couldn't have put it better myself. Stinks, doesn't it?"

Then suddenly they erupted into laughter. Doubled over, Devin laughed until he was coughing. Rusty thumped him several times on the back before he was able to settle down while the pain in his toes continued to throb. But he needed to have Rusty understand.

"They did something and mom has never been the same," he said. He stopped, eyes darting to Rusty, realizing too late what he'd said, as a hush fell between them.

Rusty felt his stomach drop! Here he was lashing out at Devin for having a normal life, a beautiful home with so many things he had moments before envied, and now — now he felt emotions he never knew he had.

Rusty, who had physically and financially struggled his whole life, but with a ton of love, not only from his mom but Zoie as well, didn't have a clue how to respond. Mutely, he looked at Devin reflecting on how strange life was.

"So now we both have reasons to become more than we are, huh?" Devin heard Rusty's question. Relief seeped through him. He didn't expect to have spoken about the things he had, but maybe, just maybe, it might make Rusty realize having a dancer for a mother wasn't that bad after all.

He felt, for a brief moment, they had caught a glimpse of the future as it reared its tiny head. Rusty came over and they hugged, a bond of friendship sealed within their hearts. After what seemed like an eternity, they parted.

Knowing they'd have to make several trips each to carry all of the firewood they had collected, they set to work and were busy in moments.

Devin still wasn't convinced Rusty's attitude about stealing was the right one but didn't want another round of bitterness coming from either of them. Keeping his mouth shut, he trudged along. He'd seen what the renegade was capable of. He felt a finger of dread shiver through him at the thought of Rusty getting caught.

Things were what they were, and Rusty wouldn't thank him for interfering. Aloud, he said, "How do you manage? Don't they know things are missing?"

"I guess, but I don't take too much at once," replied Rusty.

THE ENCOUNTER

Devin knew he needed to see this Rennie character. All this stuff with Rusty and his folks, depending on the renegade and his smuggling, there had to be an answer. Things just couldn't continue the way they were.

And he wasn't going to just get the crystal back by walking up to him saying, "Hey, you! Hand it over." Leaving well enough alone as Gramps had made them promise, wasn't good enough either. Something told him he needed to try. With or without Rusty's help, he was going to find out where the renegade hung out and talk with him.

That evening he came up with a plan, and a week later, he was on it. But the more Devin asked around, the more everyone shied away from giving an answer, making him wonder how many had had unpleasant run-ins with Rennie.

When his mom let him walk to the ancient movie theater with Rusty and the gang to watch The Vikings' Treasure, he kept a keen eye out for any signs the renegade might be around. He was disappointed, as the movie started, and there was still no sign of the renegade showing up. During the break, he headed for the boys' bathroom and spotted two older kids ahead of him. He'd seen them at the last sports competition.

About to greet them, he paused on hearing, "Just like Rennie, huh?" The voice continued, "Man, the way he just got rid of those fellows! That dude was huge!"

Devin stayed still. They were comparing the Viking to Rennie! He listened intently as the other said, "Yeah. Funny, Ned. I was thinking the same thing. I mean, Rennie's cool and everything, but the way he is, if it was back then, I think he'd be a leader or something."

"Well, last I heard," said Ned, "everyone's been keeping far away from him after what happened at the Rotten Shack. It took them two whole weeks just to repair the damages he and the ruffians made."

"Musta cost him a good deal. How do you think he got off?"

"Jake, you worry too much. Since when does the renegade pay for anything? Most likely he bribed the old barfly. He's a smuggler in case you forgot."

"Well, that explains a lot then," said Jake.

And that was exactly what Devin thought. No wonder no one would tell him where the renegade hung out. Seems the Rotten Shack was well named, he concluded.

"But what were you doing down there anyway?" Ned suddenly asked. "You coulda asked me to come along."

"It's not like I planned it. Dad insisted we needed firewood," replied Jake. "And we have a garden down in that area. Stuff's always missing. We needed it for this weekend's sale. We'd just gotten there when a bad commotion broke out. A lot of shouting and cussing."

Devin thought it was funny Lexi hadn't said a word. She was always reading The Village Beat and never failed to fill them in on the latest gossip. He listened again, focusing.

"Well, I want to see it sometime. Look at you, fifteen, and you've been there already," Ned finished.

"I didn't go inside," retorted Jake hurriedly. "And don't get no ideas 'bout going there 'cause if you get caught, that's the end of us, man."

"Why?" asked Ned.

"Well, what if something happens, and you get blamed for smuggling? That's a rough crowd."

Ned chuckled, clapping him on the shoulder, "You worry too much, bro. Leave it to me. I'm seventeen. The old crow only worries about his profit. Not who visits his shack." He laughed again, and Devin heard them leave before resting against the door of his stall, his heart beating fast.

He found it interesting that the brawl had never made it to the newspaper. The news people were very nosey. It was hard to believe someone knew and didn't tell.

"Well, here I come, be warned, Rennie. You're no Viking to me!" Easing himself away, Devin went back to his seat just as the movie resumed but was unable to focus, his mind wandering. He needed to find where the Rotten Shack was and what he'd say once he found the renegade.

Lady luck was with him sooner than he anticipated. Devin was pleasantly surprised to find the innkeeper of the Hibiscus Inn making an effort to spruce up the building.

"What in the world had gotten into him!" Devin asked no one in particular as he stood gazing around the inn's dilapidated yard.

"Oh, get this," Rusty said. "He's paying us to clean. Pretty decent too. Mom said . . ."

"Mom's gonna have much more to say if you don't get to work, Master Rusty."

The others grinned as Rusty's mom approached and mussed his hair.

"I was just explaining to Devin," he began when his mom shook her head at him, giving a slight nod to the open doorway.

The boys scattered immediately and became busy.

"Hi, Miss Ginger," Devin said, giving a quick little wave of his hand.

"Hey, Dev," Ginger returned. "Nice seeing you here. How's everyone?"

"Fine, thanks, Miss Ginger. I didn't mean to interrupt. I wanted to see if Rusty could hang out for a bit, but he said they all got jobs now."

She gave him a quick smile, nodding in agreement. "For now. Since word got out your family accepted us, folks have been busy visiting the inn. Business has really picked up."

"Oh, I see," said Devin. But he didn't have time to ponder upon it too much as a group of villagers filed past and entered the inn, their faces agog with curiosity. A few even leaned over the railing of the porch, straining their necks forward in an effort to see into the forest beyond.

"Don't worry 'bout them, boy. It's human nature!" He jumped as the innkeeper came up behind him. "Sorry, Mr. Heeb," Devin replied, wanting to kick himself for gawking.

"They can't help themselves, is what it is. Anything different becomes fashion 'round here. I've been 'round long enough to know that. Don't let them worry you. Come, we got stuff to do." Mr. Heeb turned and led the way over to the back where the once lush garden was overgrown with weeds and bushes.

Devin found he was happy Mr. Heeb had decided to employ Rusty and the others. Maybe other people might start employing the Gypsies too.

As they pulled weeds and cleaned trash, Rusty went in to see his mom from time to time and once showed up with a mug of lemonade. Devin took a glass and wandered down a little path he found. It led to a little alcove that was very peaceful. Taking a deep gulp, he felt the coolness seep into him and closed his eyes, enjoying the quiet. Spotting a tiny bench, he walked over and sat down.

A few moments later, he heard a whisper. Startled, he listened and had almost given up when he heard it again. A ragged whisper. "Tonight."

A second voice whispered, "You sure?"

"Yeah," said the first. "Heeb went outside for a bit jus now. Seen him talking to a kid. It's been decided. The boat comes in at eleven. The tide is what we wait for."

Devin sat as if turned to stone, unaware he was holding his breath. Someone was planning something big. And it was happening later tonight!

"Everyone's gonna be there?" asked the second voice.

"Yah. That's the word. Everybody's fed up. Said he's sayin' we be sorry if we think about not showin' up. You believe it? After what happened at the Shack and all. I'm tellin' you eidder we do sumtin' or . . ."

"Well," said the second voice, "eidder way, we're done then. 'Cause if we don't help him, we're in trouble. Guess I'll pass the word out. You sure it's tonight?"

"Sure," said the first voice.

"What do we bring?" asked the first. "Just y'self and yuh muscles. He's not gonna go down easy. We need all the help we can git."

As silence filled the air, Devin was almost ready to get up when he heard, "Oh, yeah. Bring dat rope we got. It can hold a boat. Think it can do the job."

"Awright, sure," said the second. "Hope we don't live to regret this."

"Hope so. Hope so," said the first as rustling sounded and Devin heard them hobbling along the bushes, their voices receding.

Devin felt his mind reeling from what he'd just heard. Here he was trying to meet the renegade, and his own people seemed to be plotting to double cross him or do something drastic to him. They had said it was going down tonight. At eleven. He had some time, but he still didn't know where the Rotten Shack was.

Finishing his lemonade, he headed back up the path and spotted Hunter as he rounded a corner. "Ever heard of a place called the Rotten Shack?"

Hunter blanched, his face turning pale. "What you want to know 'bout that place for? You don't need to be going down there," he said.

"I was curious. Heard two kids at the movie theater saying it got messed up a few weeks back. I didn't see it in the newspaper," finished Devin quickly.

"You won't find it in the newspaper," Hunter answered. "The bartender is as rotten as the place's name. He doesn't want the authorities knowing anything."

"That bad?" said Devin. "How come you know about it? Been there?"

Hunter grinned. "You forget we live in these woods. If you know where to look, you'll find anything. Guess I'll have to tell you. Just don't go looking for it. You don't know what those men are like," he said.

When Devin didn't say anything, he gave a quick look around before saying, "Nobody at camp is supposed to know I told you this. Okay?"

Devin nodded. "Okay, I promise."

Hunter nodded. "It's down by the lake."

"Lake? What lake? I didn't know there was a lake around here," finished Devin.

"Told you. If you know where to look . . ."

"Yeah, I know. You'll find anything," finished Devin.

Hunter grinned again.

"Well, there's a small waterway that connects the beach to the lake. That's how they manage to get their loot to safety. If you follow this trail,"—he pointed to the one they were both standing on, —"to the end, it takes you past an alcove to a small deck at the little stream. Mr. Heeb has a boat himself. He goes down there and buys his supplies and stuff."

"Mr. Heeb!"

"Shh."

"Sorry, sorry," Devin lowered his voice, seeing how rattled Hunter became. "You just caught me by surprise."

"Yeah, well don't go shouting again. You'll get us both in trouble," said Hunter.

"Sorry," said Devin again, almost whispering.

"Anyway," continued Hunter, "Mr. Heeb gets his things, and he pays. Real clean. No funny stuff. The renegade doesn't bully him. We've watched him every time the boats come in."

"Do you know why?" Devin asked.

"Everyone wants to know, but nobody's telling. And Mr. Heeb don't know we know anything."

"Are you all going tonight then?" Devin asked, thinking he could have tagged along.

"Nah. Too much to do, and we got enough stuff from you folks."

"Right," said Devin. "Thanks, man." And he meant it! He couldn't believe his luck. Not only did he find out where the Rotten Shack was, but he had also found a way to get there. If he was lucky, he'd be able to see the renegade!

He stayed an hour more, helping out, debating whether he should ask Rusty to go with him or not. But since he was the one worried about Rusty stealing from the renegade, he decided against it. Rusty's folks had enough to deal with already to get even more mixed up in his scheme. He knew better after going through their Judgment Circle. He'd just have to go alone.

Devin was surprised to see two hours had passed since he had spoken to Hunter. Knowing he'd need some rest, if he was going to be up later, he said good-bye to everyone and headed home.

Rennie's men were planning something funny, and he had a bad feeling about it, but he might be able to search if they were otherwise busy. Rennie had to have the crystal stashed somewhere. That voice had said something about a rope, and Devin didn't want to think what that could mean. He focused on what he'd need for the trip.

With evening approaching and having showered and dined earlier, Devin took a small bag out of his little cupboard in his room. Stuffing a flashlight and a sandwich, he added a length of rope and left the few odds and ends he normally carried around in the bottom of the bag.

Since he'd told Lexi he was sleeping over by Rusty's, he had no problem leaving earlier than planned. She was too busy learning a new dance to even worry about him. And with their parents having gone to some neighboring towns and villages to get seeds to replant crops from the recent loss, it made things easier for him.

At the last moment, Devin stuffed his pocket knife into the bag and left. For good luck, he took the necklace the circle of Elders had given him and put it on. Stopping by his cousins' home, he stayed an hour puttering around until it was dark enough for him to leave unseen and then set off.

He had no trouble getting to the Hibiscus Inn. Once there, he needed to find a way to the back. Mr. Heeb was busy tending to his customers, but he had eagle eyes for a wife and

Devin didn't want to chance her spotting him. Waiting until he saw her through the window, taking care of a particularly drunk fellow, he darted to the tool shed at the side. Waiting in the shadows, he inched his way along and soon got past any lingering light.

His dark clothing offered good protection and his long sleeves and long-legged pants kept the bugs and flies off him. His old sneakers, soft and comfortable, made very little disturbance as he hurried along. The last time he checked, it was about nine-thirty.

Devin carefully checked to make sure his little bag was secure around his shoulders. He was feeling sorry he hadn't brought his walking stick and as he approached the little alcove, his muscles tensed. Those fellows had said a boat was coming in and Hunter had told him Mr. Heeb bought supplies from the renegade.

He hurried along as quietly as he could, nervous in case he couldn't find the boat and wondering if Mr. Heeb would be leaving his customers soon. It was going to be disastrous if he got caught.

Finding the boat tied securely to a post at the little lake, Devin was just about to untie it when heavy footsteps echoed in the distance. With his heart pounding, mouth dry, and legs like jelly, Devin looked around. He couldn't turn back now. He watched as a small light bobbed behind. He could leave, except he had no idea about the lake, at least not enough to try and swim away. He peered around for a tree of any sort to get to for safety but didn't have any luck.

Not even one overhanging the edge of the lake. "Stupid, stupid," he kept saying to himself. He should have waited and scouted during daylight. Whoever it was, they were almost twenty yards away when his searching hands found what felt like material of some sort. Praying he wasn't discovered, Devin hopped aboard the little boat, no bigger than a dingy and scrambled under a mound of bags and burlaps or whatever it was that he found, almost suffocating in its odor of wet skins and rotten eggs.

But then he heard the voice from inside the alcove.

"Help me get this thing outta here, Rus. Don't want Heeb to show up for a shipment at the wrong time."

Devin almost gave himself away trying to suppress a sneeze.

"You 'eard sometin'?" said the first voice hoarsely.

"Just us and the night, Wes," replied Rus. "Jus us and the night. You too worried. You don't stop bein' jumpy. You'll make the renegade know some'in's up."

"Guess you're right, Rus. But we're ready. Mor'n ready for this. Can't stand being enslaved."

"Heeb's not gonna thank us, though. You better figure out some'in' to say when the renegade stops showin' up after tonight."

Devin felt a chill in his blood. This was more than he had planned for. Their tone was ominous, and he didn't want to think what it meant. The little boat shifted violently as someone stepped aboard. Untying it from its hitch, he heard,

"Here you are. I'll meet you further up."

And they were off. Devin figured somewhere ahead was another little boat. Sure enough, about five minutes after leaving, he heard Rus saying, "Okay then, here's the rope. Heeb sure got a lotta stuff in here. Wonder what he was hopin' for. Think we can nick some?"

"Cut that out, Rus. We no thieves. Dat's the whole point of tonight! You think the way he wants us to. Jus leave the lot and let's get on with it."

"Okay, okay. Jus thought . . ."

"Never mind that now. Hand me the rope."

After some grunting and cussing, ropes were exchanged, and they were off again. Devin silently thanked the stars. He didn't know how much longer he could hold up.

They had been traveling for about twenty minutes; smoke was the only sign anyone was on board. The silence told Devin that Rus was worried too. But it was torture being huddled under the pile of stuff. And the smoke didn't help. He felt another sneeze about to escape when they came to a slow and a soft bump.

"'Ere we are!" he heard Wes saying. "Just make sure the others know not to do nothin' till I give the signal."

"Okay," replied Rus as the little boat rocked and tilted when he stepped off, tying it up to dock at a small stump.

Devin stuck his head out and gulped air, the back of his throat seeming to have become glued from the stench of the skins or whatever he was under.

Cautiously, he looked around at the busy little scene around him. At least a dozen other boats of various sizes were tied up. He checked his watch but couldn't see a thing. He needed to get out and find a hiding place. He wasn't sure what the group had planned.

Apparently, they had no fear of being discovered because there was a lot of yelling and hollering. He saw men he'd never seen before, all with the same look of hardened roughness. Anyone that had kindly expressions seemed jumpy and nervous.

Whether it was Devin's knowledge about something big that was planned for tonight or their odd behavior, or the fact they all seemed to be armed with a weapon of some sort, something told him he'd chosen the wrong night to try and meet the renegade, but there was nothing he could do to change it now. One had a club, another, a pickaxe, and yet another, a solid rock he kept changing from hand to hand.

Soon the bustling little crowd was engrossed in bargaining and loading their loot. Amidst the fetching and yelling, Devin lost no time in searching for a spot. And he had spotted it the moment he lifted the skins off his head. Where his dingy was sitting was a sturdy tree, reaching way into the darkness.

Climbing it wouldn't be a problem. Looking carefully around, he nimbly hopped out and scrambled behind its huge trunk. Securing his stuff at his back, Devin hopped up on a low-lying limb, grasped a fatter limb and shimmed his way along into darkness. Making sure he was deep in the branches, he settled himself and took a deep breath.

A second later, he let it out in a rush as the renegade appeared at the edge of the crowd, silence falling as everyone stared. Devin wondered how soon someone was going to give something away.

The night of his watch, he'd only heard a deep voice and seen the renegade in that gruff manner. Now he saw a man with hair hanging past his shoulder blades, with a face like an eagle in its intensity, staring at the group huddled in front of him. Tall and broad, the words of Ned and Jack floated back to him.

Devin could see why they thought Rennie could be a Viking. His stance was powerful, and Devin wondered if he was crazy to have thought he could talk to the man standing in front of him. But he couldn't leave now. He watched silently as Rennie snapped his hands and everyone jumped.

He took his time looking around, making Devin wonder what he was doing, and then he heard the drawl, "Where's Heeb?" Devin knew right then he would come to remember this night as the night that would change things forever.

The moment Rennie asked, Wes stepped forward and said, "He ain't 'ere yet."

"So what's his boat doing here then?" The renegade barked. "It didn't just float down here by itself. And how do you know he's not coming?"

His quick assessment of the matter took Devin by surprise. Rus uttered a sound of distress, and Wes turned on him, "Be quiet!"

"What's this?" said Rennie. Nervous silence greeted him. He slowly swung around noticing their discomfort. "Got something you folks want to tell me then, Wes?"

Devin could see trouble coming. He understood the request for numbers. One alone was no match for the renegade. If Wes was their leader, he was a sorry one at it.

"Look 'ere, Ren," said Wes. "We don't like the way you been treatin' us. And we're not gonna do this stuff anymore."

"So we're back to this again, are we?" The renegade said in a lazy drawl, sighing loudly.

"Yup, guess we are," replied Wes, the rest of the group nodding their heads.

"Really? And how do you expect to do this?" The drawl was sarcastic, cruel.

Devin saw them cringe and felt himself go tense in apprehension.

"Gonna go to the authorities? You might have some explaining to do," The renegade pointed out.

Devin felt fear enter him as he watched the little band of smugglers forming a tight circle around the renegade.

"We don't care. Better them than you. All those promises you made to us. We did this to help our families. You made us thieves when we wasn't 'xpecting it," said a man from the back of the group.

"How so?" said Rennie. "Been listening to Wes here, haven't you, Ben?"

"Is true. Didn't know you were gonna do the things you bin doing."

"What have I been doing then, Ben?" His soft question hung in the air, the atmosphere changing to dangerous.

"Don't matter. None a dat stuff matter now." The speaker was another fellow Devin saw had gotten the courage to speak up. "No use going through point by point. You rotten, and you know it. We don't want no part of dis stuff no more!"

The renegade stared at them a long time, before shaking his head, making Devin think there was a lot to what he was witnessing he didn't know about.

Rennie looked at them for a long time before throwing his head back, laughing heartily. A loud, deep-bellied laugh of disbelief that sounded into the night like that of a man who knew he held all the power.

And in that unguarded moment, they struck.

Watching, with heart in his mouth and unable to do anything, Devin sat horror-stricken as the men attacked with everything they had. A large rock grazed the renegade as he turned his head a fraction before it connected with a killer force. And like a giant, Devin saw arms and legs and bodies being flung about. They fell, then got up, and hit and kicked and grabbed.

And he fought back like a ferocious animal in their midst. His initial surprise gone, the renegade moved with a grace and fierceness that was as wild as it was uncivilized. Ugly and brutal, the savage battle held Devin transfixed, and he watched, terrified.

How long it went on, Devin couldn't say for sure but it was the sudden bright flashes of light from a powerful flashlight aimed at the renegade's face that blinded him and it took Devin a long moment as silence descended to realize the renegade was silent on the ground, bleeding and battered as he was struck repeatedly by the group.

Whether he was dead or just badly hurt, Devin could not tell. He felt bile rise in his throat. He watched as the men gathered around, bruised and hurt, seeming surprised they were able to have taken the renegade down.

"Can't leave 'im 'ere," Devin heard Wes saying raggedly. "Heeb's gonna come looking for him. He'll know by now some'in's up. Get busy, boys. Load 'im up, and let's get done with it. No celebratin'. And nobody goes to that Inn till everyone's nice and clean. Got that?" he croaked hoarsely.

The knowledge they had done what they did, brought a flood of activity as everyone jumped to obey. "'Urry up now! Don't want Heeb on us."

Devin stared, scared and helpless, unable to do anything as they tied the body up and took it over to dump it. The ones lifting the renegade, already badly beaten themselves, labored as they headed for the lake.

"Put 'im in Heeb's boat. Let somebody find him there. That'll take care of both of them. Cut him loose too. The tide's going out soon."

Like robots, they obeyed and scurried along, slipping and groaning. They reached under the tree where Devin sat in deathly silence. With much huffing and puffing, they loaded the body into the little boat and two of them waited to make sure everyone else had safely left before cutting the rope and giving it a push.

The renegade was a big guy and his weight, together with the skins that were already in the little boat, sat solidly for a while before moving at a snail's speed. The old barfly, as Ned and Jake had called him, had obviously been in the plan because he showed up shortly after to make sure nothing incriminating was left behind.

Creepy looking, with deep-set eyes and a hooknose that seemed to pierce the night-air, he looked everywhere. From his vantage point, Devin could swear he was sniffing the air.

After what seemed like forever, he grunted a few expletives, covered the ground with sand that had signs of disturbance, and dumped dried leaves and bushes everywhere.

"Dratted hogs! Now I gotta stay closed another week with this stuff happenin' tonight." Spitting rudely, he turned and walked back to his shack.

THE RIVER AT NIGHT

Devin stayed still for a few more minutes after they left, all the time keeping an eye on the small boat slowly moving away. The moment the barfly left, he climbed down as gingerly and swiftly as he could, knowing he needed to get back home. If it got further out, he'd miss his chance, and there'd be hell to pay.

Having no other choice left, he waded into the river as far as he could, then swam, making his mind blank to the slimy feel of things moving around him. It was dark and cold, but he pushed himself away quickly, with delayed terror threatening to take over.

Gasping and panting, he made it, clutching the side of the little boat. Climbing aboard, he felt it slip. They were going to sink if he didn't do something. He didn't have time to worry about sharing a boat with a dead body. He started dumping the skins, ignoring their rotten stench. He felt the shift and the boat lightened as he kept dumping things overboard.

What felt like a tarp went. Then more skins. Finally, he felt a blanket. He turned, ready to throw it over the renegade, but nearly fell over when he noticed a pair of eyes watching his every move. Devin yelped and jumped to the other side of the boat, too stunned to speak.

A second later, he was pulling the blanket away, the light from the Rotten Shack fading fast, but he was able to see the battered, broken face, and blood gushing forth. He took his pack off and found his knife. Within moments, he was sawing at the tough rope.

Grunting sounds of pain came from the renegade, but he didn't care. He was relieved. The Renegade wasn't dead. Thank God! Relief flooded him as the ropes came loose.

His chest tightened as he sawed the ropes binding the feet, and realized he felt hot, stinging tears flowing down his face. He didn't care. Fear and terror over what he'd witnessed suddenly gave him a burst of energy.

Finding the blanket, he covered Rennie and took his little bag, using it to pillow his head. Scooping water with his hands, he tried washing Rennie's face and took off his black undershirt, using it to wipe up the blood from the bruises, making himself deaf to the groans from Rennie.

When he was satisfied that no blood was leaking into Rennie's mouth, he looked around, seeing they were farther out than he'd expected. Ditching the T-shirt, he felt around and found a pair of paddles. The renegade seemed to have fainted by then which was fine with him. He'd let himself think about everything else later. He needed to get home.

Moving to the little seat, he set forth and was soon paddling desperately, praying he would get back to the inn. He felt a spot of warmth in his chest and looked down and nearly lost the paddles as he saw a glow appear on one of the little knots of the necklace. A surge of strength flooded him, and he felt his strokes lengthening.

Turning the boat around from heading out to sea, he steered it back along where they had come from, remembering what he'd seen from his seat in the tree. They'd headed off in a right-handed direction, so Devin changed direction again and headed back in the reverse toward the Hibiscus Inn. After a laborious bout of paddling, he relaxed and let the current do the work.

The blackness of the night was broken only by the sound of the river as it rushed on, the occasional glimpse of a campfire on either side of the riverbanks, or the faint glow of a shack or hut that dotted the landscape. Devin wasn't going to question what exactly folks might be doing so deep into the woods, as tonight's events had explained that much. It did give him a fair idea however, on how wide or narrow the river was, since he had no other way of gauging their position on the water. In fact, he was happy every time he spotted another dot of light, as it made his job easier in guiding them back to Mr. Heeb's place; without the light to guide him, he would have been completely lost in the wilds.

It seemed forever, but when he got back to the little post, he could tell he was being welcomed. There was a loud splash and then large hands were enfolding him, pulling them to safety. The voice of Mr. Heeb said, "Boy, I'm not going to ask questions now, but you got some explainin' to do."

Exhausted, terrified, and in need of cleaning up, he hurried up the path as Mr. Heeb had told him to. Careful to keep quiet, he headed through the back door, turned right to the kitchen, and found Mrs. Heeb elbow-deep in the sink.

Upon seeing him, she dropped the bowl she was washing. "What you doin' here, boy?" Her loud voice carried, making him jump.

"Mr. Heeb needs help. He said he needed Galeb," Devin said in a rush.

"Oh," she whispered, "no. He left 'bout fifteen minutes ago. Just the usual lot of dem drunks hangin' on."

"Well, he said something about a room," said Devin, already regretting he hadn't just gone home.

"Go," said Mrs. Heeb. "I'll send someone." Devin turned and started back, stumbling over a drunk sleeping in the hallway. As he stepped outside, he saw Mr. Heeb half-dragging, half-carrying Rennie. Without thinking, he dashed over and lifted the renegade's left shoulder, trying to support him. It was dead weight, and he almost collapsed under the heaviness.

They were straining and huffing, dragging the renegade along when Ginger came pelting up the pathway, with Mrs. Heeb closely behind. Devin nearly lost his balance when he saw Rusty's mom.

"Dev," she said urgently, "what are you doing here? What happened to you? And him?"

"No time for questions now, Ginger, if you please. No use askin' the boy either. You know he don't know nothing."

Ginger kept quiet and together with Mrs. Heeb, they managed to half-fetch, half-carry Rennie to a hidden room at the back of the inn. Devin sagged wearily in a chair he found.

Almost two hours later, things calmed down, with Rennie comfortable, cleaned, and sleeping in a bed Ginger had made up. Devin wondered what she'd say to him.

As it turned out, Mr. Heeb had retrieved his little backpack and returned it to him.

"Thank you, boy, but I think you'll be needin' this now."

Devin stared at it a moment, before reaching out and taking it.

"Give me your promise, you'll never talk about what happened here tonight," said Mr. Heeb.

With Ginger, Mr. Heeb, and himself there, Devin nodded. "I promise, Mr. Heeb, but I was trying to find out why The Ren—— Why he took my grandfather's crystal?"

"That, I can't say, boy. That I can't say. But I'll be sure to ask him when he comes to. Do you know you coulda been killed out there tonight?" The old man was wringing his hand, one moment nervous, the other an angry bear.

"No, not really," said Devin. "I didn't know what was going to happen. I just wanted to meet him."

"Well, now you did," snapped Mr. Heeb. "And you see why folks stay away from that place," he continued. "Rennie here is well named. He does more for us than people understand."

Devin's patience snapped. "Well, he wasn't any hero tonight. He would have died if I hadn't . . ."

"Don't talk like that, boy," said Mr. Heeb, his tone agitated. Devin fell quiet as Ginger left and brought him a hot cup of tea. The tension eased a little.

Mr. Heeb went over and stared at the renegade. Devin took his time, sipping his tea slowly, wrapped in a towel while his clothes were drying by the fire. He told them what he'd seen, heard, and done.

When he was finished, Mr. Heeb looked him over carefully, then said, "Thank you, boy. It means a lot to us."

Devin nodded, unable to say anything. That night he shared the room with Rennie, and the next morning, he headed home before anyone was awake, anxious to be back in his room.

★ ★ ★

Two weeks had passed since the night of the attack, and Devin wondered what he was in for. The first night he'd kept watch, he was unprepared, full of curiosity that had turned into fear and later gained him a friend. Now, he was nervous.

A lot had happened since the night he'd saved the renegade. He had been in the presence of violence, having witnessed a crime that gave him nightmares. He couldn't help looking for the faces of the men he'd seen that night down by the Rotten Shack.

He avoided going by to see Rusty and the gang. But when Ginger sent a message to say Mr. Heeb needed help cleaning again, he knew it was their way of summoning him, making him nervous.

Mr. Heeb was waiting as he approached and took him round back, pretending he was showing him where he needed weeds pulled. As they passed the back entrance, Mr. Heeb took a quick right taking him to the room he dreaded going into.

The renegade was propped against some pillows as he entered, and in the dim light, Devin spotted scars along his hands, neck, and chest. He was mending, but weak. As he lay there, Ginger came in with salve and left as Mr. Heeb moved over to apply it.

"I told him everything you told me, boy, but he wants to hear it from you for his self."

Devin couldn't move his gaze as the renegade stared at him. But he was aware of a strange, powerful energy emanating from Rennie.

"I remember you cutting me loose."

Devin jumped at the suddenness of the renegade's voice. "Yes," he nodded, his voice shaky.

"Why were you spying on me?" asked Rennie.

"I wanted to know why you had Rusty steal my grandfather's crystal," replied Devin, amazed he was having a civil conversation with this man.

"I did it to help someone. Someone nobody understands."

"But it belonged to my grandfather," said Devin. "And you hurt Miss Ginger's son. How could you?" He stared at the renegade.

Rennie was the first to shift his gaze, retreating into a strange silence. After a while he said, "Kid, I am sorry. My nature is a hard one. I can't change what I did, but I can apologize. And if I can fix it, I will, but right now, I have to get better first. And I wanted to say thank-you for saving me."

Mr. Heeb sat down heavily on the chair next to the bed, his face hanging in disbelief. Ginger, who'd just walked in the doorway, stood frozen and Devin thought he was in a dream, hearing the most feared person in the land apologizing to him.

"Sit, boy, and close your mouth!" The abrupt sound of Mr. Heeb's voice made Devin jump. He dropped into a chair and sat, wondering if he'd just heard it right. The renegade had thanked him!

He sat quiet for a long time, thinking over what had just happened, and was shocked to realize he'd just come to respect the most hated man around.

He listened as Rennie said, "I know how folks treat her. Anything they don't understand, they treat like lepers. I wondered what she needed with a crystal, 'specially when there's a whole cave full of them down by where she lives. But everybody's got funny ways. I know how lonely it is to be different." He stopped speaking and fell quiet again.

Devin wondered at the trouble Rennie had gone to for a stranger and felt some things were just too strange for him. Noticing Rennie's attempt to stay awake, he left saying he'd be back.

He visited Rennie several times, bringing him books and newspapers. The renegade was more intelligent than he had at first realized and slowly he became less frightening to be around.

Over the next several weeks, Devin had arranged for the renegade to meet with Gramps and apologize personally. Gramps shushed him out of the room, and after a very long meeting with Rennie, they parted agreeably.

Devin was dying to know what went on, but Gramps was firm, saying, "It's taken care of, Dev. Leave it alone."

"But . . . ," he started, and Gramps looked at him.

"Nothing," he finished, frustrated.

He had the same experience with Mr. Heeb who had his reasons for taking care of the renegade but gave no explanation. Mr. Heeb had hugged him rather awkwardly, making Devin even more curious to know the extent of their relationship.

Back at home, he kicked his dresser and yelped, hurting the same toe he'd hurt on the stump when he'd kicked out before. He'd saved Rusty, and now he had gone and saved the renegade. He never set out to be a hero, yet somehow folks were getting in his debt without him meaning to. Life in the hills was changing rapidly. He felt out of sync and out of balance. He needed to find a quiet spot and think. Nobody felt the need for him to know anything. He could scream!

The one thing he knew for sure, he wasn't going to leave it alone. He had Rusty. And Rennie had told him of the cave. He was going to find that cave somehow or the other.

RELEASE

It had taken him a while, but eventually Devin figured out that he needed to make another trip. This time he needed to find the cave.

As he got closer to the forest, he heard a "psssst." He jumped, stopping in mid-stride.

Rusty appeared beside him. "What you up to?"

"Go back, Rust."

"Not a chance, buddy!"

"Don't do this, Rust. I can't take you along."

"Why not?" said Rusty with determination.

"I can't involve you in this. If things go bad . . ."

"Fine. But I'm going," replied Rusty.

Devin sighed. He'd like the company but would never admit it. "Fine," he repeated. "Just don't say I didn't warn you."

"I won't," said Rusty.

Turning, Devin started off with Rusty beside him. Soon they came to a strange trail. Everything stood empty. They spotted footprints, old and faded.

"Looks like we're late," said Rusty. "Good thing too. You wouldn't want to bump into them now anyway," he finished.

"Who?" replied Devin.

"The smugglers. Isn't this where they hide out?"

"Oh," replied Devin. "No. I guess we wouldn't want to." Shivers went down his spine.

Rusty looked puzzled but didn't say much. Devin let him. He wasn't going to admit about his meeting with them.

As they trampled on, Rusty said, "I think you better let me lead. I think I know where you're going."

"Okay," Devin said, relieved, as Rusty hopped in front. They kept going for about ten minutes, and then he stopped.

"Ouch!" Bumping unexpectedly into Rusty, Devin felt his nose, rubbing it gently, "What's the matter?" he whispered.

Rusty pointed with a puzzled look.

Devin sucked in his breath, staring in amazement at the scene they'd come upon. The growth had cleared away, revealing a lush landscape, laden with layers of vegetation, tiny streams, and ancient trees standing invitingly before them. Rotting logs interconnected, crisscrossed, and looking like a pattern of steps all jumbled together, leading the eyes upward. Lush moss covered every nook and corner of the strange but beautiful place.

Speechless, they stared at the giant tree standing way back in the very center of it all. Rising majestically, it seemed hundreds of feet tall. A huge circle of ground lay underneath in shadows, shaded by the vast expanse of branches above, allowing approach.

"This can't be. This wasn't here," Devin heard Rusty whisper.

"What do you mean this wasn't here? This didn't just grow overnight. This place is old. I mean, really ancient. Just look at it," said Devin.

"But it can't be. I was here two days ago," said Rusty. "I was right there." He pointed to a spot almost five feet in front of him. "I was there waiting to see him come in. Their boat normally comes in on the third Thursday of each month."

For reasons neither knew, their voices had become hushed, and Devin knew he wasn't about to say anything about boats, smugglers, nor his part in any of their activity of late.

"Well, what are we waiting for? Let's go see what all this is," he said, humoring Rusty. He'd been to the Rotten Shack. He was at the river. Unless there were many meeting-points the renegade met at, he knew Rusty had to be mistaken.

Rusty drew back. "But we shouldn't," he said. "I don't know this place."

About to turn back, Devin felt a strange sensation. As if the leaves were talking to him. A faint breeze whispered around, reminding him of the night he'd kept watch.

He stepped forward, climbing nimbly up the moss-covered, fallen trees, hopping from one to the other. Halfway there, he glanced up, causing Rusty to stop abruptly behind him.

"What's the matter now?" panted Rusty before staring at the large, dark opening at the base of the trunk staring back at them. Devin felt excitement flare and gingerly stepped over the small stream running below. Making their way forward, they crossed the short distance and stood before the giant tree.

It was dim in the shade, and as they approached the cave-like entrance, Devin thought it made quite a good shelter from the elements. He looked up, seeing tiny patches of silvery-looking spider webs at various spots inside the trunk. It was cozy and would have been the ideal hangout spot had it been any closer to his home.

A sensation that ancient secrets were held in its chamber flooded Devin, and he stared in awe as Rusty whispered, "Look at that."

A small bed was tucked against the far wall, shielded from drafts, with a view of anyone approaching. They stepped inside and walked forward, examining it and saw it was made of dried branches, leaves, and layers of fern, braided with grass and reeds that grew near the little stream they'd passed. Devin admired the handiwork.

"I think we need to get out of here," he finally said, thinking if they happened upon whoever slept there, it would be bad.

Rusty trooped beside him, and as they explored further, Devin felt Rusty move up next to him. He sensed the change in the air, and stepped carefully around the perimeter, then slowly emerged back at the entrance, blinking at the sudden brightness.

Setting out, they worked around the huge trunk, reaching the back and gazed in amazement at a giant hole in the ground. The tree they had just come out of stood precariously at the very edge, its roots disappearing like a giant bundle of ropes down the dark opening below.

"How do you think this works?" said Rusty with wonder. "I mean this tree is humongous. Just look at it sitting there. And no soil in the roots. I just don't get it. Have you ever seen anything like this?"

Devin didn't have an answer, questions racing through his mind. "Where did it lead to? What lay below? How did they happen upon this tree if it never existed before as Rusty claimed?" He felt an overwhelming urge that someone or something significant was there. His heart pounded against his chest, leaving him little choice.

Thinking Rusty would think him chicken, he grabbed a couple of the ropelike roots and swung himself down, calling over his shoulder for Rusty to go home if he wanted.

Two seconds later, he felt the roots above himself shaking and swaying as Rusty joined him. Grinning in the darkness, he descended. About thirty feet down, the sunlight faded. He paused, letting his eyes adjust to the darkness. Shimming down another forty or fifty feet, he noticed a glow.

The ground only a few feet below now, he let go and landed on a heap of springy moss directly underneath. Quickly scrambling away, he heard Rusty cursing as he got tangled in the roots. Devin grinned but said nothing.

Seconds later, a body landed next to him. Quickly disentangling themselves, they hopped off the mound. Rusty slipped and made a grab, missed, and slid forward. He landed face first in a shallow pool of water. Devin reached down and quickly pulled him up, looking around curiously at their surroundings.

"Careful, Rust, you don't want to twist your ankle now." Moving away, he left Rusty dripping wet behind him, his sneakers squishing and squelching with water.

Devin had gone a few yards away when a thought occurred to him. "It couldn't be!" He stopped suddenly and turned, his heart pounding loudly as he saw the hole way above them, the roots of the strange tree spiraling down and ending like giant ropes in the small pond. It was what he'd seen in Zoie's card!

His hands became sweaty and he felt the air squeezed itself from his chest. He reached out and felt for Rusty, grabbing and shushing him.

Certainty flooded him as his eyes adjusted, and he noticed a growing presence around them.

"I don't believe it!" Rusty said, his voice high in surprise.

"What?" Devin said, feeling a coolness wafting around them moments before he saw them. Thousands of tiny, glowing dots lined the walls. Around and above, they glowed everywhere!

"Do you know what these are?" he turned excitedly to Rusty, remembering he'd read about them in class.

"Uh huh."

"Glowworms," said Devin in awe, wondering if he dared to touch any.

"This is so cool!" Rusty said, his voice whispering as they saw the glow changing hues.

"Amazing! How beautiful it is down here and we never knew of it!" Devin whispered back, wondering at what other beauties lay beyond. His thoughts went back to the dream he'd had the night Rusty had stolen the crystal, and they'd slept in his kitchen. In it he'd seen a bed of moss and . . . he suddenly froze.

Both had shown him ropelike stuff. The tree roots! The glowing orb on the bed of moss! It could only mean one thing! The crystal had to be close by. He turned and hurriedly retraced his steps, looking around for signs that it was close by. It had to be! There was no other explanation, he told himself, all the while searching for it in every corner he could see.

He felt a slight movement and looked around. Rusty was off to his left, still engrossed in the glowworms.

"That's odd," he muttered to himself. "I could've sworn this was the place .. ," his voice trailed away, and he heard Rusty saying, "I wish I had brought a bottle or something. I'd like to take some of them back home."

"Don't think they'd survive up there," said Devin absently, his mind still occupied with the crystal. He felt it was down here. Everything was telling him so.

Rusty, surprised by his lack of interest in the glowworms, approached seeing his expression. "What're you looking for?"

"The crystal," he replied.

"Why? What makes you think it'd be here?"

Rennie had told him of a cave the old woman hung out at, but he couldn't just blurt that out now. Rusty would never forgive him for having met the renegade without him.

"Didn't you say your folks worked in the caverns somewhere?"

"Oh," replied Rusty, as he stood unmoving, before saying, "They're further along." Then continuing to look around, he said, "It doesn't seem to have too much going on here."

"What do you mean?" said Devin, ears perking up. Maybe they could find a way through to the other caverns. But he continued searching the cracks and crevices as Rusty searched among clumps of odd-looking ferns and grass that somehow bloomed in this weird place.

Hearing a faint rustle and a soft whisper of movement, he cocked his head and, when he didn't hear anything else, went back to searching. It was slow going, the only light coming from the glowworms.

Rusty grunted and cursed, scrambling backward as spiders flocked from a slab of rock. He stopped abruptly, and Devin heard panic in his voice as he called.

"I'm here, Rusty. What's the matter with you?"

"Dude! You for real? Can't you feel that?"

"What? The cold?"

"No."

His tone gave Devin the creeps, and seconds later, he felt a faint movement. He searched the darkness and found Rusty who seemed frozen in fear.

"Welcome. I've waited so long."

The lilting, musical voice sounded directly behind him and he felt a thousand different thoughts flashing through his mind at once, yet he was paralyzed and unable to turn around. He felt movements but heard no footsteps, just a slight movement of air around them, and the hair on the back of his neck stood up, with his hands becoming suddenly cold and his mouth dry.

Rusty gave a sudden jump as a hand descended on his shoulder. With a yelp of fright, he bolted to the opposite side of the wall. He turned to look back and let out a piercing scream. Devin felt himself go numb with fear.

"Only one person could put such terror in Rusty," he thought, seconds before feeling a movement of air, and a hand dropped to his shoulder. Instead of fear, he felt a sudden calmness seeping into him. Warm and wonderful and cozy, as if the glowworms had begun heating up the chamber. An elusive scent wafted, making him think of honeysuckles. Slowly, he turned. He wasn't afraid anymore. Zoie had shown him. He knew from the cards what was coming. Rusty had to be wrong.

Devin felt shock flow through him which rocked him to the very core as he faced the most horrid of creatures. Rusty was right! Looking around desperately, he wondered wildly how he could have been so wrong. The cards had shown the most beautiful woman he'd ever seen!

Devin felt his jaw drop as he stared in horror at the grotesque creature before him. She seemed deformed and was haggard and unkempt, her skin looking like badly burnt rubber and lizard skin all at once. The lines on her face suddenly cracked, revealing surprisingly beautiful teeth.

"No, the cards didn't lie. It's me."

This time, he definitely jumped. She could read his thoughts.

"What do you want from us?" he asked.

"Food," he heard Rusty muttering at the back. She gave a laugh, rubbing her hands together, advancing closer to Rusty. He twitched, a moan escaping his lips.

"You can't touch me. I have this."

Peering in the semidarkness, Devin spotted a familiar sparkle and wondered where Rusty had picked up the Cross from. "Probably from church or from school." The thought flitted through his mind.

"I think so," he heard an answering thought.

"I don't eat children." Her voice was surprisingly young for her appearance. "Come. Come sit with me. I shall tell you." Without giving them a choice, she retreated quickly, seeming to float rather than walk. Curious to see where she was headed, Devin set off behind her.

Rusty moved quickly, whispering, "Let's make a run for it."

"Are you kidding? And go where? The only way out is up those roots we came down on."

"It's a trap," Rusty said desperately.

"Well, unless we grow wings, there's no way we're leaving. Besides," Devin continued, his voice falling to a whisper, "we'd have to get past her."

They had arrived at the pool of water sitting at the base of the roots, and Ole Higue was seated on the nearby rock.

"Uh oh, not good," Rusty said, echoing Devin's thoughts.

"Exactly," he agreed.

Draping a hand on Rusty's shoulders, whose ragged breathing was abnormally loud, Devin remembered she could hear his thoughts. Giving Rusty a reassuring squeeze, they waited.

* * *

"No need to fear me," she began. "Hear me first before you leave. I will not try to stop you if you want to afterwards."

"Is that a promise?" Devin said, surprised.

"On my word and honor," she nodded.

Feeling she was telling the truth, he ignored Rusty's mutterings. "Then we'll hear you out."

"So be it," she said, looking at Rusty who nodded his head vigorously. "Then come," she smiled. "It might take a while for me to tell you everything."

Devin found a large rock and leaned against it while Rusty stood woodenly beside him.

* * *

Knowing she needed their trust, she knew she had to tell the truth and as she wondered where to start, the soft illumination from the glowworms reminded her of the crystal's glow. Suddenly, it all came rushing back to her — seven hundred years falling away as she looked down at her body.

She had been taught the art of casting spells, the uses of herbs, the ability to shield, fencing, and many things befitting a guardian of the realm. But as she watched her body lie defenseless, she cringed. Nothing had prepared her for this.

The unexpected journey through the crystal beam was beyond her training, and it had left her weakened, her reflexes slow. It was a miracle she was still alive, having butchered the dematerialized form.

She touched her still-warm body and smiled, remembering the shadows' puzzlement at seeing a body but no soul. Sunlight danced and sparkled, reflecting from dewdrops collected on the grass underfoot and the dense foliage around.

Feeling quite safe, she waited until complete calm settled, before lifting herself and moving over her body. She felt her energy spark in connection and slowly sunk into form, breathing slowly, deeply, settling into the sensation of being in her body again.

But it felt confined and tight. She blinked, trying to sit up, feeling leaden, her movements slow and awkward. A strange dryness started in her throat, spreading to her lips and face, and then her arms. As the parched sensation moved along her spine and limbs, she watched in horror as her skin withered and shriveled, aging in seconds, leaving her old and shapeless. "No!" her mind screamed. "No! This couldn't be!"

In agony, she battled the cold truth of her condition, and as time passed without any signs of help, she was forced to accept her fate. She would have to proceed no matter what the cost was. But life was going to be miserable. Doubly so, now that she was a creature of unknown origins and species, God help her!

"Um."

The clearing of Rusty's throat brought her back to the present with a start. She gave him a grateful smile.

"The crystal is the key to the dimensions beyond," she began.

"What does it do?" Devin asked.

"It's the way through to other realms."

"A portal?" said Rusty in excitement.

"Yes. And no," she answered. "It is what got me here, but I think the crystal exists in each of us. A doorway if you will."

An odd laugh escaped his lips as Devin noticed Rusty passing a hand over his chest. "Idiot," he said.

"She said . . . ," began Rusty.

"Never mind, it will only confuse you both," she added quickly. "Just believe. It's value is beyond anything you can imagine."

"So exactly what—," Rusty started.

"Let me finish," she interrupted him. "Rusty, you've seen how people react to me. Ole Higue," she said, distaste making her face even more repulsive. "Me. Me, whom," she trailed away, catching their expressions as they stared at her.

"I wasn't always this way. I didn't transform properly, and it left me deformed."

"You can transform?" Devin sounded incredulous even to himself.

"Not as well as I should have. I was trying to save myself from the vilest creatures ever created."

"What creatures? And why?" he said, puzzled.

"The Shadows."

"Shadows?" Rusty squeaked.

"Entities," she replied. "They drain you of your life force."

He shuddered. "Why were they after you?"

"Saint Shade was rising in power. Many kingdoms fell under his attack. Ours was the last."

"What does that have to do with the crystal?" Devin tried following, feeling a jolt of unease at her words.

"Something was always taken from those kingdoms."

"And you think he wanted the crystal?" Feeling a hiccup in his thoughts as Saint brought an image of an old man of wisdom and knowledge, with a white beard and hair, a gentle attitude of tolerance and a benevolent smile. The Shade part though, was puzzling, mocking the Saint part of his name as Serena said he'd attacked many kingdoms and Shadows – entities of some kind that drained life force had been after her.

He felt his hiccups go straight into confusion, and gave up trying to figure it out. Whomever or whatever Saint Shade was, he hoped he wouldn't have to find out.

"I had no clue what he wanted. Our army commander was protecting me from attack and told me to get the crystal. Only after I was transported here, it occurred to me it must have been what Saint Shade wanted."

"So, you're the protector of the crystal then?" he said, trying to understand.

"We, that is, my family were entrusted with it. We've been its guardians for a long time."

"Where are you from?" Devin finally asked.

"The hills."

"The hills?" Rusty's astonishment echoed Devin, but before he could find his voice, she continued, "Yes, they are our realm, and time grows short for me to get back."

"How can you be from another realm if you're from the hills?" Devin's mind buzzed.

"Well, I should have said a different dimension. But in the hills."

"How do we know any of this is really true?" Rusty shot back.

"Well, didn't you see the purging that went on? Darkness had taken this land for hundreds of years. I've been here all this time, waiting for the right conditions to return."

"But," started Rusty.

"The odd happenings were a sign the planets had started their course. If you don't help me, everyone will suffer. Worse is to come if the Shadows find this." She patted something on the rock she was sitting on.

"You have it then?" Devin was amazed.

"Yes," she replied, taking the crystal from under a thick layer of moss.

A faint glow appeared within the crystal, and in seconds, hues of bright, white, shimmering, silver streaks began emitting, distracting them. Recognizing the bed of moss as he'd seen in his dreams, Devin stared in wonder, and as she looked at him, he felt an odd zinging in his veins.

"You must release me. I grow weak. I need to get back before the time passes," Ole Higue pleaded.

Devin felt no fear from her. The crystal was important to her for reasons he couldn't decipher even though she had told him a number of strange things. It all felt unimportant.

"You believe her nonsense? She has Gramps's crystal!" Rusty blurted out, his tone suddenly aggressive.

"It's not just a crystal, and it's not his grandfather's," Ole Higue said quietly, her voice suddenly louder.

They stared in mutual shock as she glided, stopping before them.

"I'm a Guardian of the Realm. This here,"—she pointed to the crystal—"holds the secret of many things, and I must return it, but I can't do so unless you give it to me."

Rusty goggled, stepping backward.

Devin swallowed, confused.

"But you have it," he said.

"I had it stolen, and it must be freely given to set me free. This is a different world from mine, and the crystal is loyal to you and your family. It will not grant me access unless you empower it to. We have only a short time before the planets change their positions, and the auspicious time is being lost. Darkness approaches rapidly."

Devin felt the urgency. "I have one question."

She smiled. "Only one?"

"For now."

She nodded. "Fair enough."

"If you take the crystal back, wouldn't this Saint Shade character come looking for it? I mean, it was the reason you had to leave in the first place, right?"

"Hmm . . . yes. That is true. But all the signs are telling me he didn't succeed. If he had, none of this would be happening, and the crystal wouldn't still be alive."

"Oh."

"So, this Saint Shade dude," Rusty began, "he is the bad guy who wants to take over the world?"

"Yes."

Her simple answer left them both speechless. Devin saw Rusty's expression change from disbelief to horror.

"So . . ," he began.

"So, I need you to help me get it to safety before others come looking for it."

"Others?" Devin asked in bafflement.

"The changes here will allow me to leave, but others may enter."

Dread sliced through him.

Isn't it safer here then? With us?" The sound of Rusty's voice made him start. Several things had crossed his mind, making him wonder since the crystal had chosen his family to be its keeper, would the Shadows, or worse yet Saint Shade, come looking for them? If the crystal was alive, and its powers were growing, didn't that mean his world would be stronger? Why did he have to send it back to Ole Higue's kingdom when it was destroyed anyway? They weren't able to protect it the first time. The crystal had brought her here for safety.

"You're both right, of course," Ole Higue said, nodding to Rusty.

"Both?"

Devin understood she'd been listening quietly while he worked through his thoughts. When he said nothing, she answered, "Yes."

He pretended he didn't see Rusty staring at him.

"Wouldn't it be better if I return the crystal to a place that might be barren of life? Think of the destruction and the number of lives that could be lost here?

"Great. Just great!" Rusty quipped. "More bright news."

Devin said nothing. He felt a strange emotion squeezing at his heart as he stared at Ole Higue, making him feel he would gladly change places with her. She had stuck around for hundreds of years in her deformity, suffered as an outcast, been robbed of her own kingdom, and now she was asking to willingly go back to an unknown land, most likely filled with darkness so others who had shown her little mercy might be spared.

He saw an answering understanding fill her eyes, yet she said nothing, but just waited. Finally, he nodded, unable to speak.

Without any hesitation, Ole Higue moved to the pool of water where the roots touched it and kneeled. She closed her eyes, and they could see her lips working soundlessly. Whether she was praying or invoking some ancient custom they couldn't tell as a string of strange words flowed from her.

Taking several deep breaths, he willed himself to remain calm, unsure of what to do. Moments later, a strange knowledge entered him and he bent, carefully picking up the crystal and turned, seeing her nodding at him. As he stood before her, ancient words, words he didn't know he knew, spilled out of his mouth.

As he spoke, the crystal glowed brightly, its light spreading, making him become a giant, glowing ball of silver light. Gently, he placed the crystal in Ole Higue's waiting hands. A surge of energy flowed forth, and he staggered, almost falling over in its force.

As the connection was made, beams lit up the cave. Instantly, the water anchored Ole Higue to the ground, and she shivered and twisted. At her antics, Devin backed away, the spell broken. Realization at what he'd just done hit him, and he stood silently beside Rusty.

A quivering wail erupted that turned into a tortured scream. Like claws, her hands grasped the crystal. A hole developed at the top of her head as she writhed and squirmed, a thick, black liquid spewed forth, spilling down and around her.

Rusty uttered a moan, scrambling backward. "I told you she was nasty!" His voice was accusatory, and Devin heard him praying in what he thought to be his gypsy language, since he couldn't understand anything.

Anxious to see what was happening, yet trying to listen to Rusty, he finally said, "Stop!" holding his arm up, indicating Ole Higue.

As they watched, Ole Higue became soft and pliant, and seconds later, dancing, shifting shadows started around her. The fattest, most beautiful, giant, black butterflies, with huge velvety wings came fluttering up through the hole in her head. Like links on a chain, they labored, lifting her old, ragged skin away.

A horrible moan began, escalating into a full-blown scream. They stuffed their hands over their ears as her pain shot through the cave like a knife. Rusty dove behind the rock in terror.

As her screams continued, Devin realized words were pouring out of him. He felt himself dropped to his knees, uttering what sounded like some strange prayer until his voice fell to a whisper.

As he finished, they watched Ole Higue in utter amazement. Her skin was completely gone, revealing an incredulously powerful winged being, glowing iridescently blue yet shimmering white. She hovered before them, wings fanning gently behind her, the most beautiful, wondrous being they had ever seen. He was aware of a stillness descending, filling the cave with a feeling of overwhelming happiness.

So quiet at first, Devin wasn't sure he was hearing right, but soon the musical voice echoed in his ear as words seeped into form:

"Seven hundred years I've waited
For one to come through the gate
Bound to this land was my fate
Filled with fear and hate
To be hunted and shunted
And stoned and ridiculed
Still, I waited
Hoping some would wonder of whither I came
But none pondered and figured I was here
To help their way and return from whence I came
But the glory of the Realm depends now
Not on them, but on you
Thank you for releasing me
To fulfill what was told
On Full moon's shine . . ."

As Devin watched, he knew she was the person he'd seen in Zoie's cards. They didn't lie after all.

She glided, pausing in midair before them and said, "Thank You, Rusty."

Rusty made an inaudible sound before stuttering, "Wh——who are you?"

"Serena of the Kingdom of Ohhm."

"Well, don't thank me. It's him. I would've been long gone, and you coulda kiss freedom good-bye."

Devin stared. Rusty was rude, especially after how cool things had turned out. "Just nervousness," he heard again and jumped.

Rusty looked at him, "What's the matter? Ants in your pants? Let's get out of here. She has the crystal. She's changed. Big deal."

Hot anger flared in Devin before he realized Rusty was being weird. About to say something, he heard Serena say, "You must get out, they've felt the energy. They'll be searching for it." She indicated the crystal.

"Well, go on then. You got wings. It's not us they want, right?" Rusty said savagely. "Just fly on outta here."

"Shut up, Rusty," Devin snapped as a sudden coldness washed into the chamber. Scrambling, he found Rusty's hand at the same moment every single glowworm's light vanished.

With the glowing crystal throwing an odd assortment of shadows and weird shapes everywhere, Devin made a dash for the roots, feeling Rusty beside him. Grabbing a handful, he made sure he felt Rusty climbing before he swung himself up.

Amidst much grunting and cursing, Rusty yelped and swung around, nearly falling off in fright as Serena floated up beside him, extending a supporting hand when he slipped. "Easy now, you don't want to break anything. Keep climbing."

A string of curses met his ears as Rusty struggled, and Devin grinned. But pretty soon, Devin felt his fingers go numb and a strange terror seeped into him. Pure torture echoed from Rusty as they labored up the last few yards, the clawing, cold fingers of the unknown snaking itself around them.

Devin looked around for Serena and realized she had flown on up, leaving them in pitch blackness.

Rusty gave a blood-curdling scream. Devin felt Rusty's hand grabbing at his ankles. "Move, Rust! Whatever this stuff is, we can't let it get to us!"

"Fat chance of that now!" came the ragged reply as Rusty scampered past him and blessed sunlight filtered in. Immediately, the air lightened and warmth seeped into them. Reaching the surface in minutes, they clambered up with a burst of delayed fear, moving away a short distance from the hole below. In moments, they had settled on some stumps, gulping and gasping fresh air.

* * *

When Serena finally settled herself on a nearby stump, she looked at Devin and said, "Your journey begins now, Dev, whether you know it or not."

"What journey?"

"The one you started on that full moon night," she replied.

Knowing her words were confirming the verse he'd tried reading the night he'd witnessed the crystal becoming alive, Devin said, "But it was just a book."

"What book?" asked Rusty.

"I found a book about Ohhm in Gramps' things. He said an old man they'd helped left it with the crystal wrapped in a package."

"And you read the book?"

"Just the first page. The same night you took the crystal."

"Oh," said Rusty. "That explains it then, doesn't it?"

Serena said nothing, and Devin felt he had no desire to explain anything.

"It means it is not a crime to have restored honor to your ancestors."

"Restored honor?" he began.

"Your people have always kept Ohhm going. Never think what you did was nothing. It is a crime to steal, but when you stole the crystal for Rennie, it was because of me. I didn't know Rennie would hurt you. I'm sorry."

"It's okay," he said dismissively.

"Actually, it is more than okay." Serena nodded at him. "It created a link with Ohhm and the laws of the realm. It brought back an object so sacred that a kingdom fell from its loss. That object was returned by you, a most mysterious event that none of us planned."

"But Devin's family had it. I only . . ." He tried but fell silent, realizing he was about to say, "I only stole it."

"The crystal chose Devin's family for its safekeeping, but you were the instrument to get it back to me. For that alone, the honor of your people has been restored, and you should be proud of that."

Devin remembered the conversation he and Rusty had at the picnic with Galeb. "Yes, Rusty. Your people were the Keepers of Ohhm."

While Rusty absorbed that, Serena gently reached out and touched Devin. A jolt of warmth sprung at her touch, and he felt happiness flowing forth.

"What now?" he said to her.

"You go home." She hesitated before saying, "Time is short, but you have a right to know. Those were symptoms the Shadows bring as they invade. They will know the crystal was empowered. In the wrong hands, it can do untold horror."

Rusty shivered, whether from fear or remembering terror from down in the cave, Devin couldn't tell.

Serena looked at them. "You must remember what I'm telling you, but keep it to yourself! Things that started many years ago will now come to fruition. Some families have secrets that will be helpful, but not before the time is right. Gramps is a storehouse of knowledge, Devin. Learn as much as you can from him. Everything now depends on you. I have to leave. But we'll be in touch. We'll find a way. Just be open to hearing us."

"Us?" He looked at her bewilderedly.

"Beyond here," Serena said patiently.

"What's that?" whispered Rusty, as an ungodly sound came from the opening, and the ground vibrated slightly. Devin felt his hair standing on edge.

"Quick, let's go before they get to the roots. Now move!" Serena nudged Rusty.

"What about you?" Devin asked, scared beyond his wits.

"My realm. Not necessarily home but back to where I came from."

"What do you mean?" Devin asked.

Serena looked at him. "I can't explain everything, even if I tried. I left when my kingdom was being destroyed. I don't know what's waiting for me."

Devin hesitated.

Another scream echoed in the depths below, sending shivers through them.

"Come on, Dev," Rusty croaked, "now isn't the time. Let's go!"

Devin didn't need telling twice.

"Do not return to this place," Serena warned as another screech rented the air.

Sand crumbled beneath his feet. Scrambling backward, he had a quick glimpse as she rose gracefully, fanning her glorious wings, hovered a moment at the giant branch, and waved a salute before disappearing inside. Rusty grabbed him, and they turned.

Running, falling, getting up, they trashed their way through the forest, as branches scratched at them, whacking and scraping their faces and sides. They kept going, unheeding to anything as the whirling, rushing whine of the unknown advanced seconds behind them.

Reaching the fallen log, a terrifying sucking force pulled at them, and with seconds to spare, they hopped across the log. Rusty slipped and yelled. Devin turned and dove. Grasping Rusty's hands and holding onto the log, he pulled and, with a surge of energy, got them to safety on solid ground. Another painful sucking, gurgling roar echoed before fading into silence.

Shivering, they lay huddled as everything shrank and receded, disappearing like a phantom dream. Stunned and shaken, they stared at each other, mirroring the other's disbelief.

"I told you this place wasn't here." Rusty was the first to speak, his voice cracking in stuttered whispers.

"Well, we didn't just imagine all that," replied Devin, anxiously scanning the now dense forest they'd just left. "It's there somewhere, like a portal or something. I read about stuff like this."

"Me too," said Rusty, his voice sounding odd. "Just didn't think it'd happen to us."

Devin looked over and felt a new bout of fear enter him. Rusty was pale, a thin sheen of sweat beading his face. Jumping up, he quickly moved over to Rusty, hearing him whimper.

"Rust?" Feeling carefully for injuries of any sort, he found blood on his jeans. Lifting the hem away, a strange circle of punctured gashes around Rusty's ankles stared at him, black with oozing blood and slime.

"What in the world!"

Shaking as panic took over, fear of a different kind entered him when Rusty weakly said, "I don't feel too good, Dev."

Stuffing down his fear, he ran to the stream and grabbed some reeds before hustling back to Rusty. Forcing himself to stay calm, breathing deeply, he tied them as tightly as he could above the marks and stuck a hand out. Rusty grabbed it, and he pulled.

Praying they made it home in time, he kept up a steady stream of nonsense, trying to keep Rusty from losing consciousness.

"My legs aren't working right, Dev. Get me out of here."

"I'm trying, buddy. I'm trying."

"Zoie'll know what to do."

Propping Rusty on one shoulder, he headed in the direction he thought to be the camp, reminding him of the night he had befriended him. Then he was brave, now he was filled with terror.

Feeling Rusty's head lolling around, he prayed Rusty would be okay. Knowing there were healers in the tribe was little comfort. He didn't want to think what would happen if things turned out badly. He'd tried telling Rusty to go back. Now he was hurt, which made him think of the strange marks. They weren't things he'd ever seen before.

What if Rusty never recovered? Would he die? What would his mom and everyone else say now? The Elders! He agonized.

Suddenly, he felt Rusty slipping, dragging every few feet. He'd gone quiet. Too quiet!

"You okay, buddy?"

No response. Breathing hard from having to lug Rusty, he noticed it was getting dark. Stopping, he gently placed Rusty down, seeing the deathly pallor setting in. He checked his legs. They were blue and cold.

"No! Please, don't die! Rust, don't die! I'm sorry. I'll get you home. Just don't die on me!" But he remembered the cold terror behind them and knew they had to keep going. He couldn't leave Rusty or even try yelling for help.

Half dragging, half carrying Rusty, he got a short distance and saw with relief they'd made it to the edge of the forest next to the camp.

He heard a gasp, followed by squelching footsteps and felt Rusty being taken from him. "No! Don't. Stop! You'll hurt him!" he screamed, backing away from whoever was trying to take Rusty, fatigue and terror finally taking over.

"It's okay, Devin. Listen. It's me, Galeb."

He blinked owlishly and realized he was crying. Galeb stepped into view. Devin almost fell over in relief.

"The Shadows. They got him. Serena, I mean Ole Higue, we helped her, and she . . . she . . . We released her. She took the crystal back to . . ." Devin stumbled, realizing he was babbling. Serena hadn't really said where she was going back to. She'd said to the Realm. His mind cleared.

Galeb took Rusty and swung around, saying, "Follow me!"

Devin felt a spurt of energy and straightening, his burden for the moment lifted, legs fairly bouncing over the terrain, he hurried on. He got as far as the row of Gypsy tents behind Galeb before everything faded into silence.

13
LOSS

Devin awoke to find himself staring at cheery sunlight dancing through the rustling leaves outside his bedroom window. The clock on the nightstand told him it was nine fifteen, making him wonder what he was still doing abed.

Indulging in a lazy stretch, footsteps sounded outside his door, and he watched as Lexi poked her head.

"Hey! You're awake!"

"Hey, no kidding!" he tossed back, yawning. "What's up?"

"I was checking on you."

"Why?" he said, surprised, looking at her anxious face as she stepped in and settled herself on his beat-up cushion.

"You slept forever since they brought you home."

"When who brought me home?" he said, confused.

"Come on, Dev, really?"

Wondering if she was playing some trick on him, he searched her face but only saw fear beneath her skepticism.

"Really," he said cautiously.

She nodded. "Galeb and Ginger. And you've been sleeping for two days now."

"Two days!" Devin sat up with a jerk. "I slept for two days?" he spluttered.

"Um, huh."

"They said Galeb found you dragging Rusty home. And since they didn't want us to worry . . ."

And then everything came flooding back to him.

"Rusty!" he interrupted urgently, images of the black bite marks flashing before him.

"Zoie's taking care of him. They said he'll be okay."

Devin breathed a bit easier.

"What happened to you guys? And what's with all the secrecy?"

"Secrecy?" he repeated, still trying to figure out what happened after he'd reached camp.

"They brought you home in the dark on a cart."

"Oh?"

"Yes, but since both you and Rusty had passed out, nobody really knows what happened. So, what's the deal, Dev?"

He knew Lexi was persistent and wouldn't just let things be. And he didn't want her going to pester Ginger. After a deep sigh, he began, "We went to get firewood for Miss Ginger. Rusty wanted to show me where the smugglers came in. But we found a strange place Rusty swore was never there before. And there was a cave."

"They didn't say anything about a cave . . . ," she began.

"Rusty wasn't able to talk when I brought him home. I don't know how much he remembers. But it was really a strange place."

Devin saw a flicker of excitement light up her eyes but ignored it, knowing Lexi romanticized everything. And with Rusty getting bitten . . . there was nothing romantic in that.

"Well," he started again, "it looked really old. Nothing like we've seen anywhere. There was a huge tree. I mean really, really humongous."

"There are big trees everywhere, Devin," Lexi said, giggling.

"Ya, well, this one was super, duper big, and we found an opening. It was really cool."

When she raised her brows, he rushed on, "It had giant roots hanging down in this really deep hole."

"Lemme guess," she said. "You climbed down, didn't you?"

"Yes," he said, dejectedly, knowing it was really his fault for wanting to explore the cave.

"So, what'd you find?"

He felt a moment of panic. He couldn't tell anybody what he'd really found in the cave.

"Glowworms," he suddenly blurted out, thinking that at least was the truth.

"Glowworms?" she squeaked.

"Yup," he nodded. "Rusty wanted to bring some up, but we didn't have anything to put them in."

"Aren't caves supposed to be on cliff sides or deep in the hills?"

"I didn't know it was a cave, okay? It just looked really big and deep . . ."

"And you climbed down," she finished.

"Will you let me finish?"

When she fell silent, a thought crossed his mind, and he said, "Unless I had a really weird dream?" he asked, realizing he'd just woken up.

She shrugged. "Maybe. But Rusty did get hurt. And they brought you home. And you slept for a really long time and . . ."

"Okay. I guess it happened then," he agreed.

Lexi grinned. "So?" she said with raised eyebrows.

When he said nothing, Lexi cleared her throat.

"I don't remember too much after that," he hedged.

"Reeaaallly?" Lexi stared at him in disbelief.

"It's fuzzy," he said. "And . . ."

"Yes, well. You better start remembering. It's not just about you."

His head snapped up. "I didn't know Rusty would get hurt," he began and stopped when she gave him an odd look.

"I wasn't talking about Rusty. Well," she corrected, "I mean I'm sorry he got hurt. But he's going to be alright."

"What did they say happened to him?" Devin asked.

"Something bit him, and it was infected really badly.

Everybody at camp's been taking care of him. Zoie used tons of herbs on him."

Relief flooded him.

"But I was talking about mom," she added softly.

"Mom?" he repeated. "Where is she anyway?" he asked.

"At Gramps."

"Why?" Suddenly everything about his morning was odd. Lexi was talking with him in his room when she normally avoided him like the plague. He'd slept for two days, and their mom was at Gramps.

She's not doing well."

"Huh?" said Devin.

"Well," began Lexi, "when you left to go visit Rusty, things got strange."

"Strange?" That sounded funny coming from Lexi. She thought ants floating on water were strange.

"Well, I was helping mom with the baskets for the fair."

"Yeah, I remember," he nodded. "She said to tell you on my way out, to go help. I was supposed to clean the chicken coup." He stopped, seeing Lexi's expression as he babbled.

"The weather changed really quickly after you left," she continued as if he hadn't spoken.

"It stormed?"

"Uh, huh. Really bad. The wind started howling, and I swear, Dev, I saw funny orbs everywhere. Then it looked like the clouds were angry. One moment it poured, then the sun came out and . . ."

"When was this?" he interrupted, dreading what he suspected.

"I told you, a while after you left. Then Mom got odd. She just stopped everything we were doing and went out into the garden. I mean, Dev." Lexi seemed unable to stop herself. "Mom started chanting. And it's not anything we've ever heard before."

Devin felt an odd sensation in his chest. It couldn't mean what he thought it meant. His mind buzzed as thoughts flitted in and out. He tried to make sense of what he was hearing.

"It was like mom was making things even crazier the more she kept chanting."

"What happened then?" Devin asked, fearing what he already knew.

I ran for Gramps and Celeste. And you won't believe this, but when I was going to their house, butterflies—millions of them—flew in. And swans, I mean really huge white swans, came flying by our homes."

"Butterflies?" he repeated.

"Butterflies," Lexi nodded, "Giant white butterflies . . ." She stopped abruptly, seeing his expression. "Why are you staring at me like that? I swear I'm not making this stuff up, Dev."

"I believe you, Lex," he said, still unwilling to admit it had to have been the same moment Ole Higue was being released.

But he couldn't figure out what their mom had to do with anything. Missing some of what she said next, he tuned back in and heard her say, "And by the time we got back, well, . . . mom told Gramps," Lexi took a breath, steadying herself and continued, "can you believe this? She said, 'It's time. It's done.' Then, she just sat down and went kinda funny."

"Funny, how?" Devin hadn't realized he'd shouted. Mom wouldn't! Couldn't!

"I don't know. Like she wasn't there anymore," Lexi started again. "I mean, she was just not well, I mean . . ."

"I heard you," he snapped.

"I ran for Dad, but he was gone. Celeste and Gramps . . ." her voice jerked badly. Alarmed, Devin watched her struggle. "I think she's . . . I think she's . . ." and then Lexi was sobbing.

Devin was off the bed and across the room. Scrambling her by the shoulders, chest heaving with a heaviness he didn't want to acknowledge.

"Where's mom?"

Lexi was suddenly clinging tightly onto him, racking sobs, shaking her body, tears pouring down. "They said she's dying." She hiccupped.

"No!" he shouted, disentangling himself and flinging away to the door. "No! You're lying!" Skipping down the stairs two at a time, he headed for his grandparents' home and found Celeste already waiting for him.

He took one look at her eyes, red and swollen, and was lost in a crushing hug.

"Mom . . . ," he started.

Celeste nodded and steered him to the ragged little cot in their kitchen — the same one Gramps had said the old fella had slept in so many years ago. He stared down at the frail figure struggling for breath. Leaning down, he touched her cheeks and felt a slight movement. She was pale and shrunken and her eyes fluttered slightly, a small smile touching her lips as she reached out. He held her hand and felt distressed when she whispered, "You made it back, Dev. You did it."

Speechless, he stared at her. How could she possibly know what he'd done?

"I'm back, mom. Everything is fine," he said calmly, trying to will strength into her. She took a deep breath and seemed to sink into herself, alarming him even more.

Lexi had followed and now came up quietly behind him with Celeste and Gramps.

"Dev."

He bent, hearing the whisper, but his mom had fallen quiet.

"I love you, mom," he whispered.

A faint squeeze told him she had heard.

"What happened? What's wrong?"

Celeste patted him, "Shh, Dev. Your mom will be fine. She's just weak."

"It's not true. Is it, mom? Is it? Mom!" He shook her, trying to make her answer him.

"Devin! Stop. You'll hurt her. Stop!" Lexi tried prying his hands away.

"Lexi?" the whisper stopped them both.

"Yes, mom. I'm here," they chorused.

Rae smiled, turning her head at the sound of Lexi's voice. "I'm here, mom."

After another struggle, their mom lay quiet.

Kissing her on the forehead, Lexi said, "You're going to be okay, mom." When no answer came, she cried, "Mom?"

Silence followed.

"This isn't happening. What happened? Gramps?" Devin turned, seeing Gramps unable to talk, his frame seeming to have shrunk overnight.

"It was meant to be this way, Dev." His mom's weak whisper stopped him.

"No, mom. You can't go. I won't let you. Why is this happening?"

"Don't blame anyone," her voice wavered as she reached out, and he felt her touching his face.

"Listen, Dev, I am going away for a long time."

"Mom . . . ," he interrupted, but she squeezed his hand.

"Take care of Lexi."

"I'll take care of myself," Lexi insisted, staring at Devin. He ignored her.

Rae smiled, opening her eyes, and Devin knew the truth in that moment—till the day he died—he would remember the look in her eyes. She was dying. But so much love flowed out to them, he was stunned. The only time he'd felt anything like it was the night he was connected to the crystal.

"Dev, Lex, this is what I was here for. I have to go, but you have to live."

He searched his mind for some reason, but no explanation offered itself. Long moments followed before he noticed the stillness descending. The words sounded silently in his mind, in the same unexplained way it had before in the cave. Somehow, he sensed his mom was a greater soul than he had ever known, and he needed to let her go in dignity.

Devin listened to the words whispering in his mind, silently repeating them. They were sacred and had presented themselves to him when he'd released Ole Higue. Instinct had him laying his hand on her head, feeling as if he was being led by an unseen force. He was sure when he felt a faint whisper of his mom's voice in his mind. A surge of current flowed through his hand and into her, and he stood unaware of anything else.

How long he stood silently saying the strange, hypnotic words, he couldn't tell but was only aware when he felt Gramps's hands on his shoulders. Briefly, their eyes met, and he saw Gramps's look, almost as if he knew what was happening.

Devin stayed unmoving, feeling the current wavering before softly oozing out of him. Waiting, he watched as their mom blossomed with a surge of brightness and reached out, grasping their hands tightly.

"Come," she said.

Gramps and Celeste moved, and together they joined hands with Devin. Lexi gave him an odd look, sensing the strangeness but moved closer and joined her hands with theirs. Strength flowed, and as they hugged, their mom gave a smile, her gaze lingering on each of them. "I love you," she whispered. Then slowly, softly, her hand went still, and there was silence.

Devin didn't know how he functioned afterwards. He looked at his hands, turning them over and over. He couldn't tell anyone what had just happened. If they thought something strange about what he'd done, as he suspected they did, he was in no mood to talk about any of it. He left, needing to get away, uncaring if they thought it selfish of him.

Searching for a place to be on his own, he thought of Gramps's garden, unrivaled in its glory. He finally realized that the secret to its constant flowering was the crystal's energies. That stopped him. He didn't want to think of the crystal right now.

Changing directions, he headed for the small mound in their backyard: all his mom's. While Gramps'garden was rich in its abundance, his mom's little heaven was just that—serene and peaceful! Its presence was understated simplicity. Its beauty was as soft as the moonlight she had loved so much.

He breathed deeply, feeling oddly ashamed as the emotions descending on him felt warm and comforting, not dull and full of loss. It made him wonder if something was wrong with him. He didn't feel sad. He wasn't numb. He wasn't crying. He just felt a deep peace, knowing his mom was at peace. Gazing around at the flowers sitting in open softness, he felt them willing strength into him and sat down.

A long time later, the sun having set some hours ago and the moon hanging overhead, Devin felt the air move. Lexi sat down next to him, hugging him, not saying a word.

What should he say to her? He didn't know if he was capable of talking, wondering what his mom's dying meant for everyone.

"Gramps said we'll have to start with the arrangements," Lexi finally broke the silence.

"Okay," he replied.

★ ★ ★

Two days later, busy with making arrangements, floods of people coming in and out, Lexi hustled up to him. "Hey, you gotta come see this."

Swallowing a mouthful of water, he stashed the glass in the sink and hurried after her. Halfway down the stairs, he paused seeing Celeste hug a strange woman they had never seen. "Wonder who she is," he whispered, staring avidly at the little attractive woman.

"No clue," she whispered back.

But Gramps had spotted them and bellowed out, "There you are! Come meet your aunt Sophia."

Devin watched as Lexi slowly walked forward. Aunt Sophia extended both her hands out, enveloping her in a hug.

"I am so sorry for your loss, dear."

"Thank you," Lexi replied, standing stiffly in her embrace.

"I'm your aunt Sophia. Call me Sophie if you like." She drew back, shook her head, and hugged Lexi again. "It's okay. You know, I really am your aunt." When no one said anything, she continued breezily, "I think being here will be good for me."

Devin saw Celeste nod, making him curious. Gramps, meantime, had walked over and placed his hands on Devin's shoulders.

"This is Devin, Sophia."

Their aunt turned her keen eyes on him, as if she was taking in every tiny detail. Devin returned her look and was surprised when he felt an immediate liking. He stood unmoving, feeling no matter how nice anyone was, he wasn't ready for folks to be telling him to stop missing his mom.

Aunt Sophia came up and hugged him for a long time, saying nothing. Eventually, he moved, and she stepped away.

"Good, now that we've met, I have to get busy. There'll be lots to do. Lexi, will you show me the attic?"

"The attic?" Lexi squeaked in surprise. Devin stifled a sudden laugh, turning it into a fit of throat-clearing when she glared at him.

"Ah well," he thought. "Things ought to be interesting now."

"Well, now isn't the time to be picking rooms," Aunt Sophia replied. "The attic," she said firmly. "I will be fine. You both need time to figure things out."

Okay. She wasn't going to bully them about. This was good. Devin felt even better now. She sent a quick little nod to him, and he could have sworn he saw a tiny smile before she hid it. Gathering her travel bags, he led the way upstairs. "Come on, then," he said, leading the way.

Gramps and Celeste were forgotten as Aunt Sophia and Lexi followed him. Lexi was asking a ton of questions, and their aunt recounted her rush to get to them from some obscure part of the hills she'd been in.

As he listened, he was struck by how different from their mom she was. Aunt Sophia was upbeat and bubbly, having a mischievous, saucy way, which had them finding humor in an otherwise sad situation. Her language was somewhat colorful, making them giggle.

They bumped into their dad on his way out, and after rudely greeting Aunt Sophia, he left, disappearing in a rush.

The days that followed were bearable because of Aunt Sophia. A little on the plump side, with heavy dark hair, thick eyebrows, and plump lips, there was a lucky freeness to her manner, and Devin knew he wouldn't trade her for anything now. The hardest part behind them, he remembered how she had stood beside them, silent and strong as they performed the funeral rites for their mom.

A week later, Devin felt he had held up rather well. His dad was a different story. He didn't try comforting them. He barely spoke. He didn't take any interest around their home and was ready to do violence at the slightest of things.

Gramps and Celeste told them to steer clear of him, having taken comfort when Aunt Sophia had turned up. He knew there was some story behind why he and Lexi had never heard of their aunt before. But he knew it wasn't the time for questions. Lexi had tried, and their aunt had brushed her aside, saying they had lots of time to catch up.

He thought Lexi would be fine, as she turned to dancing. He'd tried a few times to jog her memory, but she couldn't tell him anything else about the day their mom had fallen sick.

Now as he looked around, feeling a heavy silence, he had questions. Anything was better than sitting home, surrounded by memories of their mom: of her cooking at the fire pit, cleaning, and washing up at the sink, of her serving the neighbors on the nights of full moon and the annoyance that had crossed her face when she'd learned about the earthworms in Lexi's box.

Devin saw little baskets of potpourri and tiny bundles of herbs sitting inconspicuously in spots he'd never paid attention to before. Aunt Sophia had been busy but had left everything untouched. He was glad she wasn't getting rid of their mom's things as he'd secretly dreaded.

Every day that passed brought new realizations. Their mom was special too. He'd never seen beyond her being their mom. Now he wondered what her likes were and if she had a special color. Guilt tore at him as he remembered all the mischief he'd gotten away with, seeing now how he'd given her unnecessary reason to worry.

She was gone! His room was lined with her handiwork. The kitchen filled with an assortment of knickknacks she'd collected; her good luck charms as she had called them. Even the little herb garden she had planted thrived in abundance.

Devin knew all he'd ever looked forward to were the times when he could be elsewhere. His cousins, at school, maybe at the movies, and most recently he'd gotten all caught up with the gang at camp. Everyone else but their mom! She was mom. She was there. Always there!

Lexi, on the other hand, had been learning about stuff he'd thought stupid as far as he had seen. Their mom had quietly made sure he was up-to-date with his schoolwork, nudging him in learning manners—whatever little existed in the villages.

Her ways were subtle and soft. Things she liked were not made known or often spoken about. It wasn't until her passing that Devin realized how powerful her presence had been.

He had been drawn to her garden earlier, finding himself deeply content, sitting amongst her lilies. Eventually, he felt a faint flutter of wings and slowly lifted his head. And it had floated into his senses. There was no denying it anymore!

He cried. He felt his heart hurt—a stabbing pain in his chest. Knifelike and hot, it seared, ripping through his entire being. If only he could see her, hug her, talk to her! All he'd done was tune her out. He wanted to hear her yell at him. He could see her face as she looked at the mess of his room and heard the displeasure in her voice. But everything faded, and he heard nothing but silence.

Tears fell. Angrily, he wiped them away as a wave of resentment rose up. He hated her for leaving. He hated her for being a coward. She was selfish! She hadn't cared what it had done to him. He slammed a fist into the freshly hoed dirt and fell over sobbing.

In the end, it wasn't just the physical injustices that had killed her, but her strength in keeping him through it all. Their mom would have laughed had anyone told her she was strong. But Devin knew. How their mom managed to hold on to life until she saw he'd made it back he would never know. He wondered what their lives would be like now if he hadn't read the page on that fateful full moon's night. But it was done. He couldn't change anything now. It had said so:

"Once done, will not be undone."

Pain sliced through him as he remembered, grief on hold, his dad and him lighting the pyre that cremated her body. No matter what the good was, they were still without a mom.

The presence of the Elders, along with the rest of the Gypsies as they stood with the Reelms, was the highest of honors as they paid tribute to his mom. Villagers from far and wide had shown up. And Rusty! Strong and healthy once again, Devin remembered how he and the gang had quietly kept folks at a respectful distance. And if it wasn't such a serious occasion, Devin would have found it funny to see the roles reversed with the Gypsies keeping everyone else at bay. How long he cried and grieved his mom's passing, Devin couldn't really say.

Much later, his heart and chest heavy with emptiness, Devin headed back to his room and found a thickly wrapped white parcel sitting on his bed. He stared at it for a long time before approaching and picking it up. An immediate sense of presence made him turn around. He saw nothing, yet the feeling remained. With shaking fingers, he carefully unwrapped it and found a book. He read,

"For Devin, With All My Love"

Flipping open the cover and turning page after page, he gazed in admiration at the drawings she had made. Fairies and angels, butterflies and strange flowers he'd never seen before. He found a picture of a small bush abundantly covered with glowing, white lilies. The mixture of colors and hues made everything seem lifelike. It was a world of unbelievable beauty and enchantment and it made him think of Serena.

What knowledge of their world did his mom have? She had never spoken of strange lands and worlds beyond where they lived. Hers was a life filled with misery and suffering. Lexi had said that their mom said, "It's time," the day she fell sick. Now he was sure she knew something. But what?

Gramps was the one who had hundreds of stories to tell. But Gramps had admitted he had nothing concrete to go on. He felt the crystal was from Ohhm, and he was right. Serena had said so.

Devin read bits and pieces of the book along with descriptions of drawings. He never knew the extent of the hardships she had gone through, except for the little hints dropped, quickly vanishing whenever she realized she had slipped. Thoughts swirled round and round in his mind as he tried to connect Ohhm with his mom.

He selfishly pushed any guilt aside when he thought of showing the book to Lexi. She was too busy dancing, covering her grief. She had spent lots of time with their mom. And, if he was honest, he didn't really want to share anything right now.

As he flipped through the pages, pausing to admire her gift, he felt an odd thickness on the front cover. He felt around, sure, when he compared it to the back cover. Turning it over slowly, examining every inch of it, he found it neatly bounded and sealed. But as he kept at it, he felt something lay underneath the sealing.

With rising heart rate, he laid the book down on the bed, passing his hands over it. The same unknown force seemed to guide him. He kept passing his hand back and forth until he felt a jolt of energy shoot through his fingers and knew for sure then. Carefully, he found the fine line where she had glued it together and got out his penknife, praying he was right and didn't destroy the only thing he had left of his mom. Making quick work of the deed, seconds later, he was lifting off the glued page of the inside cover.

Slowly he peeled the sheet away, revealing a white paper folded in half. He sat looking at it for a while, almost afraid to see what it contained. But curiosity eventually compelled him to pick it up. He took a deep breath, then unfolded it, and read:

Dearest Devin

If you are reading this letter, it means I'm no longer around. The universe in its own way creates situations that best complete a person's destiny. My life has not been a waste if I indeed gave it for you to complete that which you came for.

You are not at fault for whatever would have brought this about. It was a great honor having been your mother. I wish conditions were better, and I'm sorry. Time heals much.

Lexi is special. I know you are young but always keep her safe.

With all that you have learned, I know you will understand I am in a better place. My book is an expression of Love I made for you. Use it in times of need. My time was served. Yours is yet to be. Embrace life and live well. Love with all that you have, and know, my dearest son, I have loved you with all my heart. I will be with you in spirit—always.

Mom

A long time later, having read and reread the letter several times, Devin softly kissed it before putting it on the pillow next to him. Lying down, he closed his eyes.

STARTING OVER

Devin spent the next several days discovering trails he'd never explored before. He took trips to the beach and sat for hours just watching the waves crash and fall over themselves. Flocks of birds, strange and familiar, soared overhead, their presence giving him a strong sense of peace.

At times, it seemed like he cried forever, followed by great waves of peace. But the pain would start all over again, and he wondered if he'd ever stop hurting. Eventually, he headed home, thinking he'd stop by Rusty's on his way.

He wondered about Gramps and Celeste knowing they must be hurting too. He'd tried visiting a few times, but Gramps was always monosyllabic, and Celeste was no better. After his fifth visit, Devin stayed away knowing there wasn't really anything he could do. They'd talk to him when they were good and ready. Aunt Sophia seemed the only normal person around. As much as he wondered what her story was, he knew well to leave it alone for now.

Reaching home, he'd taken the first step on the stairs, anxious to get to his room, when Lexi startled him.

"You're never gonna believe this."

When he turned, she handed him a little package, and he had a strange feeling he already knew what it was. Remembering his reluctance to show her his book, a feeling of shame washed over him.

He took his time going through it and was surprised to discover it was a book of herbal remedies and all things natural. It had stuff about crystals and moon glow and strange liquids and energies. Cool things. Things that spoke to him. But as he thumbed through it, he quietly admitted, "I have one too."

"Really?" Lexi was shocked.

"Yeah. It was on my bed. I guess Aunt Sophia must have left it for me."

"Can I see it?" Lexi said, excitedly.

"Sure sis. It's in my room." Clearly it didn't bother her to share and that made him feel even more rotten. Going upstairs and reaching his room, he drew it out from under his pillow and handed it to her, minus the letter.

Lexi turned each page, oohing and ahhing. When she was finally finished, he gently took it back, feeling sure their mom had known of her approaching death for some time. He still had questions but no one seemed to have any answers.

Lexi stayed awhile, trying to sound normal, never mentioning their mom directly. Eventually she wandered out the door, and he watched her go, unable to find one thing to talk about.

THE VILLAGE BEAT

The word is that a low-profile Brotherhood, shrouded in secrecy, has received a crystal thought to have been one of the seven that made up the protective barrier around the Kingdom of Ohhm.

The address we have—and contacted is:

No. 5 Village Walk,
Mystic Village, Realm Point Crossing
The Hills of Veil

We've received the following response:

"We cannot at this time confirm nor deny finds we may have made. We're unable to give further details at this time."

The Brotherhood

The Village Beat continued, "If, in fact, the crystal is from the time of Ohhm, it is an exciting time. We will continue to update any information as they become available.

We're interested in hearing your thoughts and would like any information you may have. Please contact Missy Misfit at *The Village Beat*, No. 3 Firefly Station, Foxwood."

Devin was confused. Serena had said she was from a different dimension and taking it back to her world would keep any attack by dark forces from entering and destroying theirs. Why in the world would it be given to a Brotherhood and how did the news get out?

Was he stupid after all to have believed her story? And what about what happened with everything that followed? It didn't help when he turned the page and saw his mom's death announcement. He quickly closed the newspaper and felt himself wondering if his mom would have still been alive if he hadn't released Serena.

The swirling thoughts, anger, and emotions roiling through his mind made him feel ready to scream. He needed to get away and collect himself. No one but Rusty and he knew what really happened down in the cave on that fateful day. And he hadn't seen Rusty since the news had broken so he had no idea what Rusty was thinking.

ANNOUNCEMENT

The Brotherhood
No. 5 Village Walk
Mystic Village, Realm Point Crossing
The Hills of Veil

We have been able to authenticate that the crystal which was recovered recently did indeed once belong to the Kingdom of Ohhm.

We want to recognize and thank the people of the land – the tribe of Gypsies living at the outskirts of Foxwood, for their help in such a wonderful find in recent history.

Notably in this is Rusty Keeps who's been attending Beachside Academy. While out collecting firewood, he discovered the crystal in a cave.

Our thanks go out to this outstanding boy and his people for their honesty, unselfishness, and the courage in giving up something so valuable. Most of all, we are grateful for Rusty's curiosity, without which we would not have this part of history in our midst.

Thank you, Rusty!

The Honorable Dr. Piffany
Brotherhood of the Realm

CONTACT!

Devin Reelms
Gate No. 5
Blessings Lane, Foxwood

Devin,

By now, you must have read the news and are rightfully confused! With what you know, it is best that the Gypsies' proper place in society be acknowledged.

Rusty's contribution to our adventure has restored honor to their people. It is something of great measure that will carry them forward.

Your part is not to be discounted, but it is best you keep your gifts quiet. Please give your understanding and support to Rusty and his people. Too long they have suffered, and even though long overdue, the spotlight will be more of a burden than a blessing.

Your friendship is the one constant in their world, and your family's established respectability will only aid their association.

The significance of both your actions has changed the future of the Realm, and we will forever honor you.

Much work is ahead for all of us. Be well.

Serena

Devin read the note in astonishment. He got to the end and read it again, blankly examining each word as if they'd move off the page, and he would find Serena. He flipped it over. Just a soft plain sheet stared at him. He read it a third time!

He crawled up in his bed and sat leaning against his pillow with the note in front of him. So, I'm honorable? He was relieved to hear from Serena, but it wasn't what he expected.

He was angry by the report and her letter. By accident Rusty had discovered a cave, found the crystal, and gave it to some stupid Brotherhood?

He snorted. He was the one to have released Ole Higue! It was him that the crystal needed to release her. It was he who had the dream of it in a cave, and it was to him that Zoie's card had shown the crystal!

Moments later, he slumped down, the anger receding as quickly as it had erupted. He remembered what had really happened. And a whole lot wasn't being said in the article.

"But how did they get hold of such information? And how was Serena connected to the Brotherhood? It said Brotherhood, not Sisterhood!" At least he understood what she meant. Even without her asking, he never would have spoken to anyone about what had happened.

A part of him wanted everyone to know that it was him, Devin Reelms, who gave the crystal to Ole Higue for her release. But he knew it was never going to be spoken about.

Serena asked that he give support and understanding to Rusty and his people. He wondered how Rusty was dealing with the Brotherhood publicly acknowledging him for returning the crystal and if any news person was hounding them. It would explain why he hadn't heard from him.

It also reminded him that it was Rusty who had been severely hurt by unknown forces — forces that nearly killed him. Devin himself had been affected by their presence that day back in Ole Higue's cave. But he wasn't the one bitten with a strange poison. Rusty was!

He had witnessed the horror of almost losing Rusty to their evil. He wasn't ever going to claim glory for that. In spite of the emotions swirling in him, Devin knew he must honor Serena's request.

He read the note again before putting it away in his memory box, thinking that the realm must have improved for Serena to have written to him. When she left, she wasn't sure what awaited her.

* * *

The days that followed went by with him learning that Rusty had recounted Ole Higue's release to Zoie, Ginger, and Old Rupert. So that meant he was happy to be recognized for returning the crystal. But that meant Devin was now forced to tell some of it to Gramps, Celeste and even Lexi and his aunt.

Lexi was anxious to hear of the strange language he'd spoken, but much to his own disappointment, Devin couldn't remember a word of it.

She'd latched on to Ginger since their mom's passing, and even though he liked their aunt, there were moments when he'd look around, thinking he'd heard his mom calling for him. Sometimes, he'd see a wisp of movement and think she'd just walked by.

Whatever youthfulness was left in his grandparents seemed to have faded quickly, making him regret his decision to witness the phenomenon of the crystal.

At times, it seemed as if everything had been one long dream. And with the end of summer holidays fast approaching, Lexi kept reading The Village Beat for any news.

She kept up a steady stream of updates and gossip going around but Devin didn't have any interest and did his best to keep himself busy with chores and escaping as quickly as he could to be by himself.

He left, heading for the local grocery store, hoping he'd be able to find a spool of string and paper for the kite he had been trying to fix.

ANSWERS

A vacuum of emptiness stared at him. The stupor filled his days and nights with stagnant dullness. Devin found he had no opinion one way or the other about anything. The strange numbness around his heart told him it was time he spoke with Gramps.

Grabbing the book and letter his mom had left for him, he set off and found Celeste heading for the village market. After a quick hug and ruffle to his hair, she left saying, "Gramps is at the gazebo."

Devin thought that it was a good sign she was up and functioning again. She waved to Gramps and disappeared through the gates and he turned to see Gramps watching his approach.

"I need to know more, Gramps."

Gramps sighed. "Yes, Dev. I think it's way past time you were told. But I can only tell you the little I know."

"It's more than I know now," replied Devin, plunking himself down on the small seat in the gazebo. Gramps leaned the fork against the bench before sitting down and took off his garden gloves, staring off into the distance.

Devin cleared his throat noisily.

Gramps smiled and looked at him. "Where do I start?"

"When I was born?" he replied with a chuckle.

"Actually," said Gramps, "I think I have to go a little further back."

"Before I was born?"

Gramps nodded.

"Well, go as far back as you have to, Gramps, I don't mind."

"Yes. Well, I would like you to understand why things may have led up to where we are."

He leaned forward as Gramps began.

"When I was a little boy, growing up, people thought my dad, Hums, your great-grandfather,"—he paused and Devin nodded to show he was following, "was loony most of the time."

"Like they do you," the words escaped before he could help himself.

"Like they do me," Gramps repeated, matter-of-factly. "Your great-grandfather wasn't."

Devin waited.

"He'd learned of a prophecy about Ohhm."

Devin wasn't surprised.

"What you see here and beyond were once all a part of the Kingdom of Ohhm. It's our history. Our heritage and our roots lie in Ohhm. Villages and towns have changed their names, but we can't change where we're from."

"What does all this have to do with me?"

"Everything," replied Gramps.

"How? And what's that supposed to mean?" Devin just wanted answers.

"According to your great-grandfather, we've come from a line of gifted people."

"Gifted people?" Devin wondered.

"Our ancestors were revered for having the gift of the oracle," Gramps continued.

"Oracle?" Devin almost fell off the small seat.

"The royal family relied on the gifts of its oracle. In times of war and struggle, the oracle gave advice for the protection of the Kingdom."

"The Royal Family of Ohhm?" Devin couldn't hide the surprise.

Gramps nodded. "It is said the Oracle predicted a disaster and was banished from Ohhm. She was ordered never to make predictions again."

Devin felt his brain becoming fuzzy. Kingdom of Ohhm. Royalty. Oracle. Predictions… he couldn't quite figure out which was more outrageous and which to ask about first.

Eventually, he asked, "What could she have predicted?"

"I would say it had to be the fall of Ohhm," replied Gramps.

"The fall of Ohhm?" he repeated.

"Yes, the fall of Ohhm," Gramps nodded. "The way the story goes, the Oracle made a vow."

"A vow?" Devin felt stupid, repeating everything Gramps said, but couldn't help his astonishment.

"Yes. For the insult of her banishment and being ordered to never make predictions again, she made one last one."

He waited.

"It is said she vowed that only a son born of her generation would be the redemption of Ohhm!"

Devin didn't want to believe it. For a king to turn on someone considered almost holy — someone who served his kingdom's higher good — showed he acted rashly. He felt a betrayal deep in his chest and the stirrings of unjust crept in. But Gramps was speaking again. He listened.

"My father said it wasn't unusual for children in our lineage to have all sorts of gifts."

"What gifts would those be?"

"I don't know of a specific one, Dev. Each generation has had its own set of troubles. Your great-grandfather told me he didn't have an ounce of anything in him except a case of lunacy when the mood struck him."

Devin laughed.

Gramps smiled. "If any of our ancestors had unique talents, I was never told."

"More like hushed up, you mean," said Devin.

Gramps looked at him for a few moments before saying, "Sometimes what folks don't understand, they fear. And some can't handle the truth even if they were the king."

In the recent past, Devin would have thought Gramps being melodramatic. Now he didn't think it was impossible his Grand-ancestor was indeed a great oracle. He bowed his head.

Silence followed for a while before he asked, "You think I might have the gift?"

"How could you not, Dev?" The question hung between them.

"Do you think mom knew she was dying?"

Gramps's expression saddened for a moment. "Yes, I think she knew."

"But if mom had this gift—," began Devin.

"Ours is not a talking society, Dev. Strange talents, especially in our daughters, are never encouraged," interrupted Gramps. "Your mom never flaunted any gifts she had."

"Did she have to die, though?"

"We'd never know, would we?" replied Gramps.

Devin handed over the journal and the letter to Gramps and waited as he looked at them. A long time later, he handed them back, saying, "I think your mom knew," Gramps answered. "And I think she knew what the cost would be."

Silence fell.

★ ★ ★

Devin sat clearing weeds from his mom's garden. His curiosity was deepened from the talk with Gramps of their ancestral gifts and had kept him busy with the history of Ohhm. There were few written works anywhere that could tell him more and he had to settle with the belief that he may indeed be the prophesied son born to generations of the long-dead oracle. Exactly what it meant was anyone's guess.

* * *

"Dev, where are you?" The urgent tone of Gramps's voice brought him out of his musings, and Devin looked up as his grandfather hurried forward.

"I got a letter from your Serena. It says she's coming over this evening."

"Serena? Coming over? Here?"

Gramps nodded his head at each question.

"And she sent a note for you." Gramps extended an envelope to him.

Devin dropped the small shear, wiped his hands on his pants and eagerly took the envelope. Opening it, he read aloud:

Devin,

Time is of the essence. We must meet. I am bringing someone you need to know. Please be ready with your grandfather at 8:00 p.m. We'll be at the gazebo.

Your discretion in this is a must. Be well until then.

S——

"She's actually coming. And bringing someone," he said in a hushed voice.

"Hurry up then and get showered. Might be a long night," Gramps told him. "I'm going to find your grandmother. Get Lexi and your aunt and tell them."

"She said my discretion is . . . ," he began.

Gramps smiled at him. "Go find the girls and let them know. Tell them to keep it quiet."

"Right, okay Gramps."

That evening Devin and Gramps waited at the gazebo. The few minutes leading up to the eight o'clock hour felt like the longest few minutes of his life. Devin couldn't imagine who Serena was bringing to meet them and why.

The evening felt cool and a soft breeze picked up the fallen leaves, swirling and fluttering them around. Eight o'clock arrived. A figure in white appeared in the middle of the gazebo, making Gramps clamp a hand down on Devin's shoulder.

The last time Devin saw Serena, she was glowing luminously with a pair of wings. But the lady before them now was nothing like that. She was still beautiful but was wearing a simple white gown and thick braids hanging down her back, minus the wings.

She extended her hand. "Thank you, Gramps, for receiving us. I am Serena."

"Welcome Serena. I'm honored to meet you."

Devin was surprised at how normal Gramps sounded as he shook her hand. He didn't see anyone else and wondered where the person she'd mentioned she wanted him to meet was.

"Devin, I'm so happy to see you again."

"Me too," he answered. "I didn't expect you'd actually come here."

"I didn't plan on it, but there are some things you need to know."

"Let's go inside," Gramps said, leading the way and in moments they entered the kitchen. Gramps introduced Serena to Celeste, Aunt Sophia, and Lexi, and the latter seemed to be in complete shock.

"I am grateful to you for taking care of the Crystal, Celeste," Serena thanked her. "Without it, I would never have been able to be here today."

Celeste nodded. "You're welcome, dear. If my healing was a small bit of what that crystal could do, then I am indebted to it. There's no need to thank me."

As they nodded in understanding to each other, Serena turned to Lexi who was only too delighted to meet her. "You remind me of someone I used to know many years ago, Lexi," Serena said to her.

"Really? I wonder if that means she was good or not so," Lexi giggled.

"Oh, I wouldn't say she was bad." Serena chuckled. "I'd call her pretty, smart, and sometimes—"

"Don't give her any idea she's smart." Devin felt the thought slip his mind and saw Serena swallowed from trying to laugh. He was startled when he heard another, deeper, heavier chuckle join in. Looking around, he felt an odd sensation that there was someone else in the room, but when he looked at Serena, she averted her eyes and finished, "charming."

"In that case, thank you, Serena," Lexi responded, with a huge smile on her lips as she set about helping Aunt Sophia pour fresh cups of tea.

The sound of one of their neighbors calling startled them. "Come, Lexi. Let's go get some fresh air."

"Now?" Lexi gasped, unwilling to miss the meeting of her life.

"Well, it's either an evening walk, or we invite whoever it is in here. And we can't," said Celeste, already on her way out the door. Lexi hurriedly placed the tray of teacups and saucers down and left, muttering under her breath.

Devin sighed in relief as his aunt took a seat when Serena waved her stay, glad Lexi didn't kick up a fuss. Moving to a seat, he sat down and found himself on the squishy folds of someone's lap. With lightning speed, he hopped up and was across the room in seconds, the others staring at his antics.

"Hah! A voice, rich and strong, reverberated around them as laughter shook the air, startling Gramps and Aunt Sophia who looked first at Devin and then at Serena in alarm.

"Who's there?" Devin snapped, turning accusingly at Serena.

"Devin!" his aunt hissed. "Where are your manners?" she said, reprovingly.

"Well, who is it, Serena?" Devin insisted, ignoring his aunt. He wasn't about to be told he'd just imagined the whole thing. Someone was in the room.

"Devin," Serena said with an apologetic smile, "I want you to meet Chad, former Commander of Ohhm Armies and High Chief on Tribal Relations. He sees much but isn't often seen."

Stiff with embarrassment, Devin turned to the chair and bowed slightly. "An honor, Commander." His voice came out high and squeaky, and he felt himself go red, feeling stupid when the silence went unbroken.

The sensation of suppressed laughter shook the air. When no response sounded, he tried again, "Forgive my blunder." As the moments ticked by, he stared at Serena who seemed to be focused on the vacant seat.

Finally, he heard, "Likewise, little one. Forgive me. It's been a very long time since I've had reason to laugh."

Devin felt himself relax and a smile reluctantly tugged at his lips as the image of himself flying across the room flashed before him.

"Chad, if you would give us the pleasure? We have only a short time left," Serena reminded.

Devin watched the air shimmer, followed by the appearance of Chad rising up from the chair he'd so hastily vacated and felt his jaw drop. Chad wasn't ancient, nor an old, wrinkled hermit. Instead, he was tall and massively built, with eyes like pools of topaz, fringed with heavy lashes. With high cheekbones and a square jaw, his hair hung in a thick braid. A blue cape hung secured at the shoulders of a protective armor over a silver and blue uniform, telling Devin he was in the presence of great valor.

Chad's eyes twinkled with amusement under their collective scrutiny, and when everyone seemed incapable of speaking, he approached. Extending a large hand, he greeted, "It is a great honor to meet you, Devin Reelms. We have much to thank you for."

Devin stared at the hand before slowly extending his own, feeling it become engulfed as Chad shook it warmly.

"It is good to meet you too," he finally managed to say to Chad, who laid a hand on his shoulder, nodding.

"You'll do."

Devin swelled with pride at the simple statement, watching as Chad moved on to be introduced to his aunt.

"Chad was magnificent!" The thought swirled around his mind. "What an awesome dude!"

Gramps was introduced next, beaming from ear to ear, looking twenty years younger. When Chad sat next to him, patiently answering his barrage of questions, Devin could tell

Gramps was the happiest he'd ever seen him. But eventually a pause sounded, and Serena cleared her throat.

Gramps looked up, seemingly surprised.

She smiled at him, saying, "Maybe we should start with why we came to see Devin tonight."

"Oh yes, yes. Certainly," he exclaimed. "Begging your pardon, Serena. Please go on."

"It's all right, Gramps," Serena reassured him. "We will visit again soon, but our time is short tonight."

Gramps nodded his understanding, and Devin found himself suddenly nervous.

"The crystal Devin returned to me is not an ordinary one," Serena began. "It was from a different realm. I find it amazing that it survived being in your yard."

"Why is that?" Gramps asked.

"It needed to be kept in a special nectar to stay solid," Serena explained.

"I never heard of liquid crystal," Aunt Sophia exclaimed.

"Me neither," agreed Gramps.

Serena nodded. "Not many have. Its powers are many."

"What happened to cause your kingdom to fall?" asked Devin, anxious to get to the crux of the matter.

"Ohhm had many mysterious and mystical secrets. It is one of the reasons the crystal was set up in a special fountain. Only a few were allowed within the tower where it lay."

"And," Chad continued, "Dark worshippers knew of the crystal. Dominion over Ohhm would ensure their survival, making them more powerful and terrifying than anything anyone had ever seen or known before."

"They wanted to be immortal?" Devin blurted out, unsure where the thought had injected itself from, as an alien fear stirred in his chest.

Chad nodded.

"It would be almost like drinking from the pool of eternal life for them. So yes," Serena nodded, "almost immortal . . . like anyone who tastes the food of gods. And since they serve Saint Shade, it must be he who was after it."

"My people," began Chad, "were responsible for the maintenance of Ohhm, the grounds and fountains. They had knowledge of herbs and plants and such. But a number of them were captured and tortured."

Aunt Sophia recoiled, drawing in a swift breath and sitting back in her seat as if she'd been burnt.

Chad stopped at her sudden discomfort, watching keenly for a long while. Eventually he said, "Yes, Sophia, the same creatures who tortured your husband for his knowledge of the stars."

Gramps jerked, his face becoming ashen.

Devin stared at his aunt, her knuckles white from squeezing them.

"I am truly sorry, Sophia," Chad finished.

"I went searching for you everywhere, Sophia," Gramps began, his voice strained and hoarse. "The Gypsies told me you had gone to the hills. No one ever returns once they set foot in that place. Why did you let us think you were dead?"

"In your eyes, I was already dead, Dad. Everyone was better off that way. You were already ashamed I ran away with a Gypsy. What would you have done if I had returned with Xavier? Could you and mom have been able to live with the shame? Didn't you think me foolish to throw my life away for a nobody? How would you have explained it to these foolish villagers?"

"Oh boy! Oh boy!" thought Devin, his world once again spinning at top speed. She had run away with a Gypsy! That explained how Gramps had known of Rusty's people.

But the Gramps he knew wasn't an unfeeling man. And a moment later, it was confirmed when Gramps said, "You're probably right, Sophia, but you did us all an injustice. We had a right to know you were alive. We would have respected your decision."

"Like you did when I told you I loved Xavier and wasn't going to marry that stupid quack you had picked out for me?"

"I was only doing a father's duty. I was looking out for your future."

She said nothing, and Gramps continued in a voice full of regret, "I am sorry for everything, Sophia. Truly sorry." When she still said nothing, he said, "and especially about Xavier. We didn't know. You never told us."

"And I am sorry about, Rae. I heard about it from a trader and thought it was time I paid a visit," replied Aunt Sophia.

"We are happy you came home."

Devin silently agreed, knowing his aunt and Gramps would eventually work things out. Wondering how to get back to the topic at hand, he glanced at Chad and Serena who had so far stayed respectfully silent.

As if on cue to his silent question, he watched his aunt pull herself together saying, "Well, all that is past. I'm here now. This evening is about Devin, so let's see how best we can all help him."

"Before we go on, Sophia, which tribe was Xavier from?" Chad asked her, and Devin noticed the keen look in his eyes.

"She replied with an air of pride. "He was their chief timekeeper."

Devin couldn't have been more surprised. Obviously, there were many things he needed to learn. Gramps was right when he'd said everything and everyone was somehow connected to Ohhm.

"Do you still have any of his records and charts and such, Sophia?"

His aunt smiled. "I have them. Xavier did say that someday someone would be looking for them. I just never expected it would be my nephew."

Serena breathed a sigh of relief. "They didn't get anything then?"

"Only his life," replied Aunt Sophia solemnly.

"Not many would have kept their honor," said Chad with feeling. "Sophia, would you do us the honor of sharing Xavier's works with us? It would make Devin's job easier."

"They are hidden in the hills as I couldn't bring everything with me. But can you tell us a bit more?"

"Fair enough, Sophia."

As if in afterthought, she began, "Why would they have wanted them, though? Maps and charts and the stars and—"

"Those can give them the knowledge of portals and realms and when Ohhm would rise again," interrupted Chad.

"Oh," she said quietly. "But the Dark worshippers . . ."

"Worship the dark. And Shadows use such instruments to spread darkness," Chad replied with a measured look, making Devin feel he'd just edited what he really wanted to say.

"I see."

"And it is during one of these times when their powers were great that Ohhm was attacked. When Serena went through the crystal beam, I made the only choice I had. Dozens of Shadows had filled the Tower."

Devin watched as Serena walked up and reached out, clasping her arm in his. Chad's fingers tightened in hers, and suddenly, Devin felt the love flowing between the two, the stirrings of an unknown emotion seeping into him. It spoke to him of loyalty and sacrifice and the passing of time. It spoke of things he couldn't quite name, almost sacred, making him drop his gaze, unwilling to blemish it.

"I was worried," Chad admitted. "I stepped into the fountain, knowing the nectar was the only thing to keep them away from me. It did."

"If the liquid could destroy them, why can't we get some and use it on them now?" Devin asked.

"The liquid at the time was powerful because the crystal and combination of herbs had infused it with very protective energies. The Elders who knew deep arts and had knowledge of how to create it were all killed and as you know, all the tribes had fled so it's not that easy. But it saved me. But my body hadn't been trained to be in the crystal's energies as Serena's. Her family was its guardian, not I."

"So?" asked Gramps.

"So, I mutated. The nectar was from the beyond with powers I know little about. I can appear and disappear for hours at a time."

"Cool!" said Devin.

"It becomes burdensome," Chad told him, bringing an abrupt halt to his imagination. As if to make his point, Chad suddenly took off his cape, vanished, reappearing a moment later, dressed in a heavy white robe, similar to Serena's. When he lowered his collar, Devin blanched.

An identical necklace presented to him by the Gypsy Elders lay in tattoo form around Chad's neck.

"It fused to me when I was in the nectar," Chad said to his unspoken question.

Devin felt a new respect for the gift he had received from the Gypsies.

"So, Devin really is the one?" Gramps mused aloud, almost as if reassuring himself.

"By the words of Roxy herself, Devin is the son born of her generations," added Chad, startling them. He continued, "Yes Gramps, Roxy really made such a vow, or prophecy as you should call it. It was the only time I ever feared for my own life."

"Why was that?" asked Serena, as everyone fell quiet.

"Because," Chad answered, "when your father had me take her to the edge of the kingdom and give her the news of her banishment, I was bound by duty and my position to repeat her words to your father."

"And those were?" said Serena softly. Chad's look became serious, and he finally replied, "They were painful then and still more painful now. I don't ever want to repeat those words again."

Serena grew pale, and those watching on knew she was dealing with some great burden.

"And Rae?" Gramps said.

Devin leaned forward as Serena squared her shoulders, and with a deep breath, said, "Seven hundred years in the physical form takes a toll on a body. The crystal itself couldn't boost me back."

"Did you know she would die?" Devin felt the pain and loss rising up again.

"No. No, I didn't," she replied, her voice unsteady. "I didn't know your mom would die. I only knew the planets had lined up correctly, and the time was right. I had no idea someone, or even that anyone, would die so I could get a new life. Believe me, Devin, when I first arrived here, I searched endlessly for someone who might have knowledge of my world. Or even powers they could help me with."

Devin bit down hard on his lips to keep himself from crying.

"So that's why the stories say you fly through the night. And it's why they call you Ole Higue?"

"That would be the villagers for you," chimed in his aunt. "Leave it to them to spread hogwash."

He laughed. He couldn't help it. Only Aunt Sophia could find humor at the oddest moments.

"Your mom, Devin," began Serena, "was a very loving soul. She gave her life so I could have mine."

"So that day, down in the cave—," began Devin.

"That day in the cave when I was morphing, your mom was gaining her own wings," finished Serena.

"Can we see her like you then?" Aunt Sophia said, cautiously, voicing the question Devin was thinking.

"No. I gained my wings because I did my duty. Rae is a greater soul than me. She gave her life freely for a higher good. She's gone beyond our realm."

"Now what?" The question sounded rough, his voice emotionless, as Devin sat unmoving.

Chad, who was beginning to fade, said, "You're more special than you know, Dev. You gave life to the words spoken by your grand-ancestor and high priestess of Ohhm. You released Ole Higue." After a short silence, he finished, "and befriended my people. I am here because of you. Now you'll have to lead us to restore Ohhm as Roxy vowed."

Devin couldn't believe his ears. This winged being and the preserved warrior were looking to him to restore the realm? And lead them forward? Was this some kind of twisted joke? Finally, he said, "Why couldn't it be Rusty?"

"Let's not confuse Rusty's act of restoring honor to his people with the fact that the crystal chose you to release me, Devin. And you are the many-times removed generational son of Roxy. What happened in that cave was no ordinary thing," Serena explained patiently.

"Yes, but—," he began.

"It didn't choose to release its energies to Rusty when Rennie had him steal it," she interrupted. "You were the one who drew words from the ancient language and sacred world of the beyond to empower it."

"What exactly is Devin supposed to do for you?" Aunt Sophia asked, whose head had been turning from one speaker to the other.

"Ohhm is rising. And we can't ignore the call. Only this time it will be of this world. Not protected in a bubble like it was before."

"Is that why the crystal is now in the care of some Brotherhood?" Devin finally asked the question that had been bothering him since he'd read the news article.

"Yes, partly," said Serena. "When I got back to my world, it was completely destroyed and there was nowhere to safeguard it. I had to find the next best place to keep it and not draw darkness to you, and all of Veil."

"Saint Shade and the Shadows won't attack them since now it's been leaked to the public?"

"They are not just ordinary Keepers of ancient artifacts, Dev. They're still some who follow the old ways. The crystal did its job to see Serena back to Ohhm. It served its purpose and is no longer alive. Saint Shade doesn't know that, only those of us here right now know that. But power attracts evil," Chad said.

"We can never eliminate every evil and its darkness," said Gramps, wisely.

"Yes," he agreed. "But I meant Devin is the one whose light will keep growing. And we're only as strong as he is." Turning to Devin he said, "You should wear your necklace. It will give you protection for now."

"Protection from Saint Shade?" Devin asked. "Serena said once the crystal was alive, so too will the dark rise. That's what drew them in the cave the day I released her. Does it mean he'll be after me?"

"It's why the crystal is with the Brotherhood." Serena answered. "It will give us time and you a chance to learn things to protect yourself before anyone realizes. But, Devin," Chad continued, "your mom didn't give her life so Serena would find her way back home. She did it because she knew you have a destiny to fulfill. And we will do everything to protect you."

Of all the things to have happened, Devin found himself close to tears. How could they do this to him? He was just a kid. Emotions flooded him, and questions raced across his mind, bullying for answers he didn't have.

They must have sensed his turmoil as Chad and Serena approached, and he was engulfed in the biggest, warmest hug he'd ever had. The dismal mood evaporated, leaving him with a renewed sense of exhilaration.

Stepping back, Chad said, "We must go now. We've said as much as we could. Promise you'll take care of yourself."

Devin nodded, unable to say anything. He had a lot to process.

As they headed back to the gazebo and said good-bye to Gramps and Aunt Sophia, Serena gave him a reassuring hug, and Chad touched him briefly on the shoulder. In moments, they left with a final wave.

Devin headed for his room. There was much he needed to process. He knew things were never going to be the way it was before the whole crystal came alive and everything that followed. Life had gotten scary and he wondered what exactly he was supposed to do to restore their realm. Would the Brotherhood truly be able to distract the Shade fellow and his army of darkness?

10
DREAM MESSAGES

Devin's fifteenth birthday was fast approaching. Scrunched in his rocker, staring out his bedroom window, hair rumpled from sleep, he looked as troubled as he felt. If anyone had told him a year ago, he was destined to restore a realm, he would have laughed. Heck, even he knew how ridiculous that was!

But a lot had changed over the months, and his nightmare was proof things were not as they used to be. They were more frequent now, sometimes repeating themselves. Other times, they were so dark. Devin wished for his days of innocence before any of this "Restorer of the Realm" thing. Losing his mom wasn't something he'd ever forget, especially when he was the one responsible for her death.

The clock showed it was still only four in the morning. "Another day of torture," he thought, settling deeper into the chair, his mind going back to when he'd witnessed Gramps' crystal coming alive.

He had befriended Rusty Keeps, and had gone on to become a part of their Gypsy family. But when he'd tried recovering Gramps' crystal which was stolen by Rusty by a bullying renegade smuggler, he ended up saving the smuggler from his own men when they'd tried to murder him.

Devin eventually found the crystal which was from an ancient kingdom and released Ole Higue, a creature reviled by society, who'd transformed into Serena, Princess and a Guardian of the Realm from when the Kingdom of Ohhm existed, causing Rusty to nearly lose his life.

Then another survivor from Ohhm arrived - Chad – former Commander of the Armies, complicating things when they told him he was supposed to restore the kingdom which had fallen after a battle of dark and light with Saint Shade and his army of Shadows.

Back then, Devin hadn't really thought deeply about who or what Saint Shade was or might be, but knowing how events had unraveled, he prayed he didn't find out. It felt fantastical, especially when Gramps' tale of an obscure prophecy made by a Grand-ancestor of theirs was confirmed by Chad.

Chad's words about the Brotherhood, "They are not just ordinary Keepers of ancient artifacts, Dev. They're still some who follow the old ways. The crystal did its job to see Serena back to Ohhm," stayed with him.

Devin wondered who they were and what old ways they followed. Did that mean he wasn't the only one to do the "restorer of the realm" thing? Could they not lead Serena and Chad forward, in spite of the prophecy his grand-ancestor had made? Would they help him? They'd confirmed the crystal's authenticity. It meant they were reachable. And how did Serena know they existed?

Nothing made sense. He wondered if he was going mad because it sure felt like he was losing his mind. He thought of his mom and tears fell unchecked as they did frequently these days. He wished he'd never stayed up to see the crystal coming alive.

Then Aunt Sophie had shown up and began taking care of their home. She was funny and lovable and with no kids of her own, she took great joy in being a surrogate parent to them. Her no-nonsense attitude brought spontaneous chuckles to all, and he was happy to see how Lexi had blossomed. Their aunt gave him new respect for things.

Unwilling to go back to bed and risk the chance of finishing the dream he'd woken from, Devin felt himself break out in a cold sweat, just remembering it.

He'd seen Lexi wearing a crown of dark flowers on her head. Lying on a stone table in a hollow of some kind, draped in all black. A pungent odor filled the air, and keeping his nose in the crook of his elbow, Devin spotted a goblet with red liquid.

"No!" he shouted, rushing up to her. When Lexi turned an unfamiliar gaze at him, he tried pulling her off and when she refused to move, realized she was anchored at the waist. He hesitated as footsteps echoed nearby and the voices of women giggling weirdly approached. He lunged into the surrounding darkness and stayed still.

Deep in the shadows, he watched figures dressed in dark robes, file by. With uneven gaits, each holding a goblet like Lexi's, they assembled in a circle around the table and, after raising them in offering to an unseen force, began circling her.

With them chanting and muttering an indecipherable string of words, Devin felt his mind recoil and a strange energy seep in. The darkness vibrated as an eerie presence entered the Hollow and he felt the trees withdrawing in terror and silence descending around.

A sudden shout in an unfamiliar language echoed around, followed by a sudden flash of brightness, startling the group. Lexi screamed at the same moment the group snapped out of their trance-like state. Distracted, the figures scrambling in confusion, Devin saw a ring of the ugliest women he'd ever seen glaring with utmost hate into the darkness where he stood.

Shivering at the memory and having woken with the sensation of being slammed into his bed, he realized the shout had been his, remnants of the ancient language receding quickly.

As he stared out the window, the clouds changed hues – from a dark violet to a layer of gold, the approaching sunrise showing him Gramps coming out to do his morning routine. Spotting Devin, he waved easily before setting to his daily ritual.

Devin had learned a lot having watched his grandfather's ways. What he didn't know though was what Gramps said during his rituals. Thinking he'd build the courage up to ask Gramps one day to teach him, he felt the effects of the dream easing, as thoughts of his approaching fifteenth birthday settled in.

He reluctantly crawled back under his blanket with the dawn, determinedly blocking his thoughts to everything.

20
REPERCUSSIONS

He woke up with a sense of distress. Something felt out of place, making him jumpy and out of sorts. He snapped at Lexi when she sailed in for breakfast, noisy and ready with gossip.

"You gotta hear this Dev."

"Can I at least eat first?" He retorted sourly.

Narrowing her eyes, she started to say something when his stomach grumbled. Heaping his plate with toast, eggs and potatoes, he deliberately added fruits and chicken bits, surprised he was so ravenous. Adding a spoon of sugar to his tea, he gulped indecently.

Lexi filled her own plate, ignoring him. Silence followed as they ate. A short while later, satiated, Devin felt better. Drinking his tea much slower, he looked over at Lexi who was focused on her food.

"What's got you in a twist?"

She looked up from her plate, chewed slowly, swallowed, took a sip of orange juice and kept chewing.

He swore silently.

After a long pause, he heard,

"The news."

"I just got up in case you didn't notice," he defended himself.

"People are complaining about the Gypsies."

Taken aback, Devin stared at Lexi. "Are you serious?" he finally managed.

She nodded.

Devin felt the beginnings of dread take hold. "What are they complaining about?" he tried again.

"Someone said they've been squatters all this time."

"How?"

"The Brotherhood thanking them."

"Squatters?" He repeated aloud.

"You know, the land they're on," replied Lexi,

"I know what squatters are," Devin interrupted with a snap, his mind swirling. He definitely remembered Serena's letter mentioning his family's respectability being helpful to the Gypsies. "But how?" he wondered. "What went wrong?"

"Squatters tend to well ... .squat," Lexi grinned at him.

He glowered.

"It says they have to clear off as soon as possible," she continued.

"And go where? I mean, everyone...well", Devin paused and corrected himself, "we didn't at first, but people knew.

Nobody bothered them before. Why? Why now?" Devin felt a quiet anger beginning to simmer, the thought of the Gypsies being chased off rattling him.

"From what it says," Lexi explained, "and I can be wrong, which I don't think I am" she continued, "when the Brotherhood thanked the Gypsies, it mentioned that Rusty attended Beachside Academy."

"And?" Devin was still puzzled.

"And," explained Lexi, "Rusty and the guys from camp are considered unsuitable to mix with. They…"

"Unsuitable to mix with?" Devin snapped.

"I don't know," Lexi replied, "it seems people feel their children shouldn't mingle with the Gypsies," she finished.

"But everyone was so much friendlier after the storms. Rusty told me how folks were starting to be agreeable," he shook his head disbelievingly.

"Well, someone's got issues with them," Lexi insisted "otherwise…"

"Can I see it?" he interrupted, extending a hand out for the newspaper.

"Aunt Sophie has it, and boy is she in a mood."

Devin got up.

"You okay?"

"No," he replied, before adding, "Did it say who complained?" He gathered their empty dishes and headed for the sink, mind buzzing.

"Not exactly. But there are officials scattered around Veil. You know…important folks. I bet they had something to do with it," Lexi replied.

"Well, the Housing Office gave fuel to the camp after the storms. They had to have known the Gypsies were squatters back then."

"Hey, you're right," she agreed, her brows furrowing.

Another bout of silence followed with both of them in deep thought. Devin reluctantly left to do his chores, worried about the Gypsies' plight. He wondered if they even knew what was going on, before a thought stopped him short. He'd accepted becoming a part of their family!

Devin did his chores mechanically. "Where would they go? Many were old, and the kids! They'd never make it. He felt an urgent need to talk to Rupert. Finishing his chores quickly, he headed back to the kitchen and found his aunt had returned.

"I spoke to some people I know sympathetic to the Gypsies. They think people are just mean-spirited."

"But Aunt, if they have to leave, where will they go?" Lexi's question echoed Devin's thought as she spoke up.

"Gypsies have been around a long time. They'll manage," their aunt replied without elaborating.

"But," Devin began…

She raised her hand.

"I know how you're feeling, both of you. We have to let things be. It might go nowhere. After all, they've been in that camp for too many years to count."

"Unless someone important kicks them out," Devin muttered.

"That's not being helpful, Dev. We don't know what's really going on. And you have to understand, nobody wants people living illegally on their property."

"I thought you understood…" he began, Lexi's face reflecting his confusion.

"I do," she replied calmly. "But our sympathies for the Gypsies doesn't make it okay. I mean," she said after a moment, "this is how society works. No matter how much good the Gypsies did for our history, if they're doing, or have done something illegal, it is still wrong."

Devin bristled, knowing folks were using the law as an excuse to get rid of the Gypsies. People's lack of memory of the Gypsies' part in their survival during all the strange storms a few months back surprised him. But he secretly understood his aunt's logic. Lexi was right. Somebody with power was behind this.

For the next one week, he was the first one up, keeping a keen ear out for any rumors and voraciously reading The Village Beat. When Friday arrived, he was relieved when nothing else was mentioned.

But later that afternoon, Devin was shocked when Rusty, Tyler and David, soot-covered, tattered and bruised, hobbled through their gate.

Lexi gasped, her face registering fear. "What happened to you guys? What's going on?"

"We got burnt. Someone burnt us out," Rusty answered, his voice raspy.

"Burnt you out?" Devin repeated, scrambling to help them into the kitchen.

"Every last tent we had,' said Tyler, shaking his head.

Their aunt returning from next door at the same moment, stopped, her face going through a series of emotions.

"Lexi," she snapped urgently, "get water and rags. Bring me the salve and bandages too from your mom's supply. And get the ingredients to make that poultice that I taught you."

Her manner took Devin by surprise, having gotten accustomed to seeing her always being jovial. Lexi returned with supplies and they set about cleaning the guys up.

"We had finished dinner," started Tyler "when mom thought she saw someone down by our garden. I went outside and, and…"

"Rusty and I had just returned," David interrupted, "from getting firewood when everything just flared up."

"Where's everybody?" Aunt Sophie asked calmly, while cleaning the injuries, her touch very gentle.

"I don't know," said David "Tyler found me."

"Galeb got everyone together and headed for the forest," said Tyler. "We got hurled back in the bushes. There was so much confusion." After a brief pause, his voice filled with pain, he continued, "The gardens are all ruined. All the caravans were burning…." he stopped, tears falling.

Lexi sat down, giving him a hug which he returned, crying into her shoulder.

Aunt Sophie patted him comfortingly before moving on to Rusty.

"Galeb said he would take them up in the hills till he figures out what to do."

Aunt Sophie continued cleaning the wounds, her lips clamped shut.

"We couldn't get to the road because the fire blocked the entrance." Rusty gasped in pain as their aunt cleaned the burn on his leg.

Devin felt ready to explode as he listened to their story unfold.

"Dev, will you get me as many aloe leaves you can find?" His aunt's voice broke his rising fury and he nodded, stalking off as she called out ingredients to Lexi who was busily making poultices.

Returning a short time later, he helped apply crushed aloe to the burns and bruises and tried helping everyone get comfortable.

That night, the boys slept over. Aunt Sophie left when dusk fell with her baskets of poultices, herbs and medicines and a bag she'd packed with food.

Devin struggled to hide the emotions that threatened to overwhelm him. His sleep was fitful, visited by strange dreams of unseen persons setting flames everywhere.

* * *

The next morning brought a flurry of activities as breakfast was finished. After the chickens had been fed and cleaned, their aunt gathered fruits and vegetables from the garden and changed the bandages with fresh ones, while she had Devin get the spare clothing.

The boys laughed out loud on seeing themselves. Tyler's clothes fitted but were short, David's were tight but long and Rusty's were baggy. After changing into the proper fit and being presentable, they secured the house and headed out.

Arriving at the campsite, Devin felt helpless. What had once been a pretty and picture-perfect little piece of heaven, now sat in charred ruins, the smell of smoke clinging thickly around and tiny tendrils issuing from the remains.

The huge tree in the center stood like a giant skeleton with its trunk blackened and branches drooping. Rusty was right, the once hidden entrance to the campsite, now sat in open invitation with a line of people showing up. Devin couldn't imagine the terror at being blocked by a wall of flames.

He spotted a man busily sketching a drawing of the site. A petite, waif-like woman with reddish hair, dressed in a dark-blue pair of trousers and white silk top, had watched them approach. She paused in mid-speech on seeing them, and hurried over, busily taking in the group. She had inquisitive green eyes, a tiny nose and a wide mouth.

"Hello, I'm Missy Misfit, she said in a friendly lilt. "I'm a writer with The Village Beat."

Devin didn't think talking to anyone at the moment was the best thing, but Missy Misfit stood waiting.

"We got word of a fire here last night," she continued. "Do you boys live here? Can you tell me what happened? Where is everyone? Was anyone hurt? Did someone…."

"As you can see, we just arrived," Aunt Sophie took charge. "We don't know anything."

"And you are?" Missy looked at their aunt.

"I'm Sophia."

"Sophia?" Missy waited expectantly.

"Just Sophia," repeated their aunt. "These boys are friends with my nephew. When we heard what happened we came to offer any help we could," she ended, staring fixedly at Missy.

"Oh, yes. Yes of course, I understand," Missy smiled helpfully. Turning to the boys, she said, "I see you all have bandages of some kind, can you tell me what happened?"

Surprised at her quick take on things, Devin quickly began, "That would be my fault."

"Your fault, Missy Misfit turned back to him in surprise.

"Ah, yeah," he nodded.

"And you are?"

"I'm Devin Reelms. We went fishing at Fibbing Creek. I climbed the big tree there but fell off. They went in to get me. That's how they got hurt."

Missy's expression changed in degrees as he spoke, her eyebrows shooting upwards to her hairline.

Aunt Sophia nodded, "Yes. Devin should have known better than to go climbing on that limb. Kids, you know?" She sounded overly tolerant. "I still remember the fun I had as a little girl." Her expression took on a far-away expression. "I swear that old tree is magical," she said with a conspiratorial smile, bringing a nostalgic look into Missy's eyes.

"This has to be devastating for all of you," Missy turned to the boys, her face full of sympathy now. What will you do now?"

"We have to find our families," Rusty said, gesturing around.

"Of course," she replied. "I'm sorry for your loss."

"They'll be with us till we can find out more," answered Aunt Sophia. Giving Missy a look that brooked no further question, she continued, "We live at #5 Blessings Lane if you need to contact me. I'm sure the boys are worried. If you would excuse us?"

"Of course. I'll keep in touch, Sophia."

Inclining her head, Aunt Sophia stepped away, and seconds later they blended in the crowd now gathered. Within a few minutes, they were well into the forest.

* * *

It wasn't long before they found a group of people, huddled in tiny, domed shelters made out of branches and sticks.

Devin realized that the shelters wouldn't stand against the elements for long. As tears welled up in his eyes, the fury that lay simmering within him once again threatened to explode. He made a silent vow to find the person responsible for this and knew they'd have to pay dearly. He jumped when a hand settled on his shoulders.

Hurriedly wiping his eyes, he found Elder Rupert standing by his side. Bowing, he said, "Good morning, Elder Rupert."

"And a fair morning it is, Devin. How are you?"

"I'm sorry about the fire."

"I am too, Devin. I am too."

Unsure of how to proceed, but keeping all traces of worry from his voice, he ventured, "Aunt Sophie brought whatever we could put together."

Rupert looked at him with tired eyes. "That will be a great help."

"How are you feeling?"

Rupert gazed at him with a sad smile. "As you can see, things happen no matter our age. We were lucky to have stayed so long in one camp. All things considered, I'm well."

Devin heard the resignation in Rupert's voice. Watching the old man swallow, Devin felt his own helplessness rise again.

"Did anybody see who started the fire?"

Shaking his silver covered head, Rupert replied, "It still wouldn't help even if we did know who did it. No one believes the word of an outcast."

"How can you say that, Elder Rupert. Your whole tribe just lost their homes."

"All part of the big plan. We don't have to understand it." Patting Devin's shoulder again, Rupert moved away, leaving a very distressed Devin.

He found his aunt busy with some mothers tending to their kids. She sent him with an old bucket someone had rescued to find water. He headed out to find a stream and it was nearly dark when they returned home, the boys having decided to stay with their families.

* * *

The next morning at breakfast, Devin heard Lexi mumbling as she scanned the papers. He knew well enough to let her do her thing, but it was beginning to irritate him.

"What's with all the mumbling?" he finally asked.

"Hold on. I'll be done soon."

He waited.

She mumbled again and kept reading.

He fumed.

"Ah, Section 7–Things to Note. Let's see what they're hiding now."

Devin tapped his feet.

She swore, causing Devin to stare. He'd never heard Lexi utter such an expression. He was saved from asking what was the matter when she stood up, handed him the paper and left.

Devin frowned, hating when she did that. Lexi was good at breaking things down for him. He couldn't imagine what would cause her to use such an expression.

Finding nothing unusual, he figured it wouldn't be the first time a retraction was made. They were long overdue since it happened almost every third month. The newspaper was more comical than serious and a mistake of some silly item wouldn't drive Lexi to swear. Devin read each page in detail.

When he came upon it, he sat in disbelief.

Gypsy Camp Goes Up in Flames

"We are sad to report a fire which happened outside the Village of Foxwood. So far, the exact cause of the fire that engulfed a small area by the sea is unknown. It destroyed the homes of the Gypsies who had set up camp and been living there in secrecy.

Recently being thanked by The Brotherhood for having found and returned a Crystal from the times of Ohhm, they're once again living true to their nature. Homeless from the fire, their itinerant lifestyle is causing quite a concern.

The lands are privately owned, but the recent recognition gave awareness to their squatting. While it is not yet clear how many tribes are scattered throughout the hills and where they may set up camp again, talks of eviction have surfaced among landowners.

Landowners we've spoken to are taking active interest to protect any property they had previously left unattended. Some have posted "No Trespassing" signs, and while some are putting up fences, others are buying weapons to deter anyone from stepping on their lands."

We are determined to find out what will be the outcome of this, and will keep you posted on the latest developments."

Devin understood Lexi's reaction at the Gypsies' plight. Unable to understand what people were suddenly righteous about and repulsed by, Devin felt the helplessness from before return, and with it the anger.

It was bad enough knowing the Gypsies were now homeless and forced to live in the bushes, foraging like animals and lacking basic necessities. It had driven his aunt, Lexi and himself ragged, as they took turns taking care of their own home, his grandparents and helping the gypsies with whatever they could.

The final insult came two days later when he bumped into a neighbor at the Fish Market. Old Mr. Russell, who used to visit on Full Moon nights, came up to him.

"How come yuh associatin with dem Gypsies, boy?" His loud voice carried, and people stopped, listening. "Was bad enough they turnin up at your mom's passing. God rest her soul."

"Hello, Mr. Russell. How are you?" He replied, ignoring the old man's comments.

"Well and good boy, well and good." Then without missing a beat, he continued, "Don't you go feelin no sorry for them Gypsies, boy. Your mom was a good lady. Classy. Don't mean you owe them anything."

Devin silently agreed his mom was good and classy, but wondered how they could judge the Gypsies to be evil. About to open his mouth, a woman he liked, Mrs. Targ, interrupted.

"Poor taste, they showin up at the funeral. Was up to Mr. Targ, he woulda chased them off. But I told him, "Ivan Targ, you go causin a disruption, and Rae will get up from her death and kill you.""

Chuckles echoed around them. About to give a retort, another man chimed in, "Was me, I'd turn them straight back at the gate. Them Gypsies slick. Why, I found the little rascal in me watermelon patch last Saturday."

Devin saw it was the crubbly Mr. Pooka who'd just spoken. With a jolt he understood why Hixon, a boy of ten, had returned with scratches and a large bruise to his left eye, grasping on a large melon. He hadn't given it much thought at the time.

He felt a thread of sympathy for Mr. Pooka. His was always the first garden to get plundered, it being closest to the beach.

But another voice spoke up and Devin lost all patience as he heard Mrs. Billingsworth, "You didn't get the little rat then? Such a pity."

"Nah. More slippery than an eel. The rascal got the biggest melon of the season too. Was goin to enter it in the contest." Mr. Pooka spoke with passion and Devin genuinely felt sorry, knowing him to be a good man.

"Devin. Devin Reelms." The high-pitch, strident voice of Violet Coons caught Devin by surprise. A hardened busy-body, he thought she had left to be with an ailing cousin. He spotted her pushing her way forward.

Not caring about what any of them thought, he left.

"Poor kid. What a thing to lose his mother," he heard as he started running, blood pounding in his ears.

Pushing through their gate a few minutes later, he took his slingshot. Arriving at the beach a while later, he spent the next few hours shooting viciously at the water.

21
ENCOURAGEMENT

A s the days went by, Devin spent more time in the hills than he did at home. When people saw him and the boys together, it gave him a wicked satisfaction seeing how they recoiled.

But soon he heard gossip about his aunt. Things of her past surfaced, and within a short time, memories of her running away surfaced. No one seemed to care anymore that Aunt Sophia had returned to take care of him and Lexi after their mom's death.

He remembered seeing old Becky on his way to the post office, whispering with a group of ladies. He'd paid little attention to her since she had stomped off the night of the storm.

Now he wondered. She was old enough with a memory going as far back as Gramps'. Knowing she felt Celeste had deliberately withheld healing, Devin felt it pretty rotten if she was responsible for the rumors.

When he barged into their kitchen a few minutes later, he found his aunt in the rocker, sewing. She looked up before going back to her stitching. As he stood deciding where to start, he heard voices and stared out their kitchen window at the crowd of people filing into Gramps' yard. "Damn!" he thought. Gramps was having his monthly garden sale.

"Its like they're coming to a circus or something," he mused.

"Hmmm."

"Doesn't it bother you, Aunt Sophia?"

"Mr. Heeb would say, "people will be people", reminded his aunt.

"They're too nosey."

"What's really bothering you, Dev?" his aunt raised her inquiring eyebrows at him.

He told her what he'd heard.

"We live in a village, Dev. Its all folks do. Gossip."

"Yeah, well. They can go…"

"Devin!"

"Sorry," he muttered, eyes glued to the people next door.

"You're doing this all wrong," she scolded him, eyebrows knitted in concern. "Did it ever occur to you that it might be helpful one day?"

"Helpful?" he spluttered. "How can a bunch of gossiping toads be helpful to me?"

"Well," she began, hesitated a moment, and then continued, "maybe I shouldn't have said that."

"Why not?" Devin's curiosity rose, perplexed knowing how strange adults were.

As if she'd reached some kind of agreement with herself, Aunt Sophia began, "Gossip is harmful no matter what form it takes. The more you try to set things right, the faster it gets out of control. It's like a raging fire."

Knowing her to be a normally private person, he stayed quiet.

"No one ever acknowledges what they're doing is hurtful to anyone else. Everyone has his or her take on stuff, irrespective of the truth."

"So?" He began.

"So, you're still a kid and those…those toads…well…" she paused, then went on a minute later, "promise me you'll always carry yourself with dignity."

Devin swallowed, "That's exactly what mom said to me".

Aunt Sophia inclined her head in response. "When it comes to gossip, no answer is the best answer, Dev."

"Maybe for you and mom, Aunt Sophia." In a rising voice he continued, "I'm not letting anyone do that to me. I lived with mom. I saw how she suffered. I saw how much she helped everyone. Nobody helped her. Not even….." he stopped, his chest heaving.

"Well, if you must, you must. Anger is good, but you should use it constructively. And try not to stoop to their level if it can be helped. Think how what you do will affect others."

Amazed she had acquiesced, he asked "Meaning?"

"One can always channel it in a direction helpful to you or you can distract it by focusing attention elsewhere."

"So mom...." He began.

"Your mom wasn't stupid, Devin. Her intelligence was her strength."

A flood of emotions assailed him and as he muddled through, a strange thought occurred. "Isn't that just as..." unwilling to finish the thought, he stayed quiet, the insight bringing new respect for his mom.

His aunt gave him a curious look..

"Sounds complicated," he agreed.

"You should read "The Art & Science of Conversations" by Dame Singsong. It's in your mom's room."

Devin groaned inwardly. More reading. Great!

"It isn't as intimidating as it sounds," she hurried on, seeing his expression. "Just focus on what you know for now."

Devin breathed a sigh of relief. All that heavy stuff was getting to him.

"That's the problem. I don't know much. And you have not said anything since they visited."

Unperturbed, his aunt replied, "I figured you'd ask when you were ready."

He watched her fingers nimbly work on an intricate pattern and smiled.

"Well, do you really believe all that stuff about Ohhm and that I am the one who will have to restore it? I mean..." he hurried on, "it just seems so…" he paused for a moment to search for the right word before saying "fantastic! And mom! She never told me anything. I mean," he reflected aloud, "Lexi said mom had started chanting when things became weird, and she said it was time. Like what did she mean? And Gramps said she knew of the Prophecy so I'm guessing mom had some idea about things?" Then he muttered, "Why? Like why couldn't she have said something to me?"

His aunt carefully finished some loops and knots, before putting her sewing down again.

"Why don't we look at what's happened," she began.

"I don't want to," he began….

"You need to," she interrupted, a glint in her eyes. "It might help you understand things differently."

"Okay. But.." he paused before going on, "we've heard so many stories of Ohhm and I…., well, I mean, there's no real history anywhere. No ruins or anything."

"Sometimes we don't see what's in front of us, Dev," she interrupted.

He released a frustrated breath, "I'm just a kid, Aunt Sophia. I can't think the way adults do."

"You don't have to. What I'm saying is, can you deny what happened?" she asked, staring at him.

"How can you ask me that?" he shot back, blood beginning to boil.

"To help you figure out what you're feeling. You either believe you're the one who will restore a powerful kingdom, or you don't, and live with the consequences. But nothing comes from running away, Dev."

Unwilling to budge, he felt his insides start to twist as he gazed stonily at her.

Shaking her head, she reflected, "Just look at my life. So many years lost because I didn't want to listen to anyone about anything."

"I thought you were happy." Devin blurted out.

"Oh, I was. Gloriously. Deliriously. I never regretted my life with Xavier. But look at what I gave up for that happiness," she gestured around. "Its only now, years later, I can appreciate a parent's job."

He grinned, nodding. "I know we aren't easy to be around."

She chuckled, shaking her head, "If only that was all there was to it."

At his expression, she went on, "Xavier. Rae's death, seeing mom and dad so much older, Chad and Serena, your dad being gone. And you. You have a destiny to fulfill." She laughed, shaking her head. "What's normal about all of this? But it's the card we were dealt with and all we can do is be strong and do our best."

"Oh."

"Yes," she nodded, "time has moved on and life has changed so much. I didn't realize how much I missed all of this. "But why don't you tell me what happened?"

"You mean from the start?"

"That would be a good place," his aunt laughed.

Well," he started, "Gramps told us the crystal was alive."

She nodded. When he came to the part about reading the verse, she quickly said, "Do you remember it?"

"I have the book," Devin replied, getting up and retrieving it from the small nook behind her chair. Surprised at his anxiousness to read the prophecy again, he had purposely left the book unfinished. Now he gazed in defiance at the battered cover, "Ohhm, A Forgotten Land."

Taking a deep breath, he glanced over as Aunt Sophia sniffed. She nodded encouragingly and he read it again.

When he was finished, the silence grew and he finally asked, "What do you think, Aunt?"

"Well…" his aunt began, "if as Gramps says your mom knew of the prophecy and you're from our Grand-Ancestor's bloodline, she had no idea if there are other male descendants. She couldn't know for sure it would be you. In fact, I don't think anyone could have predicted any of this, not even Roxy herself."

"But if Roxy made the Prophecy…" began Devin, only to be interrupted.

"Roxy was furious enough to make the prophecy, but not how any of this would come about. I mean Dev, think about it. Gramps told you how odd his dad was and you know how people think Gramps himself is missing a few marbles. No one could have said how the string of events would have led to our present situation."

Devin was hanging on to every word his aunt spoke, feeling another painful skip of his heartbeat when she said, "Dev, if your mom suspected you might somehow be the one to bear such a burden, how could she in good conscience tell you she would have to give her life? That she'd have to die to make sure you are able to fulfill a destiny? No one should ever be burdened with such a thing. And no decent parent would ever truly want to do that to a child. It's no ordinary thing, Dev. This is as fantastical as it gets."

Devin tasted a pain so bitter, he almost choked. Yet, he found himself whispering, "She could have found some way to let me know something, Aunt Sophie. Anything."

"Of course, she did, Dev. Look around you," Aunt Sophia gestured widely.

"What do you mean?" Devin asked, confused.

"This," she exclaimed, pointing all around them. "Can't you see how different our family is from the rest of the villagers?"

When Devin took inventory of all he could remember, he saw the truth of what his aunt pointed out. One thing he realized was how much his mom did to keep attention away from herself. But he was busy being himself... an absorbed fourteen-year-old with regular kid's issues. The truth was all around him, staring him in the face and it was his own innocence which caused him to not think otherwise.

"I still don't get why she tolerated the things she did. And why Gramps and Celeste never seemed to be able to do anything about it." This came out so unexpectedly, he wasn't sure he'd spoken aloud, until his aunt sighed unhappily.

"I'm afraid it's probably because of me," his aunt admitted dejectedly.

Devin gaped. "You?"

"Well, you know I ran away with Xavier, a Gypsy," she said, with pain in her voice.

Devin nodded.

"I suspect your dad had a different kind of ambition when he married your mom, but it didn't turn out the way he had hoped. Maybe he felt shame by association, and became resentful since he didn't get the life he was hoping for. You, Lexi, and your mom were a constant reminder of what it cost him."

Devin fell quiet. It made sense and explained the many ugly and cruel episodes he and Lexi had witnessed their mom deal with.

"How do you know all this though, Aunt Sophie, if you'd already left?"

"Xavier knew how much I loved my family. He had someone who helped Gramps around the yard tell him of the goings-on here. I've always felt badly about how it all turned out, but I still don't regret leaving."

"It still doesn't explain mom though," he tried again.

"Dev, I don't think we will know the full truth about your mom. For her to have borne a child whom we now know is to restore a Sacred Realm, means she herself was no ordinary soul. Your mom was, and remains a mystery.

A short silence ensued, before his aunt asked him to continue telling of what had happened. He did and continued, "Rusty stole the crystal for The Renegade and got beaten up. I helped him and we became friends. Then the Gypsies honored me and Zoie did a reading for me."

"She did?" His aunt was surprised.

He nodded.

"Go ahead," she replied.

"Then the weather got weird. We got snow and floods and..."

"Yes, it wasn't pleasant in the hills either," she agreed.

"I went looking for The Renegade," he paused, remembering no one knew of his expedition to The Rotten Shack, and continued quickly, "and found Ole Higue."

"Tell me of Ole Higue," his aunt said, leaning forward in her rocker.

Devin went over the details, telling her as best he could what had happened down in the cave. Remembering his promise to Serena, he finished, "Then mom died and," he hurried on, "and you showed up."

"That's everything?" she inquired.

"Well…just what Gramps told me of the prophecy by our grand-ancestor. Then Serena and Chad met with us."

"Did you ever finish reading that book?"

Her question took him by surprise. He'd returned the book to the shelf, plagued with guilt.

"No," he answered.

Aunt Sophia leaned back in her chair with her eyebrows furrowed in concentration. After a long time, she said, "How many other boys have had so many strange things happen to them?"

Devin gazed unseeingly at the scene in his grandfather's yard, her questions hanging between them for a long time. Finally, he said "It's not fair."

"It is not about fairness."

When he said nothing, she continued, "You need to listen to what I have to say, Devin."

He nodded, turning to look at her.

"In life, we have choices. Either you accept all the things that have happened, showing you that you are the one to restore Ohhm, and prepare yourself to face what lies ahead. Or, you deny your birthright. You have to choose one."

Devin swallowed at her matter-of-fact manner. She was for the most part, jolly, fun-loving, and sometimes even eccentric. He'd never seen his aunt mean business. "I, ah… what I mean is… this is awkward," he muttered, unable to finish.

She shrugged.

"Everything I've told you, really happened, aunt. And you met Chad and Serena."

"Indeed," she agreed.

"And you, you were married to Uncle Xavier. A Timekeeper."

"Yes." Aunt Sophia said, sounding bored now.

"Why are you being this way?" he grumbled, gritting his teeth at her sudden indifference.

"Many people have suffered, Dev. All our futures hang on the choice you make."

Devin got up, pacing the length of the room. Aunt Sophia went back to her sewing, the silence of the room broken only by the sound of his sandals grazing the floor. He paced for a long while.

"The choice was already made, wasn't it?" he accepted quietly.

Aunt Sophia looked up, "Let's say I allowed you to see the bigger picture. It was only a matter of time before you admitted what you feared."

"It is scary," Devin admitted.

"Yes. It is," she agreed.

When he didn't say anything, she continued, "You have gifts even you don't know of. And if what we have been told is really going to happen, then I believe prophecies aren't made if the hero is going to die."

Devin's insides tightened, hearing her voice his fear. "You think that could happen?" he heard his voice trembling.

"Heroes always have heavy burdens, but they prevail, Dev. I think Ohhm will rise because the time has come, because you have what it takes to make it happen and because the will of a force beyond anything we can imagine, wills it so. You just need to believe in yourself."

Her words hit Devin to the very core of his being, making him feel like he was worth the world. His doubts fled, a surge of confidence flowing over him.

Walking over, he knelt down, wrapping his arms around her in a tight hug. "Thank you, Aunt Sophia."

"You're welcome. And Devin?"

"Yes?" He looked at her.

"I think you should finish reading that book."

"Okay," Devin nodded. Suddenly, his worry over folks being petty vanished and he headed out the door, his heart much lighter.

"Don't be rude," she called. He waved in reply.

BRAWL

Walking home from seeing the guys settled for the evening at the tiny shelter they'd built, Devin whistled a silly tune he'd heard the kids singing.

"Gypsy!"

Startled, he turned, scanning the approaching darkness.

"Yeah you. I'm talking to you."

He spotted Frey Alton, the village bully and his gang. Knowing he was in trouble, he scanned the area for friendly faces, neighbors or anybody that might be passing by, even hoping the old post-master might still be out on his porch.

Not a soul stirred except for the bullies in front of him.

"What's with you and the Gypsies?" The mulish voice, closer now, told Devin Frey was in high form, itching for trouble.

When he didn't respond, Frey called out again, "Think you better than everybody?" The taunting, heavy voice grated on Devin's nerves.

"What's it to you anyhow?" he challenged, knowing there was no avoiding what was coming.

"You keep doing what you doing and dem rats are never gonna leave."

"They're people. Like you and me. What do you have against them, Frey?" Devin watched the others go quiet as he spoke up.

"They're parasites, infestin our lives. And you pretendin you better than everybody, helping dem out. That's what I got against them. You makin dem think we owe them stuff."

The answer sounded rehearsed, like he was repeating something he'd heard. His dad, Jaedon Alton, had been talking of getting rid of the Gypsies but exactly why, Devin still hadn't figured it out.

"I don't see you doing anything to help," he replied calmly, remembering his aunt's caution.

Incredulous laughter sounded as the group tightened.

"You serious, Gypsy? Help? Why would I want to help the low-lives?"

Devin let a moment go by, before saying slowly, "Because it's the decent thing to do."

Frey was quiet for a long time, making Devin wonder what he was coming up with. Finally, he looked around his group and said, "Gypsy here's sayin we ain't decent."

"That's not what I said," Devin inserted as the crowd gathered closer to Frey, muttering darkly, nodding at something someone said.

Devin felt a moment's fear, but stood his ground.

"So now you better than us AND you decent. Whoever gave you the idea you so noble then, yuh mom? Oh," Frey continued quickly, "I forgot, she's dead!" he jeered, his buddies cackling loudly.

"Poor baby," said one hefty fellow from the back of the group.

"Yeah," came another voice "gonna run to dat aunt of yours? Oh wait, now I remember, she's one of dem."

Knowing they outnumbered him, Devin tried keeping his anger in control. Deliberately keeping his voice calm, he said, "What's it to you whom I help anyway? I don't go about asking your business."

"We makin it our business," replied Frey pompously.

"That's why we have the law, Frey. Not you," Devin countered determinedly.

"So you gonna keep helpin the rats then?"

Dread flowed through Devin as he heard the ominous tone, knowing it was only a matter of seconds before things got ugly. "Don't see why I shouldn't," he replied in a soft, deliberate voice.

"Well guys, guess we gotta show Gypsy here why he needs to stop mixin with dem parasites," Frey said darkly.

Devin stayed still, looking for a sign he could still leave in one piece when he heard, "Hey, Gypsy how 'bout letting us be friends then?" The unexpected question caught him by surprise, and he peered in the darkness trying to see who it was that had spoken.

"Do you mean that?" Devin asked hopefully, thinking it offered a way out.

"Sure," came the answer. "We can be friends. And Lexi. Lexi can tend to me any day. We've needs too. Com'on man, it's the decent thing to do. What'd you say?"

Vulgar laughter erupted around, followed by jeers and lewd suggestions.

Someone chuckled directly behind him and he spun around in time to see a burly fellow by the name of Riza Boyd rushing at him.

What followed reminded him of the night he'd witnessed the Renegade being attacked. What he lacked in strength, Devin made up for in agility, and as Frey closed in on him, he nimbly hopped aside. A sickening crunch sounded as Frey and Riza collided.

Devin didn't have time to savor their stupidity. In moments, he felt blows reigning on his face, arms and legs. Pain blinded him as someone squeezed his throat, his vision wavering. He kicked and jabbed. Rolled away and was tugged back. Striking back, he managed to land several punches that elicited groans and shrieks, but they kept attacking him.

As suddenly as he'd been grabbed, he was let go, the unknown attacker reeling back, yelling in agony. Gasping, Devin watched as the group paused, someone had a light out yelling for whoever it was bawling to shut up. "You gonna wake the whole neighborhood up. Cut the mewling out."

A moment later, Devin felt the air go deathly still, the silence finally broken when the light showed a kid's flesh burnt where he'd choked Devin.

He stared in confusion. He hadn't even touched the person who'd been choking him. He touched the necklace, gasping as realization hit him.

"What you got there Gypsy? Meddlin with witchcraft now?"

As they came at him, Devin didn't care anymore. He needed to get out alive and no promises to Aunt Sophia or Gramps or anyone else was going to keep him from saving his hide. Pushing everything noble from his mind, he fought, using every tactic that came to him, foul means or not. They were out for blood and no one was coming to his aid.

Whether it was the last few weeks of being in the hills and developing his muscles, or some inner reserve of strength or the help from the necklace, when Devin felt his hand touch emptiness, it was the only time he stopped moving.

It took him a moment to realize they were either gasping for breath, wincing in pain or were out cold. How he did it, he didn't know, but he didn't wait around to figure out. He left, hearing sounds of people approaching. He dashed behind a clump of bushes and waited, trying to keep his breath calm and slow. When he heard Jaedon barking harshly at his son, Devin realized the incident had been planned.

Thinking fast, he slid deeper down the side of the road, hearing the commotion picking up. Without hesitating, he slid and felt his way along the little stream that ran alongside the street.

It guided him to the bridge at the head of the street leading to his home. Crawling under the bridge, he came out the other side and stayed silent. Moments passed and he was about to start out when he heard a sneeze. Freezing, he waited, while ignoring the throbbing and bruises that had begun to swell up.

He first heard a voice and then footsteps moving away. Nimble as a goat, Devin hopped up and saw a retreating back fading in the darkness.

In less time than he could have imagined, Devin reached home, breathless and grateful. Somehow he felt a lot better. The pent-up anger of weeks now had been what saved him tonight and Devin didn't doubt they'd have visitors in the morning.

Devin slept in his mom's room, feeling a sense of comfort after everything that had gone on. He awoke to loud voices in the kitchen below. The clock showed it to be only seven-thirty in the morning. "Who had come calling this early?" he wondered. Then he heard his name.

"Well, well. If it ain't Saucy Sophie after all these years? Lookin mighty nice Sophie," Jaedon Alton brayed in loud humor.

Dervin nearly fell off the bed. The sound of Jaedon Alton's cronies exchanging pleasantries with his aunt roused his curiosity. Having generally gotten along with everyone before Frey spread his poison, Devin's anger grew. Those creeps had no place in his home, much less being around his aunt. He'd seen enough of their brawling, bullying, and lewdness to know this was bad.

"Thanks, Jadeon. I've been around for a couple of weeks now." His aunt's chirpy reply gave Devin pause. She sounded totally unfazed by the tough company crowding below.

"Oh, I heard," he brayed again. "Life in the Hills must have agreed with you."

"It did. You should try it sometime."

She sounded a bit too sweet to Devin's ears. He winced as laughter erupted again. "Me? Nawh. I got everything I need right here in Foxwood."

"Life in the village must really agree with you. How is Lizzie? Frey looks a lot like her."

Snickers echoed in the room.

"Shut it!" Jaedon's ugly snarl brought immediate silence.

Devin grinned. How his aunt had come across Frey Alton was a mystery to him. He slid waist-down from the bed, his ear to the floor.

"I married Jill. Lizzie ran away with Chester. Always was a stupid chick." His brittle voice told Devin he was still burning from that insult, but he had no time to savor the revelations as talking continued.

"All these run-away brides- Lizzie, Charlotte, me."

Devin grinned.

"I'll have to congratulate Lizzie and Chester. I can't believe they are together after what you did."

"She just got with him because he's rich." Jaedon barked. "She wouldn't know love if it..."

"If it what, Jaedon?" interrupted Aunt Sophie, "looks like Chester?"

"Awww, cut the reminiscing out Sophie. I ain't interested in going down memory lane."

"Just down the beach road?" She asked.

Silence descended.

"Look," he started, the bully back in place, "we got no issues with you. It's ..."

"Just get to the point, Jaedon," Aunt Sophie interrupted. "Our family is in mourning, in case you forgot. And I don't have time to entertain this early in the day."

"We're here to arrest Devin for doin witchcraft on the kids last night," he stated with rough satisfaction.

"What?" Devin scrambled back onto the bed.

"Doing witchcraft on kids last night?" His Aunt repeated with a chuckle. "Where do you come up with these things, Jaedon? Why in the name of everything holy would Devin do witchcraft on anyone?"

"Laugh all you want, Sophie. He did witchcraft." Jaedon's voice rose, the ugly edge in his voice making Devin uneasy.

"That's a strong accusation against a kid, Jaedon."

"That's not normal stuff kids do, Sophie, going around burning skin off of people. He's doing Gypsy witchcraft."

"That's ridiculous! Devin told me he and the boys had a scuffle because they don't like us helping the Gypsies."

"Treating them like royalty more like," he mocked.

"My dad's been doing it for years. In fact, he helps your family all the time," Devin heard his aunt reminding Jaedon.

"Nothing to do with me," he dismissed. "What my old man and your dad's doing is their business."

Throats cleared and shuffling sounded. An awkward pause followed. Devin knew many had at some point been the recipient of help from his grandfather over the years.

"I see." His aunt's reply hung a long while in the silence. "And nine against one in a fight is gentlemanly?"

"Devin's no hero." Jaedon's belligerence made Devin angry.

"And you are?"

"I'm standing up for what is right, Sophie. Devin did a bad thing and we're making sure he don't go around doin this stuff again."

"Its strange you're in such a hurry to arrest Devin. By what authority are you arresting him? And what proof do you have that Devin performed witchcraft?

"Don't you lecture me on what I'm doing when you been with the low-lives in the Hills! Maybe it's you teachin him all that dark magic!" Jaedon's shouted reply stunned Devin.

"Careful now Jaedon," the nervous voice of Riza Boyd's dad cautioned.

"Boys sometimes fight, Jaedon. I remember you started that fight with Kitty Floyd and she whipped your butt. I didn't see anyone arresting you for being a bully."

Laughter erupted, and Devin felt a slice of wicked humor at his aunt's words.

"Kitty Floyd beat you?" The hoarse voice was unfamiliar to him.

"Shut it, all of you. This is about what Devin's doing."

"Yeah, she slapped him silly and told him…."

"Cut it out Sophie. Playing with witchcraft isn't funny," he interrupted.

"she'd tell everyone he had a puny…"

Guffaws exploded and Devin stifled his own laughter.

"Make fun of me all you want, Sophie. I'm not leavin here without Devin."

A strange thought sparked Devin's curiosity. Why was Jaedon Alton so determined to arrest him? Suddenly he wasn't worried anymore. Something else was really going on, and by golly, he was going to figure it out.

Feeling it was way past time he went down to the kitchen and faced them, he paused on hearing his aunt's steely voice.

"Show me proof Devin performed witchcraft and how you know what it is."

"How in the world are folks able to judge what was or wasn't witchcraft anyways? Seems the whole village was crazy", Devin thought.

"You should have stayed in the Hills, Sophie and left things for us real men to take care of," Jaedon mocked.

"Real men don't let their young sons do their fighting for them, Jaedon. Making Frey pick fights and throwing people in jail when he loses? Grow up, Jaedon. Stop holding a grudge because I didn't run away with you."

When no one else spoke, his aunt said, "If you're done accusing me of things you have no understanding of and Devin for doing witchcraft, I suggest you gentlemen show yourselves out."

Devin heard a flurry of movement as the group of men hurried out of the kitchen. He hopped to the windows and stayed behind the curtains, peering out, spotting the group as they headed up the street, their backs straight and their expressions wooden. He had no doubt that Jaedon Alton was out for revenge now. He'd have to watch his back.

23

THE BEEKEEPER

Devin felt that he needed to know exactly what his mom knew and let his mind flow. Her books, drawings and notes all pointed to knowledge of things beyond. What those were, still remained a mystery.

He couldn't fathom how she'd helped so many in the villages, had the refinement beyond the mindset of the locals, abused by a brute of a husband, yet still kept her life so private.

The village was rife with gossip, always embroiled in each other's family drama, and yet folks were clueless about the intimate details of her life. Not that he wanted a story, but considering the norm, Devin felt frustrated. He needed to keep his mom's memory and life in dignity; but for the love of all things sacred, there had to be someone who knew something!

Lex said she was chanting the day he'd released Ole Higue. Did she speak the ancient language which had flowed to him? Or was she just saying one of Gramps' prayers because she was unwell? Her books spoke of things beyond Foxwood and the ordinary.

"Hey Dev, would you mind going to Honeysuckle Farm? Mr. Fleming said last week he would hold two jars for us", said Aunt Sophie.

His musings broken for the time, he hollered back, "Sure, Aunt Sophie. Gimme ten minutes."

Leaving the last pile of leaves he'd gathered to pick up later, he dusted off, after he had washed his hands and gathered his knapsack.

Finding his bicycle, he took a few old hand towels, and set off. Honeysuckle Farm was a good distance from home, and he knew if the jars weren't packed properly, they'd be broken by the time he got back.

Grabbing his walking stick, he set off. Pedaling his way through the streets that led up to the bottom of the valley, he headed west to the road that would take him to the edge of the village. Whistling his way along, he arrived about an hour and a half later and found Mrs. Fleming collecting fresh honey.

She asked him to go around back to their storage shed since she was handling bees.

He waved to let her know he'd heard her. Leaning his bike against the hedged fence, Devin walked a short distance and found the old bee keeper shuffling through his jars and bottles of honey, checking off names and quantities for families who'd ordered and were waiting to pick them up.

He seemed ancient compared to the last time Devin remembered seeing him, and he felt a moment of sadness stroll through him.

Having lost his mom, Devin wondered how long these old folks whom he'd grown up knowing would be around. Celeste and Gramps had seemed to have doubled in their age, and all around he was being faced with the realization of how things he once took for granted were no longer so.

A stroke of genius flashed through him as he remembered Serena's words about many families having knowledge and would be of help to him.

When the pleasantries and order were complete, he made the payment and was delighted when Mr. Flemming asked him if he'd be willing to help with the restocking.

"Sure, Mr. Fleming. Show me what you need done."

The old man beamed and happily put him to work, climbing the ladder to restock the higher shelves and checking for rodents and helping with the bottles waiting to be filled, all the while exchanging stories about the farm and life back in his home.

"How are you holding up, Dev?" Mr. Fleming asked, making Devin realize it must have been his aim all along. He surprised himself and asked, "I'm okay. Can I ask you some questions about my mom?"

Mr. Fleming blinked at him, scratched his head a bit, and then nodded. "Let's get comfortable then, Dev. This might take a while."

Devin shimmied down the ladder and followed him as he led the way into the kitchen. He got two cups of freshly brewed tea, took one and handed the other to Devin and headed outdoors to the waiting swing.

When they'd settled down, he sipped his tea for a short while and said, "What would you like to know, Dev?"

"Why did my mom take such abuse from my dad?" he blurted out.

"Well, son," the old man said, "every marriage has its share of misunderstandings. I can't say I know for sure, but I have a fair guess that your dad became resentful about how things turned out."

"What things?"

"Your grandfather was pretty influential back in the day. A figure of prominence. Your dad probably felt he had a chance of benefiting by marrying into the family. Mind you," he continued quickly, "I'm not saying he didn't love your mother, but his family wasn't the kind you'd want to claim friendship with."

"So, he wanted respectability and influence?" Devin said, "but if that was so, wouldn't Gramps have known of his true intentions?"

"Yes, for sure, son. Your grandfather is quite a smart man, but he likes believing in giving people chances. I think after the scandal of your aunt taking up with that gypsy fellow, no insult meant," he added quickly, "I think he was relieved someone showed interest in his other daughter. And it might have worked to your dad's interest if your mom's interests were the same."

"What'd you mean?"

"Well," continued Mr. Fleming, "your mother was a lovely child when I knew her. She grew into a wonderful person but she had quite a fascination for unusual things."

"Like what?" Devin was quick to ask.

The old beekeeper smiled before looking off into the distance, almost as if he was peering into the recent past, lost in memories. Finally, he got up and said, "come. I can show you."

Startled, Devin hopped up and followed, his heart racing and palms suddenly sweaty.

The old man led him to what looked like a forgotten part of the farmhouse and, reaching up over the doorway, took a large key that had a layer of dust covering it.

Wiping it on his overalls, he opened the door to reveal a small chamber filled with a very large wooden table covered with bottles, tubes, jars, canisters, open notebooks, and large sheets of paper with drawings and pictures.

"What's this?" Devin whispered.

"Your mom's."

"I don't understand, Mr. Fleming," he whispered gazing in fascination. "What does mom have to do with this?"

"This was her secret, Dev. Your mom had a very curious mind. It's been this way since she was last here. Couldn't begin to tell you the number of happy hours she spent dabbling and testing her little heart away on things even I couldn't understand."

Devin stepped in and walked up to the table, gazing over, under, across, below and above. He couldn't believe he'd finally found something about his mom's life.

"What does it mean, though?" he suddenly felt an unwilling moment to disturb anything. It felt like he was about to trespass on something holy and sacred. He felt inexpressibly excited, a pull to dive into everything before him tugged within, yet he stood in wonder and gazed.

"I call it alchemy. She was fascinated with this stuff."

"Alchemy?" Devin repeated in surprise.

"I mean," the beekeeper said, "it's what I call it. She had a very bright mind and would tell me things about the stars and moon and the tides and you name it. She could tell you stuff that you knew somehow never existed. But she said it and the next thing, something weird would happen and it was exactly what she said was so."

"Interesting," thought Devin. "How did my mom get started with all of this?" he gestured to the contents of the room.

"Oh, she'd been stung by a few bees when she came to get honey like you're doing now. She wanted to know how poison, venom and so on worked, and how the medicine used to help soothe the stings helped. After that, there was no holding her back."

"Is that what Gramps meant when he said no one spoke about gifts their kids would have, especially if they're a girl?"

"I think what he meant was how unconventional your mom's interests were. Learning about stars and the belief about the effects of the moon on our psyche, are things unlike those that a typical girl is usually focused on."

"Mom really learnt about all those things?" Devin asked. "How though? Where did she learn such things?"

"I think Old Mr. Tibbles had quite a collection in his library. She used to spend a lot of time at his estate. And you know? It was quite fun having her around. We didn't have kids of our own, and it gave us a lot of happiness watching when she'd come up with some herbal concoction of some kind. It was like all the stars would light up when she was happy. Quite the little alchemist, your mom."

He fell quiet, lost in memories, but Devin was checking the little chamber. He felt that it explained the two books she'd left for Lexi and himself. Clearly her mind was full of exquisiteness.

Mr. Fleming spoke, bringing Devin out of his musings, "Your mother was a wonderful human being with a generous heart and had the kindness I wish many more had. I don't know what I can say to make you feel better. She had a lot of hidden knowledge."

"And dad was upset because my mom wanted to learn?"

"More like he thought she'd be a social butterfly, whatever little existed in this part of our world, and with your grandfather's influence, he'd have quite the life. When your mom showed little interest in those kinds of pursuits, he became bitter."

Aunt Sophie had said almost the same thing to him. She wasn't quite off the mark, and now hearing Mr. Fleming say it, Devin felt the old anger returning.

"He was a brute and a bully. Why didn't Gramps do anything about it?" he wondered aloud.

"He did. But your father is an insecure, vindictive, manipulative and controlling man. He found other ways to retaliate. He thought he'd get a fancy life when he fooled your grandfather into letting him marry your mother, but he didn't know your mother's joy lay in simple things. Things that eventually led her to discover that story about the prophecy of Ohhm."

Devin gasped. "You know about that?"

"I was the first one she told."

"How?"

"Your mother had the gift to charm the birds off the trees if she chose," Mr. Fleming smiled. "She said it's a story she'd heard from your grandfather who was told about it by his dad, and that old fella he helped a long time ago had given him a book. Something was in there that led her to keep searching for what it meant.

"Yes, but everything that happened…"

"I know Devin. But your mother showed me a book that told her things. Not that she had powers and such, but when she said all the things she was learning, I told her to put it away."

"Why?"

"Well, with so many stories around these parts, I wasn't sure if someone had put a charm on it and might have led her down the wrong path. I mean, we had Dark Worshippers who preyed on young girls."

"Oh." Devin fell silent, not having the heart to tell Mr. Fleming that he himself had found that book and everything that had followed.

Something the old beekeeper said a few minutes back clicked and he stopped abruptly. "What do you know of Dark Worshippers, Mr. Fleming?"

"Just that they're an evil lot who everyone should stay away from. There's a rumor of one of them living somewhere in the wild. Seems something bad happened with the lot, and he went sour. He split ways."

He happened to glance over at Devin and something in his expression made Devin guard his thoughts.

"Don't you go meddling with such things or people, Devin," he admonished, suddenly seeming regretful of having said so much. "Curiosity is a many-edged sword and there's no telling what'll happen now."

"You have my word, Mr. Fleming," Devin reassured him. "I won't go looking for trouble."

Mr. Fleming stared at him for a few seconds, and after seeming satisfied, nodded.

"Very well. I don't believe your mom would have tolerated lies. I'll take your word for it."

Devin, in truth, was ecstatic! This was the first true thing he'd learned of his mom, and he couldn't be more pleased. There was nothing he'd do now to jeopardize any chance of learning more.

Still a mystery in many ways, his mom's only crime was in being innocently attracted to what he was learning were the more secretive subjects that weren't easily available in the valleys, with folks who themselves knew very little about.

"You can have the lot," Mr. Fleming's voice jolted him in surprise.

He stared. "Have the lot?" I can't take this stuff."

"Why not?" Then before he could answer, the old man replied, "Tell you what? Anytime you want to, you can come by. This is all yours now. I'll be sure to let Mrs. Fleming know and we'll leave the keys right where we've always left them before."

Devin was beyond happy, especially when a ray of sunlight glinted off a glass bottle, making the substance within shimmer and dance at him.

Knowing his aunt would be wanting the honey, he decided to head home and visit another day to check his mom's things out properly.

Thanking Mr. Fleming, they locked up and he loaded his bottles up into the basket. Shaking hands, he left and waved goodbye. His heart light, legs pedaling like the wind, Devin was as happy as he could be after the months of sadness at his mom's death.

He was looking forward to his next visit to Honeysuckle Farm, excited to see the kinds of things his mom was working on. He flew homewards, lost in musings at the unexpected discovery. Before he knew it, he'd entered the foothill road leading back to Foxwood.

* * *

A blaring honking startled him, and Devin clamped onto his brakes as two burly men rose up on the road before him. Nearly crashing into them, he was barely able to avoid his bicycle flipping over, but heard the loud crack as the glass jars jostled against each other.

But he had little time to worry about that. Jaedon Alton appeared and waved a paper at him.

"Got you now, you little rat! Sophie's not here to save you!" The unshaved, leering face of Jaedon Alton broke into a smile that showed his stained and crooked teeth. The burly henchmen grabbed Devin who realized there was no escaping this time.

Jaedon's stink breath hit him like a sack of sand when he came close and said, "witchcraft is a crime, my boy. Yes, it's a crime. And you're going to pay for hurting those kids."

With that he made a gesture and the men got a sack and pulled it down over Devin's head. He heard his bike being loaded up in a vehicle of some kind and he was led and shoved roughly into what he figured was the backseat of Jaedon's truck.

He was jostled and bumped as the truck drove on. He averaged they'd been driving for at least forty-five minutes before slowing down and coming to a stop.

Knowing his aunt would be worried by now, Devin wasn't sure what they intended to do to him. He got a surprise when the sack was pulled off his head, and he was pushed forward to stand in front of the gates of Tumbleweeds – Center for Delinquents.

TUMBLEWEEDS

Devin was at a loss to figure out what would become of him now that he was taken by force and dumped at a center for delinquents. He hadn't realized the level of hatred Jaedon Alton had for him, but now that he did, it wasn't going to be of any help to him.

He tried asking the others about the center, having never heard of it before. But it remained a mystery as no one knew of its existence before arriving at it. He stopped, figuring it was better to stay invisible and not bring undue attention to himself.

Given the barest of accommodations, he counted at least fifty other kids of different ages as house-mates. Angry expressions and resentful attitudes seemed to be the norm with so many locked up, rightly or wrongly so. A by-product of survival, he realized.

After the first few mornings of being everyone else's entertainment, it didn't take them long to figure out he was not to be messed with. They left him alone just as quickly.

After an altercation with one of the older boys from a room across the hallway, who kept calling him odd names, Devin tried being friends. It didn't go over well, especially when the guards thought he was trying to form a rebellion. Taken away from the tiny room he had, he was stuck in an outside shed with even worse conditions.

The kid who'd started it all by jeering and mocking him, wasn't spared either and Devin saw he was also being led to another adjacent dilapidated shed across from his. Victims of unknown reasons by their jailors, Devin knew friendship was the better way to go and soon decided whatever the kid did from that point on, he wouldn't react.

★ ★ ★

Several weeks after his imprisonment, as he called it, there was a commotion outside the assembly room. Everyone had gathered for mid-morning snacks, having been outside since early morning doing the gardening chores. Sweaty and covered in the smell of outside, a collective groan echoed at the delay, everyone having worked up appetites and being short on patience.

But no one was more surprised when the Administrative Staff of the facility walked in with an official from the courthouse, along with sheets of paper, calling for order and silence.

Approaching the head of the room by the window overlooking the garden below, with a burly security guard by his side, Mr. Hank Holden, the Warden of the Center went on to read a lengthy document that was mostly lost on everyone with the legal jargon he was rattling off.

As he was winding down, he announced, "As a result of a motion by the courts, permission is hereby granted that everyone be released into the care of "Benefactor A", who shall forthwith be held in confidence at this time, and all will then be released and into the care of said Benefactor for the next part of their stay in detention."

It took a few moments of confused silence before a ripple of whistles and hoorays started up. He blew his whistle to call for order and with great effort, seemed to hold onto his temper in the presence of the court official as witness. Wishing everyone well, he claimed it was a great privilege to have been a part of their time at the center and how the time spent would help them settle into better futures.

That brought a round of audible cursing from some of the kids that Devin knew were mistreated and he couldn't say he blamed them. He was curious to know who this benefactor was to wield such influence of having everyone released. Somehow, something had triggered the plight of what had been going on at Tumbleweeds. But he wasn't about to argue with their good fortune. The few friends he'd made all came up to him to say goodbye as they were led out, and the rest either waved in farewell or called out about seeing each other on the other side.

The warden himself came to escort Devin to the outside and release him into his aunt's care who gave the man such a blistering tirade of insults for his part in Devin's imprisonment, that Devin feared it would erupt into a volcanic proportion.

Not wanting her to be accused of inciting violence, he quickly said, "Aunt Sophie, it's over. Let's go home."

She stopped mid-sentence and gave him a huge hug. "Thank God you're okay, Dev! Yes, let's go home before I'm arrested for what they did to you."

★ ★ ★

Much later and after hours of sleep, a good meal, and sitting comfortably with a cup of tea in his rocker while gazing at Gramps' garden, Devin sighed with appreciation for the many things he'd taken for granted. He knew there was no avoiding his aunt's grilling about what had happened since he'd gone to get her honey at Mr. Flemings'.

When she finally joined him with her cup of tea, Devin told her what had happened, which she seemed to have suspected as much.

"How did you manage to get me home, aunt?" The court official said it was ordered and permission was granted for all of us kids to be released into the care of some Benefactor."

"That fool Jayden Alton decided to come gloat to me about you finally having to pay for what you did to his son and the kid whose skin burned off. I told him I would get him arrested for lots of old crimes.

He finally confessed where they'd dumped you and I just happened to arrive when you were being led out. I didn't know about any benefactors or anything else. And since the Warden didn't ask who I was, I.. well you saw how it went."

Devin was relieved he'd made it back home safe and sound, but now his curiosity was at an all-time high. He also knew the other kids would know he didn't make it to where they were all supposed to go and sooner or later, someone would say something. He didn't know what to expect since the courts were involved. Did that mean he and his aunt would be in further trouble? He sighed. Things just got a bit more complicated than he had expected.

His aunt, however, didn't seem to care. She was just happy he was back home and that was the end of that.

"So where is Rusty and everyone else?" He finally inquired, unsure if he was hurt or angry that no one seemed to have missed him when he was gone.

"They've disappeared. A High Guardian from an old estate with hundreds of acres, deep in the wilds, offered sanctuary to them after what happened. It's all everyone talked about. The courts granted permission, thankful for having the burden taken off of its hands," his aunt continued. "It worked out well for everybody here. They couldn't wait to get rid of them, since they created such a stink about squatters and thieving gypsies."

Devin felt a surge of suspicion flowing through his mind. "Who's this person, Aunt Sophie?" he asked. It was too coincidental the same thing happened with him and the others at Tumbleweeds.

"Serena Goodwill," is my guess,' his aunt replied.

A sudden bout of laughter overtook him and Devin heard himself muttering "this ought to be rich."

"Yes. That's what I thought myself," his aunt agreed.

But he felt it was for a completely different set of reasons. Adults never seemed to stop surprising him and he wasn't about to try and figure out their weirdness. A part of him was relieved the Gypsies would now have a place to call home, wherever the wild lands were, but the other part of him felt awash in loneliness - he'd never see Rusty and the gang again.

25

THE KEYS TO ETERNITY

A week later, as he was helping Gramps with his seasonal sale, a little group approached them. He wondered if he chased them away what would be their reactions, since he knew they were really coming out of shameless curiosity rather than a true interest in buying anything.

His recent arrest was still a hot topic in the gossip zone. He decided to wait in the shade of a nearby tree, rather than proving them right by how rude he might be and spoiling things for Gramps.

Surprisingly though, Gramps had a brisk sale going. Jars of jam, baskets of eggs and fruits from his orchard went at a steady stream. Many had questions about Gramps' gardening secrets but Devin just smiled, knowing Gramps was never one to talk about his gardening.

Many times, he'd heard him muttering quietly among his plants. Sometimes he'd see stuff like salt scattered at the roots of plants. Once he'd found cracked shells. Another time he found powered crystals in the supplies room, sometimes old tea leaves.

Even if Gramps suspected he'd been nosing around, he never said anything. But it was eerie how he would point out the very thing Devin had seen the next time they did gardening.

After almost an hour, folks trickled out in ones and twos and when the last one had finally departed, Devin set about helping Gramps dismantle the small stand, packing things away.

As he fetched and carried things into the storage shed, a silver streak flashed in the limbs of the huge tree at the front of the yard, distracting him. Gramps looked over curiously.

Starting towards the tree, looking from the gazebo underneath the giant limbs that held a thick canopy of vines covered with tiny flowers, to the tree itself, Devin couldn't place where the silver flash had gone. The effect of the garlands of flower-covered vines swaying gently in the shade distracted him with their stunning beauty.

Of unknown origins, the tree had stood sentinel since before Gramps had moved onto the land, growing in abundance with each passing year.

"You could climb it if you like, you know."

Surprised, he looked around, spotting Gramps. He smiled, knowing the tree had always been off-limits. "How come?"

"I was young once too," replied Gramps. "things have changed, haven't they, Dev? And, I think you might really like it, you know?"

"Are you sure Gramps?"

"Absolutely," nodded Gramps, smiling, eyes twinkling. "I've always wanted to try, but old bones, you know? And you never know-adventures don't call now that I'm old. You'll need to tell me what it's like up there."

Finally, he said, "Thank you Gramps."

Gramps nodded, turning to gaze at the huge tree before heading back indoors, calling over his shoulders, "Let me know how it goes, okay?"

Excitement coursed through Devin. He slowly approached the tree. Hands suddenly shaking, he gazed at the massive trunk. It brought the memory of Ole Higue's tree to mind. Serena's words, "I think the crystal exists in each of us. A doorway if you will," floated into his thoughts. She'd also said the crystal had been sourced from another realm, in liquid form.

The sudden intrusion of the future sent a sliver of anxiousness coursing through him. Restoring Ohhm to its former glory, especially when he hadn't a clue where to start, had him gasping, with dizziness assailing him. Clutching the trunk, Devin sat down, leaning his head back.

A white butterfly landed next to him, settling on a bluebell swaying cheekily in the breeze. Closing his eyes for the feeling to pass, he waited. Zoie's reading surfaced.

Opening his eyes at the sudden rush of thoughts, a feather floated lazily by drawing his gaze away from the butterfly. It landed at his feet. Another blast of dizziness hit him. Eyes scrunched together, images of a gigantic tree - luminescent white, loomed before him. Rising majestically with giant branches extending in thick abundance, a shaded alcove sat underneath, layered thickly with pristine white leaves that beckoned invitingly.

Like a giant magnet, it drew him forward and he moved, unaware of walking. Closer now, he gazed in wonder at the millions of white, shimmering leaves dancing before his eyes. Thousands of white pods hung lusciously like bunches of grapes.

He had never seen such fruits. Stepping closer to examine them, a small pod exploded, shooting sparks at him. He jumped.

He reached out, trying again, touching a pod from the bunch next to his nose. It glowed, a needle of warmth shooting up his finger. Jerking his finger away, he watched the glow dim.

Devin tried it several times, unable to figure out its meaning before looking around curiously. Where he stood at the tree was the center, seven spectacular pathways leading off into unknown vistas. Each avenue was lined with uniquely massive trees. A faint humming sound filtered in. Unable to place its source, Devin wondered if he should dare to venture forth.

A pod exploded nearby, splattering him with a milky, white juice. A tingling sensation crept along his fingers and he watched in amazement the bruises and scratches he'd gotten from gathering firewood healed themselves.

Rudely he came to his senses, looking stupidly around for a moment, blinking in confusion. The butterfly was long gone and the shadows had lengthened. Disappointment flooded him, knowing it was too late to try to climb now. The crick in his neck as he straightened had him wincing. He had fallen asleep!

Stooping to pick up the feather, Devin froze, hand in mid-air. Staring at his outstretched hand, the scratches and bruises were gone. His mind raced. It was a dream, that's all. Turning his hand this way, and then that way, seeing it smooth and blemish free, he felt a tremor go through him. Thoughts zoomed in and out of his mind, each discarded for another, before going blank.

★ ★ ★

How he got to the dinner table, Devin couldn't say. Neither could he remember what he ate. He left before Lexi could rope him into some chore and wandered into his mom's room.

Sitting down on the comfortable sofa, silent for a while, he slowly brought his hand forward, gazing at it, unable to believe what he was seeing. Leaning back, he looked around at his mom's room. He would never have come to her if this had happened when she was alive. Now, he needed to show her his hand. He wanted to hear what she would have come up with. He knew now she had strange gifts. It especially frustrated him that she wasn't around to talk to.

His gaze fell on a book on her desk. He crossed over, picking it up. The title said, "The Keys to Eternity" by Ashaun Gibbs. Flipping through it, excitement flared. Intrigued, he sat reading about symbols and colors. Turning the pages, information about elements and dimensions and vibrations unfolded.

Engrossed in the book, he heard a muffled "ouch" sound outside the door. Stuffing the book under the cushion next to him, Devin scrambled for an old newspaper clipping sitting on a pile at his feet. A second later, Lexi appeared at the door.

"Oh. Hey, Dev. What are you doing here? I didn't know you were home."

"I was looking to see if mom had notes on how to care for her lilies."

"Oh, we're going to get…, what?"

Devin had to keep his jaws locked from laughing.

Her eyes darted around the room, settling on him suspiciously, before she said, "Gramps'll know. Why don't you ask him?"

"Mom has loads of notebooks in here. Gramps' grumpy."

"Suit yourself. I came to get a scarf. Aunt Sophie said it might get cool."

"You're going out?" he said, relieved.

"Just to Red Hawk Court. Aunt Sophie's teaching me how to make fish stew," she finished with a flourish.

"Cool," said Devin, "you're making dinner," wondering if he should mention how folks had been down at the Fish Market.

"It is going to be edible, you know," she injected loudly.

"I didn't ....," began Devin but she had brushed rudely by him, scarf in hand, calling "I'll make you a special Fish Gut Pie," before disappearing out the door.

"Ugh."

After she had slammed out, he settled down, knowing he'd be alone for a while. But something seemed different. Devin tried finding the page he'd left off at, only to find maps and charts and images of the most beautiful lights in motion, swaying and twisting, bending and rising.

Flipping back to see the title, he read, "Keys to Eternity," by Ashaun Gibbs. Checking to see if he'd gone ahead to a different chapter, he found the contents had changed. The chapter he'd just read continued on. He thumbed ahead. The chapter now went past page nine.

He found information on herbs and plants and read about the properties of water. Absently the thought inserted itself "Books don't write themselves." The way the chapter continued on from where he'd read before was bizarre.

Almost an hour later, engrossed in "Impact of Energy Cords," a topic beyond his understanding, Devin examined his hand. A tiny thread of fear mingled with awe crept through him. He closed the book, huddling down.

Serena and Chad had said knowledge would be revealed soon. Could this be a clue? His hand healing on its own was weird. He couldn't figure out what it meant.

He turned, the book falling off his lap. He started at the thump as it hit the floor and he realized he must have been dozing. Turning on the small lamp beside him, a thought occurred.

"What if? Nah, it couldn't be...well, what if?" He picked it up and it opened on "Trees of the World."

Devin never knew so many different types of trees existed. Almost ready to give up, he turned the page half-heartedly and gazed at the heading:

"Mystic Trees and Their Properties"

"Legend has it that the Isle of Aurora is rumored to have the elusive Angels' Balm. It is said to contain life-giving properties, when mixed with liquid moonlight.

The Great Gylfi, known as the fiercest and wildest albino griffin of ancient times, is believed to be the Guardian of this sacred tree which many have sought throughout the ages. Revered as a divine creature, and friend to the pure in heart, it is known to appear in times of need.

Little is really known of this mystical realm and its inhabitants. It has never been mapped and its existence has never been proven. The question is – does it really exist?"

Devin sat for a long time, his mind wrapped around his dream and the unique healing. He wondered if he had dreamt the elusive Angels' Balm.

No descriptions of the tree were in the book. The image of what he'd gotten was the closest thing to another realm he'd ever seen. It still didn't give him an answer to how his hand was healed. And what was he supposed to do if he was ever able to get the Angel's Balm?

The Brotherhood came to mind. He remembered the article from The Village Beat mentioning someone had verified the crystal being from Ohhm. Maybe they might be able to help him un-muddle things.

Getting up, he rummaged through the basket of old newspapers Lexi collected. This was one time he was glad of her hoarding of things. A minute later, he wasn't so sure when he came upon advertisements of creams and cosmetics.

After turning several more pages, he paused on seeing that the Logan Estate was having a sale as old Mr. Tibbles, even more ancient than Gramps or Celeste, had died.

Devin was surprised as he hadn't heard anything of a funeral, seeing Mr. Tibbles had died the day after his own mom had passed. An odd emptiness entered him. Mr. Tibbles, he remembered from when he and his mom had visited him as tiny and wizened, with long, white beard and sparkling eyes, always full of joy.

The mansion had many nooks and crannies with a great kitchen and the biggest fireplace he'd ever seen. Not that anyone ever used fireplaces in Foxwood, but it gave the home a sense of grandeur and Devin remembered the pleasure his mom took in visiting. He himself had spent many happy moments at the Logan Estate.

A conversation Mr. Tibbles and his mom had floated to mind.

"You think he will ever understand," the spritely voice of Mr. Tibbles had brought a tortured look to his mom's face.

"I pray he does. I don't know how much longer I can go on. He's still so little…just a child," she had continued.

Mr. Tibbles had nodded comfortingly. "Yes, yes. But you should teach him just a little." He'd gestured for Devin to sit with him on the old bench. Then looking at Devin, he'd said, "Your mom has some things she needs to tell you. It might sound strange or funny. Or like a story out of a book, but you must learn, won't you?"

Devin had nodded.

"Go on then, you can go to the swing," patting Devin on the back, he'd shooed him off. Devin had sped away, completely forgetting everything. Now he wondered, "Was mom talking about all this stuff? And Mr. Tibbles…had he known?"

He remembered Liam, the great-grandson who'd played with him whenever he visited and figured he needed to visit the estate soon. Continuing his search, he focused on finding what he needed.

Some items had been highlighted, circled, and crossed out. Obviously, Lexi hadn't bought any of the fripperies. After going through more copies of The Village Beat, he eventually found what he was looking for.

A flutter of trepidation went through him. He'd purposely avoided reading further along in The Village Beat about the return of the Crystal, as it also had his mom's death announcement. A part of him still wished he had been recognized for finding the Crystal, but he ignored it. "Get your priorities right, Devin," he muttered to himself.

Skimming through the article, he found the announcement and turned to Page 14.

"We have been able to authenticate that the crystal which was recovered recently did indeed once belong to the Kingdom of Ohhm.

We want to recognize and thank the people of the land – the tribe of Gypsies living at the outskirts of Foxwood, for their help in such a wonderful find in recent history.

Notable in this matter is Rusty Keeps, who's been attending Beachside Academy. While out collecting firewood, he discovered the crystal in a cave."

Devin skipped ahead until he came to another similar article.

He put aside the newspaper and debated how to proceed. After deciding what to do, he got up and moved over to the desk. Writing a quick note, he addressed it to:

The Honorable Dr. Piffany,
Brotherhood of the Realm
#5 Village Walk
Mystic Village, The Realm

With Lexi and Aunt Sophia gone to the fish market, he headed to the small post office. Dropping his letter off, he collected a bundle of mail awaiting delivery as their mailman was out sick for a week, and conveyed thanks to the withered, old postmaster.

He skipped over a pile of cow manure, his thoughts repeatedly turning to the mysterious Brotherhood. Had Chad not told them of the Brotherhood himself, he would have thought their existence an old wives' tale like everything else in the villages. If he got a response from his letter, he was willing to think they might just be okay to help him. Chad had said they followed the old ways, whatever that was. The only thing old was Ohhm. Devin knew he needed to find a way to learn what that world was about.

Hopping out of the way to see Slink ride past, he suddenly remembered The Renegade. The last couple of times he visited, Mr. Heeb was jovial, saying, "Hey Devin, how you doing?"

"Good Mr. Heeb. How're you?"

"The Missus and I are doing well, thank you. And business is good. If you're looking for your friend, he's still away."

After the third time of the same, Devin ceased, wondering what had happened.

"Hey, Dev."

He turned, spotting Zubida, his classmate for the last several years at Beachside Academy.

"Oh, hey."

"How've you been? I'm sorry 'bout your mom," she continued in her breezy manner.

"Ah… yeah. Thank you. I've been okay."

"I heard that your aunt turned up and she's taking care of you guys now."

Devin nodded.

"Zubida!" A call came from her home. "Zubida!"

"Coming, mom," she hollered back, waving at Devin before disappearing through the gate.

He felt awful. People had been snubbing him a lot, and now that Zubida's mom kept her from talking to him, Devin was pretty miserable.

School had reopened with him still at home. When his aunt had written asking for details and an explanation, the school had replied with a firm:

"We regretfully, are unable to accept Devin Reelms now or anytime in the foreseeable future as a student and reject your request that he attend our school. He has a record with violent behavior and has been found guilty of practicing witchcraft. These are not qualities and behavior that are allowed or accepted at our school."

Bitterness filled him and Devin had left the room. On finding himself in his mom's garden, he'd settled down among the blooms and slept under the stars that night. At dawn, he was up doing yard work, no closer to a solution to what to do with life.

When he finally decided to go indoors, he remembered the bundle of mail and found it, thankfully dry, under the flower bush he'd fallen asleep next to.

INVITATION

The day went by with him doing chores and it was much later that Devin heard his aunt calling him for dinner and asking him to wash up. He was ready within minutes and headed in. Dropping the bundle of letters on the table, he stopped.

"Dad! You're home. When did you get back?"

Hugo looked up wearily at Devin. "I got in a while ago. I leave again in the morning."

"The morning!" exclaimed Lexi, coming up behind Devin with a huge platter of rice and beans, and their aunt directly behind with a huge bowl of roasted chicken.

"Devin, go get the salad please," she said.

He returned, salad bowl in hand and after setting it down, he took his seat. Seeing his father back, weary and even smiling, Devin thought it was the most humane he had seen him in a long while.

"Sophia, I have to say, I didn't expect any of this. It's really good of you to take care of the kids."

"Don't mention it, Hugo," she interrupted. "You can't be everywhere at once. And I'm really enjoying the kids."

"Hey, where's my Fish Gut pie, Lex? Devin turned to Lexi.

"You louse!" Lexi shot back at him. "And you said...."

"Cooking, snipping, growing," their aunt laughingly inserted. "Hugo, I swear these kids will keep me young to the end of my days. You can see it's no trouble for me."

"You're kind to us, Sophia. I know how ugly I was to be around. I'm sorry. I., what I mean is, thank you for all you've done."

Devin took helpings of the dishes, focusing on his plate.

"Hey dad, you got home just in time. Devin got the mail," Lexi chirped, passing the bundle over to him.

His expression brightened, taking the opportunity to compose himself.

"And who're you expecting to be writing to you?" He asked, loosening the string on the bundle of mail.

"Depends on whom she's impressed," Devin couldn't resist.

Lexi glowered at him, tossing her head. "At least some are impressed," she wiggled her eyebrows at him.

"Kids," their aunt interrupted.

Their dad waved at them, going through the mail. Devin kept a keen eye on the pile of envelopes. He'd been too distracted by Zubida to pay attention to the mail before. Now he spotted a very elegant envelope and was curious to know who could be writing to them. Local folks couldn't afford such luxury.

Lexi and his aunt dawdled over dinner, their dad quite comfortable. Devin couldn't rush him. After another five minutes of anxious glances and anticipation mounting, his dad finally had the heavy envelope in hand.

"What's this?"

Lexi paused her chattering, her interest perking up. Aunt Sophia glanced over at Hugo, eyes darting back to the expensive envelope as he opened the envelope and unfolded heavy sheets of expensive papers.

A series of expressions crossed his face as he flipped through the sheets. When he was finished going through them twice, he carefully put them down, pushed his plate away, and leaned back in his chair.

"What's all that about, dad?" Devin ventured tentatively.

He passed the envelope over with the sheets of paper and sat back, his expression thoughtful.

Devin took them and read:

To: Mr. Devin Reelms
Gate #5, Blessings Lane
Foxwood Village, The Hills of Veil

Angels' Academy
#7 New Age Road
Realm Point Crossing, The Hills of Veil

Dear Devin:

In view of the recent happenings, we are pleased to inform you that you have been accepted at Angels' Academy.

Our curriculum, though somewhat unusual, nevertheless, offers a varied, fun-filled and unique approach in paving the way for tomorrow's youth.

Classes are scheduled to start on arrival. Enclosed, you'll find a list of school supplies and directions to our school. Let us know your decision, should you decide otherwise, so we may give this opportunity to another worthy angel.

With kind regards,

Serena Goodwill,

High Guardian and Chief Council

Devin read the letter a second time, moving on to the most unusual list of school supplies he'd ever seen.

"What is it, Dev?" Lexi's voice sounded urgent. He passed the letter to her, still staring at the list.

Supplies List
Angels Academy - Exclusively at Celestial Village

- Ruler, Pencils, Compass
- Notebooks and Paper
- 1 Pouch - Assorted Crystals
- 1 Pouch - Assorted Metals
- 1 Carton Herbs (Assorted Canisters)
- 1 Pouch of Essential Vitamins

Books

Creatures - Mystical, Mythical & Magical – By Rowena Hills

The Life of Plants, As Told by Plants – By Reynold Hawkins

Hidden Energy – By Robby Ley

Introduction to Water – by Roxi Boone

Strange Customs for Everyday Living – By Ravindra Singh

Charting the Stars, A Beginner's Guide – By Oswald Fawdry

His mind raced to the "High Guardian" part. He'd suspected right about Serena being the benefactor who'd gotten him and the other kids at Thumbleweeds released. He looked up in time to see several expressions flitting across Lexi's face as she finished reading, and passed it to their aunt. He glanced at his dad, seeing him staring off into the distance.

"Well," Lexi's voice finally cut into his thoughts, "is there a letter for me?"

Coming out of his reverie, their dad looked through the pile. Devin cringed inwardly. The envelope had given him a clue, but nothing had prepared him for this.

"I don't see one," said their dad. "Might come in the next batch. Give your aunt the letter, Lex. Let's hear what she thinks."

Lexi got up with a casual air of finishing dinner and left, taking her plate. Devin wasn't fooled. He needed to stay out of her way.

"Devin, why don't you help put the things in the sink? I have to talk to your dad about this now since he's leaving again in the morning."

Devin didn't need telling twice. Gathering empty plates and dishes, he scooted by, placed them in the sink and fled to his room.

Life was going to be rough if Lexi didn't get an invitation. But he couldn't help the happy jitters filling him. He'd been dreading having to constantly see Frey and his gang every day at school. He hoped with all his heart their dad said yes to the offer to the new school. But try as he did, he didn't get any more ideas on what to expect, and surprisingly, he fell asleep into a dreamless slumber.

Morning dawned quickly. His dad was short in his goodbye, saying, "I told your aunt to do what she thinks best. She told me what's been going on.

"Oh, yes. There's been…" Devin reply was cut off when he heard,

"I'm disappointed. I think this…this alternative school," his dad said, "might be the answer."

Devin was careful to keep his expression blank, feeling his heart shriveling.

"I already said goodbye to Lexi and your aunt."

"Sure dad," Devin said, seeing a strange look in his dad's eyes. "Have a safe journey."

His dad left, ignoring him and Devin felt betrayed. If Aunt Sophia explained everything, his dad had to know people were being nasty. He'd wrongfully been taken to Tumbleweeds for defending Lexi's honor and for his family helping the Gypsies and his own skin. What didn't his dad get?

He closed the door and went back to his room, wishing someone was around to talk to. He still had no idea where Rennie had disappeared to, and since no one was telling him, Devin felt he needed to do his own thing. With that thought firmly etched in his mind, he examined his options until a startling thought hit him. Until his aunt decided when he would be heading off to Angel's Academy, Devin knew it was now or never.

27

A DESPERATE JOURNEY

Devin knew Aunt Sophia's charts and maps were too valuable. He hadn't brought any along, memorizing them as best he could. Something was guiding him on. His aunt's description of her cottage wasn't hard to find but it was quite a distance into the hills and it was rough terrain.

Grasping the wrapped object under his shirt with fierce protection, Devin was careful to stay hidden along the way, constantly watching his back and peering ahead for signs of anyone or anything threatening. He had started out early, knowing sunlight would be a much-needed protection. At least from the Shadows.

Now as he stepped through the tunnel made by bushes his aunt had so lovingly cared for, he watched the fat trunk of yet another tree his uncle had marked. It was a wonder no one had found it before, Devin mused.

His Uncle Xavier had written that the horn Devin had was from a Unicorn he'd saved. Having stumbled upon the Dark Worshippers at their moment of sacrifice, he had spoiled their offering. In return, the Unicorn had gifted the savagely sawed-off horn to him. He had written, if the horn were ever seized by force, the result would be a severe curse. Since it was a gift directly from the unicorn to his uncle – it needed to be protected at all costs.

The little he'd read, Devin hadn't really believed unicorns existed, thinking someone had just written stories for kids. But a lot had happened since his experience with the crystal. He didn't think things were so strange anymore.

He wondered if the Shadows' eventual brutal act of torture to his uncle was because he had interrupted their sacrifice, gained a powerful object, or because of his knowledge as the chief Timekeeper. Maybe his uncle had deliberately spoiled their timing. Another person in his family to have sacrificed their life, Devin reflected. He wondered how many more would have to die for him to succeed in his destiny.

He'd never ventured this far into the hills but had made good time – it was almost noon. Catching his breath, he gazed at the valleys below. Lush streams, steep hills, thick vegetation, and a feeling of being on top of the world made it hard for him to understand that evil-worshippers thrived within range.

If he found the circle of mosaic stones, he might be able to see what Uncle Xavier meant. He'd gotten an idea that had brought him to the Navigational Clock, and if he was lucky, he might be able to test it.

Fifteen minutes later he stopped, staring in awe. He'd reached the ruins! Built on a huge circle of land at the top of Lookout Hill, his uncle had used the ground as the base. He'd said the Navigational Clock was a tool of the heavens to receive messages of Time unfolding. A giant sundial lay in disgrace before him.

As Devin approached, he saw the damage was extensive. Destroyed in rage by the Dark Worshippers, many of the markers had been shattered. He counted twelve pillars. Each had a different astrological symbol carved on it. What hadn't been dislodged or damaged had been set on fire. Everywhere showed proof of great loss. The little remaining symbols and inscriptions were useless to him.

According to his uncle's notes, he had been able to tell the seasons, the time of day, when to plant crops, the moon cycles, charting of the stars and many other things.

Unmindful to everything else, Devin strode forward determinedly and started pulling heavy weeds. They came free and he found signs depicting the heavens made directly on the base. Searching meticulously, he came upon the center mosaic base, and peeping out of heavy weeds, the gnomon sat conspicuously absent.

Excitement surged through him. Taking deep, calming breaths, and with trembling hands, Devin took out his precious package, unwrapped it, examining the horn carefully. Leaning forward, he inserted it in the gnomon's place and watched anxiously as it sat silent.

Minutes passed as he looked around, unsure of what to expect. Disappointment grew and Devin sighed - he had tried. Reaching over to retrieve it, hand on horn, Devin heard a faint musical note. He paused, glancing around. A soft vibration started under his feet and the rocks glinted. The pieces of mosaic rocks started melting, swirling together. Before he could react, a vortex opened up and he felt himself carried forward swiftly.

Catching glimpses of the scenery in a blur, the clear tube of space forged its way on. Devin flew forth for a short while, before feeling a change in the air. A second later, he slid forward onto a thick layer of grass, grasping the horn tightly.

Examining his surroundings curiously, an insect flew by and he swatted at it. He didn't recognize anything. Everywhere he looked was covered in lush foliage. Tucking the horn into his waistband, he covered it with his shirt and set off.

Spotting a pathway, he followed, finding himself walking parallel to a small harbor. Suddenly he stopped, staring at a gigantic white butterfly boat, with huge wings curving upwards on each side, rising to meet the transparent sails billowing gently in the breeze sat before him. Sitting in splendor, the gossamer-like quality of the boat beckoned in invitation. Devin watched, enchanted as the water sparkled and shimmered in reflection.

A thick rope of vines hung over the side, covered in huge Morning Glories. Carefully watching for signs of life, a thread of nervousness kept him still. Someone had to be around. Such a splendid boat had to have an owner. He couldn't afford to make any mistakes. Too much depended on him. The horn had worked. What he didn't know was where he'd arrived.

After waiting for a while, he saw no signs of movement and sprinted forward, making a lunge at the huge vine. Climbing up wasn't difficult and in seconds he was aboard. It took him a minute to get accustomed to the gentle sway.

The inside, like the outside, glistened softly, leaving a dusting of sheen on his hand. Rising at the bow, the butterfly's antenna stood before him like the hands of a compass. It was the coziest thing he had ever seen. Overall, the boat was sturdier than it looked.

He felt a rush of unsteadiness and grabbed the tendon-like rope, anchoring the sails. Pulling himself to the railing, he saw the vine had been dislodged and the boat was no longer moored. Devin felt another vibration under his feet and watched as the sails billowed out, picking up speed.

Going back to the antennas, he took hold of them, pulling and twisting. He soon got the hang of it, steering with ease. The boat responded to his touch, leaving little wake.

Approaching open water, they clipped briskly forward. Water splashed over the side, gliding off as it did on the feathers of the ducks he had back home.

"Mom knew the cost. Mom had faith in me." Thinking along these lines, Devin felt a moment's guilt about leaving without anyone's permission or knowledge. Chad and Serena had left specific instructions with Gramps and Aunt Sophie.

But he was going nuts. The gypsies had moved far away, Rennie had disappeared, and he was rejected from school.

He'd been in his mom's room when he overheard his aunt talking to Lexi.

"You know, Lex, if things are going to be revealed to Devin, I'm really worried."

"Good stuff, right?" Lexi sounded scared, and Devin, listening, prayed his aunt would stop talking.

"I was hoping I would never have to talk about this. But now things are so different from when I arrived." A short silence followed before she started again, "Your uncle was tortured to death. I don't know how I managed to live through it. Now I understand things a little better, especially after that night."

"You mean when they visited?" Lexi said.

"Yes," replied Aunt Sophia. "I keep seeing your uncle's body in front of me. And now Devin's in the middle of things he shouldn't be."

"He never tells me anything." Lexi said, sounding angry.

Devin couldn't help feeling guilty. But he'd given his word and no matter the cost, he wasn't going to break a promise.

"Don't hold it against him," he heard Aunt Sophie saying, "after all, he doesn't know enough himself."

"He knows enough." Lexi replied stubbornly.

"Lexi, you have to understand. It's a lot for anybody to have to handle. I don't know what I would do if some strange people showed up with bizarre stories and told me I am supposed to save mankind. Come on, you have to see Devin doesn't even know what's involved. That's why Serena and Chad are here. They don't even have all the answers."

"Hmmm…" Devin heard as he sat still, listening. And he wasn't disappointed when he heard Lexi's voice.

"So, when Devin starts knowing things and he can't tell anyone, how are we supposed to tell them he had an epiphany?"

Devin grinned. Lexi had to have the last word.

"Well, I guess I hadn't quite thought of that. I'll have to talk to Devin."

"Um hm, that's what I thought" replied Lexi, "good luck aunt. Just so you know, you'll need a really good reason for Devin to tell you anything." Her doubtful, sarcastic tone had Devin bristling.

"You know Lex, I told you so you would understand why I'm so worried. Stuff's really serious and I don't think I like your tone."

"I can't help it. Devin got us in this mess. He should have just left this well alone."

Devin felt his insides squeeze on hearing Lexi's blunt words.

Apparently, so did his aunt when he heard her astonished, "My goodness, Lexi. You almost sound like you hate Devin. What's going on?"

"I feel he had something to do with mom's death. I don't know why, but I just do."

Devin felt his shock first turn to anger and then guilt. Now he had to add Lexi to the long list of people he'd somehow managed to offend for simply being a curious kid and landing in a heap of trouble.

When heard the sound of her crying and listening, his sense of guilt only intensified.

As ever, his aunt was the voice of reason when she replied slowly, "Well, Lexi, I hadn't expected that. But why do you think Devin had something to do with your mom's death?"

Devin flinched, but listened.

"I just know it. The day mom was dying, he did something. I saw how he held her. I know he knows more. And what about what happened to Rusty and him in that cave? No one would tell me anything. Not even Gramps. Every time I ask, he says we only have now and to focus on the present. What's done is done."

"Well, that's true. We can't and shouldn't try to undo anything. There are some things we are better off not knowing. Did you ask Devin if he made your mom die?"

"Well, no… not really. I just.. well, I mean.."

"That's my point," replied Aunt Sophie. "Nobody's going to benefit if you walk around angry. You need to tell Devin how you feel and ask him straight up what he did."

"Then he'll hate me."

"He might. I still think you should ask, rather than blame him for something he had no control over."

Devin felt tears burning his eyes. He'd have to remember to thank Aunt Sophia.

"He'll still hate me," Lexi insisted, her tone petulant. Devin heard Lexi give a huge sigh, sounding like she was ready to launch into another of her complaints.

"Look Lex, I can't speak for Devin but listening to you I wonder if it's a sign."

Devin heard movement and, "Pass me those towels. I can fold while you pack."

"A sign?" Lexi sounded perky now.

"Well, Chad did say they're only as strong as Devin. He told us to let them know if anything unusual happens."

"How's that supposed to be a sign?" Even Devin was curious.

"Lexi, I lived many years with your uncle and learnt a lot of things. One of the first signs is when people close to each other start behaving weirdly. Hating each other, if you know what I mean."

"You think that's what I'm feeling?" Lexi was a bit louder now.

"Well, aren't you?" countered their aunt.

When the silence continued for a while, their aunt said laughingly, ""Um hm, that's what I thought."

Lexi giggled. Devin heard their aunt chuckle and smiled.

But it had given him something to think about, unlike Lexi. Their Aunt must have had the same thought – wondering if they would be visited by Shadows. He hadn't seen any signs of them so far. He would have felt them. And Chad had said the shadows couldn't exist in sunlight.

He knew he'd have to talk to Lexi whenever she came with her questions. It was better she knew. It would be awful if she got lured into something bad.

Only a few people knew of his connection with the crystal, Ole Higue and the gypsies. Somebody would have to deliberately betray them, if it came to that. And Devin knew he didn't know enough of what lay ahead. No one did. Lexi was his sister and he needed as many friends as he could have. But it was stifling to be under watch all the time. He needed to do something.

Shaking his head, Devin took comfort by telling himself, "At least I'm not just sitting around." He was supposed to be leading them forward. He wasn't sure where, "And now is as good a time as any," he continued, especially when the anxious feeling only eased when he had set out, following the feeling nagging at him.

A huge island loomed ahead and his doubts eased on spotting the first marker – an island shaped in the form of a butterfly. He'd read that the people of Ohhm believed souls rested at Butterfly Island, before moving on to The Lighted Cove – the place where souls later ascended to meet their source.

A musical "whoosh" vibrated loudly. He jumped, pulling violently in reflex. The tone resonated long after it had issued forth, echoing into the distance.

Righting his course, Devin looked around and stared as one of the sails above him sat in the shape resembling a large morning glory, acting like a horn.

"Okay. So much for being undetected," he muttered, his heart rate slowing back to normal. Wondering what it meant, Devin looked around anxiously. He didn't need any monsters and shadows or any kind of delay now. Praying the portal stayed open for his return, he watched carefully for signs of company.

He felt a sudden rush of air and a second later, huge butterflies rose up like a giant cloud over the island they were gliding past. Within moments he was surrounded as they formed a thick canopy, dancing with shimmering beauty around him. Fluttering in and around in all shapes and sizes of whites, he watched in amazement.

Pinks and blue and colors he'd never seen before, they hovered, covering his boat. Landing on him, settling everywhere, he blinked and stared as they kept him company.

Devin tried focusing on what he'd read on the chart and notes. The timeline so far was good. He didn't want to jinx himself. The butterflies were still with him, their presence comforting in the unaccustomed silence the further along they sailed.

A while later, a prism-like gleam appeared ahead of them. The shifting rainbow lights swirled in waves and arches, creating a hypnotic dance in the sky above them. As they approached the lights, he felt movement and scrambled to hang on to the antennas, feeling a pulling suction. He watched as the sails fluttered down, forming layers of wings. The boat became airborne, its curved wings working effortlessly upwards.

The blanket of butterflies flew forward, steering the wind current. Hanging onto the neck, the antenna moved in a swishing motion and before long they had slowed and Devin slid onto solid ground.

Standing ungainly for a moment, his legs wobbly after the long journey, the huge butterfly sat silently before him. Doing the only thing that came to mind, Devin sank in a deep bow and said with heartfelt gratitude, "Thank You Butterfly."

In reply, the butterfly fanned its huge wings, rose gracefully and did what looked like a downward flap of its wings like a return bow. A second later, the others flew back, settling on it, and as one they rose, before disappearing through the lights.

His legs feeling boneless, Devin sat down abruptly. The knowledge that he was totally on his own in a strange place finally sunk in as he gazed at the extraordinary landscape before him.

Knowing his only choice was to keep going, he gathered himself and started forward. Not a soul stirred. Keeping his eyes focused on the path ahead, Devin labored as the land gave way to a steep incline, the scenery becoming increasingly more beautiful.

The cool air had a softness to it that had him taking deep breaths. He immediately felt a difference in his energy and picked up the pace.

After about an hour of climbing, he found a small sign with several arrows pointing in different directions. One said "Generational Garden," with the arrow pointing straight ahead. The other said "The Hall," with the arrow pointing left and the third one said "Aurora Pools," with the arrow pointing right. Intrigued, Devin looked around. What did he do now? Closing his eyes, he let his mind settle and felt a faint movement by his shoulders. Opening his eyes, he saw a butterfly fluttering ahead of him, flying in the direction of the Generational Garden.

He figured it was as good an answer as he would get and started forward. The gentle breeze had settled down and the further along he walked, the landscape changed and the path opened up ahead, lined with the most magnificent trees he had ever seen.

He walked on and could have sworn he heard faint whispers and giggles and a few times little dots of silvery lights appeared on many of the limbs he passed.

Devin continued admiring the scenery, his mind quietly absorbing the beauty around. He passed a small log with a beautiful harp sitting on it. Too tempting to pass up, Devin debated for a moment, and before he could change his mind, he reached out and picked it up. It felt delicate and alive. He strummed a string.

Rather than a sweet note, Devin heard the imagined whispers, giggles and invisible movements in the many trees go completely still. The quiet in his brain was uncomfortable and thinking the harp wasn't working, he set out to replace it, but halted when he heard delayed musical notes echo in the distance.

Startled, his grip tightened on the harp as the notes rose in waves. It was unlike anything he'd ever heard. The cascading notes rushed like a tidal wave around him. The air vibrated and he felt unable to focus on anything else as a hazy rainbow of colors swirled by. It suddenly stopped and brought Devin out of the strange spell.

About to replace the harp, Devin stared in shock at a huge set of white paws resting before him. He lifted his gaze from the paws and slowly raised his eyes up, his mind busy trying to figure out what kind of creature sat before him.

He realized the harp had alerted it. He couldn't avoid it now. Inwardly shaking, he raised his head and saw sitting before him the most beautiful creature he had ever seen. His breath caught after realizing it was an albino griffin.

Instinctively, he bowed as a pair of purple eyes watched him.

A sensation washed over him and he was aware of acceptance. Straightening, Devin saw a tendril of white mist swirling from himself and curled to merge with the rainbow energies of the griffin.

Only then did he hear a very deep voice say, "Welcome, Son of Rae."

"You know me?"

"As I have throughout the millennia."

"How?"

"Some links are forever. Others, for a short time. Ours span thousands of years."

Devin digested this bit, wondering how he was linked to it. "My name is Devin Reelms. I am in need of help."

"Devin Realms."

"No, not Realms, Reelms," He corrected. I'm told that I am to restore the Kingdom of Ohhm."

The air vibrated as if it laughed at him, even though it continued staring at him.

"It is known to us," the griffin finally said.

"Us?" Devin repeated, looking around.

"Us," repeated the griffin.

"Let me introduce myself. I am Gylfi, Guardian of The Generational Garden."

"The Gylfi I read about!"

"I didn't know you had knowledge of my world."

"I didn't. I mean…," amended Devin quickly, "I read an article in a book."

"What kind of book is this?"

"A book I found in my mom's room."

"And what is this book called?" Gylfi's stare was piercing, making Devin doubt its status as a friend.

"The Keys to Eternity, By Ashaun Gibbs."

"Ah."

That didn't sound encouraging.

Eventually the griffin said "Only Souls have come here. Your presence tells me of things I may not speak of. Grave things."

"I didn't know I would end up here. Where is this place anyway?"

Here is where all the Generational Trees are. Souls of families over thousands of years, Lineages return to their sanctuary."

He hadn't imagined the giggles and whispers after all!

As if reading his thoughts, Gylfi pointed to a luminous orb that had floated in. They watched as it hovered for a second before settling high up in the branch of a majestic tree. He watched Gylfi give a slight nod of its beak in acknowledgement.

He told whatever came to mind.

"Come, let us walk so you see this place you've come to."

Gylfi led the way with Devin asking, and it answering his endless questions and Devin felt the worries falling away from him.

The path was velvety soft, covered in white sand, fragrant grass growing on either side, stretching as far as the eyes could see. He picked up a handful of sand and felt the sensation of liquid silk pouring through his fingers and felt an unexpected warmth filling him at the sudden contact. He took his shoes off and wiggled his toes in it, thinking of the beach back home.

Soon they approached an intersection that connected with a circular trail and he watched as Gylfi raised its head up high, releasing a loud, long musical note that echoed everywhere and eventually faded into nothingness.

Devin saw many avenues of giant trees, wondering at the stories they held. He felt he was walking through time and wondered about things he'd never thought of before. It was strange and familiar at the same time and found himself confessing, "I unknowingly set a prophecy in motion and released Ole Higue when I returned a crystal to her. And I caused my mother's death." The last came out in a whisper, his voice cracking.

Wondering what made him tell Gylfi so many things he was never to talk about, Devin closed his mouth.

"Such are the ways for some," Gylfi said and Devin felt something blossom deep in his chest. He didn't know what it meant but suddenly, Gylfi dipped into a deep bow to him. Devin froze!

As the moments passed, Gylfi rose and his brain started functioning in slow motion.

"Come with me, Devin Reelms. Tell me what you're looking for to have come here."

"I was looking for answers that no one has. I'm told I'm the one to restore the fallen kingdom of Ohhm. Maybe I can find something to destroy the Shadows."

"Yes, the Shadows," The griffin padded softly beside. "You're highly gifted to be able to visit this Island of Souls and the Generational Garden. There must be a reason for this. Think, Devin."

"Is it possible I can see my mom here?"

Gylfi paused, then in a gentle tone said, "Do not lose your focus, Devin Reelms. Your mother has her duty. She gave up herself for many reasons. Do not try to distract her. You will only cause more heartache and problems."

"I just wondered if…"

"It's only natural. But you have to do your duty also."

Gylfi turned, opened its wings and engulfed him in a hug.

Devin felt a strange sensation seeping through him, the pain of losing his mom fading to peace.

"Yes?" Gylfi's voice prodded his mind.

"Yes," he repeated. It stepped back and they walked a short distance when it dawned on him. Could it really be? It had to be it!

"The Angel's Balm! I dreamt about it. And I read in mom's book. It has to be mixed with liquid moonlight. That's it! It's here somewhere! Why else would the horn have brought me here?" When Gylfi said nothing, he repeated, "It's here, isn't it?"

Gylfi gazed at him. "Yes, it's here Devin. Many mystics and masters have searched for it for thousands of years. It is not something given easily. This is a great burden to bear."

"But I don't seek it for myself, Great Gylfi. I am trying to restore a realm. Surely that must count for something," he said.

THE GENERATIONAL GARDEN

"Come, you've traveled far and your task is not an easy one." Crouching, Gylfi waited. It took Devin a moment to realize he was meant to climb on its back!

He approached and with feet on either side of Gylfi's back, he held the griffin's neck and with a flap of its magnificent wings, they were airborne.

"Keep your eyes open, this is not to be missed."

Unprepared for the beauty below as Gylfi flew on, Devin spotted a glistening white hill in the distance.

"What's that?" he shouted, nearly losing his seat when his voice echoed loudly back at him.

"The Manor Hall."

"You rule here?" He finally asked.

"I protect all of this. Many secrets are guarded here. Try not to fall off. We're about to descend."

Devin felt his tummy do a summersault at the drop in the altitude and within moments they touched down on a dais in the courtyard. The walls of the Manor sparkled and shimmered with what seemed to be crushed crystals mixed with an unknown substance.

"You need food and rest, Devin. Our little helpers will see to your needs. Let's go find you a little one."

He followed Gylfi. Expecting to see lavish decorations and grandiose furnishings, he was surprised to see a great hall supported by tall pillars. A giant statue of Gylfi on a majestic base sat before them in the center and he counted twelve other bases set in a grand circle, each with a sitting statue of a griffin.

Gylfi chuckled. "You are permitted inside, Devin. Feel free to look around and get acquainted."

Devin didn't need a second invitation. With quick footsteps, he was in front of the first statue. A tiny inscription read "In Honor & Gratitude". As he went around the circle, he read the same thing for each.

"They're all guardians here?"

"Were," Gylfi answered.

"Oh."

A little figure darted forward, bowing deeply before them. "Welcome, Great Gylfi. Welcome, honored guest."

The deep voice took Devin by surprise. The creature itself was unlike anything he'd ever seen. No taller than three feet, the creature was covered in white fuzz, its ears curved on top of its head, like little horns. It had huge eyes.

It had spoken to Gylfi but was looking curiously at Devin.

"Devin Reelms, this is Ocie. Ocie, meet Devin Reelms."

Unsure if he should bow, Devin dipped his head in acknowledgment, saying, "Hello, Ocie. It is nice to meet you."

"Likewise, Devin Reelms." Then turning to Gylfi, it said, "We will make Devin comfortable, Mistress. Everyone is gathered at the Chamber."

"I will see you later then, Devin," Gylfi said before turning and padding away.

★ ★ ★

With the dawn of morning, Devin was awoken by Ocie moving about his room, humming an unknown but very cheery tune. Ocie danced across the room and stood at his bedside.

"Ahhh. You're awake, Master Devin.

Devin stretched and slowly got up, brushing his hair off his face. He went to the floor-to-ceiling window and gazed out at the spectacular view extending as far as the eyes could see. Lush hills and valleys beckoned invitingly, the shimmering mist sparkling in patches where a river appeared in a hide and seek manner.

"What do you have to eat in this place, Ocie? I'm not sure what to ask for."

"Let's go and you can see what we have and then decide, Master Devin. Everyone wants to make something delicious for you."

Devin made a quick job of the morning rituals and was soon dressed before following Ocie to breakfast. There he met a number of the same strange little creatures as Ocie and was delighted at their antics to keep him entertained.

The food was light and delicious but nothing like he'd had back home and if he had to name any, he couldn't. There were dishes that looked like fruits and honey. Nectars and unfamiliar juices. What felt like wafers, melted in his mouth and the only normal dish he could say with any surety that came close to what he had back home, was the steaming brew of a delicious drink that tasted like a blend of tea and rich flavors of flowers and herbs all mixed together.

Devin drank several cups and watched as the little creatures busied themselves for the day. It was a cozy and comfortable feeling and he felt their love for everything they did.

Basking in the cheery atmosphere, he was surprised when Gylfi padded into the scene and watched in amusement at everyone. After a few minutes, she finally said, "Okay, little ones. I have to take your pet away for now. I'll bring him back later. Now can we go?"

Devin realized she was talking about him and quickly got up. They came to attention and Ocie bowed and nodded. "Excellent, Mistress. We look forward to seeing Master Devin again soon."

She motioned to the rest and waited respectfully as Devin nodded, thanked them and followed Gylfi. Once they exited the kitchen and headed back to the main hall, she set off on a brief tour and showed him the Manor. Eventually, she led him outside and onto a beautiful pathway that extended into the distance with the same sparkling crystal-like sand.

"Very few have ever been able to obtain the balm. It was long before my time as the Guardian here," Gylfi spoke.

"Why would it have revealed itself to me?"

"That is still yet to be determined."

They soon arrived at a breathtaking view of the magnificent white tree he'd seen in his dream. It stood in splendor in the center with pathways extending out and disappearing in every direction. It shimmered and sparkled, alive with vibrancy. Devin saw the familiar bunches of pods and blossoms, more beautiful than in his dream. He stood speechless before its presence.

Gylfi led the way forward, stopping under the massive branches extending out in greeting. Devin felt a fuzzy euphoria filling him and the images he'd experienced in his dream once again played in his vision.

He realized Gylfi was attuned to what he was experiencing and watched as she walked forward, seeming to be in deep commune with the Tree, her reverence clearly visible.

"Proceed with your wish, Devin," she said, then moved aside.

Devin wasn't sure what exactly he was supposed to do or say, but found himself bowing and felt the silent flow as the unknown language released into a flow, before receding into a long silence, drawing him along with it.

Unsure how long he was in that state, a wave of sensation washed over him and he opened his eyes, seeing Gylfi's eyes widen and followed her gaze.

A shimmer danced within the bunches of grape-like pods, sparkling before them and Devin felt like he'd stepped into his dream again. As the images played, he opened his palms and waited, watching the magical moment when a massive bunch of pods slowly released. The gossamer-like droplet sealed itself and sat nestled in his palms.

Devin stared at it for a long time, feeling the same warmth and energy as he had before. Overwhelmed, he thanked the tree and saw Gylfi doing the same. Soon, they started the long walk back to the manor.

On arriving back at the hall, he found Ocie and the others standing in complete reverence. Ocie left and soon returned with a silver silken pouch with tiny ropes and with Gylfi looking on, Devin placed the pod inside, securing it.

"This is indeed a momentous occasion, Devin. Even for me."

The hours that followed were merry and unlike anything Devin had ever experienced. The little beings had created a seat of honor for him along with a special space for the Balm to sit on.

Ocie carved his name, along with a replica of the Pouch like a trophy of some kind and gave it a place of honor next to the statue of Gylfi in the Grand Hall. Then she whispered to him, "Master Devin, you are lighting a whole new realm. We are most happy."

Devin wasn't quite sure what to say, so he just smiled and let them enjoy their celebration.

Soon Gylfi rose and everyone fell quiet. She padded to the center of the Hall and called to the others on the pedestal. Devin was surprised when he saw Essences of the others emerge and alight. She bowed to each one and told of the events that had transpired and Devin found he was suddenly the focus of all of their gazes.

Gylfi motioned him to enter and he did, bowing before each and waiting in respectful silence. What followed was unlike anything he'd ever experienced and he listened to each of their good wishes, and gave his own thanks. They engaged again with Gylfi and soon returned to their individual perches.

Knowing he needed to get back home, he thanked Ocie and the rest for their hospitality and was surprised when Gylfi padded up to him. It took him a moment to realize she was escorting him back to see him off and after climbing up, she flew for a while.

Devin watched the Manor Hall disappear and in a short while, they arrived back where he'd played the little harp.

Gylfi lifted her beak and suddenly the air was filled with musical notes that echoed around the land. In a few minutes, huge, golden lions began appearing from each of the pathways, heading towards them.

Greeting Gylfi, they waited until she addressed them with instructions to keep the Isle protected and told of her intended journey. They each bowed before returning the way they'd arrived.

It took Devin a moment to realize Gylfi meant she was accompanying him all the way home. "Thank you, Great Gylfi. I will take great care of the Balm. You don't have to leave," he said, unwilling to think he'd again caused yet another situation he hadn't planned on.

"It is my duty to now be with you, Devin. This is not an ordinary event that just happened. It has to be protected and we are already connected. This goes much farther than you understand."

Devin didn't know what to say. So, he settled for a very small "okay" and secured the silken pouch Ocie had given him firmly to his waist and climbed up, becoming airborne as they flew on.

BLOOD MOON

"How do you propose we get back to your realm, Devin?" He heard her inquiry in his mind.

The images of his journey to her home played in his memory which she followed until they saw the prism of light appearing ahead. Passing through the dancing, swaying colors, and over the in-bound scenery in reverse, they reached the little harbor with the Butterfly Boat.

Gylfi descended and landed in the meadow he'd arrived at.

"Quite a journey you made, Devin."

"The horn brought me here."

"Well, let's see how we can get back to your home. Time's passing."

He dismounted and they walked to the tunnel of bushes he'd arrived through where he spotted a sundial sitting near the entry-port.

She padded over and watched as he removed the horn and after he climbed onto her back, he placed it as the gnomon, keeping his mind focused atop Lookout Hill where he'd left from. Within moments, he felt the swirling sensation starting to build. Soon, they were flying through the tunnel of light. They flew forward until he felt the sensation changing and a small slit in the field opened up ahead.

As the whoosh of air propelled them forward, he had the sensation of falling before Gilfy extended her wings and they were airborne. Soon though, she slowed and they landed with a soft thump into the night where a full moon hung in red hues above them. Something felt off. Devin shivered at the sudden change in energies they'd just arrived from.

Gylfi, however, was sniffing the air. "There are dark and dangerous things happening in your world, Devin. You took a very risky trip," Gylfi said.

"I was looking for answers," he muttered, sensing a bit of censure in her tone.

"Yes. What you've achieved is commendable, but with the vast unknown, it was a bit foolish to wander into the wilds without guidance."

"Not you too," Devin said in a huff. "There is no one with answers. And trying to figure things out on my own with no help isn't the easiest thing to expect from a fifteen-year-old."

"No, indeed. A sorry state. What will you have me do now that we've made it safely back to your land?"

Devin couldn't have her fly into his yard and announce "Look everyone! I made a new friend. This is Gylfi!" He hadn't thought what it would mean to have her here. And he couldn't just tell her "thank you. You can just fly back to your realm."

"No, you couldn't Devin. But it was I who insisted on bringing you back home. I will take you home before I come back to these wilds. I will stay low-profile and keep my presence a secret. But we must secure the Balm."

Devin felt a heaviness inside his clothes and as he withdrew the pouch. He felt something was different. When he opened it, he saw it wasn't the shimmering, magical liquid he'd obtained, but a sparkling, solidified crystal sitting in the palm of his hand.

"What happened?" he asked in astonishment, looking up at Gylfi.

"It solidified coming into this realm, Devin."

"How am I supposed to be able to use it now though?" He felt disappointment flowing through his veins and a dip in the happiness he'd returned with.

"Just a hiccup, Devin. You'll find a way to liquefy it again. No one will be able to use it if it falls in the wrong hands."

Suddenly he was filled with foreboding. Lexi flashed in his thoughts and he felt himself break out in a cold sweat, remembering the nightmare he'd witnessed. Did something happen while he was gone? Was she in trouble? He prayed not, but the feeling wouldn't leave.

The nightmare played itself over again in his memory. He shivered, assailed by the knowledge it was real this time, no dreams or nightmares could describe the fear and terror coursing through him.

"Those are dark things to be burdened with Devin. Who is she?"

"My sister," he answered, realizing Gylfi was also seeing the images.

"Come, let's get you home and see if all is well."

Devin returned the pod to the pouch, secured it and they were soon airborne, flying into what had suddenly become an ominous flow of uncertainty.

"Look, something's happening below," Gylfi said after flying for a short while. She circled and hovered over a clearing below. Devin sensed they'd stumbled onto something he wasn't going to like but he felt a deep compulsion to see what it was.

Lexi flashed in his thoughts again as they continued descending onto a sturdy limb of a large tree.

Immediately he was assailed by the eeriness coiling around the entire woods. It was thick with a sense of dread. Devin shook off the busy thoughts crowding his mind and focused, taking deep breaths to steady himself.

Sounds echoed below and they watched as cloaked figures walked into the clearing where he spotted a raised platform with Lexi lying atop it. He almost lost his balance and felt a cloak of energy tightening around him, keeping him immobilized.

Gylfi was keeping him from acting rashly as images flashed in his mind, showing him a Black Circle they had created around the perimeter of the clearing. Fast and furious, the images kept changing. How to get to Lexi without making their presence known, he wondered. He knew he had to protect Gylfi's presence as well, but there was little either could do without revealing themselves.

The witching hour was almost upon them as the Blood Moon approached fullness. Devin felt panic rising. He feared they were about to lose Lexi with his nightmare beginning to turn into reality. He watched helplessly as a line of weirdly giggling females made their appearance and began their dark offering, chanting into the unseen force.

Gylfi sent him images as she flew down onto the platform, shielding Lexi's body, letting out a scream at the circle of worshippers. Her voice echoed far into the night and Devin heard the ancient language pouring out of him and watched as chaos broke out.

The figures snapped out of their state and went scattering and scrambling in all directions, disoriented and confused, their sacrificial ritual offering disrupted.

Devin didn't waste time on any of them. Lexi was coming out of her trancelike state as she turned her eyes and a dull recognition flared.

Without tools of any sort, it took some work to get her untied and off the platform. She seemed drugged and was slow to respond, unable to walk properly.

Devin couldn't imagine what would've happened if they hadn't reached in time. As the ropes came loose, Lexi leaned into him and he helped her down. It was maybe a good thing she was still dazed as he knew there was no way she'd allow herself to be tied securely atop Gylfi's back.

Just then, bright beams of light flashed and screams of terror echoed around them. Devin froze. Were the worshippers returning? A figure shot out from the woods into the clearing, saw them and took off, followed by a beam of light and a figure in white robe. They disappeared into the night, with screams echoing, the beams of light shooting deep within the forest.

"Let's get out of here, Devin. It's getting dangerous," Gylfi's urgent thoughts flashed in his mind.

He agreed, but resisted since she wouldn't be able to carry both him and Lexi. He sent images of his home and insisted Gylfi take Lexi to their aunt and sent memories of himself traveling and landing up in her world, reminding her he'd take care of himself. After a moment's hesitation, she took off.

Devin felt his bravado falter for a second, knowing it was unwise to be on his own in a forest with dark beings at war and having disrupted their ritual.

He didn't waste time. He hopped off the platform as echoes of terror filled the night around him. A large fire erupted ahead of him and he turned, plunging into the forest, comforting himself that he was wearing the necklace.

Whatever they'd interrupted, Devin knew it was bad. As he kept moving with no proper sense of direction to tell him where his home was, he realized the dark now knew a powerful force was also present in the land.

With that thought in mind, he sent Gylfi images of himself making his way in the forest, having distanced himself from the worship circle.

She sent back images of the terrain below her and he knew it would be a bit before she reached his home. Things had gotten complicated. He remembered the conversation with his aunt and felt the weight of what still lay ahead of them. Mostly him. He hadn't expected Lexi to get kidnapped, much less being offered as a ritual sacrifice.

That alone was enough to drive anyone crazy. And Gylfi's presence now was a predicament he hadn't planned on. Again, he'd been driven to seek answers when no one was there to help him and ended up in a more dangerous situation than he'd ever imagined.

He stumbled over a root and the heavy pouch of Angel's Balm shifted, reminding him he still carried it. That stopped him. In the rush of rescuing Lexi and evading the beings alive in the forest, Devin had completely forgotten he still had it on him. He would have entrusted it to Gylfi to take it safely to his home.

What was he to do? He slowed his steps as he noticed the shouts and beams of lights had gone quiet. Did the warring forces stop? Were there others about? He knew he couldn't remain where he was. After a few minutes of quiet, he decided to move on. When a soft glow lit up several feet across from him, he felt a familiar one starting on his chest.

It couldn't be, he thought. But sure enough, the figure of Chad appeared.

"Devin! Thank God you're okay."

"Chad."

"We were hunting tonight. The worshippers had a big event planned and it got interrupted."

"It was Lexi they were offering."

"Lexi! Good God!"

"We managed to get her in time."

"That's good. All the more reason why you shouldn't be wandering here.

Devin went on to tell Chad what had happened and was surprised when Chad said, "The Gylfi? She's here? This is good news indeed."

"You know Gylfi?"

"She's known to us. I'm happy to find you and know Lexi was saved. The others will be happy to hear Gylfi is among us. Come. We have to get you home."

They'd reached a small clearing by then when he saw images of Gylfi seconds before she landed in front of them.

Before he could say anything, Chad dipped into a deep bow and Gylfi walked up to him. She seemed to be having her own conversation with Chad which surprised Devin but he kept a respectful silence.

Soon, Chad turned to Devin saying, "I leave you in good hands, Devin. I have to get back to the others. Gylfi will see you home."

"Thank you, Chad. It's good knowing you're around."

Chad nodded, squeezed his shoulder and after making sure they were airborne, set off into the night.

Gylfi stayed close to his home that night and after checking in with his aunt who said they would speak in the morning, he checked in on Lexi and saw her resting comfortably.

Devin took time to get a cold shower, and after tucking the large pouch of Balm next to him, he fell into a deep sleep.

The days and nights that followed, Gylfi went on many trips, sometimes meeting with him in the woods, other times gone for long periods. Devin had taken Lexi to meet Gylfi properly.

She thanked Gylfi for saving her after getting over her initial fear, but was happy to get back to her room. Devin let her. She had been through a lot and he figured she would talk when she was ready. Aunt Sophie was good with her. No one said anything about what happened to their grandparents.

FENWICK HOLLOW

It was time for him to get ready. With Lexi's kidnapping and near sacrifice, Devin was worried about leaving for school. But a late invitation arrived for her and he was relieved. He'd secretly been dreading that the village bullies might have harassed her if she were left alone while he was gone.

Now, with both of them at the new school, she would be safe. He knew she still suffered nightmares and his aunt had been pretty good at helping her. He hoped the new school would help her recover and forget the ugliness she had faced.

Saying fond farewells to their grandparents, they set off with aunt Sophie in Gramps' jalopy and soon reached the unpaved trail given on the directions. It stretched in a long, winding journey with turns and twists through unfamiliar pastures and stretches of deep forests.

They struggled for what seemed like hours before arriving at a juncture. They went past and kept going for quite a while before arriving at the abandoned farmhouse. Signs announced "Private Property–Keep Out!" and "No Trespassing." A smaller one informed anyone wishing entry or permission to "Contact the Office of the Solicitor – Foxwood."

Galeb sauntered out from behind the farmhouse where he must have been awaiting their arrival and waved in greeting.

"There you are!" Aunt Sophie said. "I was beginning to worry if any of this is true."

Exchanging warm hugs, Galeb waved it away, "A good way to keep the busy-bodies away." Then he greeted Lexi who'd been relatively quiet but returned his hug. He looked at Devin who mouthed "later." Galeb nodded.

Until their aunt's greeting, Devin realized she'd hidden her worry well. He felt regret on being clueless, but figured now she'd have more time to help their grandparents with both him and Lexi away.

Galeb helped with their luggage and walked with Lexi, doing his best to keep up a stream of conversation. After some time, her mood lightened and she was smiling, becoming quite animated, much to Devin's relief.

Lexi's memories were a bit fuzzy. She only remembered the women approaching her for some help, and small fragments of being rescued by him and Gylfi. Beyond that, she still suffered nightmares. Devin hoped she'd soon get over the horror of what had happened.

Galeb led them down a path through a covered archway covered in vines and wildflowers. "From here we go by boat," he said, leading them down to a small dock where several small, leaf-shaped boats bobbed in welcome.

They hugged their aunt goodbye, promised to be good, and wished her a safe journey back home. They watched as she nodded, looking brave and blowing kisses while their luggage was stored aboard.

Galeb took the oars and steered them into the current and focused on navigating the way. He kept Lexi entertained with funny answers to her endless questions. Devin let his mind wander, happy to let them talk.

The river branched off in a number of directions, with Galeb pointing out where to avoid when they go out on their own. Devin, engrossed in his musings, missed it. By the time he realized what Galeb said, they had already passed. He shrugged, telling himself he'd ask later or figure it out when or if he had to go back on the river.

About forty-five minutes later, Galeb steered them into a small inlet and docked. A fleet of the same small, leaf-shaped boats bobbed and a welcome sign greeted them.

With their boat secured and luggage in hand, he led them up the widening path where a set of arrows pointed the way uphill. They walked for about fifteen minutes before coming to a crest and gasped at the beautiful sight below.

Fenwick Hollow sprawled below in a horse-shoe shaped village. Tiny pathways stretched in all directions. Lined with abundant wildflowers, hugging the landscape, appearing in brief spans at a time, they vanished in short gaps that led to tiny cottages, before continuing on to unseen corners.

They started down the path and passed a sign saying "Welcome To Fenwick Hollow". Devin felt his mood lift as they passed through the village and folks called out to Galeb in greeting.

"What happens if others find the boats and come through?" Lexi asked.

"Some have gotten through, but it's pretty wild. They most likely get lost at the juncture.

Devin realized his wandering mind had made him deaf to Galeb's talk.

"I get wooley-brained too," Galeb said, "you'll learn the river soon."

"I was curious if folks would try and follow us."

"Because you've been sent to a bad, bad place?" Galeb chuckled at Devin's surprised expression. "Ya, we heard."

Devin decided not to worry about it. It was too pretty to think about the foolish villagers. He focused on the beauty around them and watched the tiny streams bubbling by, giving way to lush gardens, wells and the surrounding forest. Birds twittered and chirped, butterflies danced by and bees hovered in search of nectar.

Wares and trinkets sat displayed in stalls, tinkers fiddling at their craft, and the womenfolk bustled by in colorful garments as they tended to stalls and canopies packed with assortments of jars of jellies, fruits and vegetables.

Intricate needlework and goods sat in display. It was charming and full of warmth and friendliness. He thought the villagers had given the Gypsies a better home than if they'd allowed them to live in their little caravans and shelters, struggling as they had.

He was happy how things had worked out, but Devin knew people would get curious and once they found a way to see the haven Gypsies now called home, things would change.

The Brotherhood thanking the Gypsies had caused misery for them and with the court granting Serena permission to have them at Fenwick Hollow, it was better than he expected. He remembered he'd never gotten a reply to the letter he'd sent off to Dr. Piffany – if that was an actual person, he corrected himself.

Knowing they still had to get school supplies and become acquainted with their new home, Devin walked on. They'd reached the busy part of the village and he spotted a huge tree standing sentinel in the busiest part. A surge of cheering went around a small group gathered at the base where a burly young man with wide ears, shaggy hair and large hands stood smiling.

Juggling little orbs, he offered them to Lexi who giggled. They were entertained for a little bit before Hunter, Rusty and a group of boys from camp showed up. Hugs and slaps on the back were exchanged in a happy welcome.

Devin asked about the guys he'd shared time with at the center, but Galeb told him they'd chosen to go back to their own homes after Serena had met with their parents.

"Hey, I know you!" the juggler said, watching Devin like a strange bug. "Aren't you the kid who had the old goats in a knot? Boy! I never seen them so busy with themselves."

Turned out he was a cousin of Galeb and Devin smiled at his comment.

"I'm Devin Reelms and this is my sister, Lexi." Devin greeted him as Quentin extended a hand to them both. "Good to meet you. Welcome to Fenwick Hollow."

"Nice meeting you, Quentin," he said, liking him.

"What's that?" he asked, seeing a slide around the trunk of the tree and looking up. He was surprised to see a platform with people emerging out of the trunk through a doorway, placing their luggage on the slide and then descending on a set of stairs wrapped around the huge trunk.

"Folks arrive here several ways," Quentin said.

"Oh."

Lexi meantime was excitedly checking out the various booths lining the street. Galeb called and Devin said a hurried goodbye to Quentin and went over to Galeb. Walking on, they soon arrived at the supply store, got everything they needed and stopped for refreshments on the way back.

Refreshed, they headed up the street and went along several more before finally arriving at The Academy.

It was built on old ruins of some kind and had been updated to accommodate the needs of the school. A mixture of old and present as far as Devin could tell. It was said, whoever built it, flowed with the natural layout of the old foundation.

With a beautiful white exterior, several small towers and a main one with roofs that sparkled and shone in the evening sunlight, it looked and felt enchanted. A sign said "Angels' Academy".

Serena welcomed them and led the way through the entrance and up into the main hall with soaring ceilings etched like the heavens, giving a feeling of stepping into a beautiful realm beyond the stars.

Huge pillars with lamps shaped in the form of stars and moons lined the hallways. The whole atmosphere was alive and throbbing with a sense of warmth. Hallways extended in different directions and doorways labeled with signs showed the library and classrooms with terraces leading outside to pretty gardens and beyond. There were stables and an animal sanctuary. But it was already late and in the quickly fading light, Devin couldn't see very far.

Everyone was excited and eager to explore. Serena was gracious but firm and told them they'd have to wait for daytime.

He'd kept an eye on Lexi and could tell she was happy. She was given a room with some of the other girls she was busy making friends with and he had one a little distance from the others in a different part of the building. It had hues of sapphire blues and silver — simple and comfortable but elegant at the same time.

Once settled, they all met in the hall and Devin was surprised at the number of students attending.

Rusty and the gang all sought him out and listened to Serena's welcome talk. She gave general guidance, introduced them to the staff and spoke of being respectful to each other, and shared knowledge about the grounds and lands outside and what dangers they might encounter if they ventured beyond certain points.

She encouraged them to allow each other to learn and grow with kindness and consideration. She spoke a little of restoring honor and dignity. It was brief and since it was already late, they had a very tasty dinner in the eating hall and Devin, like everyone else, was happy to head to his room.

Tomorrow would take care of itself and classes were to begin in two days' time.

31
LESSONS

The start of classes was interesting and unusual as the invitation had said. Teachers encouraged and welcomed questions and interactions.

Back at the village, the subjects were structured and rigid, learning limited only to what was written by some unknown authority. Here, it was completely the opposite, and Devin realized he was the one ignorant of much. He developed a healthy respect for his fellow students and that night as he prepared for class the next day, he looked over the schedule they'd been given.

Monday	-	The Stars, Energy & Astrology – Dome 3 – Mr. Ley
Tuesday	-	Herbs, Plants & Gardening – Greenhouse C – Ms. Hawkins – Aqua Life – Lake Pristine – Mr. Boone
Wednesday	-	Animal Care – Paddock 1 – Ms. Abbott Customs & Beliefs – Dome 1- Mr. Hills & Elders
Thursday	-	General Studies, Arts & Crafts – Mr. Fellows & Ms. Whimsy
Friday	-	Sports, Extra-Curricular Activities & Trips

By the end of the second week, they got a new addition, Snyder Stein, and Devin was surprised to learn he was an outsider and the son of a high official. He knew there was a story there and one to stay away from. But it was hard to witness the arrogance Snyder brought with him.

Mr. Hills was talking of a strange practice in some remote part of the region when Snyder began interrupting, being rude. Mr. Hills indulged him for quite a while, until he firmly steered back to the lesson and Snyder felt snubbed, standing up and raising his voice.

"My father is the District High Commissioner and my family goes back to when this place didn't exist. You're the teacher but are refusing to answer my questions?"

The class went quiet and Mr. Hills stopped what he was doing, put down the book he was reading and looked directly at Snyder. "Young man, I'm of the Gypsy Tribe, otherwise considered an untouchable but capable of teaching without favoritism. Your father knew this when he asked that you attend our academy."

Snyder, red-faced and huffing, seemed ready to have another go at Mr. Hills who continued, "If you feel you cannot learn in this environment, I suggest you take it up with the District High Commissioner."

The silence was broken only by students doing their best to move out of the line of vision between Snyder and Mr. Hills.

Devin watched in amusement as Snyder, angry and embarrassed he'd been exposed, sat down in a huff, muttering rudely, his air of superiority deflated. The episode, however, made Devin question the wisdom of Serena allowing him admittance.

"Very well, Snyder. I'd like to think you exercised understanding and know all of us are here for the purpose of learning and will leave all prior prejudices outside my classroom and the academy."

32
REBELS' CLAN

The days went by with Devin and Lexi adjusting nicely to their new life.

Soon though, stirrings of unhappiness began to emerge. As the days went by, things got more complicated. At first, Devin figured it was just adjusting to new life but then he began to notice slights, whispers, and snubs aimed at him. Sometimes randomly, other times deliberately.

He tried to ignore it as much as he could even though it was starting to get under his skin. When it became too much, he decided to ask the next person who was rude to him what exactly he'd done to deserve their bad behavior. A group of kids were whispering but immediately averted their gazes when they saw him looking at them. One fellow made a rude sign.

He decided to go and confront them. But before he could go face them, a girl in the lunchroom let out a god-awful screech on finding a ferret on her table. The poor thing was more scared than she was, scrambling from table to table causing quite a distraction and Devin lost the opportunity to confront the kids.

One kid finally managed to get hold of it and took it outside, releasing it back in the woods. Devin sighed. "Well, that's that," he thought, heading back to class thinking Galeb might be able to give him some idea about what was going on.

But when he went looking, he could not find any trace of Galeb. It was his third attempt in as many days to meet him but he still couldn't find him. He decided to stop at the stables. He'd heard talk in the lunchroom and wondered if the rumors were true about Galeb having secretly joined the Rebels. He didn't want to believe it but where else could he be?

Shaking off his misgivings, Devin decided to try Rennie whom he'd met the first full day he'd arrived and learned he'd been given a small cottage on the far end of the Sanctuary. They'd had quite a long talk with Devin filling him in on all that had happened since.

Rennie was happy to see him, and told Devin he was happy to be at the school. Serena had invited him to stay, having heard about what had happened between him and the smugglers.

Now, as Devin headed over to the tiny cottage, he found himself surprised at Rennie's abrupt greeting. Feeling snubbed, he hid his disappointment and deliberately kept his voice light. "Do you happen to know where Galeb is? I've been to the stables and looked everywhere. I can't find him."

"Sometimes you gotta run with the pack to understand their ways."

"What?" Devin wasn't sure he'd heard that right. "It's true then?" Pain sliced through his gut. "Not Galeb too," he thought. "How could he?"

"You're smart, Devin. You can figure it out," Rennie said, his tone a bit warmer. "I can't break confidences."

They'd talked about so many things, Devin wondered what exactly Rennie was referring to.

"But…."

"But nothing," finished Rennie. "Things are what they are and you should get to class."

"Sure Ren," Devin said. Something was off. Didn't Rennie know classes were over for the day? "Thanks. I'll be off."

"See you Devin," Rennie said, stepping back inside the cabin, closing the door soundly in his face.

"See you, Ren," he said and turned to leave. Rennie was entitled to his life but his behavior still hurt. Devin left it alone and headed to the docks for the boat race everyone was hyped about. It had sparked a lot of talk since his arrival.

He felt after what happened back home on the river with Mr. Heeb and the Renegade, he'd at least try it for the fun of it. What remained of the day was still nice and had enough hours of sunlight, with a gentle wind and coolness that made it perfect for the race.

As he made his way to the little harbor, he saw a crowd had assembled and by the time he reached, everyone was already aboard their little boats. He hurriedly got into one and had barely settled in when the shout went up and everyone was off.

Before long, Devin found himself with company as kids in other boats sped up and fell back and in the spirit of things, he rowed along, focused on navigating the waters now more turbulent than before, filled with more boats than normal.

As his muscles began to strain and he tried to keep his boat from capsizing, Devin realized that he hadn't paid proper attention to the path ahead. It took him only a few minutes to realize that something was strange as several of the boats kept blocking him from all sides and he couldn't get past them.

The swift current and their deliberate blocking steered him into a small opening on his left and the shouts of his friends encouraging him on, got lost. The silence penetrated his mind and he looked around at the unfamiliar cove he'd ended up in.

Devin sighed, knowing it would be useless to get back in the race. The current was strong and fast and as Galeb had told him the first day he'd arrived, the river was filled with countless places folks could get lost in. Then he saw the other boaters bobbing right along with him and he felt himself being steered towards the shallow end of the cove.

He felt a moment's panic on seeing several well-muscled guys who he thought were the rebels waiting to welcome him. He realized that he'd unwittingly strayed into trouble.

With deep breaths, he allowed the brisk strokes to carry him forward, even as he kept a brave smile on his lips. The tiny boat bumped as it reached the water's edge, and the others pulled in on either side of him, bumping him from behind.

He looked around, scanning his surroundings, realizing the group had chosen this particular cove for the privacy it offered.

"Join us, Gypsy," the mocking voice of a buffed young gypsy drawled in insulting welcome. "It's what they call you in the village, isn't it? Quite the hero."

Loud, jeering laughter greeted his words and Devin felt himself going tense.

"What do you want? Why did you bring me here?"

"You rowed yourself here, Gypsy. I'm Alifair, Leader of The Rebels," he said, laughing loudly and giving an overly dramatic bow. "We were in the boat race like you."

"Yes, but you fellows here kept blocking me and it was the only choice I had left," Devin felt he had to explain.

"Too bad you weren't paying attention, Gypsy. If a boat race can lead you so easily into our little meeting, it makes me wonder why the old goats trust you can lead our people, Gypsy."

Fury engulfed Devin. "My name is Devin Reelms. And I don't want to lead you or your people."

"Tsk, tsk. So quick to desert our tribes? You were quick to accept the stupid offer to become one of us. Why did you?"

"Maybe," said Devin, carefully holding his anger in check, "you should ask The Elders why they did such a thing."

"I did," came the growling answer, and Devin could have sworn he heard frustration in his voice. "Because you didn't hand over the brat to the authorities. And yeah, your family's been supplying our folks with grains and food. We heard it. That's what they said. But they didn't have to make you family. And," he sneered, "we got by well enough before you came along."

"I know." Devin felt the words slip out.

Silence hung between them for a long time. When Alifair finally spoke, he said, "careful, gypsy. I think you calling us thieves." His eyes glittered as he advanced, even as the others carefully stepped back, away from them.

Then it came to him. Devin remembered seeing their little group and ugly stares when he was made a member of the gypsy family at the festival back at their camp. Something stirred in his memory and he tried remembering what he'd heard.

"You're bringing disaster to us here. Wasn't it bad enough when you caused trouble in that village of yours?"

Devin knew they were looking to start trouble. But he already had enough to deal with. He realized that he had to find another way out. But he was far from the academy with little way of escaping unless he planned to swim back all the way. But there were too many of them to let him escape.

A thought occurred and he realized, Alifair said The Elders weren't telling why they'd made him family. He didn't feel duty bound to confess anything to him or anyone.

Rupert and Rennie were right. Sometimes power could be corrupting and he could see Alifair was out to prove himself. Setting Devin up to impress his gang, trying to gain the real reason for him being at Fenwick Hollow and bullying him, told Devin Alifair was more talk than action.

But he'd seen the knockdown, dragged out fight that had gone on between the villagers and a set of rebels. They were still Gypsies at heart, loyal to the last and Alifair wasn't someone he would choose to start a fight with. He didn't believe in fair fighting if his was the group that fought with the villagers.

Back in the village, Devin had the help of darkness and being on land for that fight with the village bullies. Here he was surrounded by no less than a dozen rebels and a boat that was bobbing uselessly. At least three miles from the Academy.

"I called you no such thing," he said directly to Alifair as he stuck his face into Devin's. "I simply agreed with you that I knew you got by well enough before I came along."

Devin almost missed the twitch that told him Alifair had lost it, but instinct had him stepping aside. The force of Alifair's fist carried him forward and he fell face down in the water.

Laughter erupted and Devin had to suppress a chuckle himself at the sight of Alifair slamming fist first into the ground. He knew though he had to avoid a fight at all costs. Alifair got up and stood glaring at him. The others watched, unsure of how to proceed and Devin felt his awareness expand, sensing where each of the rebels stood.

"You'll pay for that, Gypsy," he growled, advancing, wiping water from his eyes.

"Here goes nothing," Devin thought. "I tried, but now I gotta save myself." And the next moment Alifair was at him.

He called out to the others, "Gypsy's mine. No one touches him."

He was ripped and well-muscled, slippery as a snake and Devin knew he was in for the fight of his life. The rebel leader had a grudge and he wanted Devin to suffer.

They fought, slugging each other painfully. Up, down, Devin landed a punch that knocked the wind out of Alifair, who fell over gasping. He looked on helplessly as Devin, breathing hard, stood looking down at him. When Devin did nothing, his face contorted in fury. The others gazed at Devin, unsure if he'd follow through and go at him.

Looking at each of the rebels to see what they would do, no one could meet his eyes nor step forward to help Alifair. He wouldn't accept their help anyway.

"If that's all you wanted to say to me," Devin spoke to the group, watching Alifair, "I suggest you speak with The Elders. They have the answers you're looking for. Good evening, everyone, I'll be on my way."

Carefully, he backed away and was about to step into his boat when Alifair rushed at him. "Uh oh," the thought zipped through his mind.

Closing his mind to everything else, he felt the heat on his chest. Alifair was ugly in his fight. Nothing like fairness existed in his being and Devin felt a strange animal energy envelop him. He was numbed to whatever pain Alifair inflicted, caring only for his survival. He was aware of hands pulling him away from Alifair as he trashed the rebel. When the fog had cleared, he gazed at a whimpering Alifair.

The others had finally stepped in and pulled him away. Devin shook his head, trying to clear his thoughts and gazed at his hands. He didn't regret what had happened. He hadn't gone looking for a fight. And he knew he was justified in fighting. The words of The Renegade floated to mind, and he laughed out loud.

Suddenly, he understood and it made him laugh even harder. He doubled over, gasping at how crazy his world had suddenly become. And as if his thoughts had conjured up The Renegade, Rennie walked into their little group.

"Bit far from school and the race for you to be, Devin," The Renegade greeted him.

The silence that followed was loud enough that even Devin felt the rebels' fears grow in desperation.

"Nawh Ren, we had a bet and Alifair was showing me some moves. We're friends," Devin replied.

"Is that so?" The Renegade asked, looking around the group.

Alifair nodded, giving Devin a strange look.

The others looked on in alarm, unsure of how to proceed.

"In that case, I'll have to let Serena and The Elders know. Devin, now you can travel without fear of any of these rascals causing problems," Rennie indicated the small group of warriors.

Heads nodded vigorously and Alifair gave another pained shake of his head.

"Well, seems like we have to get going then," Rennie clapped his hand at them, making them jump. "Boys, I'll leave it to you to see Devin's boat safely back to harbor at the Hollow. Alifair, you can't just sit there. Seems like you lost this bet, am I right?"

Smothered laughter greeted his question and Devin kept his gaze fixed on Alifair. He knew someone would pay dearly, but he won't be responsible for that.

Without hesitating, he walked over and extended a hand. Another silence descended around the group and Alifair gazed at him for a long while before carefully raising his hand. Grasping it, Devin pulled him up and gave him a steading hand as he caught his breath, wincing in what must be pain.

Stepping back, he bowed to Alifair in recognition of a fellow warrior while observing the Gypsy custom. Alifair took a moment to recover his shock and did a bow in return. When he could stand straight again, Devin could see pain in his face.

"Well, good evening then," Devin said, "see you around." He started walking towards the forest, completely ignorant of where he was heading.

"Good evening," echoed the clamor of voices behind him.

"Evening boys," Rennie called, following him and after a small distance from them, he said, "That was quite decent of you."

"What do you mean?" Devin asked, trying to keep the alarm out of his voice.

"Relax, I happened to have heard quite a bit."

"How much?"

"Enough," came Rennie's short reply.

"When did you get here?" Devin asked.

"Long enough to know you were in big trouble. I was going to step in but it seemed your way was more effective."

Devin couldn't believe his ears.

"And worth the entertainment," Rennie laughed loudly before sobering up.

"Where did you learn to fight like that?"

"Like what?" Devin hedged.

"Listen Dev, I've been in a few brawls in my lifetime. I know fight. And what you did back there was not a regular fight. You seemed possessed."

"I felt possessed," Devin replied truthfully, shocking both of them.

Rennie gazed at him for a long time, "hmmed" and nodded to himself, "Right then, I think we need to get you cleaned and fixed up before you go back to the Hollow."

Rennie led the way forward while Devin followed, with both falling into deep silence.

Devin never spoke of the fight to anyone, but he noticed a change in the behavior of the kids around classes. Somehow news had gotten out, and it was a nice change to not worry about further attacks and rudeness.

He eventually found Galeb in the gardens one afternoon and they headed for the little gazebo where food was always available. He told him what had happened and Galeb sighed.

When he finally told Devin what started it all, Devin felt a bitter taste in his mouth. "Why?" He thought. "I don't want to be a hero, Galeb. I never knew any of these things would happen. Mom died because of what I did," he muttered in torment, "I don't want recognition."

"We know. Stop blaming yourself for what happened, Devin. No one has control of how life unfolds."

"I insisted Rusty stayed home. I told him," Devin felt the threat of tears behind his lids and blinked. "He wasn't going to let me go by myself."

"I would have done the same, Dev. Friends have each other's backs."

"I never intended for any of this to happen."

"Devin," Galeb said patiently, "you need to let it go. Whatever is going on with the rebel lot," he grinned, "will sort itself out. It does get a bit wild when new warriors are vying for leadership."

"If it weren't you becoming part of our family, trust me, they would have found another cause to disrupt and cause chaos. This is kinda normal with our kind. It's why outside folks think the way they do about us. Alifair is proving them right when he and his gang go around doing stupid stuff."

"So, I'm a convenient excuse for his bullying?"

Galeb laughed. "Even Alifair didn't expect things would come to this. Now he's raised the bar for himself and they'll have to prove themselves. He's probably even crazier now."

Devin tried keeping his worry to himself. With his mom's death and their grief, things must have been put on pause for a little bit, but it had sat simmering with Alifair and his little band Devin realized.

And their displacement with the fire didn't really help them, or maybe they were hoping they'd never see him again. Devin remembered the article he'd read and dismissed it at the time about folks questioning whether the Gypsies themselves hadn't been doing things to gain sympathy from the public.

Now he questioned the little voice in his mind. Could Alifair and his little band be so unhappy about him being made part of their tribe, they'd been willing to burn their own tribe out to get back at him and gain the favor of the Elders? What would they gain? Something didn't feel right.

He didn't know he could have refused their invitation of becoming a part of their tribe. He had realized too late that the Gypsies managed with or without anyone's help. He felt worse, knowing he was the cause of the split of the rising stars of their tribes.

Now, Alifair's latest stunt of attacking him, would cost him any gain in recognition he'd so far earned. The first mark of a great warrior was that of humility but he'd only exhibited arrogance and bullying in place of friendship.

"What happened?" He asked after the long pause.

"The Elders and Rupert kept to the ruling that you were family. Alifair left in fury and went on a rampage in retaliation for being burned out. He said you didn't deserve any honor. Gypsies took care of themselves. But Rupert said the Elders had spoken and their word was their honor. That you were family."

"What happened?" Devin felt worse now.

"He left, infuriated, calling anyone who believed in him and the injustice that was done to leave. Quite a few had left with him."

"So, what happens now?" Devin wondered out aloud.

"Only time will tell. Eventually, he'll come back. Only now," Galeb laughed, "he'll have to tell them how right they were in making you family."

Devin sighed. He didn't need enemies, especially within the tribes. Lexi and him were here because of what had happened when he'd befriended the gypsies.

"Many in the past would leave for long periods. But they always ended up back in the tribes. Just the way it is." Galeb paused, then finished, "whenever he shows up and explains his actions, the Elders will decide. Until then, just let it be. You're family now. Infighting happens. Most find their way back. Other times, not. It doesn't matter. The Elders decree."

"I still feel bad."

"What you did was a very noble thing, Dev. And its not lost on Alifair. When you extended friendship after he attacked you its something he'll never forget." Galeb patted Devin on the shoulder before getting up. "I have to get back to the gardens."

Devin nodded and waved him off. He knew he had some explaining to do himself and whether he liked it or not, he wasn't going to shy away from it.

He took a walk and found himself at the door of Elder Rupert's home. When it opened, Rupert greeted him warmly and welcomed him inside. It was a vivid contrast to the wagons and caravans they'd had back in Foxwood, and Devin was happy to see the strained expression no longer prominent on the Elder's face.

"So how may I help you, Devin? I sense you're here for more than pleasantries."

Deciding on being frank, Devin asked, "Did you make me part of your family just so I would be bound by loyalty? Did you think Gramps or I would ever have done anything to expose or put the tribes at risk in any way?"

Rupert took a while before answering, and when he did Devin felt outrage followed by hurt. "It did cross my mind that by offering you a place in our tribal families, it would keep you from betraying us."

"I became friends with Rusty even before I knew anything about your tribes!"

"It's not that simple," Rupert replied. "We knew by offering you what we did, it would cause you to exercise loyalty to us. When we heard Zoie's reading and the many journeys ahead, we knew we needed to protect you."

They were protecting him?

"Is that why I was given the necklace?"

"Yes. It's not an easy task making those. They're particularly rare. It might be one of the reasons the rebels," he chuckled, before continuing, "are so upset. The cards showed you are the one to bring the light back to our people, so yes.

Many things are changing and no matter how brave the boys in camp are, you're the one taking us forward. I'll do my best to keep them in line, but you'll have to use your smarts and kindness, no matter what, to keep them from disrupting our people. I'm not what I used to be and young bloods are always foolish in their ways."

Surprised by Rupert's words, Devin felt his anger disappearing, only to be replaced by worry.

Feeling like no better time than the present to tell his tale, Devin told Elder Rupert of what had transpired between him and the Rebels. When he'd finished, a long silence followed and he was beginning to worry when Elder Rupert spoke.

"When Rusty told us what happened in the cave, your power with the crystal and knowledge of the ancient language, and how you released Serena, we knew for sure it was the right thing to do. Now hearing how you handled The Rebels," he chuckled loudly before continuing, "they will realize why we did what we did."

Devin didn't know what to say. The matter was settled and Elder Rupert wasn't going to add anything. He thanked him for his time and understanding, gave a small bow and left.

33

A STAR IS BORN

The days that followed were interesting and fun. Lexi had settled in nicely and had made quite a few friends. Devin had told Serena about Lexi's near sacrifice when she'd spoken to him in private.

She was troubled and concerned. "We don't know what they gave her to drink so we'll have to keep a close eye on her."

"She's been pretty normal," Devin was quick to say, then remembered Rusty's after effects when the Shadows had bitten him. Serena nodded, having followed his thoughts.

"I will meet with the Elders to let them know what's been happening."

He told her about his meeting with Chad the night they'd disrupted the sacrificial ritual and how he'd seen him to safety.

"I'm happy he found you."

Devin debated telling her about his other trip, but in the end, he knew it wasn't something he could keep hidden for long. He told of Gylfi but omitted the fact that he'd obtained the Balm. She was once the Guardian of the Crystal and would most likely know what to do, but something kept him from talking about it.

She was intrigued and asked many questions.

Devin told of Gylfi's world and the things he saw.

"This is amazing, Devin. Where is the horn? Is it safe?"

"I brought it here and it's safe in my room."

They talked for a long time and eventually Serena was satisfied that all was well. Promising she would visit Lexi, Serena bowed and left. Devin felt his heart lighter than it was for a long time. It felt good to have unburdened a lot of what had happened.

* * *

Now as he sat with Rennie, things had settled nicely since the last time he was at the cottage. He was surprised when Rennie repeated, "That was pretty decent of you as I said before," Rennie said.

"What was?"

"The truth about why you guys were mud wrestling the day I found you and the rebels at the river."

"I have enough enemies already," Devin replied.

"True enough," Rennie replied.

"What's going on?" Devin inquired.

"Well," Rennie replied with a grin, "your new found "friends" have come up with some interesting news."

"Interesting" meant a lot of things to Devin, but he had the good sense to keep quiet.

"I'm meeting them at dusk over at Embers," Rennie answered as if that explained everything.

"Embers?"

"A hangout. It looks like embers from a giant campfire, sitting in the middle of the valley. First thing folks see as they get off the mountains - all aglow and welcoming."

"Sounds cozy," Devin needled.

"It is," Rennie agreed.

"Lemme guess, I can't go with you."

"Save the sarcasm. And good guess. You can't go with me," Rennie agreed. "But only because I need your help here."

"Here?" Devin exclaimed, gazing around the cottage in puzzlement.

"Well, not exactly here. In the forest," Rennie called over his shoulder, already gathering items he'd need for his trip.

That didn't make Devin feel any better. "Doing what?"

"Something fun," Rennie grunted as he stuffed an unending number of items in his knapsack and then continued as if he hadn't finished explaining from before.

"Weird stuff's been going on at Fellsmere. The Hunters have been finding Peacocks and serpents killed."

"Elder Erik's Clan?" Devin searched his memory from the Judgment Circle, still trying to make sense as Rennie hopped around in explanations.

"One and the same," Rennie nodded. They think dark worshippers have struck.

"No!" Devin blurted out, reliving the horror of Lexi's near-sacrifice. "I thought that was ...."

"Ya, I know. But something or someone is busy."

"Any chance it's locals starting up trouble?" Devin voiced his doubts. After all, someone had set fire to the Gypsy's camp. The niggling thought was always with him that soon someone would want to know where the Gypsies had disappeared to. Gossip was the way of the villagers when they didn't understand things.

"The villagers don't have the guts to," Rennie assured him. "They like their creature comforts too much to come this far into the wilds."

"It could be a trick to lure you away from The Hollow, Rennie," Devin said in afterthought.

"The Villagers don't know where I am. They don't even know that I'm alive, remember? The Clans are at peace. Erik wouldn't send for help if it weren't serious. And even if that were the case, I'm curious to know who would try."

"When things get strange, it makes me wonder," Devin said. "The Gypsies now have homes and no one to blame for stuff. Maybe folks are trying to start something."

"Well, with your grandparents and aunt still back in the village, we can't risk anything that will make them think we're on to them if that's the case. Until I check things out, we'll have to leave it alone."

Devin sighed. "Fine. I'll leave it alone. But I'm still curious about the real story between you and Ole Higue."

It was Rennie's time to sigh loudly.

"Dev, Dev, Dev. Didn't anyone tell you it's not always a good thing to ask too many questions?"

"All the time," Devin nodded. "Would you prefer I stay ignorant? What if I hear some version of your story and don't know the truth from fiction?"

Rennie shook his head. "Where do you think of these things?" he said, exasperated.

"So, you gonna tell me then?" Devin grinned at him.

"Only so you get the right version. I frankly don't care what stories folks come up with. I care what happens with you."

When Devin said nothing, he continued, "The night I turned my back on the group I belonged to, I trekked into the forest. I was tired and hunkered down in a remote corner of the hills.

"And?" Devin prompted after a lengthy silence.

"I had ventured into the bizarre. Me, a Master of Stealth, was captured by the Shadows."

Devin recoiled, his insides freezing.

"They were about to sacrifice me when Serena rescued me."

"You mean Ole Higue!"

"Yes, Ole Higue," Rennie nodded, then said. "Mr. Heeb was a trader back then and he was captured as well."

"Mr. Heeb!"

"I was being forced to kill him. I refused and managed to set him free. He fled and I was his replacement."

"What!"

"Ole Higue saved me after Heeb escaped. That's how I know her. Returning the crystal to her was the least I could do for her, for saving my life."

"Oh man! I'm sorry, Ren."

"Me too, Dev. Just wish we didn't have to meet the way we did."

"All that's over with."

"I should have told you what happened after you saved me that night down by the river."

Unsure of what to say knowing he'd wondered what had caused Rennie's men to mutiny, he waited.

"The truth is," Rennie continued, "I was once a part of a group of men who did things the High Officials ordered us to do to defend our land. I did dirty work in the name of honor. They took glory when I and my fellow brothers suffered the consequences. When things went bad, they would claim no knowledge of us. Or they'd claim we were rebels."

He paused and Devin wasn't sure if he was supposed to say anything. He knew there was a story to The Renegade.

"It happened too many times and I was being robbed of my conscience. I finally went rogue and left with a bounty on my head. The villagers I tried helping, turned on me because I couldn't disclose what I planned. I knew where the chambers of food were being stored for the high officials and was going to take from them since they enjoy while everyone else suffers.

After what happened, your aunt offered me to stay at her home and I stayed dead until Serena asked me to come here and help with the academy. And now it's not really over. Seems the worshippers are at it again. I'll know when I get to Embers. Let Serena know why I had to leave and why you were out tonight. She'll understand."

"Right," Devin nodded, spotting Rennie kneeling and removing a floorboard. Retrieving a pouch, he took a handful of the contents and returned it to its hiding place.

"Why the heck," Devin wondered, would Rennie go wandering off into the night with supplies and precious gems, if he was going on a trip to learn about doings of dark worshippers?

"A man does what's necessary. Some people don't play by the rules."

"I….."

"Don't waste time on things that don't matter."

"I know that," started Devin….

"No, you don't," interrupted Rennie, stuffing more items into his knapsack.

"I just thought…" Devin began.

"Stop thinking and help me get these together," Rennie pointed to a number of baskets lying by the table nearby. Filling each with all kinds of nuts and seeds, a mixture of fragrant mixed herbs that hung in abundance from the cabin's roof, he became busy with his task and Devin had no chance to wonder exactly which marble had gone missing from his friend's head.

He kept running back and forth, collecting and packing as Rennie called items out. Trudging through the garden, gathering bundles of lavender and roses, Devin noticed Rennie scanning and reading through an aged book.

From time to time, he'd wander off into the kitchen and return with fists-full of ingredients that he set in a gleaming bowl which sat on the table.

"That's interesting," thought Devin as Rennie called out more items he needed. He scurried out the door, his curiosity at an all-time high trying to figure out what Rennie was up to.

He found the hanging moss Rennie asked for and snipped some. A gentle breeze blew by and an unfamiliar fragrant wafted in. Unable to place its source, Devin felt a sense of enchantment settle in. He shook it off, but it persisted, and he decided to check it out.

Sniffing along, he spotted a tiny trail as the scent intensified. Winding itself in a series of circles and spidery-web kind of design, Devin came upon a small clearing and found a shrub he'd never seen before. Covered in white flowers, they glowed luminously, striking a sudden sense of familiarity.

As he gazed at the unusual flowers, the picture in Lexi's book his mom had drawn for her, flashed before him. How could his mom have known of this plant, he wondered? Did he dare disturb this pretty plant? After a few minutes, he felt it safe and reached out and gathered a number of blossoms.

"Thank You," he whispered and after collecting moss and the rest of his things, he headed back to the Cabin.

"Those are amazingly beautiful. Where did you find them?" Rennie's tone surprised him.

"If you know where to look….," he left it unfinished, a cheeky grin lighting his face.

"Well, I'm impressed. Your aunt's notes say those are extremely rare to come by."

He went back to mixing herbs, honeysuckle, and rose petals in his bowl. Adding some powdery substance, he took a dropper and counted seven drops of some kind. Seeming satisfied with his mixture, he started putting things away.

"You still haven't told me what all this is about," Devin reminded him, as he watched Rennie wash his hands over by the sink.

"I know," Rennie nodded, walking over and disappearing briefly into the bedroom. Returning after a few minutes with a long, rolled bundle in his arms, he gently laid it down, and began unfolding it. Devin was amazed to see a carpet of moss, dried vines and an assortment of leaves and grass.

Rennie looked over at Devin and said, "You'll have to wait until about eleven o'clock tonight, and take this," he pointed to the blanket he'd unfolded. "Go through the meadow at the back of the cabin, past the stream, and head on over to the waterfall. Once you pass that, go for about a quarter of a mile and turn right, you'll come to a small meadow where you'll find the Moon Pool I showed you once."

After checking to see if Devin was following, he continued, "Take the baskets of nuts and seeds I've gathered with you. Leave them near the pool. Then find a sheltered spot and spread this blanket. Sprinkle the mixture I've prepared onto the blanket. Make it look as natural as you can. Then leave."

Devin decided to humor his friend. Nodding his understanding, he said, "In the middle of the night?"

"Yep." Rennie replied.

Being alone and unprotected, late at night in the forest by himself? Devin felt the stirrings of something serious, sighed loudly, but left it alone. Too many times he'd gone off and done rash things with painful results.

Rennie looked over as if reading his thoughts, and asked, "I do have a really good reason for asking you to do this for me, even though I know it must look really silly."

Devin shrugged. After the many recent screw-ups he'd made, he wasn't in any position to get angry at Rennie. "I won't ask questions."

Rennie nodded. "Thank you. You've had quite a few adventures on these kinds of things Dev, so I'm not really worried. Are you? I mean," Rennie continued, "You went into the unknown looking for me and Ole Higue, remember?"

"Yeah, I remember," Devin said. "I don't have a problem helping you out. But wandering out in the middle of the night on my own is a bit careless, isn't it? Saint Shade's hunting me after all."

Rennie looked visibly shaken and Devin gazed at the horror on his face, a coldness entering him. He'd just been shooting in the dark. Stumbling on the truth, however, left him cold. But he couldn't make Rennie feel responsible.

"I'm sorry, Dev. But how did you know?"

He shrugged, "I suspected after what happened with Lexi. The worshippers specifically chose her. Maybe they were hoping they'd get me if I went looking for her."

"You're right," Rennie nodded. "I tried telling Serena exactly that. But the stories keep changing and Serena doesn't know which is the truth. I'll know more once I get to Embers. For now I have it on good authority that Saint Shade is otherwise occupied."

Devin's heart skipped a beat. "For real?"

"Yep," Rennie nodded without explaining further. Going outside, he returned with his skin smeared with mud and grime, all signs and scents of herbs and flowers gone.

Devin felt a bit unsure what Rennie meant about Serena. He'd just been to see her and she hadn't said anything to him about Saint Shade and now Rennie was heading to unknown parts.

"Remember, when you get there, do exactly what I told you to do, then leave. Get back here as soon as you can."

Devin nodded to show he understood but his throat was tight with unspoken words as he watched his friend head out the door.

"I have quite some distance to go. I'll be careful and be back soon." With a quick wave, Rennie was gone.

Sending a prayer out to the universe for Rennie's safety, Devin decided to find dinner and get some rest as it would be hours before he headed out into the night and the forest himself.

* * *

He followed Rennie's directions exactly as he'd been given and set off with his supplies of things he'd helped prepare, all the while wondering what exactly it was that Rennie had him doing.

He had agreed and it was too late to change his mind. When eleven o'clock struck, he gathered the blanket and set off through the meadow at the back of the cabin. With the light from the full moon, he trudged along past the stream and kept going, heading for the waterfall. Soon he was over it and kept going, all the while keenly alert for signs of anything unusual.

Careful to keep his attention on his footing, and not wanting to twist an ankle or crack his skull on any of the slippery rocks along the waterfall, the terrain proved to be quite different at night, but he got through. Making it safely past the waterfall, he kept going for the quarter mile as Rennie had said and found the tiny trail. Turning right, he found the pretty meadow and approached cautiously, unsure of what exactly he'd find.

On finding the tiny Moon Pool, he looked around and found his attention caught by a low whinny, over and under a patch of trees. He quickly walked over and with the filtering moonlight through the leaves, he quickly set about unfolding the blanket of blossoms and leaves they had made, spread it out and sprinkled the mixture on it.

Feeling satisfied, he took the basket of fruits, nuts and seeds he'd slung over his shoulder and set it down close by. Content with his handiwork, he took a minute to catch his breath before turning around to leave, having peered into the shade and every nook and cranny he could see, with no idea as to why exactly he had to do what he'd done.

But just as he had taken his first step to head back, the whinny sounded again and he paused when a glow beyond the trees lit up.

"Take the baskets of nuts and seeds I've gathered with you. Leave them near the pool. Then find a sheltered spot and spread this blanket. Sprinkle the mixture I've prepared onto the blanket. Make it look as natural as you can. Then leave."

The words echoed again in his thoughts and for a split second, he was rooted to the spot, his mind racing in panic. He wondered if dark worshippers had already infiltrated the area, and if he had been spotted. But the whinny sounded again and he felt an odd pain flooding him.

Either way, he couldn't stay where he was and wasn't too keen on turning back. Shaking off the pain engulfing him, Devin moved as silently as he could towards the shelter of trees where the whinny was becoming more urgent.

Finally, he made it under the heavy overhanging branches and stared in amazement. There at the base of the tree, a beautiful white unicorn lay on her side, about to give birth. She moved, her coat shimmering in the moonlight that had been filtering through the branches and he felt a surge of excitement racing up his spine. Moving softly lest he scared her, he found her looking up, her ears twitching on spotting him. For a while, they stared at each other.

A rush of pain flooded him and he sank to his knees. The baby was about to be born but she seemed to be in some trouble. He murmured comfortingly so she wouldn't fear him and wondered if she could hear him the way Gylfi did.

She must have because a sudden band of energy relaxed around him, the intensity of pain lessening. She lifted her head, neighing softly and watched him crawl forward and reach over to try and calm her.

"It's okay, Beautiful. It will be fine," he kept whispering, rubbing her head as she nuzzled his hand. He moved closer and kept rubbing her head, careful not to touch her horn.

It was the most magical thing he'd happened upon and as amazed as he was, Devin didn't feel it was strange to be sitting with a mother unicorn with her head in his lap, about to give birth.

He was hit with an excruciating band of pain and she whinnied painfully, making him realize something was wrong. Extricating himself and putting her head gently back on the ground, Devin remembered the times he'd helped Gramps with goats and sheep birthing. It was a normal thing in the village.

As if she understood, the mother unicorn breathed noisily and whinnied again. Devin didn't have anything he could use as he'd seen Gramps doing, so he set to work, quickly setting himself down and began the laborious task of helping the baby unicorn out of the birth canal.

It took a long time but he was successful and after the rush of the baby coming out, he carefully moved away and let the mother do the rest.

Moving back along the path, he went back to the Moon Pool and cleaned himself up. He found a dried gourd shell and filled it up after washing himself as best he could. Satisfied, he quickly made his way back to the trees, careful to keep the water from spilling, and found the mother unicorn and her newborn babe still bonding. He approached and placed the water nearby.

She paused and looked at him and he swore he felt her thanking him. Soon she moved around and allowed the baby to start suckling. Devin knew she would be at the mercy of the night. He got up again and backed away, unsure she was able to read his thoughts of being right back.

He rolled back the blanket of blossoms and everything else he'd left under the nearby tree and brought them over to where she and her baby lay. She was completely comfortable with him and within moments he was able to spread it out where she nudged the baby over and they nestled comfortably.

She didn't seem eager to explore the baskets of goodies he'd brought, but he knew she'd expended a lot of energy giving birth and her priority was the baby. As if she understood, she whinnied again and he moved over. She lifted her head and nuzzled his hand as if she were saying "thank you".

Devin's mind was working furiously though, completely blown away by what had happened. He knew at some point the reality of it would settle in, but right now he had to think about what would be the next step.

A long time after sitting with them, he came up with an idea. Seeing the little one had snuggled down with the mother unicorn, he decided to try and communicate with her the way he did with Gylfi. Sending her thoughts of what he intended, he got an instant reply, not images, but sensations and emotions filling him – from dread and worry for their safety, to the uncertainty of her being away from her herd.

Devin sent her images of Gylfi in return and what he felt would be the best thing to do. Time was passing and the hours had flown by. He didn't want to leave her alone for long, but he needed to get back to Rennie's before morning.

She seemed to relax at the messages she received and in moments she had flashed her happiness and gratitude. Devin moved over and petted her, careful to still keep his hands away from her horn and the baby. He moved a few feet away and closed his eyes. Suddenly there was a whirling gust of wind and Gylfi landed squarely in front of him.

"Devin, what are you doing out and about at this time of the night? And in such a place? You must know the danger…." She stopped as Devin stepped away, revealing the mother unicorn and her newborn babe.

"Ahhh, I see your predicament," Gylfi nodded in the moonlight. "Hello, my beautiful one. What happened that you strayed from your family?"

Devin only got a gist of what they exchanged. It was lengthy and animated and after a while Gylfi turned to him. "Things are serious, Devin. You must hurry and get back to safety. There are Dark Beings about in the night, and she was being hunted. The rest of her herd was able to get past the shield, but she wasn't so lucky. If you hadn't come along when you did, we don't know what would be the outcome. I will get her back safely across to her realm but you need to get to Serena and let her know the Dark Ones are close by. Students must not venture out. Now hurry and go."

Devin sent images of comfort and farewell to the Unicorn and her babe and nodded to Gylfi. Bowing, his heart and mind at odds with leaving them behind, but also with the news of what was happening, he set off at a trot, praying that he would make it back to safety in time to give Serena Gylfi's message.

SAINT SHADE

Rennie! He halted in his tracks, remembering Rennie had said the Rebels sent news of sacrifices over in the Embers area and he was sure Saint Shade was occupied elsewhere. As if he'd conjured Shade, Devin felt the air shift around him and he was surrounded by dark, wispy figures. His breath left him in a rush while dread and panic flooded him as one detached itself from the group and advanced.

Devin felt rooted to the spot, the meadow echoing with strange sounds. He reached in his mind and felt the warmth flooding him, the ancient language flowing forth. But a shout from the figure seemed to lock his thoughts and he went completely blank.

Immobilized, he stared as they all came closer, dressed in black, smelling foul and rotten as gleeful laughter echoed around the bunch.

"Isn't this precious?" It paused, realizing something was strange. Devin wasn't their actual prey. "What's this?" He asked again, moving even closer and leaned into Devin, sniffing.

The stench of rotting flesh and his inability to vomit made Devin feel like he was going to faint. But the figure withdrew. "Yes, Master will definitely be pleased with this one. He smells of sunshine and sweet meadows." He sucked another deep breath that made Devin see black, his breath ready to snap from his body.

"I think this one here will definitely spare us from losing that unicorn. Too bad, but..." he stopped, turning back and stuck his face into Devin's. "You smell the same! Hahaha... this is rich, Brothers! This one here can tell us. Come, smell for yourself."

Devin found himself surrounded by the circle of hooded, shadowy figures, all vying to sniff him. He must have passed out, because the next thing he knew, he was being bounced and jarred, uncomfortable and sick.

He found himself atop a magnificent black horse, his hands tied securely in place and he was being led into the night and the unknown. His mind was working again and he was able to catch bits and pieces of their conversation, realizing they needed him unharmed to give as a gift to their Master.

With him being the consolation prize, Devin knew he was in grave danger. He remembered when he'd saved Lexi. She was bound and lying on a stone surface. Those captors were women. Here, it was an all-male group, and from the snippets of their conversation he had heard, he couldn't tell if they knew who he really was or if they had picked him up just because he smelled of the unicorn that they felt was valuable.

The only person he knew to be so feared would be Saint Shade, but Rennie said Shade was far away from the meadow where he'd left Gylfi, the new mom and the baby in.

Devin tried pushing away the terror that was threatening to take over him and focused on figuring a way out of his predicament. He was sure that if by morning, Gylfi returned and didn't find him, she would go in search. But he couldn't risk her being captured either. The Shadows as he named them, obviously had ventured far and had managed to penetrate the veil that protected the school when they tried to capture the Unicorn.

He closed his mind to her and the baby. If the shadows were able to shut him from using the ancient language, he wasn't sure what else they could do.

Did he just happen to be at the wrong place at the wrong time? The Shadow had smelled the unicorn on him. He couldn't and wouldn't call on Gylfi and endanger her either. She needed to make sure the mother unicorn and baby made it to safety.

Devin focused on staying on the horse, having had little experience riding one. But his mind was busy. Mr. Heeb and Rennie were at one time made victims to be sacrificed. Was that what was to become of him? He was in serious trouble and still couldn't see a way out.

They traveled for what seemed like hours. Devin was parched and tired. Morning had dawned and passed. Midday went by and still they kept going. Through alien territory and strange landscapes, some amazingly beautiful while others barren and bare, desolate and dark. But just as he was about to collapse, they crested a hill and he stared at the beauty lying in the valley below them.

They had reached a pretty estate set at the foothills below. He felt a strange emotion fill him when he realized they'd reached their destination. What exactly they had in mind for him, filled him with dread.

They descended and within moments he was rudely pulled down from his seat and pushed forward to the entrance of the manor before them. The door opened inward and they stepped inside. His eyes adjusted to the interior and Devin was struck at the coziness of the house. But he had little time to take in his surroundings or enjoy any rest he might've been expecting.

"Move," the raspy voice prodded him from behind.

He felt a shift in his emotions and sensed a presence. Looking around, he saw he was being studied by the most handsome man he'd ever seen in his life.

The Shadows, as he thought of them, hurried forward, rasping, "Our Lord, we've brought you a present."

"Explain yourself, soldiers. My orders were specific. Nothing will spare you if I find this gift of lesser value than what you were sent to obtain."

He's of the same essence of that which you seek, our Lord," the Shadow replied, bowing.

Devin stared at the man as he shifted his gaze from his soldiers, his expression changing to a mixture of interest and curiosity.

"Is that so, Soldier? There is only one such said to be hidden in the realm. You're saying you brought him to me?"

"Indeed, our Lord, you'll find it quite so and more. We offer him as the Highest Gift you could want."

"Indeed. We shall see, Soldier. Anything less and you will regret it."

The Shadows rose and turned, watching their master approach him. Devin felt his insides doing cartwheels, his mind refusing to accept what he suspected. It was bad enough he'd been careless and gotten himself kidnapped. But this! A shudder coursed through his body.

The man meanwhile approached him and, like the Shadows, sniffed deeply and took a sudden step back. Devin saw a series of expressions crossing his face.

"In all my travels, across all the lands and realms, never have I come across something so amazing," he muttered to himself. "Unless the universe is playing a joke on me."

He leaned in again and closed his eyes, taking slow, deep breaths. As he inhaled, he seemed to become intoxicated. As he drew deeper and deeper, Devin felt a sucking sensation around him and cringed. It was slimy and repulsive and he felt a strong urge to vomit.

He kept himself calm but felt his insides clench when the man said, "You're spared, Soldier. This is unexpected, but delightfully so."

The man was truly beautiful. Devin realized he'd been impressed with Chad, thinking him the most magnificent man he had ever seen. And Rennie, another person that impressed him with his savage fierceness, build and beauty; darker and more rugged than the specimen that stood before him. But this man was magnificent!

"This is an unexpected pleasure, Son of Prophecy. It's an honor to finally meet you. I'm Saint Shade."

Devin blanched. Very few knew it was him that had released Ole Higue. Saint Shade knew of the prediction but how did he know Devin was called Son of Prophecy? He felt himself go cold as unfamiliar emotions flooded him, his heart thumping painfully against his chest.

"No need to panic. Calm yourself. Come, come now. Let's get acquainted. I've heard much about you. Your birth was prophesied from a very long time ago. I wondered if there really was such a person. You're a legend and a hero of the realm. I am fortunate, very fortunate to have this long-awaited meeting." Shade laughed again, interrupting the flow of thoughts.

"Then you have the advantage over me," Devin replied, ignoring the title. He frankly wasn't sure what to call his archenemy.

Saint Shade tsked at him.

"Now. Welcome again, Son of Prophecy." Then seeing Devin's expression, he gave a bark of laughter. "Well, that is who you are, aren't you?"

"I'm Devin Reems from the Village of Foxwood."

"You're the one who will fulfill your Grand-ancestor's curse. So, join me, won't you, and let's take this realm back! You will go down in history, Devin. Imagine ruling this land alongside me."

Devin's insides twisted, fear taking over. He was a curse? He was to restore a world back to darkness? An endless tunnel of betrayal spun before him. Could it be? Did someone twist the words of the prophecy? It was hundreds of years ago that the prophecy was made. Who other than Chad, who'd personally escorted the Oracle in her banishment, had heard the prophecy? And how did it become known? Could they have misinterpreted its meaning? He'd never questioned any of these things before. Now he wished he had. Was Saint Shade correct?

As Devin grappled with the questions churning for answers, Shade laughed.

"I see you doubting yourself. Didn't your High Guardian," he broke off laughing again at the title and flicked an imaginary speck of dust off his cuff, "tell you the whole truth?

Devin kept his emotions in check as the sniffing continued. The sense of time fell away as the words of the prophecy floated across his mind again and everything that had followed flowed.

"Soldiers, thank you for your good work. Meet the Son of Prophecy."

Throwing his head back, Saint Shade broke into maniacal laughter of a joke known only to himself, the sound echoing across the great chamber and floating out into the valley.

Stamping and jubilant cries broke out from the shadow soldiers. Shade was still caught up in his jeering laughter to the Universe. It went on for a long while and just as Devin thought they'd forgotten about him, he found himself standing in front of Shade, unsure how, since he hadn't felt himself move.

His worry grew but he kept his face expressionless, the pain slicing deeply. Rusty! What had he revealed? So much had been happening, he couldn't remember when he'd last seen Rusty.

Since the public acknowledgement for returning the Crystal, he'd first become a hero but that had quickly changed when they were burnt out from their home. Devin knew he didn't know what effects the Shadows poison had on him. Rusty had healed but could he have become a part of them? Would he have betrayed him? It didn't make sense.

A blast of pain shot through him. How he managed to not howl, Devin couldn't say. He just felt a numbness filling him and watched a calculating look enter Shade's eyes. None of it mattered. Saint Shade had found him.

Fear gripped him. Maybe if Shade had been yelling and threatening, he could have gauged his next move, but a wave of nervousness and uncertainty flooded him. He needed to keep his wits about him.

"What is your secret, Son of Prophecy? Greater men than you have tried defeating me. I cannot believe You, a mere boy, has what it takes to get rid of me. I…I who have been to the ends of the earth and back and sacrificed and," abruptly pausing, he looked around before continuing, "done much more than you can ever imagine…" he trailed off into a thoughtful silence.

"I don't claim anything," Devin replied.

Shade walked up, then went around him in a circle, gazing up and down at him. Devin felt like a specimen as Saint Shade hmmed to himself.

"For you to be the one to restore the realm, you have to have something special about you. What is it, Devin? Be a part of my family. Come join us and let's regain what has been ours all along."

"I don't understand what you mean," Devin said in the silence that followed the offer. He wasn't sure Shade would take kindly to being rejected and didn't trust himself to just say no.

"Ahhh, I see how this is," Shade nodded, an edge to his voice. "But… I will not underestimate the value of youth. After all, that is what this is about. Isn't it Devin?"

His breath inches away from Devin's neck, laughing softly, he said, "Not a boy still, yet not quite a man. Roxi must be laughing at me."

When Devin stayed quiet, Shade sneered, "Surely you've heard the pitiful account of Roxi, the High Priestess and Oracle to the Kingdom of Ohhm!"

Devin wondered if Chad was the only one to have heard the prophecy Roxi made, how did it get out? And the story Gramps told of his father, Hums who'd talked of the prediction. There was a missing part to the whole story Devin realized, but he didn't have the time to figure it out. He needed to deal with Saint Shade.

Shade's expression went dark and Devin watched as all traces of humor were wiped clean as Devin continued to stay silent.

"Say nothing," he told himself. "Just look scared. Show you're paying attention." The thoughts kept rolling around his mind, making him thankful for the bitter lessons he had so long hated, remembering the price they'd all paid.

Tears built at the back of his eyes. How frustrating it must have been for his mom to try and teach him things no child could understand. And how hard it must have been to know she would never be able to explain it to him. Devin felt strength fill his spine. Lifting his head, he stared directly at his enemy.

"Ah, the famous House of Evermore trait. What nobleness!"

"House of Evermore?" Devin wondered. Is that whom his lineage was from? He'd have to go searching, but first he needed to get out of this predicament.

Shade came closer, his mocking voice adding to Devin's resolve. But he drew back, the stench of evil hitting him strongly.

"Don't go there, sonny. I like games. Just not this time."

"What do you want from me?" Devin asked.

Astonishment passed over Shade's face. With hands clasped behind his back, he was quiet for a good while, making Devin wonder if he was going to answer when Saint Shade began speaking.

"The secret," Shade replied.

Devin was confused. "Secret?"

"How did Ohhm begin its rise again? Only secret wisdom would be the reason."

"Why do you want this secret wisdom?" he asked, completely confused.

"Because it is my birthright."

"Your birthright?"

"Indeed, Son of Prophecy." Shade laughed mockingly. "My ancestors were driven from their homes for having the secret to everlasting youth. Brutalized and hung. They paid with their lives."

"By whom?" Devin asked, unsure as to what to believe. He didn't know if what he was hearing was the truth, or just a trick that Saint Shade was playing to earn his sympathies.

"Some within the ancients believed the knowledge was to be limited to a select few. They prided themselves superior," he grimaced, flicking an invisible speck of dust off his shoulder, "and the rest of them felt betrayed for being denied."

Devin was surprised at the almost normal conversation Shade was having with him, and was beginning to think he'd misjudged him, but the small voice kept him quiet.

"The knowledge they gained studying the mysteries were repaid in death. Death, Devin! Your mother died. You know what that's like to lose someone you love. Imagine that a thousand fold. Hundreds of lives lost. Why? I'll tell you why. Because the few who found the secret of youth became a Superior Breed and chose to destroy the ones who they felt were unfit.

Devin felt the unjustness of what Shade had described, but something felt off.

"Yet the only surviving Mystic myself, I've been refused that gift. And you! You dare to think you've achieved what I haven't been able to? I, who've studied, traveled, slaved and done everything under the sun, moon and stars to learn, and it's still been denied to me! But you!"

Shade's voice had fallen to a quiet whisper, his eyes piercing in intensity and Devin felt he was staring into pools of evil.

Shade spoke, taunting and boasting and Devin felt his anger simmer into sadness for the many who'd suffered at the hands of Shade. No one deserved to have lost their lives because Shade couldn't accept something that wasn't meant for him. No wonder the Mystics never gifted him the secret he so wanted.

Devin didn't feel blessed with having to restore a realm. If anything, he'd been met with nothing but heartache and tragedy since the night he'd witnessed the crystal coming alive. He couldn't say what made him special other than an obscure prophecy that had led to great calamity followed by another angry prophecy made by his grand ancestor.

He just happened to be that one kid who went looking for trouble and found it. He had lost a mother, been betrayed in the worst possible way and given a burden no boy should have to bear. And this creature had the nerve to question his right to the sacredness withheld from him. Devin had nothing to do with how the prophecy unfolded. It chose him. Why couldn't the fool get that!

"Ah, let it out there, boy. I felt the guts in you there a second ago. Come on, come on. The mystics wouldn't give the gift of youth without you having some kind of something in you."

Devin stayed quiet. Could his grand ancestor, Roxi truly be from these very mystics that Saint Shade was claiming he was from? What did that mean for him?

"Now I've put you to thinking. Good, good. Take your time and tell me what you come up with." The voice crawled down his spine and he jumped as he felt a hot, sticky breath on his neck again. "Unless you're as stupid as you look? Could it really be that you have no idea what I'm talking about?"

Devin had a fleeting hope to keep up the stupidity act when a sudden, blinding pain exploded like liquid fire in his head that had him doubling over. He fell forward in agony, barely hearing Shade's voice above him saying, "Yes, yes. I wondered when we might get to this."

Devin was unsure how long he laid in excruciating pain, but as he felt it beginning to subside, he opened his eyes, only to find himself staring into the blackest pool of hatred he had ever seen.

He felt himself falling into the depths of evil, the coiling, life-sucking stare drawing the life out of him, and a sensation of being pressed by an unseen force, terror so indescribable, he scrunched his eyes closed, unwilling to breathe. But he had to open them just as quickly as he was pulled into strange, terrifying scenes of horror.

Saint Shade was ten feet away, gazing at him in utter hatred. "I was having misgivings a moment ago," he said, his voice friendly and quiet, as if what he'd just done never happened.

Devin knew Saint Shade was cruel, cunning, and diabolical. A walking, breathing, evil entity that stood before him. He wondered how long Shade would keep up the torment and if he had any chance of escaping.

"Maybe I'll keep you alive and see who shows up to save you. Maybe mommy dearest will rescue you from the beyond."

"Shut up!" Devin shouted. "Just shut up, you demented demon. Don't you dare speak about my mother. You don't know anything about me. Or my family. Just shut up!"

Blind with fury, he lunged forward only to find himself flung backwards. Pain exploded as he was flung again, his head connecting with the edge of the trunk, and he sunk into blackness.

How long Devin lay like that, he wasn't sure, but he came awake with a deep, throbbing pain in his head and his vision blurry.

Unsure where his archenemy was at this point, he lay still trying to get his bearings and then heard "Impressive. I'll just have to find other ways to test your powers then, Devin."

The sound of the door opening distracted Shade. A Shadow hurriedly entered, bowed and had a whispered conversation with Shade that had him swearing loudly. "Go, get everyone and gather everything we need. We'll get on with the ceremony as soon as everything is ready." Pointing to Devin, he said, "We'll need to get him prepared and ready. See to it."

"Yes Master," the Shadow's raspy voice replied.

"It seems I shall have my dream fulfilled this very night after all, Son of Prophecy. But first there is something I need to take care of." He turned and left with the loud thud of the door vibrating behind him.

Devin sat up, feeling his body raw and bruised. "So that was Saint Shade," he told himself. What did Shade mean he had to get prepared? That sounded ominous. He had to find a way out. They'd traveled a long way and many hours. Where this was, he hadn't a clue, but it didn't matter. Saint Shade wasn't going to get his way, whatever he was planning.

The door opened and a burly guard came in, shouting, "Let's go!"

"Where?"

"You'll find out soon enough," the guard laughed loudly.

Keeping his mouth shut, Devin followed him out the door and around the courtyard, past the stables and finally to a small rustic hut at the far end of the compound.

"In you go then," the guard said, stepping aside, motioning him in.

Except for an old cot in a corner and a wooden table and chair with a bowl of what looked like a month-old supply of fruits, it was empty and bare.

"All yours," the guard laughed again before slamming the door, leaving Devin alone with his thoughts.

They must be very confident that he wasn't going to escape, Devin figured. If he was the highest prize and Shade's soldiers were saved just for offering Devin to him - and Shade knew him as the Son of Prophecy, how come he was stuck in a hut for safety?

But it was a much-needed respite from them and he needed to think. His head was throbbing, a massive headache making him fade in and out. He went over to the cot and sat down and soon heard the guard outside ordering someone to stand guard by his door, followed by a rush of activity and loud calls.

He got up and peered through the window. A busy sight met his eyes when he spotted figures rushing about in a frenzy of activities. The darkness outside wasn't helping and he felt panic rising as he remembered Shade's words about a ceremony.

Trying to stay calm, his mind flooding with ugly thoughts of every kind, Devin knew he couldn't give in to the possibilities swirling around his mind. Shadows and Saint Shade weren't a combination to take lightly. He had to find a way out.

Stay tuned for
Part II - Shades of Light